From the acclaimed author of
Touch the Sun and *Comes the Rain ...*

The Pony Wife

In the mid-1800s, the storms of change cast a shadow across the American frontier, threatening the fate of the native tribes who lived there. And into this world, a child was born. . . .

Her name was Dark Moon, for her mother gave birth under the tainted light of a lunar eclipse. According to tribal superstition, the child possessed strange and mysterious gifts that could be used for good or for evil. But as Dark Moon's powers grew stronger, she was feared and shunned by her own people. Only one man had the strength to love her—but Dark Moon was torn between her tribal duties and her heart's desire. And when the white man came into their world, she was her people's last hope to survive. . . .

Author Beverly Bird presents a breathtaking epic novel
of passion and power, tragedy and triumph,
hatred and love—the story of a courageous woman
you will never forget.

D1370645

Also by Beverly Bird

COMES THE RAIN
TOUCH THE SUN

THE PONY WIFE

BEVERLY BIRD

JOVE BOOKS, NEW YORK

THE PONY WIFE

A Jove Book/published by arrangement with
the author

PRINTING HISTORY
Jove edition / June 1995

ISBN: 0-515-11629-7

A JOVE BOOK®
Jove Books are published by The Berkley Publishing Group,
200 Madison Avenue, New York, New York 10016.
JOVE and the "J" design are trademarks
belonging to Jove Publications, Inc.

PRINTED IN THE UNITED STATES OF AMERICA

10 9 8 7 6 5 4 3 2 1

For Jami and Tani,
who really do talk to each other,
and who both would have had
the courage to go all the way
and claim it all.

Prologue

We-lu-poop, Moon of Cold Weather, 1855

THE PAIN CAME in on her again, a crushing thing that tightened over her until she thrashed. Vixen set her teeth against it, and felt blood burst from her tongue where she bit it.

The whole village was in the longhouse now, watching her with furtive glances. The people gathered at their own private hearths as the wind spirits roared outside. Strong Cub would be at one of those fires, although Vixen could not think who would offer him a place to wait. They were interlopers here. Her own people had cast them out several snows ago when she'd chosen him for her mate. He had never found his *wyakin,* his path to the spirits, so that he might have a guide protector and a medicine name.

Once, as a naive girl, Vixen had truly believed that he could overcome such a staggering disadvantage. Once, as a young man, Strong Cub had vowed to her that he would. But he was not a good hunter, and he could not fight, and when she had learned to accept that, he had hated her for it.

She clawed for the arm of the midwife who hunkered down beside her. "When this babe comes out, you must take it away," she gasped.

Broken Bird looked horrified. "You talk crazy with pain!"

"No. If you do not do as I ask, my husband will kill it."

The midwife looked doubtfully at the other hearths. "He is at Four Goose's fire," she muttered, "bragging of the son he will soon have."

"But it will not be a son. I have made medicine."

Another pain crashed through Vixen's body. She did not have much time now. She had to convince her.

"A boy child would need a strong father to teach him the things a warrior must know, so I worked against one. Strong Cub's anger will be horrible. I do not care for myself, but this babe should not suffer his temper."

"So you would forsake her?" Broken Bird demanded angrily.

"It is the only way." Vixen girded herself against another pain. "Tell Strong Cub that the babe has died. Please. Keep her in your lodge until the next sun-coming. By then, he will beat me so badly that Looking Glass will finally banish us from this band. You know he has been dwelling on that."

Broken Bird did. The headman was her brother.

"Sit up," she urged her. "We must go now, before you can no longer walk."

Vixen said no more. In the end, Broken Bird would either help her, or she would not. But Vixen knew she would kill this child by her own hand before she would let Strong Cub near her.

In the whole nine snows of his life, Water Calf had never seen a storm such as this.

He turned slowly, his head moving from side to side. There was no rain, nor any clouds. But the air had frozen abruptly, and thunder rumbled from somewhere far away. It made something strong and strange move in his belly.

He gaped up at the moon, certain that one small edge was missing from a moment ago.

He squeezed his eyes shut and waited, shivering as the icy gusts blasted him. Then, finally, he looked again, and his eyes bugged.

More of the moon was gone.

Now fear touched him, trembling in his belly, making his bowels feel soft. He began running in a wavering gate that was all his unsteady legs would allow.

He burst through one of the doors cut into the side of the earthen longhouse. Both Vixen and his mother were gone to the birthing lodge now, and his own family's fire was way to the front. Water Calf opened his throat and shouted to be heard there.

"The moon!" he cried. Then he looked back out at the night. Not even his fear could keep him from knowing what happened to it next. He ran outside again.

One of the men at Four Goose's hearth chuckled. "So who shall be the first to rush out after him into the pile of pony dung he has waiting for us?"

Strong Cub's gaze moved from one man to another, and helpless rage began to twist his gut. He knew what that boy was doing. The people would be distracted by his trick, and recognition of Strong Cub's new son would be overlooked.

Looking Glass gathered his coveted buffalo robe about his shoulders, and Tenku, the band's shaman elder, went with him to investigate the child's call. Four Goose and his cronies stood also, and Strong Cub struggled with himself.

If he went out there, perhaps *he* would be the one to step in the dung. Perhaps this joke had been aimed at him all along. It was a very real possibility, but his curiosity was strong.

Finally, he got up and moved toward one of the doors. A knot of people were jammed there.

"Move now, move!" he shouted. "This is the night of my son's birth! The spirits are talking to him! I must see!"

The people ignored him, making no move to let him pass ahead of them. His anger began to hurt his throat.

"Get out of my way!" he shrilled, and finally, a small path cleared for him. Strong Cub shoved his way outside.

When he saw it, his spine tingled. Tahmahnewes, Great Spirit Chief, it was true! The powers were talking to his son!

A quarter of the moon was gone now, but it had happened in a queer, rounded way, almost as though another, darker, moon were converging upon the real one. Surely this was a magnificent omen of the child who was soon to be. Strong Cub crowed his triumph and looked toward the women's lodge where Vixen gave birth.

He could not imagine why he had been denied his own *wyakin*. He did not know why he could not dream. But this child would have power even stronger than his wife's father, the great *tiwats* headman Toolhoolhoolzote who had thrown them out.

He began trotting into the frigid wind, toward the women's lodge. A high-pitched sound whined from his throat as he rejoiced. Broken Bird came out, clutching a small bundle wrapped in a woven grass mat.

"Let me see. I must see him!"

Broken Bird's gaze snapped up, and her face fell. He was almost upon her before she recovered. "Get back!" she gasped.

The eyes of the others began leaving the eerie sky, moving in awe to the babe who had been born beneath it. Broken Bird began retreating toward the lodge where no man would ever dare enter.

"He is dead, Strong Cub. It would not be good for you to look upon him."

An unearthly cry came from the man. It was a sound of such agony and denial that many knew a spasm of grief for him beneath their own horror. Broken Bird backed through the door opening.

Crazed, Strong Cub came after her.

She screamed and lashed out with her free hand, raking her nails down his cheek. The man struck a violent blow against the side of her head and she reeled, stumbling over Vixen's prone form. She lost her grip on the babe and it squealed lustily as it hit the ground.

The cry dumbfounded Strong Cub. His jaw went slack as he stared at the grassy bundle, then his gaze moved to his mate and the midwife.

"He lives. You lied!"

He snatched up the child. Vixen howled as she had not done throughout her ordeal, but now it was too late. Broken Bird knew he would kill them all.

Strong Cub tore back the bunting and found his healthy daughter. He knew then that there would be no redemption this night, no honor. The magic moon had given him a girl child.

He hurled the babe aside so that she hit the lodge wall with a sickening thud. Broken Bird screamed again, but she knew no warrior would break the taboo that Strong Cub had spurned. No man would come inside this place to help them.

Strong Cub grabbed a heavy boiling stone from the hearth and descended upon Vixen. The woman made not a sound. There were only the pulpy noises of his blows as the rock crushed her bones and her flesh.

Sobbing, choking back the sound of it, Broken Bird began to crawl behind him. She reached the door before she heard him grunt in satisfaction, and she tried to move faster. Strong Cub caught her braid and hauled her back. The stone came down, smashing her crown, but the stunned women outside saw the desecration of their special place. Howling in rage, they rushed the door.

Sod flew as others hacked at the walls, bringing them down with stone pestles and antler scrapers and anything else within reach. Now the men could have helped them, but Strong Cub was already doomed. They fell upon him with their tools, swarming over him until Broken Bird could see no more.

She put her face to the blood-spattered ground and prayed.

Water Calf rested on his haunches on a spit of high ground overlooking the icy, clear-watered Kooskooskia. A few women worked beside the river, grimly bathing what was left of the squaw Vixen. Strong Cub's body had only been dragged up into the hills, left for whatever animals might take pity upon him and return him to the Earth Mother who had scorned him.

Water Calf shuddered at such a fate.

He was pretty sure Tahmahnewes smiled on him. He was blessed with strong kin and blood ties to the headman's hearth, and he always brought back hares and spawn fish when he went out to look. The girls seemed to like him. His father, Culmuh, said they followed him because he was strong and sturdy. His mother said it was because he had good eyes. Still, who knew which man Tahmahnewes would ultimately, capriciously, choose to deny a *wyakin?*

Hushed, fervent prayers began to rise up from the people who continued to stare at the sky. The moon was completely gone now. Water Calf sprang to his feet to go back inside.

When he passed the shattered squaw lodge, a horrible sound came from within. He yelped, skittering away from it, then his face flamed. What sort of warrior would he be to fear the wind? Tenku had chanted the Pasapukitse to blow the ghosts away; what else but the shivering gales could cause such a suffering sound?

Could it?

He sucked his belly in and stepped into the mess. The sound came again and he inched toward it warily, then his jaw dropped.

The babe!

In the horror of the night, it had been forgotten, this child who had been born beneath the vanishing moon. And it was not dead after all. One tiny leg stuck out from beneath the clumps of sod and splintered branch frames, and it pumped indignantly. As Water Calf looked around for someone who might be able to explain all this, it let out another lusty howl.

He squatted down and pulled on the leg until it was free of the rubble. The babe wailed louder. And it was a girl child.

The band's sick and orphaned children were always taken to his mother, but Broken Bird could care for no one now. Scowling, Water Calf plucked this one up by the arm and went on toward the longhouse anyway.

He slipped inside through a door at the rear, then he grinned in satisfaction when he saw Silver Cloud's fire. That squaw had a babe; she would know what to do with this one. She was away now, probably outside watching the moon, but Water Calf knew she would return. He laid Vixen's girl child beside the cook pit.

He backed away and went outside again. The night was a milky gray now that made him stop and twist about in confusion. All around him, the others stared too, swaying and moaning in reverence.

The moon was coming back, and the icy gales had faltered. It was almost as though Tahmahnewes was showing his pleasure that the babe was safe.

Water Calf shook the crazy idea from his mind. She was only a girl child, after all.

Part One

1

Toose-te-ma-sah-tahl, Moon of Migrating for Roots, 1855

THE CAMP DOGS barked excitedly as the ponies were driven in from their snow season in the hills. They were a motley herd in this season of first warmth, the foals wearing patched coats of newborn winter fuzz, the stallions scarred and bitten. Still, they moved with their tails flagged and proud, as though they knew they were the very lifeblood of the People.

They are glad that it is finally time to move on, Silver Cloud thought whimsically. The band was late in its travels this season. Looking Glass, their headman, had been off over the mountains to buffalo country, and he had just recently returned to lead them on.

An unconscious smile softened her face as she stood balanced on another squaw's shoulders, tugging on one of the big teasel mats that made up the longhouse roof. The riverine home would be left open to the elements during the warm moons, so that the wind and rain could sweep it clean. In the meantime, the people would follow the chinook and steelhead salmon. When the snow melted in the high country, they would migrate up onto the plateau in search of the bitterroot and camas and kouse that were the other staple of their diet.

In various meadows all over the land, the Nez Percé bands would come together and camp for a while. Perhaps, Silver Cloud thought, she could get one of those other squaws to take Vixen's babe from her care.

She looked down at the orphan, tucked in her cradleboard

near Rocker, her own toddling son. It was not so much that Silver Cloud minded tending to her, but she knew her husband wanted the child gone from his hearth. He said that her powers, if ever she should possess any, would be dangerous.

Silver Cloud chewed her lip, watching her. It was true that there were times when the babe's strange, blue-black eyes seemed to focus and stare at nothing, when it looked as though she were communing with the spirits although she could not yet talk. She was the spawn of a man who had been scorned by the power givers, born on a night when the moon had gone away. Her very coming had brought death to the Hasotoin band.

Silver Cloud shook her head. All that notwithstanding, the child was a poor, forsaken girl babe, one she could not quite bring herself to abandon.

She rolled the teasel mat into a neat bundle and jumped down to gather up the orphan's cradleboard. She pulled Rocker onto her other hip, though he tried mightily to wrestle away from her.

"Ride my own pony!" he squealed.

"Not this journey, little one. We go far."

"He is strong enough," her husband chided. "Let him ride by himself and be a man."

Silver Cloud shrugged. She did not think it was a good idea, but she disagreed with Cut Nose only over those issues she deemed very important.

She whistled for Rocker's little red pony with its silver spots. She transferred some of her packs to its back, hitching the orphan's cradleboard to his saddle as well. Perhaps the full load would keep him from trotting dangerously away from the others as he was so often inclined to do.

At last, she mounted and looked back at the rushing Kooskooskia. "Heal well, Mother," she whispered. "We shall return."

She pulled her pony around and trotted to catch up with the other squaws. Now and again, her eyes strayed to her boy, riding proudly behind a throng of older youths. Then she pulled a camas cake out of one of her buckskin parfleches and munched contentedly.

The first scream to split the air was thin and startled. The second was pitched with panic, and it made the root meal go dry in her mouth. Silver Cloud knew that cry intimately, knew it in the deepest place of her heart. Her gaze flew to her son again, and she found him struggling with his red pony.

His colt began to heave and rear. But he was a good little rider; Silver Cloud knew that. She gathered her breath to call to him to stay calm, and the cake lodged hard in her throat.

She could not breathe!

She clawed at her neck as Rocker's pony plunged, finally sending him out of his little saddle. Then the sides of her vision began going dark, so that she could barely see as the others reacted. A squaw dismounted and ran to Rocker, where he lay small and limp in the grass. The midwife's boy rode to catch the red-and-silver pony, and to save the cradleboard.

Suddenly, Silver Cloud understood.

The orphan had done this terrible thing to them.

She could not understand why, when she had worked so hard to help her live, but she knew it with a foul, rancid superstition that chased her down into darkness. Everything the people had said about the babe's powers was true.

Near dawn, the howls of mourning began to crack hoarsely and fade into exhaustion. In the stunned quiet that followed, Water Calf watched the sun rise over the river again.

He twisted around to look at the peoples' lodges, his long black hair snaking across his naked back. The mat-covered summer huts were strewn haphazardly across the valley. Cook fires glowed here and there, pale, cold orange in the quickening dawn. Many people still sat at them, murmuring quietly to each other.

Water Calf got up to wander past them. They talked about the orphan babe as though she had done something bad, he thought. They wanted to hang her in a tree and leave her for dead. But he had been the first to reach Rocker's colt, and he knew that the girl child had had nothing to do with its panic.

He came to the last knot of grass huts, where his kin sat at the headman's fire. He squatted down behind his mother, leaning forward to peer over her shoulder. The orphan was still there, nestled on his mother's lap beside his own infant sister.

When her eyes wandered around to him, they seemed to stop and focus accusingly.

"She did not do it," he blurted. "I saw. She did nothing."

His mother looked back at him, her gaze sharpening. "Tell us," she urged.

Suddenly, he had everyone's attention. Culmuh, his father, looked skeptical, but Looking Glass studied him thoughtfully in that way he did when something was important. His seamed face was haggard in the dawning light, and his snarly gray hair formed a fearful nimbus about his head. Water Calf lived in awe of his uncle, and he was suddenly nervous to have his attention now.

"I rode fast to the pony when I saw it jump," he rushed on. "This is the time when the snakes come up from their holes to bake on the rocks. And that is what I saw when I reached the boy. *Ch-ch-ch-ch!*" He moved his hand back and forth, fingers flicking. "A *wexpus,* the one with the rattling tail, hanging from the pony's leg, here, below the knee. That babe and his pony disturbed its slumber. That is why the animal is lame this night."

"Go see," Looking Glass snapped, and his son, Young Looking Glass, ran off to the herd.

A few moments later, Young Looking Glass came back. "There are two fang marks on his shin. The heat is just now going down."

Culmuh scowled. "If that child is strong enough, she could call animals. She could talk to a rattlesnake and tell it to strike."

"She is a babe!" his wife chided.

"She is of magic blood," contributed Helps Another, Looking Glass's wife. "Toolhoolhoolzote, her grandfather, can call whole herds to come to him."

"But she is yet too young to show us if she can or not," Broken Bird insisted. "I say let her grow old enough to defend herself against these words of yours."

The others frowned at her, and Broken Bird flushed. It was true that she had nearly lost her life helping to birth this child. There was an ugly dent at the back of her head that she would carry forever. Still, she felt a strong, instinctive need to protect her.

"I can care for her now that the other squaw is gone," she went on stubbornly. "I have milk."

Looking Glass thought, then he shrugged. "If Broken Bird is willing, I see no need to disallow it. We have no proof that the babe killed Silver Cloud and her son. She may stay with us for now."

He pushed to his feet, his old bones creaking after the long night. But Broken Bird was not yet content.

"It is time she had a name as well, so the spirits can find her if she does not survive."

Looking Glass groaned, but he was not known to deny his sister much. "So be it."

He thought a moment, remembering the frightening night when the orphan had come to them. There had been magic in that sky; he was wise enough to know it. He was wary of it, deep down undecided as to whether it had been good or evil. But he was a man who had learned the value of patience. He would not condemn her yet. He would honor the spirits who had sent her to them in such a way; it seemed the safest thing to do.

"She will be Dark Moon," he decided.

A great clatter rose in the air with the next sun-coming. Willow lodge frames were lashed into travois, and the teasel mats that had covered them were rolled up again. The Spirit Chief had again taken life from the Hasotoin band, but what remained still needed to be fed and sustained. The chinook still ran, and other bands would be gathering at Tolo Lake, so Looking Glass's people moved on.

The orphan's cradleboard stayed with Broken Bird. Squaws' eyes darted to her burden as they passed, but they did not slow down to ride beside her and gossip as they usually did. Soon

Water Calf realized that this trouble would spread to him as well. One boy, Wahlitits, sneered openly as he joined his friends.

Water Calf did not like Wahlitits. The youth had seen fourteen snows and had found his *wyakin*. He should have been riding with the warriors, learning, listening, earning his stature. Instead, the youth spent his time here, boasting of his accomplishment.

"This sun it will be Broken Bird and your wee sister to die," he taunted.

Water Calf felt his belly tighten. A true warrior would not retort against one of his own, though, oh, how he wanted to.

"Broken Bird will bring destruction to all your kin if she keeps that babe," Wahlitits persisted. "Perhaps we will even have a new leader. Then you will not think you are so special, the headman's nephew!"

Suddenly, Water Calf thought of another way to retaliate. "Are you afraid of her, of the orphan?" he challenged.

Wahlitits snorted in disgust. "I am a warrior."

Not yet, not until you do something to prove it, Water Calf thought. "Come with me, then, to see her. Touch her."

Wahlitits's lower lip jutted out. "I do not wish to die."

"What true warrior is afraid to?"

Water Calf split off from the boys, riding back to Broken Bird. He did not think Wahlitits would follow, and indeed, all he heard behind him were hoots of excitement from the other boys.

"I will take that little one from you so you can ride with your friends," he offered his mother.

Broken Bird's eyes narrowed on him shrewdly. "*Your* friends will think you are very brave."

"They will think Wahlitits is very silly," he countered. "And perhaps they will stop fearing the orphan."

Broken Bird shook her head in resignation. He was a clever one, she thought, and she was grateful for that. A strong warrior needed to be innovative.

She lifted the cradleboard strap from her saddle and handed the babe over to him. Water Calf galloped back to the others.

They scattered warily at his approach, and Wahlitits's narrow face flamed as he whipped his own mount around to stay clear of the child.

"This only proves you are crazy!" Wahlitits shouted.

Water Calf rode closer to him, then closer still.

"Come with me!" Wahlitits called to the others. "Leave this crazy one to die by himself!"

The others hesitated. Nothing had happened to Water Calf so far, and indeed, his actions seemed to be the braver of the two. After a moment, one of the boys crowed loudly and leaned low off his pony's flank to scoop up a handful of dung. He hurled it in the direction of Wahlitits. It landed harmlessly at his pony's hooves, but the others caught on, hooting and laughing as they raced about, gathering up manure of their own. The missiles rained in on Wahlitits until he had no choice but to gallop off.

"You will suffer for this!" he yelled back. "You do not even have a *wyakin* to protect you!"

But I will, Water Calf thought stoutly. I will have one someday, and it will be far stronger than yours.

Gradually, the boys came back to ride beside him again, though they maintained a wary distance from the cradleboard. Still, in his belly, Water Calf knew that few of them would ever forget this sun. It was good, very good, for a warrior to have followers.

He grinned down at the babe, then his heart jolted. Her strange, blue-black eyes were angled up at him, and he thought she was smiling conspiratorially.

The band reached Tolo Lake with the end of the next sun. Looking Glass's people drew in quietly, looking about in fresh alarm. The moon for traveling was well spent now, but only a handful of others had gathered here at the traditional first spot to take fish. Something was wrong. Water Calf saw their eyes go to the orphan babe, as though she somehow had caused it.

Looking Glass waved a hand for some of his closest comrades to follow him to the small encampment, and impulsively,

Water Calf kicked his pony. His mother shouted for him to come back, but no one else chastised him and his heart swelled eagerly.

The people gathered were from the small band of Lean Elk, a young, renegade headman. His people tended to wander through Crow country, far to the east.

The women began rushing about to put dried fish and berries on a mat. Water Calf decided it was best for him to hang back, just close enough that he could listen. But for some time, the men only ate in silent camaraderie, ripping off hunks of the sweet, stringy fish so that his own mouth began to water for some.

Finally, Looking Glass looked idly to Lean Elk. "You are far from home," he observed.

Lean Elk chewed and nodded. "I would learn what comes of this white-skin council our foolish brothers partake in," he explained. "I have come to wait here until they return from Walla Walla with news."

Looking Glass's eyes narrowed. "I have heard of no council. I have been gone to take buffalo."

"I heard rumors about a moon ago, but I decided not to mingle with the *xayxayx* people, those white-skins. Tahmah-newes does not approve of their angry god. He wants his people to rely on their shamen and their *wyakins,* to cross the mountains to hunt and make war on the Sioux and the Shoshone, as we have always done."

Looking Glass nodded thoughtfully. "Do you know why these white men wish to speak to us?"

Lean Elk made a disgusted gesture with his fish. "It is that man Stee-vuns whose parties appeared in some of our villages last robe season."

Looking Glass frowned. "That man went west. He said he was looking to make a trail there for his iron horse to go to the big water."

"He lied. He has returned, and now he would council with our headmen. I think he would put an iron horse here as well."

Looking Glass felt his belly go sour.

"I have been all over, and I have heard much about this

white man, Stee-vuns,'' Lean Elk went on. ''When he left here at the end of the snows, he visited the Lahkayyou, the Yakima. He tricked them into signing away their lands for his iron horse. Now they will go to war to get it back.''

War. The feeling in Looking Glass's gut got worse. He knew what came of warring with the *xayxayx*. The Crows had been driven from the best of their lands when they fell to the soldiers. Traditionally, the *xayxayx* had been met hospitably if guardedly when they wandered onto Nimipu land, then they had been urged on their way again. Why would the other headmen council with them now?

Looking Glass got abruptly to his feet again. ''We must go to Walla Walla,'' he decided.

Lean Elk looked appalled. ''You would join them?''

''I would stop them.''

He had known terror of those iron horses from the first time he had seen one roar through buffalo country. He had known always that the belching metal beasts would bring evil and destruction to any country they went through.

They were not for Nimipu land.

2

THE EXCITEMENT THAT Water Calf felt at going to the council place died abruptly when he saw it. It looked as though some spirit-thieving monster had sucked the life out of these *xayxayx,* leaving pale, dry husks of skin.

He looked quickly at the others to check their reaction. The warriors were calm enough, and Looking Glass appeared strong and unflappable. But some of the women and boys hung back. Water Calf guessed, like himself, they had never actually seen these white-skins before. Not many had ever ventured into the deep country of Looking Glass's Hasotoin territory.

The prairie was thick with grass here, swooping down to a thin, cold creek that strayed from the Walla Walla River. The white-skin shelters hugged the bank, coveting a lush place his own people would have left clear, to be used by all. Their lodges were not grass thatched, but similar to the buffalo cowhide his uncle possessed. They whirred with a snapping, intrusive sound as the wind rippled across them. In front of one were some planks balanced atop thick, upright branches. Nearby, he could see the mighty tree that had fallen to make the thing.

White-skins, the *xayxayx,* gathered at that table. His people's headmen sat before them on robes. Camps were spread across the country, and squaws and warriors and elders watched from there, staring intently at the council.

A murmur snaked through everyone as they became aware of Looking Glass's presence. Some of the headmen pushed to their feet to look back at the newcomers in mingled surprise and embarrassment. Water Calf's pony was jostled as his friends moved up close behind him, as though waiting for him to go closer before they dared it themselves.

He felt stronger now, watching his uncle and father. All the warriors had painted themselves for this encounter, and crimson and white slashed their faces and chests. Eagle feathers were woven into their ponies' manes and tails, and beads and deerclaw bells hung from their bridles.

Suddenly, they rode straight for the white men, beating their horses into a gallop. Water Calf's heart leaped in surprise, then he yipped and kicked his own pony. He dashed about the peoples' camps, his friends following him eagerly.

When the warriors reached the desecrated tree they wheeled about again, whooping. Water Calf laughed aloud at the whiteskins' stunned faces.

"My people, what have you done?" Looking Glass demanded, "While I was gone, you tried to sell my country. I have come home now. Is there left to me a place to pitch my lodge? Go home to your lodges. I will talk to you."

He whipped his pony about angrily. The headmen began gathering up their robes again, some with apologetic glances at the white men. No one had made more dangerous trips over the mountains than Looking Glass. His influence was far stronger than Lawyer's, the only headman to remain behind with the *xayxayx*.

Water Calf trotted close to his father. "Will they give the land for that iron horse?" he asked.

Culmuh scowled for a long time before he answered. "We have stopped the talk. For now, that is enough."

Looking Glass's people settled between Old Joseph's Kahmuenem camp and that of Toolhoolhoolzote's Pikunanmu band. As the sun went down, it was almost as though they had never left Tolo Lake, had never moved on without fishing and feasting. There were the strong, mouth-watering smells of eel and sturgeon sizzling over the pits. Warriors and boys took to the plains to race their ponies. When his own gelding began heaving, Water Calf left the contests and led him back toward the camps.

There was hunger in his belly and a good feeling in his heart. He paused at the herd, rubbing the sweat off his mount with handfuls of grass. Then he squatted down to chew on a blade of it himself, chuckling as foals chased around him, bucking and playing

They were all strong limbed and colorful, but Water Calf knew that nearly all of the males would be castrated and most of the females would be culled, traded away before they could reproduce. Only the most exceptionally colored animals were permitted to breed.

When the animals quieted again, the babes sought out their mares so that they might nap in safety at their hooves. For some reason, that made Water Calf think of the orphan babe, without a mother to love her. Her own true kin were here now, but the haughty old Toolhoolhoolzote had only stared through his granddaughter as though she were invisible when Broken Bird had tried to present her to him.

Scowling, Water Calf pushed to his feet and spit out the grass. He went back to his kin's fire and peered unobtrusively over his mother's shoulder. The orphan was there, cuddled against her chest, nursing. But to Water Calf's way of thinking, she was doing far more howling than suckling.

"What is wrong with her?" he demanded.

Broken Bird answered him with a small, worried frown. "I must feed your sister first, and there is never much milk left for this one. She is hungry and frustrated."

Water Calf scowled. "Could that make her starve?"

"She is a strong one, and some milk is better than none."

It was not much of an answer, and he thought of more questions. How had Silver Cloud been able to feed her? What of real food, like the camas-thick broth Broken Bird made for him when his belly was sick? His mother sighed as though she read his thoughts.

"That other squaw was able to stop nursing her own son to provide for this one. Her babe was old enough, ready to be weaned, but your sister is not. And Dark Moon is not yet big enough to take anything but milk. She spits out everything else I try to give her.''

Water Calf looked down at the child's scrunched, angry face. It was not his worry, he decided. The warriors were counciling about the white-skins, and now that the racing was over, he wanted to hear.

He left his mother and moved toward the big council fire. But when he passed the pony herd again, his feet seemed to stop of their own volition.

If the orphan could not have a mother of her own, perhaps many mothers could fill her belly.

He scrubbed his hands over his face. How his friends would laugh at him if he did what he was thinking! They might even stop following him, and that would be disastrous. Without a following, he might find his *wyakin* only to become just another average warrior.

He moved toward the council fire again, then he stomped one moccasin against the earth. The idea would not leave his head.

Milk was milk, he thought. If he took a little bit of nourishment from a different mare each sun, the orphan would not starve and their foals would not feel the lack. He bit his lip and looked back at his kin's hearth. Broken Bird was even now carrying the babes into her grass lodge.

The men were still talking, and he knew they would keep doing so until the moon went down. He had time.

He sat down and untied a moccasin, feeling foolish as he hopped back into the herd on one foot. He picked a pony who knew him, one of his mother's mares. But when he first tried to grab her teat, she squealed and snaked her neck around at him, her teeth bared.

Water Calf jumped back, then her foal scrambled to his feet to nudge a drink of his own. With his little body pressed close to hers, the mare did not seem to know who was actually tugging on her udder. Water Calf tried again, this time splashing a long stream into his moccasin.

The longer he was able to get away with it, the more he grinned.

Finally, he backed away, swatting her happily on the rump. She gave him a level, unamused eye, as though to tell him she had not truly been duped. Water Calf laughed and went back to his mother's lodge.

Dark Moon was laced into her cradleboard, still wailing, but his mother had gone back to the fire. He squatted down beside the babe, dunking his fingers into the milk and dribbling it upon her lips. Her eyes went even bigger as hunger gripped her anew, and she opened wide to squall again.

"No, Screamer, wait!" Impulsively, he took a gulp himself, then leaned over her to squirt it into her while she was wide-mouthed.

Dark Moon sputtered and coughed, but she swallowed. Water Calf gave a whoop of satisfaction and repeated the process.

When his moccasin was soggy and empty, he was left with a thick, bitter taste on his tongue and a dozing babe. He slipped quietly outside again, spitting at the ground and scrubbing his mouth as he glanced around. No one paid him any mind.

He grimaced at his moccasin. He was not eager to put it back on his foot. He moved away from the lodges, toward the river, and hurled the shoe as far as he could. He tugged the other one off and dropped it in the water. He would catch a good reprimand from Broken Bird for losing them. Next sun-coming, he thought, he would steal one of her sheep horns. She would not be happy about that either, but it could not be helped.

Curled in his bedding against the next chilly sunrise, Water Calf listened to the sounds of his mother feeding the babes. A private grin crossed his face as Broken Bird cooed to Dark Moon. There was slight confusion and concern in her voice. It was not his imagination, then, that the babe did not seem to squall so loudly this dawn.

When Broken Bird had gone outside to work at her summer hearth, Water Calf pushed his robe back and crawled over to the little one. She began gurgling expectantly when she saw him. Could she have learned that quickly that he represented food? He did not know much about babes, but he did not think their minds were supposed to work that accurately. He backed away from this one.

"Not now, Screamer. Later." He half expected her to begin wailing again, but she only watched him with those strange, nearly blue eyes, as though she understood and would wait.

Nothing would keep him from the council this sun, not even the hungry babe he had dubbed Screamer. This would be the time when his uncle spoke to the *xayxayx*.

He went outside. His friends were already at the pony herd, where the sun turned the dew on the grass to silver sparks of light. They went chest to chest with wagers over the games and races that would come, but Water Calf turned the other way. When the bands finally found the salmon runs, there would be time enough to play.

He scowled at the *xayxayx* place, then he went the long way around the camps to the river. This was a real council, and he did not think he could get away with joining the important men. He slid down the bank, then waded quietly back toward the spot where the noisy white-skin tents were. The water was icy with the first of the mountain runoff and his teeth chattered. When he reached the desecrated tree, he dropped to his belly and crawled back up to the prairie through the tall, wet grass.

Many were already gathered. Looking Glass came last. The small magic mirror that gave him his medicine lay flat against his forehead.

He looked sternly around at the *xayxayx*. "It was my children who spoke yesterday," he announced. "Now I have come to talk."

Before he could say anything more, Lawyer approached the gathering at a trundling trot. The white men looked confused, their gazes moving between one headman and the other.

The *xayxayx* chief stepped forward. "Which of you is in charge?" he demanded, and a trader man translated.

Lawyer's face began to stain red and he turned to the man Stee-vuns. "I would speak. I can fix this." Water Calf thought he sounded desperate, not like a warrior should at all. But then, it was said that Lawyer had laid down his bow when he had started talking like a white man, following that *xayxayx* god.

"These men are our friends," he said earnestly. "They do not want our good lands. All they ask for are border countries where none of our villages or rivers are located. This council has gone many suns before you came. The white men have promised this, but you were not here to hear it. They ask for little, and give us much in this treaty they offer."

Looking Glass growled, "I have heard of their treaties. I have met people from the East who have been stripped of their lands, so that they must live like tethered animals on plots allotted to them. They must beg to go hunt even the lowly deer. And what of the Yakima? They gave what they thought was little, to this very man. Now they must fight to reclaim what the Spirit Chief once granted to them solely!"

"You say they give much!" someone called out to Lawyer. "What?"

"They will protect us from their trespassing brothers." Lawyer shouted to be heard over the growing murmur of debate. "White-skins will not be allowed in our country, as they have infested the lands of those people over the mountains. If we do not take this treaty, there will be no protection. Then roaming *xayxayx* will fill our land, as they have done to others before us."

"And will they call our country a re-ser-va-shun?" the headman-shaman Toolhoolhoolzote sneered.

"Yes," Stee-vuns interjected. "But it is all the same land you have now. We wish simply to set the place apart for you, away from the railroads that will run around your country."

"I will show you our re-ser-va-shun." Looking Glass snatched up the map that lay on the white-skins' table. He drew his mark over the whole expanse, the traditional Nimipu country as Tahmahnewes had given it. "This is our country. This is where our women and children stay and prosper while we travel free across the mountains. *That* is what I will sign to."

"That is all we ask you to sign to," Stee-vuns assured him.

Looking Glass left the talk, and the others drifted off behind him until only Lawyer and Old Joseph remained. Lawyer turned fretfully to Stee-vuns.

"I will sign." He was convinced that cooperating with these men, taking up their ways, was the only way his people could survive. Besides, it had been a long time since he had dreamed, and he was growing afraid without his *wyakin*. This seemed the safest path for him to choose, one where a spirit guide was not so vital.

Stevens took in a deep breath. "Good, good. Now I want your heart to be true, and I want you to make your mark."

"I will get those presents?"

"Personal benefits and payments, yes, as head chief, since you led these talks before your friend interrupted. In addition, payments will be made to your tribe in the form of improvements to your reservation."

"And that is the land we have always had?"

Stevens nodded impatiently. "Your traditional land, within the land you have disclaimed. Your fort will be just south of the Clearwater, with soldiers there to protect you against any whites that might try to come in. But let it not be forgotten that you've promised to stay there and refrain from molesting those men coming through with the railroad."

Lawyer bristled a little at that. No Nimipu had ever harmed a white man, not in all the generations that had passed since those Lew-us and Clark people had turned up lost and hungry in their land. Still, he made his mark.

Old Joseph leaned over the table to inspect the map again, to make sure his beloved Kahmuenem, the Wallowa valley that had been his father's and his father's before him, was not included. He saw that the white-skins indeed took only the country surrounding those lands claimed by Looking Glass, White Bird, Toolhoolhoolzote, and himself. Huishuis Kute's territory was so far south it was not a consideration.

Old Joseph thought that that would be all right.

"I want no presents," he said sternly, signing. "Just keep your people far, as you promise."

Hidden in the grass, Water Calf frowned. With a boy's pure instinct, he decided he did not trust Stee-vuns's smile.

3

Tay-ya-tahl, Moon of Hot Weather, 1860

DARK MOON LIFTED her nose into the sweltering wind and felt her belly cramp up at the smell of all the food here. Something almost like a smile lit her face.

"Go then," Broken Bird said to her, wrestling the last side of her teasel mat onto the branch frame of her summer lodge.

She had parfleches full of dried fish taken at Tolo Lake, but she knew the child would only nibble nervously at that food if she offered it to her. She hated staying in camp, especially these large communal gatherings when the Nimipu met in the summer moons. She tended to keep to herself where the constant suspicion of the others could not touch her.

Broken Bird's face tightened with anger. Such treatment was more than any child should have to suffer. Tahmahnewes, this one had seen only five snows!

"I said go!" She waved an arm at her. "There is nothing for you to do here. Do you see work?"

Dark Moon shook her head, her long, black hair flying in a snarl of motion. She skittered backward, her heels hitting a pile of Broken Bird's camp supplies. She fell hard over them, and a boy passing behind her hooted and snagged a handful of her hair.

"The babe killer cannot walk!" he bellowed loud enough for his friends to hear. "We must help her!"

He tugged cruelly on her hair again. Dark Moon flipped over onto her knees in a reflex so fast it startled even Broken Bird. A thin sound came from her throat as she fought him, whip-

ping her head back and forth like a camp dog trying to work
a piece of meat from someone who would take it from him.

Broken Bird snatched up an antler scraper and waved it at
the youth angrily. His grip fell away and raced off again. Dark
Moon was gone in the same moment, fleeing as though a spirit
monster were on her heels.

She did not stop running until she was well outside the
camp. She squatted down in the grass behind some shelters,
scrubbing one hand under her nose to dry her sniffles.

Babe? she wondered. Killer? For a moment she nearly cried
in frustration because she could not ever remember hurting a
wee one, and could not imagine why anyone would think she
had. Then her belly demanded her attention again, clenching
up tightly at the good smells of meat here.

She stood, cocking her head, listening for the telltale growls
of the dogs. The sounds finally came to her from between two
lodges to her right, and she moved cautiously in that direction.
She spotted them and moved in as naturally as the wind that
spun up eddies of dust all around them. When she was very
close, she dropped to her hands and knees and gave her own
growling sound. A young wolf fell back, eyeing her curiously,
and her hand flashed out, snatching up the meaty bone he had
been working on.

She leaped to her feet again, running on, and circled the rest
of the sprawling camp. Much of what she scavenged was useless, eel skins and offal, but she was able to gather some roots
and a not-quite-rancid hunk of sturgeon as well.

She headed out for the herd. The ponies nickered and shifted
to allow her to move among them. She nickered back, imitat-
ing their sounds. Most times, it was a game she loved, pre-
tending the ponies could understand her, and sometimes they
truly seemed to do so. Now, however, she was very hungry.
The Hasotoin had been traveling for several suns, and she
could never get much food when they were on the move, eating from their dried stores.

She deposited her cache in a small pile, then she shrugged
out of her tattered doeskin and squatted down, naked, to knot
it into a sack. The sun felt delicious, baking down on her. In

spite of the big fishing and root camps the season brought, summer was her very favorite time. She was free to wander then, to take care of herself.

She began to relax, humming a soft little chant under her breath as she worked. She moved through old White Bird's Lamtama band ponies, then she went to those of the Pikunanmu band, her voice dying unconsciously there. She had often heard it said that Toolhoolhoolzote's Pikunanmu were her real people, that her mother had come from them and that the *tiwats* Toolhoolhoolzote was her grandfather. But Toolhoolhoolzote did not want her to live with him because she was a babe killer.

Dark Moon shook her head. She did not like to think about that because it made her belly feel bad. Instead, she turned her thoughts to finding just the right hard balls of dung, carefully slipping them into her dress sack so they would not crack.

She ran back to her little pile of food and stripped the grass away from a small circle of earth. Then she dug out some of the dirt and buried the roots, laying the torn grass over them. Water Calf had made her a fire starter, and she untied her shift again, pulling the tool carefully from her belt. It was a very special possession, the only thing in the whole world that was truly hers. She worked it over the grass, biting her lip in concentration.

Smoke, and finally a small flame, licked out. She smacked her hand down upon some of the manure, pulverizing it, and sprinkled the powder on top of the grass so the fire would grow. Finally, she placed the remaining balls of dung atop the little blaze, careful not to extinguish it. Now she would need some sticks, to hold her meat and the fish over the flames so it could cook. Green wood would be best, because that fish would have to smoke for a long while to get the stink out of it.

She stood again, studying the prairie, shaking out her shift and slipping it over her head again. She had finally decided on a distant, straggly knot of trees when movement flickered at the periphery of her vision.

She looked around sharply to see men riding toward the

camp. No, not men. Boys, older than the one who had pulled her hair, but not yet warriors because they did not carry a full complement of weapons. She began to sink down into the concealing grass, then she recognized one of them.

Water Calf!

Her heart soared. He and his friends had wandered away from the main band two whole suns ago. Broken Bird never seemed scared when he did such things, and Culmuh was always proud to welcome his son back because he brought game and wonderful stories that proved his bravery and his worth. But Dark Moon always waited tensely until he returned safely to them.

She ran toward him, her long, skinny legs pumping furiously. He reined in his speckled pony, motioning his friends to go on without him. She came abreast of him, then she felt as though all of Mother Earth fell out from beneath her moccasins. Water Calf was scowling.

She began moving backward again, and he sighed.

"Wait, Screamer. Here. I have brought you something."

He reached behind him to the rump of his pony. An antelope carcass was lashed there, and an assortment of smaller game hung from the leather straps. Her eyes widened in disbelief as he pulled a hare free and tossed it to her.

All of it? It was all hers, the pelt and the meat and *everything?*

"I had a good hunt," he said, reading her stunned face. The gift would keep her busy as well, he thought, so perhaps she would not follow him so relentlessly about the camp this sun. He had seen fourteen snows now, but the little orphan kept to his heels as if he were her playmate. Sometimes he almost regretted feeding her all those seasons ago, establishing such a bond.

"Broken Bird can show you how to take those brains out and use them to tan the fur," he went on.

Dark Moon's small mouth worked. She was too overwhelmed to find the words to thank him.

"Screamer."

She did not know why he called her that, but she looked up

at him worshipfully. He was so pretty, she thought, then she
remembered that he hated it when she said that. Once he had
pushed her away from him, shaking his head. But he did have
eyes that seemed as deep as Tolo Lake, and she liked looking
at him, just as she liked watching a perfect pony run.

"I always try to bring you something," he went on.

"Yes." Her voice finally came, high and uncertain.

"When I *can* bring you something, I will seek you out to
give it to you. You do not have to come running to me and
my friends as soon as we appear."

He had told her that many times before, and she felt
ashamed for forgetting. It was just that sometimes, when he
had been gone for several suns, her excitement at seeing him
again overcame her good sense.

"I will remember next time," she vowed fervently. "I
will."

He finally smiled at her, lightening the world for her again.
As he trotted back to the camp, she hugged the rabbit to her
chest, watching him adoringly.

Water Calf took the remaining carcasses to his mother. He
grinned easily while Culmuh bragged over his kill. It did not
take very long for the commotion to draw a crowd of young
girls. He sought the eyes of the one he decided was the prettiest. She was slender and straight, with a narrow waist and
high breasts. Her eyes were direct and flashed in the sun.

"This antelope ran to me and gave me an arrow," he joked.
"It held its hoof to its heart so I would know where to shoot."

The other girls looked at each other and giggled, but the
one he liked best only lifted her chin with a sure smile.

"And the rabbits and squirrels?" she countered. "Did they
leap into your lap as you rode?"

Water Calf laughed, a good, deep sound that made at least
one girl shiver. "No. I had to chase those down. Who are
you?"

He knew, of course. He had seen her around before, but she
had never approached him. He had not bothered to seek her

out, either, because he was rarely short on female companionship.

"They call me Cloud Singer now," the girl answered. "I am daughter to White Bird who leads the Lamtama."

Now. So she had found her *wyakin,* he thought. His confidence, usually so strong a part of him, flagged a bit.

Soon, he told himself. Surely Looking Glass and Culmuh would send him in search of his spirit guide this season.

Cloud Singer pulled on the arm of the girl who stood beside her. "This is A-yun. She would like to meet you. She is daughter to Lawyer."

Ann, of the *xayxayx* name, blushed scarlet, and Water Calf smiled at her to put her at ease, but his attention went straight back to Cloud Singer.

"*You* do not want to meet me?" he teased.

"I already have," she shot back, and he decided he liked her quickness as well.

They were jostled apart as more and more people began to gather at his kin's summer hearth. The boys he had gone hunting with carried pieces of their own kills, and the livers were shared proudly with the appreciative girls. Broken Bird cut off some of Water Calf's own roasting antelope and passed around the pieces.

The crowd began wandering down to the river, away from censuring adult eyes. Water Calf had been shocked, a few seasons ago, to learn that his own father and mother had once come here as well, that the river gatherings and the antics that went on there were no secret to anybody.

The boys squatted down on their haunches near the water, and the girls sat among them. Water Calf leaned one shoulder against a tree, chewing on a twig to clean his teeth.

After a while, the jibes and dares began, the air filling with young male voices like the barks of elk in rutting season.

Trinkets were promised and bartered while the girls blushed and giggled among each other. Water Calf moved closer and stood behind the other boys.

"I will do it if you do it," he heard Cloud Singer challenge Ann, and he knew fleeting regret for Ann. There was something simple in her eyes, a deep-running eagerness to please. Ann would obligingly go first, easing the way for her friend without even realizing she was being manipulated.

"I will give you my whole antelope hide if you do it first," he heard himself call out to Cloud Singer, and he was immediately appalled at himself. How would he explain such a thing to Broken Bird? But already the others were gasping and looking around at him, and it was too late to take back the dare.

Cloud Singer's eyes met his appraisingly. Water Calf realized with a sinking feeling that somehow, he had reacted just as she wanted.

She stood slowly while the boys began to hoot even more loudly. With a quick, graceful shrug, she dropped one shoulder of her dress. She undid her belt with long, slim fingers, still holding his eyes. When the top of her doeskin was loose enough, she pushed the other shoulder away as well.

The shift fell to her waist, exposing her breasts. She did not giggle and hurry to clap her hands over herself again as most of the girls did. Instead, it seemed to Water Calf that she actually straightened her spine, pivoting slowly to show herself to the others.

Finally, she pulled her dress up again. The boys began to roar even more loudly, especially Young Looking Glass. She turned away, wandering prettily down the river, back toward the camp as Ann scrambled eagerly to her feet.

Cloud Singer stopped in the concealing shadows of the next copse of trees, smiling to herself. She had wanted to go first. Each subsequent girl would be goaded into removing more of her clothing, into outdoing the last one. She had no intention of being one of those. She had learned that boys seemed to want most that which they could not have. Still, it was her opinion that it was always a good idea to give them a little glimpse of what they were missing, and she enjoyed feeling their eyes on her.

Cloud Singer turned away again as silly Ann let her doeskin slide all the way down her body, pooling at her feet. Tomorrow, she was sure, Water Calf would come to her father's camp, looking for her. Playing the boys' game briefly, with all the dignity she could muster, had been worth it.

She had wanted Water Calf to come looking for her for a very long time.

4

THE SEASON TURNED, and Water Calf finally gave up hope that he would be sent out to search for his *wyakin*. The camas roots were picked, the salmon had spawned, and his people were home again in their Hasotoin longhouse. He knew it would be difficult for him to make it into the hills and back before the Weekwetset, the Dance of the Guardian Spirit. That was when all the youths who had found their *wyakins* revealed their new names. The rite had to take place before the cold truly came, and no one had yet spoken a word to him about spirit protectors.

He dwelled unhappily on that as he hunkered down beside Culmuh to scrape a root cake from the ashes of his mother's fire. When his father finally spoke the words he had been waiting for, he only looked at him blankly.

"You should go. It is time."

Water Calf swallowed down his cake. "Where?" But then he knew, because his uncle came from his own hearth to stand over them. "Now?"

"Now is the hardest time, and therefore the best of times," Looking Glass said mildly, and then Water Calf understood. He had not been sent at the peak of the summer, when the suns had been warm and the nights mild, because that would have been a mediocre triumph. His uncle and his father wanted more for him, and they obviously thought he was strong enough to earn a superior dream and reputation.

A little thrill went down his spine, then came a sobering thought: *If he dreamed.*

"Is there time?" he asked, but he was stalling, and he was immediately ashamed of himself. He stood up without waiting for an answer. He would be back before the Weekwetset, and he would have a dream. He was strong, of good blood. He had been waiting for this chance, working toward it, since the time he had first walked.

He pulled on the string of his leggings, letting them drop to the warm ground of the hearth. He held his arms high to Tahmahnewes, to show that he had no weapons. But, oh, Spirit Chief, already the cool air brought puckers of goosebumps to his naked flesh, and he was not even outside yet. A tiny, stricken sound came from behind him, startling him. He whipped around to find the orphan squatted in her usual spot, on a pile of bedding away from the others, near the wall.

"You think I am weak, that I cannot do this?" he chided. Dark Moon shook her head wildly.

"Then make sure you cook up much food for me, for we will celebrate when I return."

She would do that and more, Dark Moon vowed.

As he left the longhouse, she got up from the bedding, her fist wrapping tightly around the beloved rabbit paw that hung about her neck.

"Where do you go, little one?" Broken Bird asked.

"I must wait for him."

"Oh, child, no." But Broken Bird saw that she would not stop her. The orphan was so solemn for her snows, and accustomed to taking care of herself.

"Promise not to leave the camp," Broken Bird urged. "And take some cake."

Dark Moon took a tiny, crumbly portion. How she had managed to grow so much taller than the other children was a mystery, Broken Bird mused. She certainly did not eat enough to keep a bird alive.

The wind outside was strong and damp, and Dark Moon went only as far as the pony herd. Soon the horses would begin wandering up into the hills for the winter, and she would miss

them terribly. But for now, they stood close to each other,
sharing their body heat as their rumps faced into the gusts.

She dropped to her knees and crawled beneath the bellies
of a docile pair of mares. She would wait right here until Water
Calf came back, she decided. Nothing on Tahmahnewes's
earth could make her seek comfort as long as her friend was
suffering somewhere also.

The wolves, oh, Tahmahnewes, the wolves!

By the third night, she could not bear them anymore, those
haunting, predatory howls as the animals roamed the hills. But
when they fell quiet, terror made a weak, watery feeling swim
in her bowels.

Were they quiet because they had eaten? *Had they eaten
Water Calf?*

He had no weapons with him, and he was not allowed to
fashion any. He did not need to hunt, because he was not
allowed to eat. She thought he must be even hungrier by now
than she was, and her own belly was beginning to twist with
the hurt of it. She scowled, remembering that hunger was good
when you were looking for your *wyakin*. When it got very,
very bad it made your head grow light and open. The hardship
would make Water Calf's thoughts float up into the air. Then
the Great Spirit Chief could catch them and turn them into a
vision, if he so chose.

A mare grunted and dropped clumsily down into the grass
to doze. Dark Moon crawled to her and cuddled up close
against her as rains came with the dark. The relentless downpour began to chill her bones anyway. She hurt, oh, Tahmahnewes, she did! The cool wind buffeted her sodden dress, and
an ache started deep within her.

*Water Calf. She had to do this for Water Calf so that he
did not become like that man who had been her father.*

Her eyes drifted closed, but she caught herself, forcing them
open again. She sat up and pushed her small chin out stubbornly, widening her eyes so big they hurt. She hugged herself
and thought of a fire.

Water Calf had one. That was allowed, she remembered.

She tried to make herself stand, to get wood, but her limbs felt like a tree that had died, heavy and broken. It hurt too much to move, so she sighed and lay down in the mud again instead.

She would just think about a fire, she decided, and that would make her feel better. Sometimes, on cold nights, she pretended she was closer to Broken Bird's hearth than she truly was. It always worked, making her feel warmer. Dark Moon closed her eyes tight and concentrated hard.

Comfort crawled in on her treacherously. Oh, Great Spirit Chief, she did feel warmer. She did not dare stay like this too long, or she knew she would sleep. But just for a moment, just for a little time . . .

A big, speckled mare came close and stepped over her, shielding her body from the elements. Thank you, Tahmah-newes, Dark Moon mused. No more rain. Just the fire in her head . . .

She was not sleeping because she would not let herself. She could not be asleep because she knew she was not supposed to do that.

She watched the fire she had built in her mind.

It flickered gently, and it was a magical fire, because the rain did not put it out. Was the rain back? Yes, she was sure it was, even though she could no longer feel it. She saw it plopping and glistening on the leaves. And there—that was thunder, rolling out with dark, warning anger.

The trees began to scream. Their branches crashed above her, rackety and whipping. But there were no trees where she lay with the herd, and that made her frown.

Water Calf!

How had he gotten here? He was supposed to be out looking for his *wyakin!* Panic gripped her and she called to him, then she saw that he *was* looking for his dream vision. He sat very still, just on the other side of her make-believe fire. His eyes were closed and his hair was flat against his head as the cold rain cascaded over his skin.

There was another crash, closer, and she wondered if a tree had fallen to lightning. Water Calf was deep inside himself, and he did not seem to hear it. She stood up, and now her legs were strong and fine. She would find the tree herself. It seemed important.

Thunder rumbled again, too close, much too close. It was more like the growl of an animal, one with a big, deep chest. She looked around, and then she saw it.

A bear.

Oh, Tahmahnewes, it was so big, bigger than anything she had ever seen before! Horror made her cold again. The bear was close and angry, and fear robbed her air. She saw his yellowed claws, long and deadly, and his teeth, far up in the air over her head. His fur was wet and matted and bloody.

Rogue! Now she did scream, and the sound was so loud in her head! But neither Water Calf nor the grizzly seemed to hear her. The bear lumbered past, crashing through the brush, drawn by the fire, moving toward Water Calf where he sat still and silent and unaware.

Noooo!

Her terror lifted her, spun her, filled her with the lightness of air. Terrified, she flung her arms out, her small hands flailing for something to grab. Instead, her claws raked through the branches, sweeping down through the brush, clearing a path. Everything was different! Grandmother Earth was too far below her, her feet too far from her head. Hunger and pain were wild inside her. She watched Water Calf through the golden, measuring eyes of the bear.

She was *in* the bear!

Desperation wailed through her, the wildest, biggest part of her true self. *Not Water Calf, not him!* She screamed again.

Hands dragged at her, pulling her awake. Somewhere inside herself, she felt herself falling, spinning again. Something sharp and deep rushed through her head, bringing agony.

The bear . . .

But he seemed to be gone now. The last she felt of him was her own fear, sudden and inexplicable, prickling the hair on his matted nape.

''No, child, no! This is enough!''

Broken Bird's voice came to her, first from far away, then

closer. Her hands were warm and sure, lifting her off the wet ground. Dark Moon put her arms around the midwife's neck, wrapped her legs around her waist, and sobbed.

Far off in the hills, a rogue grizzly's whine was whipped away by the wind. He plunged back into the brush, away from the terrible, intuitive danger that seemed to leap suddenly at him from the flames of the once-luring fire.

Water Calf was so deeply wet and cold he did not hear. Wonderful colors flowed in his head, blue and rose and the golden green of midsummer grass. He watched them, rapt, pushing the outside world away.

All about him, the storm roared.

Part of him still knew that, and for some reason it reminded him of the night the orphan had come to them. For a moment, he thought he heard her call his name as well. Her voice seemed to sap the last of his strength, taking it away when it faded. Exhaustion dragged him down, into a place deep inside himself.

Another gust of wind came, stronger than any yet, and he fell slowly over under its force, curling up on his side.

The colors in his mind changed, growing sharper, forming images.

War.

He saw his people, bloodied and wounded, many nearly naked. The crack and clatter of the trees above him muted and merged into gunfire. The People were running. He went along behind them, knowing he had to, knowing he had never had any choice. He had to guard them, protect them, until they were gone to some unknown place of safety, a place he could not see.

The sound of thunder grew louder, relentless, steady. *Hoofbeats.* He whipped around again, and saw the coveted Nez Percé herds galloping toward him.

They were wild, their hides frothing, crashing about and into each other. The squaws caught them up. Mounted, they fled faster, and he ran with them until a single pony surged close to him, making his steps falter.

It was a mare, sleek and beautiful, solid black unlike anything the People had ever bred. He stared at her, at her tangled, whipping mane. It grew longer and longer, into a woman's sleek, straight hair. Her wild eyes and flared nostrils blurred into each other, streaming like paints left out in the rain. But he made her out clearly now, a stunning, ethereal squaw, flying on hooves of lightning.

He ran with her, with the pony woman, faster and faster. His feet flew as impossibly quickly as her pounding hooves, and he knew, by the smile in her eyes, that she would save them.

5

WALTER CALF STIRRED from a deep sleep on the damp ground. He sat up, dizzy and disoriented, then he remembered.

He had dreamed.

He gave a bark of exultation and sprang to his feet, but his legs were hollow and weak, and he swayed, grabbing a tree for support. Common sense came to him in a frustrating rush. It was a long way back to the Hasotoin village, and he had no pony to carry him. If he tried to go to his people now, he would not make it.

He slid down again and propped himself against the tree, and groped about for some rocks. He pulled a small pile of the missiles close to his right hand, and then he went very still to wait. Dusk came back before a grouse settled low in a tree within his range. He hefted a rock, measuring its weight, eyeing the angle and distance between himself and his prey. With a small grunt, he let the rock fly.

It hit the bird squarely, felling it. Struggling up again, Water Calf made his way to it and twisted its neck.

He buried the bird beneath the hottest embers of his fire, and when the feathers singed and smoked, he dragged it out with a stick. He forced himself to eat slowly, allowing his stomach to adjust to the onslaught of food. He did not dare vomit it.

Finally, sated, he lay down to sleep.

He felt stronger when the sun came again. He stood, and his legs held him more steadily. He eyed a moderately worn path down the hillside. The trail meandered wildly through the most passable terrain, easily twice the distance of a direct descent. He decided against taking it. He was impatient to be home.

He pushed his way into the brush, finding footing on a smooth fall of rocks. But he had gone only a short way before the stench of something dead lifted the hair on his nape.

He followed his nose. Soon he found tracks to lead him on, large, claw-gouged indentations in the mud. He looked over a precipice and found a grizzly far below him, twisted forage for the death birds.

An odd, uncomfortable feeling nudged at the back of his neck.

He went on, nearly gaining the valley before his thighs and calves began to tremble again. He watched for fresh sign of water so that he could camp through one more sleep, and found it just below him in the riotous autumn colors of deciduous, creek-thriving trees.

His eyes narrowed. A sinewy wisp of smoke hung there as well, then was caught and scattered by the wind.

Smoke?

His feet began to move more covertly, avoiding twigs and whispery clumps of grass. He moved catlike into the copse. It would be his own people, with ponies . . . that was all that made sense, but a little, clawing animal scurried around in his belly, telling him it was not so.

Shoshone? Blackfoot? But no war party would venture so far from its homeland in this late season, not unless dire vengeance demanded such a risk. None of his own people had been over the mountains since the spring. The Hasotoin had done nothing recently to incur such wrath.

He stopped, easing his way down into the brush to slink closer. Then he saw them, and his heart staggered.

Xayxayx?

For a wild moment, he considered that he was still dreaming, that the grouse and the rough trail downhill had all been part of his vision. Then came the certainty, wilder still, that he was awake. There were white-skins here, dirty men with stringy hair and pallid, watery eyes. They had appeared on his dream trek, and he knew, somehow, that they and his *wyakin* were intertwined.

Adrenaline surged in him, hot and ready to meet the challenge. But when his hand moved deftly for his knife, it slid over bare skin instead.

No weapon.

He bit back a frustrated growl and went flat on his belly to wait. As the interminable sun fell, he watched the *xayxayx* perform a strange ritual over the creek. His eyes narrowed as they pulled shiny, gold flecks from the water, raucously calling to each other in their twangy tongue. Somehow, they had sneaked in here, to Nimipu land, into the deepest heartland only the People knew.

That man Stee-vuns had promised this would not happen. Betrayal and disbelief made his blood pump harder.

Shadows began to crawl into the creek bed. The white-skins settled into their camp. They passed leather flasks, filling their shallow, metal bowls with food from a kettle. Drinking from the flasks made them louder, and then they slept abruptly.

Still, Water Calf waited.

When the moon was straight above him, he pushed to his feet again, his legs screaming with the effects of more forced inactivity. He let the tingling pain pass through him and grinned suddenly. The *xayxayx* were crazy, he thought, perhaps as crazy as he was for daring this coup. They had come uninvited, yet they left no sentinels out while they slept.

There were six of them. He moved silently into their camp, stepping among their prone forms. His heart hurtled into his throat when one stirred, but his hands were steady as he slid their rifles out from beneath the wadded clothing and blankets they laid their heads upon.

His grin widened as he gathered up their supplies as well. He took the few little pouches of their metal that he could find. Two of the rifles were gleaming and new. He laid them on the bank atop one of the blankets, and emptied the ammunition from the others, holding a single knife in his teeth. He slid everything else into the creek. The gentle current caught the stuff and coaxed it downstream.

He knew he would have to leave them afoot. Looking Glass might choose to come after them, and he wanted to make sure that they would be traveling slowly and painstakingly if that were the case. He turned to their picketed mounts, his pulse thundering.

But, oh, what a sweet rush it was, this new sense of danger!

He knew that when their ponies stirred, they would wake. He glanced at them one more time, then he crouched down and used the knife to slice quickly through their hobbles. One by one, the horses began to wander. Their sounds were furtive at first, a snort here, the stomp of a hoof there. Then came the shout he had been waiting for, groggy and alarmed as a miner sat up.

"Eeeeeiiiiiooooow!" The war cry leaped into Water Calf's throat, as naturally as though he had always voiced it. The ponies bolted and the last one, still hobbled, struggled helplessly. His adrenaline screamed as he brought the knife down through that last tether as well. He grabbed up the blanket with the guns and the ammunition, then he snagged the last pony's mane and scissored his legs up and over its back.

He did not quite make it.

Hands as hard and strong as any warrior's caught him about the calf, fingers biting into his tender muscles. Pain howled up into his thigh. He tried frantically to kick the grip off, but the *xayxayx* had not just been on a *wyakin* search and he was stronger. Water Calf fell with a grunting burst of breath onto the hard ground, his heart starting to pound.

How had this gone so bad so quickly?

Terror made his throat burn, then the white-skin's hard-soled moccasin came down there, choking off his air. High above him, he saw moonlight glint off the blade of a knife. As blackness swam over his vision, it occurred to him that maybe he was not so special or blessed after all. Maybe it did not matter that he had a *wyakin* and followers, or good, handsome eyes and strong kin.

Something in their eyes told him they would kill him anyway.

*   *   *

Dark Moon was miserable sitting so close to Broken Bird's fire. It felt as though everyone, all down the long row of longhouse hearths, was watching her. She kept her eyes down, trying to ignore them, but she could not shut her ears.

Helps Another, Looking Glass's wife, gave a low keening sound from the next fire. "He is gone from us, gone," she moaned. "What has happened out there?"

The storm was long over, but Water Calf had not returned. Dark Moon knew his kin thought him to be dead, and she knew that many blamed her, the babe killer. It was not right that she should have been found in the pony herd, unconscious and wailing, in the worst part of the weather. They wondered what spirits she had spoken to out there while Water Calf made his vigil.

More men came to Looking Glass's hearth: Tenku, the *ti-wats* shaman, and Four Goose and his cronies. She flinched when Tenku spoke.

"She has already killed four, if you count those two who gave her life. Now perhaps she has taken your nephew. She is a danger to us all. How much longer will you let her stay?"

Dark Moon felt hot, righteous anger fill her throat. She had done nothing, at least not to Water Calf! But she could not tell them that, because she truly did not know for sure. She struggled to recall what had happened out there in the herd, but, oh, she could not remember! It was just like that babe they said had died. *She could not remember!*

Old Looking Glass spoke to her almost kindly. "Did you dream out there, little one?"

"Bah!" Broken Bird protested. "A child of five snows cannot dream!"

"Did you?" snapped Culmuh. He was angriest with her of all. He had been so very proud of his son.

Dark Moon felt a single tear slide out from the corner of her eye, no matter how hard she tried to fight it. "No," she whispered, and prayed very, very hard that it was true. Because she was almost sure that if you dreamed, you remembered it.

"Then what did you think to do out there?" Four Goose demanded.

Oh, Great Spirit Chief, she had only wanted to help her friend!

She scrambled to her feet, no matter what Broken Bird said about staying warm so that she would not fall ill from her ordeal. She looked wildly at the midwife, the other person she loved so much she would have done anything for.

"He is well!" she blurted. "He lives."

She ran back to the bedding against the longhouse wall and buried herself in it. It did not occur to her that soon everyone would wonder how she knew that as well.

The white-skins dragged him closer to their fire.

The man who had caught him wrapped a meaty fist in his hair and pulled him across the rough creek-stone gravel. Water Calf took his breath in, then let it out with a surge of rage and what energy he had left. He kicked out, twisting savagely, nearly getting away before another miner landed over his legs with a grunt.

"What the Christ's he doing running around naked?"

"You don't see no cur dog wearing clothes, do you?"

"What're we gonna do with him? He already trashed everything we brought."

"Tie him up."

They were short of rope, so they used their reins, wrapping them so tight around his wrists Water Calf felt the leather dig into his flesh. The blood was hot and stinging.

"Maybe we better not do nothing with him. Cripes, Jonesy, we ain't got no guns no more. Think his friends'll come looking for him?"

"This here's Injun land," another warned.

"We got those two guns he didn't sink."

The white-skin with the knife drew it slowly down his chest. It sliced cleanly, burning painfully, more blood welling there. "Always wanted to carve up one of these bastards, ever since Dakota Territory," he said. "They think they own the damn country."

"This ain't Dakota Territory," someone reminded him darkly. "Ain't no soldiers for miles."

"Nope. Just us, all of us, and one of him." Savagely, he plunged the knife down. It pinned Water Calf's hand to the dirt where it was stretched over his head, bound to the other.

He jerked, but managed to choke back on the agony. They expected it of him. He would not give them what they expected. That could not get him free.

He waited until they leaned close over his face, hunting for reaction, for tears, then he jackknifed his legs up, cracking one cleanly against the back of the head.

The white-skin yowled in rage. Water Calf girded himself against the pain and yanked his arms up. The knife left the ground but stayed in his hand, dangling from the meaty part between his thumb and his finger. He got the hilt between his teeth and pulled.

Blood sprayed. He spit the knife away and finally, he did scream, not in suffering, but in a feral sound of fury. He rolled in one quick motion, coming up on his feet again. His legs threatened to buckle. He heaved himself sideways before it could happen, landing on the bank again, then he rolled down into the water.

He let himself sink into its dark, concealing depths, holding his breath. It was barely enough to cover him, but it was enough. He kicked gently with the current and let it drag him downstream, over the rocks and silt of the creek bottom.

Finally, when his chest ached close to explosion, he came up again, taking a quiet breath that made his head spin. He heard them shouting among each other, but he did not think they would come after him, not now. Many had spoken in the voices of cowards, and it would require too much determination to begin scouring the creek bed to find him.

He moved silently up into the blackness of the trees. He found one of their ponies there, munching on the tangles of grass.

This time when he heaved himself up, belly first, he made it. He threw his leg astride as the animal startled and skittered, his bound hands in front of him. When the sun came again, he would find a sharp rock to sever the reins. For now, he needed to get away. He guided the animal with his calves, sending him back in the direction of the far, clear trail he had spurned earlier.

Distantly, he heard the other mounts crashing back up the hill. In a spurt of inspiration, he kicked his own pony into a gallop and went after them.

When he had most of them herded in front of him, he laughed aloud, suddenly, strangely exhilarated. He knew in that moment that he had found something just as precious as a spirit guide and his reputation.

The elders were wrong, and with a little thrill of fresh terror for the sacrilege, he was wise enough to admit it.

He had found the courage and the fire within himself, and that was more valuable than any *wyakin*.

6

THE HASOTOIN WERE grimly beginning their Weekwetset when he rode in, driving the *xayxayx* ponies ahead of him.

The squaws' hands went still over their big ceremonial cook fires. Huge eyes followed him as he galloped to his kin's outdoor Weekwetset hearth. A child cried his old name as he reined in, and he looked down to see the orphan.

For no other reason than that life felt clean and pure now that it was firmly his again, he leaned low off his pony and hurtled her up in front of him. Dark Moon squealed and clamped her arms around his neck.

"You found it! You found your dream!"

"Hush." He put a hand over her mouth, but his eyes almost crinkled shut with his sudden grin. "I will sing of that later," he reminded her.

He dropped to the ground, taking her with him, and the Hasotoin swarmed in on him. An elbow caught her in the back of the head, and someone shoved her out of the way. She fell into the mud with a grunt, but she found her knees quickly and scrambled away, crawling back through their legs.

Behind the throng, she stood again, hopping up and down to try to see over their heads. But she could not find Water Calf anymore, and a new and appalling thought occurred to her. She had promised him a feast to celebrate, but so much had happened while he had been gone that she had forgotten!

She looked about wildly, and her gaze fell on the golden brown grass flowing out toward the hills. She ran that way, stripping her dress off as she went. Wild berries flourished in the hills almost until the robe season was full upon the people. She could get some of them, and make them into cakes.

Water Calf went to his uncle's hearth. The old man waited for him there with a crowd of his cronies and warriors.

Looking Glass watched him approach with a lingering smile of satisfaction. The soft, almost pretty quality was gone from his nephew's face now. In its place was a hardness to his jaw, a vaguely gaunt look about his eyes. It was the mark of a man who had suffered and survived, who had looked death in the eye and grinned at it before he disdained it.

"More has happened than just a vision," he observed.

Water Calf nodded. "Yes."

"Tell us."

Water Calf sat carefully. This was a council, the first he had ever been asked to partake of. His heart almost hurt, it was so full of relief and satisfaction. He had dreamed all his life of being a great warrior. This was the most auspicious start he could imagine.

With meticulous detail, he told all he had seen of the *xay-xayx* and recounted what he had done to them. He did not mention what they had done to him. His wounds were evidence enough. His left hand was puffed to twice the size of the other.

Some of the men chuckled at his ingenuity without a weapon, but his uncle only scowled at him thoughtfully.

"Such intrusions were supposed to have been prevented by Lawyer's treaty," Looking Glass mused finally.

"We should leave now, track them!" a younger man shouted. "We should kill them all!"

Looking Glass thought about it, then regretfully shook his head. "No."

There was a chorus of outrage and discontent. The headman forced his strong voice over it.

"Listen to me! Each man here can do as he likes. I cannot stop you. But those who would ride out angrily know little of white-skins' war! I have seen it. I know its fruits. It would cause unconscionable trouble to ambush these men. It would bring the wrath of all the *xayxayx* down upon us. Like the Crow, we could lose our lands. Like the Cheyenne, our villages could be burned, our women attacked. Hear me. These white-skins with their iron horses are like no enemy we have met before. We must handle them skillfully, carefully, with words, not with our bows.''

"You would find them and talk to them?" someone demanded incredulously.

"No. I would travel to Lawyer's Lapwai country when this feast is over. I would council with his white-man a-gent there about this breach of the *xayxayx* word.''

He stood, ending the council, and Water Calf got angrily to his feet as well. If this a-gent was anything like what he remembered of Stee-vuns, he did not think his uncle's approach would do much good. He wanted more; he wanted vengeance, even more for their trespassing than for their assaults upon him. But Looking Glass was one of the wisest men the Nimipu had ever known. If he thought they should wait, then it was so.

He turned away to go back to the place where the dancing would be. His blood still ran hot. He would sing of the war he did not dare advocate . . . yet.

Dark Moon gathered a good horde of huckleberries, then she sat down to rest, drawing her knees up close to her chest as the twilight chill fell. Everyone was back at their Week-wetset hearths now. Even from here, she could smell their food. She closed her eyes, concentrating, picking out each different aroma. Three were wild carrots and onions, and roasting fawn. The hearths would be piled high with dried blueback salmon and kouse-root cakes as well. The Dance of the Guardian Spirit was more than just a time for the youths to tell their new *wyakin* names. It was a rite to honor Tahmahnewes, to bring nature, the People, and all the animals into spiritual union so the difficult winter hunts would be good and the weather kind.

She did not want to go back there very much. She was

happiest here, watching the festivities from a distance, but she had promised Water Calf this food. She gathered her dress sack closed and wandered back through the tall grass.

She came up behind Broken Bird's hearth. Water Calf was already out there in the center of the ritual circle of fires, singing of the *wyakin* he had found. Broken Bird and Blue Prairie and Helps Another stood watching him proudly. A small knot of his friends watched as well.

She would wait until those boys left, Dark Moon decided. She spilled her berries on the ground and pulled her dress over her head again, crouching down to watch from the shadows.

Water Calf's dance was strong and eruptive and wonderful. Her heart swelled for him as he cried out his new name. Twelic Sepe, Thunder in the Wind. Thunder . . . something worked at the back of her mind, then faded.

When it was over, his friends went to meet him, laughing and hooting and slapping him on the back. Dark Moon scooped up her berries and inched closer to the hearth.

Broken Bird was pleased with her work. "Oh, that is good, little one. Here, come, you can help me mix them with the kouse mash."

Dark Moon nodded, but her eyes darted warily around the fire before she took another step closer. One of the boys remained. He turned about as Broken Bird spoke to her, and now she recognized his face.

Wahlitits. Her heart thumped.

He was not a boy after all, but that young warrior who stayed to himself, without a following. Panicked, she started to scramble backward, but it was too late. Wahlitits caught her by the arm, twisting it painfully up behind her as he pulled her off her feet.

Something snapped and grated in her shoulder, and she screamed.

Somehow she managed to clamp her teeth down on her lip. Wahlitits had tormented her before. The more she cried, the more he seemed to like it.

"You brought him back!" He shook her, making agony explode from her shoulder. Oh, Tahmahnewes, she could not stand this! But she had to, because suddenly, she was not sure if he was truly angry at her, or at Twelic for returning. She knew uncertainty was the most dangerous thing of all. When it happened, she had learned to keep very quiet.

"Did you grow afraid that Looking Glass would send you away to live with the wolves?" he went on. "Why did you change your mind and spare him?"

Suddenly, Broken Bird was upon them. "Wahlitits!" she snarled. "You forget yourself! You are at my hearth, and you are not welcome here to hurt my kin!"

"Kin!" He spat the word with contempt, but he dropped Dark Moon hard. She groaned as she hit the ground. "She is kin to the spirit monsters, that is what I say. Ask her what she said to those spirits while your son was out in the hills!"

He stomped off. Broken Bird helped her to her feet again. "He has hurt you badly," she muttered. "He is no man. He behaves worse than a boy."

"His words bear thought," Helps Another observed darkly. "How is it she knew Twelic would come back?"

"It does not matter. We must get Tenku. I think this hurt is more than I can fix."

She released her, and Dark Moon sank to her knees again, looking at all the wonderful berries she had brought Twelic. Wahlitits had crushed them with his feet. She scooped up a handful of the mess with her good arm, unable to stop the hot tears that spilled down her cheeks.

She did not belong here at the hearths. She would go back to her ponies. The ponies liked her.

Before Broken Bird could react, she scrambled to her feet again, clutching her broken arm close to her belly, and fled.

7

Keh-khee-tahl, Moon of First Harvest, 1863

DARK MOON STUDIED the herd as she did every morning, shrugging her long hair back where it blew into her eyes. The warriors would not go up into the hills to drive the horses down for another moon yet, but the beasts were far more intelligent than anyone gave them credit for. Already some of them were returning, responding to the gathering warmth in the air and longer visits from the sun.

One red-and-brown stallion had appeared while she slept, and he had brought with him a handful of mares. Dark Moon recognized him; he belonged to Culmuh. Broken Bird had persuaded Culmuh to allow Dark Moon to care for his ponies. The responsibility—such an important one!—made her feel worthy in a way that was new and good.

She hurried to her charges to welcome them. She ran a hand over the stallion's withers, murmuring to him with the whinnylike sound that made the other children laugh at her. But the pony understood; his head came around sharply and his ears pricked forward. He nudged her with his muzzle.

He sported a few gouges and scars that had not been there when he had left in the autumn, but that was to be expected, she thought. As for his females, they were all heavy with babes.

She left them and started warily back toward the village, watching the people who gathered wood and washed in the river. She hurried past them, her head down, and found Broken Bird inside at her longhouse hearth.

"Culmuh's red stallion has come back. Do pony babes come out the same way real babes do?"

Broken Bird thought about it. "Faster," she decided. "Are all his mares ready to drop?"

Dark Moon nodded, but she scowled. She had never birthed a pony before. Usually, the mares went down in the darkest, quietest part of the night, and they pushed their babes out all by themselves. But what if these did not? What if she had to help?

She cringed at the thought of Culmuh's anger and disgust with her if something went wrong.

"Do not worry," Broken Bird said, reading her mind. "I will help you the first time, and show you what to do. For now, you could give them some thistles. That will make them happy while they wait."

Dark Moon nodded eagerly. She started to pull her shift up to make a sack as she always did, but this time Broken Bird came to her quickly and caught her arm.

"You must not do that, little one. Not anymore."

Dark Moon's big, blue-black eyes went to the midwife. She truly did not understand, Broken Bird thought. But then, it was sometimes hard for even her to remember that Dark Moon was only in her eighth spring.

The midwife's eyes ran down her long, lanky body. Already, the girl stood as tall as her chin, and she was beginning to ripen as well. She possessed a gamine, coltish prettiness, more pronounced because she was so innocently unaware of it. Her face was a perfect oval, and her eyes were that unique indigo color. Her look, even Broken Bird admitted, was exotic and strange.

It was beginning to concern the Hasotoin greatly.

It was not good that someone born as she was should look so different as well. Broken Bird cursed the fate that would not let the orphan grow up like her own daughter, still so round and soft. Tahmahnewes had indeed cursed Vixen's daughter, she thought, marking her with a gamine beauty well before the time for such things.

"Wait," she went on. "I will give you a basket. I have one

that is not yet packed away to travel. That way you will not have to use your dress.''

Dark Moon took it doubtfully. She sensed that this kindness was more than it appeared, but she shrugged the mystery off because she was more concerned with her ponies.

She left the longhouse again, the gazes of the others following her, tickling the back of her neck. Only when Twelic crossed her path did she hesitate.

He wore a sharp, acid look that told her his thoughts were far away. He had that look a lot now that he had seen seventeen snows and was truly a warrior.

''What is it?'' she ventured, because to talk with him even for a moment would make the whole sun shine brighter. At worst, he would smile at her and merely shake his head.

But this time his eyes came to her and focused slowly.

''I think Looking Glass will talk this morning,'' he mused, almost to himself.

Dark Moon grinned. She liked it when he spoke of important things, as though it mattered that she understood. ''Why?'' she asked.

''He has been frowning for nearly a moon now, ever since Toolhoolhoolzote's Pikunanmu messenger came here to visit. Whatever is troubling him will have to come out soon, and I think it will be this sun. Do you see the way he looks almost relieved this morning, as though he has come to a decision of some kind?''

She didn't, but she would not have admitted it for all the berry cakes in the camp. She nodded sagely.

A brief smile flashed across his face. ''Go do your work. I must see about this.''

Instead of going to his mother's hearth, he paused at the headman's fire. Dark Moon watched him for a moment, thinking how strong and sure of himself he seemed as he crouched down beside the fire. In a flash of instinct beyond her snows, she understood suddenly that that was one of the reasons why he was so nice to her. He truly did not care about following the mood of the others if it did not sit right on his own heart.

Finally, she turned away and went out for her thistles.

"You will eat with us this morning, nephew?" Helps Another asked as Twelic settled beside her.

Looking Glass interrupted. "Yes, he should. Twelic, call your father as well." He looked around for his own son. Young Looking Glass was nowhere to be seen.

"He is still down by the river," Twelic offered.

"Find him, too. Tell him to bring Four Goose and Tenku, and all the young men who have any coups, any fighting achievement."

Twelic nodded, considering briefly that this would exclude Wahlitits again. It was the way of things, the decision of Tahmahnewes and the powers. They decided how a man should dream, and how many opportunities he should have for proving himself.

Of course, he, too, had helped Wahlitits's ignominy on its way. The warrior's reputation had never fully recovered from that sun long ago when he had shown such fear of the orphan. Men could not safely follow a coward, and women did not want to mate with one.

Twelic found Young Looking Glass and passed along his message, then he returned to his uncle's hearth to eat heartily of Helps Another's salmon jerky. The others began to arrive before he finished, but Looking Glass continued to eat pensively for a long while before he spoke. When he did, it seemed at first that he was only making an idle observation.

"Three snows have passed since my nephew encountered those white-skins on his vision quest. Three springs have come since we went to talk to Lawyer's *xayxayx* a-gent."

There were a few irritable murmurs. Lawyer had proven to be a troublesome and selfish thorn in their sides. He had been quite busy lately earning quantities of the white-skins' precious yellow metal. His Lapwai Nimipu sold the miners stock and hides and hunted for them. They thought their gold flakes would be very important medicine in the future, and they were hoarding them now.

Largely because of Lawyer's self-serving position, Looking Glass's talk with the a-gent had not gone well. The white man had merely assured him that the miners would not be permitted any further south than the Kooskooskia, and Lawyer had strongly backed such a compromise. He did not want the miners driven out.

Looking Glass had agreed to granting the white-skins this limited passage. He was still reluctant to incite trouble with them, although his patience with them was wearing thin.

Now Toolhoolhoolzote's band had sent a messenger with word that disturbed him greatly.

"That a-gent is either weak or a liar," Looking Glass went on. "The Pikunanmu headman tells me that the white-skins have found more of their gold metal in his territory now. But Toolhoolhoolzote's country is not within the land which we agreed they could look through."

The murmurs grew louder. Looking Glass's next words turned them into a roar.

"Now the a-gent wants us to come back and make a new treaty.

"Let me speak!" he roared over the confusion. "I have no interest in attending another talk with those men. I do not want to encourage their pleas with my presence, nor do I believe my influence will sway that cowardly Lawyer. But before I make a decision, I want to know what our other headmen think. I want to know just how far these *xayxayx* miners have spread.

"I would like one of you to lead a small party along our Kooskooskia to check on the activities of these thieves who would steal from Mother Earth. None of our hunters have seen any white men for three snows, so we know they are not coming this way. But it can no longer be denied that they are out there, and I would like to know exactly where.

"Twelic, choose five other men. You have witnessed the *xayxayx*'s habits and have some idea of their paths. Find them again and tell me what they are doing. Go to White Bird, Toolhoolhoolzote, Old Joseph, and Huishuis Kute as well. Ask them if they will be attending these talks."

Twelic felt his heart gallop suddenly in his chest. *His first mission, all his own, to lead.*

He would not fail his uncle. Perhaps he had only been chosen because he was kin, but he thought it also had much to do with his last encounter with the white-skins. Either way, he would return from this trip knowing every belch the *xayxayx* gave to despoil Nimipu air.

"I will leave this sun," he declared, rising, then he looked around at the other young men pressing in on him. At once, they began shouting at him, eager to be chosen.

"Swan Necklace," he began, calling to one who stood behind the throng. The youth had no coups yet because he had seen only fifteen snows, but he was big and burly and he was very good with an arrow. Twelic liked him and would give him a chance to earn his stature.

He picked three others, then hesitated. There were several he admired, many more whose favor he would like to keep. But Looking Glass would give him only five.

Suddenly he became aware of Wahlitits pressing in close, trying to catch his eye. The idea of choosing him was almost laughable, but the disaster inherent in it helped Twelic to keep a straight face. Wahlitits was a volatile, unpredictable warrior, desperate by now for his first coup. He could not risk him trying to prove himself on this mission.

"Thunder Dance," he finally decided, and grimaced as the others groaned and shouted. But he left the circle and went among them to try, somehow, to explain why he had chosen as he had. Somehow he would make them believe that this mission carried no great importance.

Wahlitits angrily threw the fish he had been gnawing on into the fire. His throat worked and his eyes blazed as he followed Twelic's progress, but only Dark Moon noticed.

She returned through the first door and hesitated, surprised and panicked at the uproar of men there. But she guessed immediately what had happened. She clutched Broken Bird's basket so tightly against her chest she nearly crushed it.

Twelic was at the center of the confusion. His eyes were bright and hungry. He had been chosen to go out this season.

However would she last the summer without him? There would be no kills to supplement what she could scavenge, no smiles to make her heart shine like the sun. The prospect made her feel shaky and hollow in a spot deep inside herself. Then Wahlitits crashed into her on his way out of the longhouse, and she stumbled backward.

For once the warrior did not even seem to realize who she was. His gaze was still angled back toward Twelic.

What she saw in his eyes made Dark Moon feel even colder.

8

THE FEEDER RIVER emptied into Tolo Lake in a cascade of twitching silver and blue. Already fires leaped in the dawn, smoking strings of the salmon's sweet, pink meat.

Dark Moon salivated as she watched, but she had work to do before she hunted up food scraps. Twelic had asked her to keep a special watch over his little herd while he was gone. Broken Bird had not even needed to persuade him. Culmuh's ponies were healthy and their coats shone in the sun, so Twelic had thought of asking her all by himself.

It was a chore that made her heart almost hurt with gladness. She headed out eagerly toward the ponies, keeping behind the lodges and away from the bustle of the bands. Most of Twelic's mares had newborns suckling at their sides, but one was still so swollen with life she stood listlessly, her head down, her expression seeming beleaguered.

Dark Moon went to her first, crooning to her, and saw that she was sweating. Wet patches stood out on her neck and over her flanks. She bent over and found waxy knobs of hardened milk tipping her udders. She knocked one away with her fingernail, and fresh milk promptly beaded there.

"Soon, now," she murmured to the mare, and the animal gave a long, groaning grunt.

Very soon, she decided, and panic fluttered in her belly again. Culmuh's mares had indeed done their birthing in the middle of the night, but this pony was late, and that alone seemed different and troublesome. It was big, too, she thought.

This was the fattest mare Dark Moon had ever seen.

She would ask Broken Bird to look at her, she decided. She ran back toward the lodges, too preoccupied now to take the long way around. Wahlitits stepped onto the path, blocking her way.

"Where do you hurry to?" he demanded.

Her gaze darted helplessly to the herd, then back toward the lodges. "I . . . must get help."

"I will help you."

He would? Dark Moon's eyes came back to him. He wore a thin smile on his long, angular face. His mouth was a gash, turning up at the corners as though it pained him. Something about that smile made fear squiggle in her belly more than anything he had done to her yet.

Her gaze went longingly to the herd again, and this time she saw Twelic's mare go down.

She ran for her again, half expecting to feel Wahlitits's hard, cruel grip in her hair, dragging her back. But nothing happened, and contrarily, that didn't seem good either. She reached the herd again, out of breath, and risked a look back at him. He watched her, but made no move to follow.

She bent to the mare again. There was no time now to find Broken Bird, not if this birthing happened as fast as the midwife said. Already, two sturdy little hooves were beginning to poke out of her, slick and shiny with membrane. *Please,* she prayed, *please let her be able to do this herself.* If something should happen to one of Twelic's ponies while he was gone, she was very sure she would die of the shame.

Wahlitits's smile shattered just as soon as she turned away. Still, he kept his eyes on her until he became aware of the others watching him.

"What do you look at?" he snarled at a squaw working nearby. She promptly dropped her gaze.

"The babe killer asked me to help her," he went on, and cursed them all, every one of them, for not listening to him. The bitterness in his throat actually curled his tongue. Twelic had done this to him, Twelic and his uncle, the great, wise headman who had not asked him to lead the mission after the white-skins. He had seen five more snows than that arrogant young warrior and he was far more deserving of the honor, but Looking Glass never chose him for anything.

No one chose him for anything, not since Twelic had taunted him with the orphan's cradleboard. As though he were the only one who was ever afraid of Vixen's mongrel daughter!

"You all know she kills!" he screamed, and now they started to give him a wide berth on the path. "She does not scare me!"

It was what he had meant to prove by intercepting her, but she had not been grateful for his goodwill. He had intended to show everyone that he was not the coward they thought he was. Perhaps he had not touched her cradleboard on that sun so many seasons ago, but he had decided it was not too late. He could befriend her now, and he would regain the respect that had been his when he had first found his *wyakin*.

The orphan would cooperate next time.

He would make her.

Dark Moon felt despair push up in her throat, hot and thick and terrible. *What had she done wrong?* Oh, this pony babe was not right!

She hugged herself and watched as he tried to stand. His front hooves folded under him and he pitched forward. A cry hitched her breath.

At first, everything had seemed to go well. The mare had pushed and strained, and more and more of his little legs had appeared. But then nothing more had happened. Impulsively, instinctively, Dark Moon had wrapped her hands around his limbs and helped to pull him out.

It had *seemed* right. In that place deep inside herself where she felt things, Dark Moon was sure it was just the right thing to do. And when the mare had pushed again, the whole foal had squirted out, shiny and wet. The sack had broken and his little nose had twitched for air. The mare had done everything else by herself, standing up, breaking the cord that held her to her babe. All was well until the foal tried to stand and nurse.

Then she saw that something was terribly wrong with his legs. *The legs that she had touched.*

It had happened again. Oh, Tahmahnewes, it had really, really happened this time! She *was* a babe killer!

She looked back at the camp. If people saw, Looking Glass truly would make her go away this time. He would know that the Hasotoin spoke true, that she really did kill things. She keened low in her throat, terrified.

Oh, Tahmahnewes, if she could only stop this little one from dying, she vowed she would never, ever, ever touch another living thing again!

She scrambled to her feet, her heart pumping. Somehow, she would have to fix this little boy colt so that no one ever knew she had marked him. She bent, gathering him up in her arms, grunting and staggering.

He weighed nearly as much as she did, but she had to get him away from the herd. She struggled toward the river, and his mare followed quizzically. She reached the screen of river trees and dropped the babe, gasping.

She had to find a hidden place, a place where no one ever went. She took another deep breath and dragged the foal down into the water. He began swimming in the wobbly, struggling way that most newborn foals walked. The mare followed them along the bank.

Finally, they came to a cove sheltered by more trees and some tangled, wild brush. Heaving, getting leverage under herself with her heels and wrapping her arms around his neck, Dark Moon pulled the babe out again, onto the river sand.

Now what? She wanted to cry. Instead, she pulled one of his bent little legs onto her lap.

She bit her lip, studying it. After a moment, she crawled over to the mare and ran her hand lightly along her leg as well. She touched the back and then she touched the front, and then she understood.

Triumph leaped in her, but it trembled quickly away again. She knew what was wrong, but she could not imagine what to do about it.

The sinewlike pieces at the back of his legs were shorter

than the bone in front. His hooves curled back toward his belly, even when he was lying down. The mare's did not do that, because both her tendon and her bone were the same size.

It all reminded her of a warrior's bow, and she scrubbed her hands over her eyes, thinking. If she wanted to straighten a bow out, she would cut the sinew, easing the tension on the wood. But she could not cut into this little one's legs. She blanched at the prospect.

Sinew stretched with use, though. Weren't Culmuh and Twelic always replacing the strings on their bows with new, taut strips?

Suddenly, she knew what she had to do.

She would use the hides from the kills Twelic had given her. She stroked the foal one last time, whispered a fervent promise to him, then got up and hurried back toward the camp.

Four suns later, Dark Moon gently unwrapped the furs from the colt's legs. Her breath was hard and still in her throat, and she squeezed her eyes shut, afraid to look. Finally, she forced them open again, and the air burst out of her in a glad rush.

It had worked! His hooves did not curl under when she took her hands away!

When she had first forced them straight, his pained struggles had made her heart quail. But she had kept at it, wrapping sticks against the backs of his legs with her furs so that they could not curl. His tendons had stretched and grown softer, just as she had prayed they would.

She helped him get up to nurse. He wobbled, staggered, and fell over again. His legs were straight, but they were not strong.

Dark Moon groaned helplessly and dropped down to sit at his side. The mare watched them sadly.

"There is a way," she told her. She could not give up now.

She looked down at the river again. Perhaps if he worked his legs in there, where they did not have to hold his full weight, then they would grow stronger. She stood again, hauling him down into the water.

The foal struggled with the current, his nostrils flaring. He

was weak enough that he did not make any progress against
the tide, but she thought that was good. He could work and
work without going back around the bend where the people
could see him.

"What is wrong with him?"

Her heart knocked up into her throat and she spun about.
Wahlitits was up on the bank, watching her.

"N-nothing."

She felt sick with the fear that whooshed through her. Even
if Wahlitits left right away, he would tell the others what he
had seen!

"Why is he in the water?" he demanded.

Dark Moon shook her head mutely.

"He should be killed. What good is a pony who cannot
walk?"

"*No!*" Her voice came back in a thin shriek. She launched
herself to the bank, putting herself between the foal and the
warrior. "Go away!"

Go away. Anger exploded suddenly in Wahlitits's head.

She was a dirty snip of a girl, an outcast born under a vanishing moon. Did she think he did not know she ate the offal
from other fires? Yet she stood there, wet hair tossed back
arrogantly, thinking even she was too good to work with him.
He lashed out suddenly and grabbed the hair that so irritated
him, as sleek-wet now as the fur of a river otter.

Dark Moon screamed, then she choked on the sound. He
spun her about and slammed her hard against one of the trees,
her head whipping back and knocking solidly against the
wood. She wrapped her arms tightly around herself so that he
could not get a grip on them, remembering the cracking, searing pain from the last time he had hurt her badly.

He let her go and turned back toward the colt. Something
wild and desperate erupted in her own heart. No matter what,
she could not let him hurt Twelic's foal.

She howled and threw herself at him. Wahlitits turned back
on her, his fist swinging easily. It caught her against the side
of her face and stars burst in wild glory.

She sank slowly to her knees. "Go away," she moaned

again. Her begging would excite him into hurting her more, but oh, Tahmahnewes, that would be all right if only he left the pony babe alone.

He looked down at her bent head, his blood pumping hotly. She would not even look at him.

"We will go back and tell Looking Glass what you were doing," he snarled. "Do you think I do not know? You have put a curse on that poor animal! We will tell him that and see what he thinks should be done with you!"

And suddenly, Wahlitits knew it would work. He did not need to befriend her to show the others he felt no fear of her. He would have her cast out instead, once and for all, and they would thank him. They would follow him for saving them from her evil.

He reached down for her again, trying to get another hank of her hair. She wriggled away from him. Frustrated, he kicked her hard in the ribs to make her be still.

She could not get her breath to scream!

She rolled over onto her back, hugging the explosion of pain in her ribs, trying to gasp. Her chest felt solid, hard, then finally her breath came, rushing into her with a burst of agony.

"I will go away. Please, let . . . me . . . go."

It was what he wanted, Wahlitits thought. He wanted her gone, but she would take even the glory of that away from him if she just slunk off into the brush like a wounded animal.

He would not let it happen.

He grabbed the front of her shift to pull her up, and the tattered old skin tore, a swatch coming free in his hand. He stared at it, his breath coming hard and fast, and then he looked back at her.

Her indigo eyes were wild now, huge, filling her whole face. Her wet hair was matted with sand. But Wahlitits did not see any of that. His gaze moved down to the place where her torn shift fell open, and fell on the delicate new buds of her breasts.

They rose and fell, rose and fell with her panic, and that excited him even more.

The anger in him grew into something else, something hot and squirming. Now he knew what she was truly afraid of, why she was so willing to go away. Like the other squaws, she would do anything to keep him from touching her. But this one—this offal-eating mongrel—had no right to think she was too good for him. She was the spawn of a man who could not even dream.

He made a grunting sound and yanked on her shift again, tearing it farther, clear down to the edge that tangled above her knees. Then he gave a bark of triumph, because he was right! It was just as he had thought as he had watched her scurry about the camp; that ragged, dirty dress hid secrets . . . dark secrets, beautiful secrets, nestled behind the baby-soft tufts of ebony hair just beginning to show at the juncture of her thighs.

He would have her. The idea exploded in his head, and he knew it was the best thing to do. He would take her, claim her, prove that she had no evil that could harm him. Then he would spurn her as she had tried to spurn him, and toss her, trembling, her arrogance broken, at Looking Glass's hearth.

He fell beside her, laughing in an eager, high-pitched sound. He drove his knee between hers to force them open. He waited for the disgust, the panic to come into her eyes . . . *wanted* to see it, wanted to remember every squaw who had ever turned away from him because this one—this dirty, little snip—had ruined his reputation. But her eyes would not focus on his, and her only sound was a whimper, her only response a twitching shudder that seemed to come up from her very soul.

Anything, anything, to get him to go away, to make him leave her alone.

Dark Moon watched the treetops as the first dry, hard pain shot through her from her most private parts. Up and deep, harder and harder and tearing, but she could bear it, she *could*. It was just like what the stallions did to their mares, nothing more . . . nothing more. . . .

She clung to that as each thrust pushed her a little farther toward the water, the sand scratching her skin, her air leaving her in little grunts.

The mares did not scream, did not cry, and she would not do it either.

When it was over, Wahlitits stood again, his breath fast. He bent to pull her to her feet, to do as he planned, to take her to Looking Glass. Then his hand fell back.

An eerie coldness touched him between the shoulder blades.

What was she looking at?

She lay very still with her limbs sprawled, her eyes blue and deep and watching. . . .

Watching and seeing nothing he could see. His gaze followed hers to the sky, then he backed away, leaving her, running.

From the nearby copse, other eyes watched him go.

Young Looking Glass scowled, a tangle of conundrums making his belly feel sour. He wished he had never chosen his own spot to fish upriver, where his catch could not be compared to the others. He wished he had never heard that mare snort and wondered what a pony was doing out here, so far away from the herd.

The orphan finally stirred, rolling over in the sand, curling up there. She was alive, then. Relief swept through him. That was one problem he did not have to deal with.

But what of Wahlitits?

He looked back the way the warrior had gone, and finally he shrugged. He had forced himself on her, an incomprehensible shame no warrior would ever bring upon himself. But Wahlitits was not much of a warrior, and the orphan was not even really a squaw, just an urchin who moved with the band, silent and hungry, a worrisome threat to them all.

She was not worth getting involved in a messy, tangled problem over. More than anything, Young Looking Glass hated problems.

He turned silently away from the copse, closing his mind to what he had seen.

9

Dusk crashed across the sky with the spectacular purple and pink of a dry spring. Dark Moon watched it with focused concentration.

Do not think about what he did. Do not think.

The dark came, and with it, a scratching, biting cloud of gnats. They tickled her eyes and her ears and swarmed busily around her thighs. She sat up, brushing them away, and her hands came away sticky with her own blood.

A mewling sound worked up in her throat and she scrubbed at herself frantically, then, abruptly, she went still again. She had much to do to make things like they were before. She *had* to make things like they were before.

As the moon came up, she dragged the colt back to his mare. She wrapped his legs again with the sticks and the fur, then she eased her way down into the river to wash. Finally, she shrugged into her savaged dress again and made her way back to the camp.

Broken Bird looked up from her hearth just as she reached the outermost lodges. The midwife's eyes narrowed.

Something was very, very wrong.

The girl came directly through the camp instead of skirting around it like she usually did. She walked slowly, carefully, putting each bare foot in front of the other as though she expected Mother Earth to fall out from beneath her steps. Finally, she drew close enough that the midwife could see her face.

One side of it was purple-red with a ghastly, growing bruise. Her eyes were vacant.

"What is it? What has happened to you?" Broken Bird reached a hand out to stop her progress.

"I need my robe." Her voice was as careful as her gait. "Then I can sew this dress back together."

She looked down at her torn doeskin. Scowling, Broken Bird followed her gaze, and then she knew. She saw the fresh blood on her thighs, and something at the very core of her went hot with rage.

"Who did this to you?" she hissed.

Dark Moon shrugged. "Wahlitits. He hates me most of all."

She gathered up her robe and began to turn away, back toward the pony herd. It was so dark now, and the smells from there called to her, hinting of comfort and safety. But Broken Bird had her arm and she would not let her go.

"No. Go inside, little one."

Her voice was like the stones that ringed her hearth, and Dark Moon flinched. *She knew.* Wahlitits had already told what she had done to the pony.

"I fixed him," she pleaded. "He will be fine soon."

Broken Bird felt fear twist in her heart. She looked around quickly. Wahlitits was at his own hearth some distance away, eating alone, as always, with his eyes down, on his fish. The orphan had not cursed him, then. Broken Bird felt her skin heat at her own uncharitable inclination to believe the worst of her.

"Hush," she answered. "You must not say such things." She pushed the girl into her lodge. "Wait here. I will get Tenku."

"No!" Some spark came to Dark Moon's eyes again, a wild kind of panic. Broken Bird remembered the last time she had called the *tiwats* to tend to the orphan, when Wahlitits had broken her arm. Tenku had helped her only at the midwife's insistence, and he had not been gentle or kind.

Broken Bird closed her eyes helplessly. It was a vicious, endless trail. The Hasotoin feared the orphan, and though she had tried—Tahmahnewes, how she had tried to make them see reason!—no proof, no one staunch voice would ever make them change their minds.

The girl did not need any more torment now, from any of them. "I will do my best to help you myself," Broken Bird said.

She pushed her down upon some bedding to inspect the damage Wahlitits had wrought. It was no worse or better than she had feared. Physically, she could be fixed, just as a tiny squaw birthing a big babe could be mended.

But what of her heart, her head?

As she worked over the girl, Broken Bird's fury grew. She waited until the orphan dozed fitfully, then she went outside again to find Helps Another.

"If she wakes, do not let her leave the lodge."

Helps Another looked as though she would offer some argument, but she fell wisely silent at the midwife's expression.

"I must speak to my brother," Broken Bird went on.

She found him at the council fire near his own tule, or cattail, lodge, enjoying a smoke with several of his cronies. He was in a good mood.

"Little sisters never change," he chuckled, "not in all Tahmahnewes's seasons." He waved a hand at Four Goose and Tenku and the others. "Leave us for a time."

The old men grumbled about women and left. Broken Bird sat in Tenku's place.

"What? No food? Once you bribed me with berry cakes. What do you want from me this time?"

"You must make Wahlitits go away."

He was a man who hid his emotions well, but now his jaw dropped. "I admit that he is a poor warrior, but I have no cause."

"He has violated the orphan."

Looking Glass was silent for a long time. "You have proof?"

"Dark Moon has told me."

"That is not enough."

Broken Bird felt her anger rise all over again. "She would not lie! And I mended her. *I* saw the proof."

"You saw proof that she was molested. You do not know by whom."

"Who else?" But that was a question fraught with too many answers. She changed tactics. "This band's disdain of her has gone much too far now. Something must be done!"

"Nothing *can* be done."

Looking Glass was angry as well, and he felt something squeamish curl in his own belly at such a heinous affront to a child. But he thought of Eagle Robe, Wahlitits's father, a good man who did not deserve to be shamed on such flimsy evidence. He thought of the way things had always been done.

"You must make an example of him!" Broken Bird pressed on. "You must show the others that they cannot torment her without fear of reprisal."

She felt someone step up behind her and looked around, but it was only Young Looking Glass, approaching the fire for something to eat.

"Think, sister, think of the position you put me in," her brother answered. "Your words are good, and perhaps the orphan speaks true. But it is only her claim against that of a warrior. No one can be punished under such circumstances. It is not the Nimipu way."

She knew it was not, and the midwife felt frustration hurt her head.

"Call him," she insisted. "Get that weak-bellied boy who calls himself a warrior and ask him yourself."

Looking Glass nodded. He could give her that much.

"Get Wahlitits," he said to his son. "Put that fish down. You should have speared your own. What did you do all sun?" he grumbled.

Young Looking Glass swallowed a morsel and went to do as he was told.

"It hurts my heart that he is so lazy," Looking Glass mused when he was gone. "Always letting others do for him, the easy way, not like your boy."

Broken Bird's chin came up. "If Twelic were here, he would thrash Wahlitits."

But Looking Glass only shook his head. "No. Twelic is full of fire, but he is wise."

The warriors came back, Young Looking Glass eyeing his father's fish sullenly, Wahlitits looking about at them with an odd, careful expression.

"The orphan says you have hurt her," Looking Glass charged coldly. "What have you to say?"

Contempt flashed in the young man's eyes. "You would believe a babe-killing mongrel?"

"I believe my sister. You would call *her* a liar?"

Wahlitits flushed. "Our midwife has a kind heart," he amended. "She would not suspect anyone of lies, and would innocently repeat them as true."

"You deny this accusation then?"

Wahlitits scoffed. "I am a warrior. I have no time for one such as her."

Looking Glass watched him. "Go, then," he said finally. "But do not darken my hearth again."

Wahlitits looked as though he would protest. A mottled color came to his face, then he wisely shook his head and turned away. He could not speak of the colt with the bad legs, he realized bitterly, not without admitting he had seen the orphan this sun after all.

He stalked away, and Broken Bird turned incredulously to her brother. "You know he is lying, yet still you do nothing!"

It remained that there was nothing that he *could* do. Broken Bird hated it even as she finally accepted it. Wahlitits would walk away from this unchastised, and she knew that soon another warrior and another would use the orphan according to his own will. It was permissible now, unpunishable, as long as no other saw. Men were like wolves, she thought viciously, snarling and swarming over a doe once it was down.

"Aye," she whispered low beneath her breath. She had truly come to love the girl, she realized. She had suckled at her breast; she was one of her own.

And like one of her own, Broken Bird knew she had to protect her, even if it meant rending a hole in her own heart.

"There is one other way you can save her."

Looking Glass looked at her sharply. She had accepted the inevitable, but he knew from her tone that she would not be dissuaded a second time.

"Send her away," Broken Bird went on. "Away from these close-minded Hasotoin. Find her a new home, a fresh start."

The headman was startled, then he felt an odd guilt. It was something he could do with good conscience, something that assuaged his own troubles as well. He had much to worry about these suns, without the girl sent to them by the vanishing moon. He would not mind being free of the responsibility of her.

"I can see that that would be good for her," he said carefully.

Broken Bird's eyes began to shine.

"Yes, that could be an answer," he went on. "She will never have a normal life here. Sentiment and superstition have worked against her for too long. People have long memories, especially those who have been bereaved."

Broken Bird gave a last, token protest to the idea that had been hers in the first place. "Every band saw that moon go away," she muttered.

"But no other lost Silver Cloud and a toddling young warrior. No other saw blood spill at the same time."

"It was all so long ago. Eight snows."

"And with each snow, the memory has festered and grown, larger than truth. You know that."

Broken Bird did, and now her tears spilled over. It had not helped that the orphan had had that spell when Twelic had found his name. Every small, inconsequential thing she did stoked the fire.

And now this. Somehow, Broken Bird knew, the People would twist this as well.

"I will begin speaking to the other headmen right away," Looking Glass promised. "Many bands are here, and we should be able to find the others at the camas prairie when we go."

Broken Bird got to her feet, then looked back. "But not Toolhoolhoolzote," she warned.

The headman raised a brow. "It is where she belongs."

"No. You will have relief from the trouble of her, and it will be good for her in the end. But make sure it *is* good for her, or I will fight you anyway. Toolhoolhoolzote's people will scorn her as well as ours do. They have already cast out her mother, and they will not forget that she carries Strong Cub's blood."

Looking Glass nodded his agreement.

It was done.

Broken Bird found the orphan awake, pressed up against the lodge wall. Her fingers dug like claws into the woven teasel and tule. Helps Another sat in front of the door.

"It is the only way I can make her stay," the old woman muttered grimly.

Broken Bird nodded. "It is all right now. You can go."

When Helps Another left, the terror went out of the child. Oh, Tahmahnewes, she is so like a wild animal, Broken Bird thought, like one of the ponies she loves. She cannot be trapped, and she is trapped here, in this band, whether she knows it or not.

It made her feel better, made her decision sit more softly on her heart.

"Little one," she said quietly, and the girl's eyes darted to her. "It is going to be better now."

Yes, it would be, Dark Moon thought, as soon as she could get back to the herd. She began inching toward the door.

"Wait." There was no way to buffer the decision, so the midwife merely blurted it out. "I have spoken to Looking Glass. He is going to help you find a new home where this sort of thing can never happen to you again."

A new home?

"You are a good girl," Broken Bird rushed on. "You deserve to marry, to have babes, like every other squaw. Oh, little one, that will not happen here! The only way you might have such a chance is to go somewhere where your past does not haunt you!"

"Nooooo!"

She had done nothing to Wahlitits, nothing! But he would win, he would take everything from her. Now even Broken Bird hated her, and Twelic would be gone to her as well . . .

. . . *Twelic.*

He would help her. He had to help her!

Life with the Hasotoin was not sweet, but it was predictable, it was understandable, and it was all she had ever known! She shoved past Broken Bird and ran from the lodge, horror and fear eating up every part of her soul.

THE PONY STUMBLED, but Twelic offered him no respite from their grueling pace. He had been gone more than two moons now, and he was anxious to be home.

He did not rein in until his small party came upon a rise. There on the root prairie below them, the grass lodges of several bands were sprawled. Cook fires leaped invitingly.

"What is it?" Swan Necklace asked querulously. His enthusiasm at being chosen for this mission had waned considerably since they had started out. It had been more work than he had anticipated, riding and stalking the *xayxayx,* with little excitement to break the monotony. Twelic had not allowed them to raid the mining camps they had found, though he knew his careful guidance irritated the younger members of his party.

Thunder Dance was the exception. "Are our Hasotoin here, or do we ride on until we find them?" he asked easily.

Twelic squinted into the darkness, trying to decide, then something caught his attention at the corner of his vision. He turned that way and saw the orphan.

She stood outside the pony herd, but she did not leap at the sight of him this time. She stared at him as though silently beseeching him to come to her.

Something was wrong, he thought, but he could not grant her his attention now. He kicked his pony again, and the tired animal trotted on. The Hasotoin were here.

Boys hurried from all directions for the honor of taking his pony. Squaws watched from their summer fires, those without mates calling seductive invitations in his wake. Later, the memory would make Twelic grin with pleasure. Now he ignored the commotion to go straight to his uncle's hearth.

"You have earned the right to relax and eat with those you left behind," Looking Glass observed, but Twelic shook his head and sat.

"Later. We must talk."

Looking Glass was pleased with that response. "Wife!" he called. "Bring me my pipe. There is someone here I would smoke with."

A smoke with the headman. No matter that they were kin, it was an immense honor.

"So tell me," Looking Glass said finally. "What did you find?"

"The nearest *xayxayx* are a long sun's ride west of here, along the river."

Looking Glass's good humor soured abruptly. So close. It was worse than he had feared.

"From that place on, there are more of them than those of us who can rightfully claim the land. Their camps reach all the way to Lapwai country. Where the Snake joins the Kooskooskia, they have begun to wander south. Some of them have gone as far as the Salmon, where that last strike you heard of is located."

"Toolhoolhoolzote's country," he said tightly.

"Yes. That is the place. But the worst of them are near Lapwai, where the Snake meets the Kooskooskia. They have brought these giant smoke-belching boats there. They carry their stores and supplies. There is a big lodge there, too, to hold it all."

Boats? A lodge? "Lawyer has allowed this travesty?" he demanded. It was incomprehensible, yet how had so many of these white men invaded in such a short time, unless it was for Lawyer's hospitality?

"I have heard that he complained to his a-gent," Twelic offered, "but then he agreed that the boats could come to his territory, provided no more of the big lodges were put there.

The a-gent promised to bring sol-jers from the fort to see that the white-skins took no further liberties. But I watched the *xayxayx* miners stray beyond this point, and the sol-jers did nothing to stop them.

"I was told that this all happened just before the snows. Now Toolhoolhoolzote's and White Bird's countries are overrun with these white-skins. They have turned their stock onto the headmen's grazing grounds. White Bird put up fences to mark his land off from them, but they tore the pickets down and used them to enclose the places they have claimed for their own. Some of his warriors have been killed also. When the miners' ponies stray, White Bird's and Toolhoolhoolzote's people are accused of stealing them. The *xayxayx* attack them for it, even as they take their fine Nimipu ponies for their own."

Looking Glass cursed Stee-vuns roundly, knowing that it had all begun with that smoke-belching beast passing by Nimipu land.

Twelic did not want to go on, but knew he had to. "The boat place has become a village now," he explained. "There are many, many dwellings there. That is what I saw. Toolhoolhoolzote and White Bird have each been to Lapwai. They have demanded that this place be torn down, and that those old treaty words be enforced. That is why the white-skins want a new treaty."

"And all those other leaders will go talk to them about it," Looking Glass muttered. It was not a question, and Twelic nodded uncertainly.

"Toolhoolhoolzote and White Bird will be there to demand the removal of these men from their lands. I saw Old Joseph, and he will ride to Lapwai as well. He fears that if this invasion is not stopped now, soon the *xayxayx* will find their way even into his distant country. Old Joseph tells me that Huishuis Kute will go talk for the same reason."

"Has there been fighting?" Looking Glass asked. "Have we spilled any *xayxayx* blood?"

"My men did not, and there has been no other killing that I have heard of."

But soon it would happen, Looking Glass thought. Their warriors were only men, after all, and it was man's nature to fight back when he was pushed too far.

The headman stood, swaying slightly under the weight of responsibility. "Tell the others to come here when the moon rises," he said. "We will talk more of this then."

"Where do you go now?"

"I must speak to my *wyakin*." But he thought he knew what it would tell him.

In the end, they would all go to the treaty talks.

They would try to have the *xayxayx* removed from Tahmahnewes's land.

They would try, and they would fail.

The squaws worked to move out with a decided lack of enthusiasm. Twelic sat at his uncle's fire, watching impatiently as they loaded their ponies. His own gelding was ready and waiting for him, cropping grass a short distance away. It had not taken him long to pack. Owning too much, being burdened down by too much, made him feel trapped and itchy. He liked to move with the freedom of the wind that had granted him his name; he needed to rely on his own skills and wisdom.

"Do you think there will be fighting?" Young Looking Glass asked suddenly from beside him.

Twelic looked back at him with a raised brow. "If there is, you will not be ready for it unless you begin loading up."

Young Looking Glass shrugged as Twelic eyed his possessions, a massive pile in contrast to his own. "I need a wife."

Twelic held his tongue. He had been about to advise that his cousin do something to earn one. But in truth, Young Looking Glass would not need to, and they both knew it. Some sun, heredity would push him into his father's moccasins and he would become leader of the Hasotoin. No other accomplishment would be necessary to lure a squaw to his lodge.

"I was thinking of that one who is daughter to White Bird," Young Looking Glass went on.

Twelic was startled, and vaguely put out. "Cloud Singer? She set her eyes on me once."

"You should have acted while you had the chance."

Twelic shrugged and stood up. He would like to have known Cloud Singer better, but it seemed to him that a wife was the most cumbersome possession of all.

"Perhaps she will be at this treaty talk," Young Looking Glass mused. "I was disappointed not to find her Lamtama people at any of the gatherings this season."

"White Bird is more concerned with the *xayxayx*." It seemed impossible to Twelic that any warrior could forget that.

"So do you think he will come to Lapwai, then?"

"Yes. I am told that all the headmen will be there."

"Good. Then perhaps we will finally be able to find a home for that orphan there as well."

Twelic stared at him, a cold stillness permeating his gut. "The orphan has a home," he reminded his cousin flatly. "She is of my mother's hearth."

Young Looking Glass shook his head. "No. It is better that she go away. Then there will be no more trouble with our band."

"What trouble?" Twelic demanded. He knew that they said she had had something to do with his difficult *wyakin* search, and he was equally certain that she had not. But something told him that Young Looking Glass was not speaking of that now. Something else had happened since he had been away.

"What is she accused of?" he persisted.

Young Looking Glass blinked at him. It had happened nearly a moon ago, and had been best forgotten in the first place, but obviously Twelic had not yet heard.

"Wahlitits found her down by the river while she was caring for one of your foals," he explained. "He beat her again, and threw her to the ground and took her. It was strange the way she stared, as though she would curse him and kill him later for what he was doing to her. There will be more death here if she stays. You will see."

Awkward memories of that sun came back to him in detail, and too late Young Looking Glass realized how much he had revealed. "That is what I have heard, anyway."

Twelic turned away abruptly, his eyes hot and scouring the

camp. He could not find Wahlitits, but he guessed where the warrior had gone. How often did a man need to bathe when he did no hard work to make him smell?

He finally found him hunkered down at the edge of the river, steadfastly chewing the wild mint that he would rub over his skin, as though that would lure some indiscriminate squaw. *And if that does not work, you will force a child.* Rage exploded in Twelic's head.

He ambushed him from behind, barreling into him, so that they both sprawled in the water.

Wahlitits struggled up, his hands slipping and sliding as he grappled for a stranglehold on Twelic's neck. Twelic pounded him squarely in the jaw, sending him splashing backward again. Wahlitits was thin and wiry, and that gave him some advantages in fighting, but Twelic knew he had more solid strength, and in that moment, he ached to use it.

Wahlitits's sneer was more pitiful than irritating. "Such a respected warrior," he gasped, "attacking one of his own!"

"What did you tell my uncle?" Twelic demanded. "How did you convince him not to cast you out?"

Satisfaction filled Wahlitits's eyes. In the end, the final triumph was his, if not in all the glory he had first imagined.

"Your orphan will be the one cast out!" he crowed.

Twelic lunged for him again.

He heaved the slighter warrior onto the bank, pounding his head against the sand, one fist in his hair. "What did you tell him?" he demanded again.

Wahlitits managed to shrug. "It was my word against hers."

Twelic brought his other fist down. Blood burst from the warrior's nose, spattering.

"As it will be my word against yours. Who do you think the council will stand behind this time if you tell them that it was I who thrashed you?" said Twelic.

Wahlitits did not answer, though his heart writhed with new fury at another ignominious blow to his pride. They both knew the council would never believe him over Twelic.

"I . . . will . . . kill her for this," he managed, hatred filling him, making his blood burn more hotly than the pain from his nose. "I will kill your precious little mongrel."

"No." Twelic only gave him a hard, grim smile. "I will see to it that you never have the chance."

He found her in the herd, concentrating fiercely over one of his foal's legs. Twelic knew instantly that it was the one she had been trying to help when Wahlitits had set upon her.

Briefly, guilt churned in his belly. If he had not asked her to tend to his ponies, if he had taken Wahlitits with him . . . but no. It went against his grain to give up, but there was nothing he could do to protect her anymore, not now that he would be away from the camp as much as he was here.

"Screamer," he said quietly.

The orphan lunged to her feet, away from the pony, as though she had been doing something wrong. Her indigo eyes were wild, but then they filled with light as she recognized him.

"You will help me?" she whispered, and his belly hurt worse.

His mother had said that she did not want to go. He cared enough for her to take the time to convince her that she must, but in that moment, she made him feel ashamed for failing her.

Twelic hardened his jaw.

"Please, you must tell Broken Bird to change her mind!" she went on. Suddenly, in a burst of inspiration, she whirled about and grabbed the foal by the neck, hugging him hard. "Look, Twelic, please, I fixed him!"

"You cannot spend your whole life caring for ponies!" Twelic snapped. "You should be tending a husband and your own babes!"

"I will marry you," she begged. "Then I can care for your babes and your herd as well. I can . . ."

Surprise flushed his face, and she trailed off. She did not understand. He and Broken Bird were the ones who kept insisting that she needed a mate.

Then Twelic laughed, a belly-deep sound that crashed through her, making her hurt like she never had before.

Twelic sobered at the look on her face. "Screamer," he said more quietly. "You have seen only eight snows. If I were going to have wives, I would have ten of them before you were old enough to mate."

She began to shake her head in sick denial.

"You must find a boy elsewhere, someone of your same snows. You must go somewhere else so that he will see you as you are, never hearing of these stories that haunt you."

Her eyes flashed back and forth, betrayed, searching for some escape from the hurt. Frustrated, he went on more fervently.

"I will never marry," he said, and he knew, in that moment, that it was irrevocably true. And though she was a child, he found himself trying to explain.

"All I have ever wanted is a warrior's life. I want . . . I *need* to ride after the buffalo and enemy tribes. How unfair that would be to a woman, to love a man who would rather be roaming places even the wind has forgotten than be home with her!" He had seen the fullness of his country now, had tasted it, on his own without a superior warrior to make his decisions for him. And he knew, suddenly, that he would never be able to let it go.

He wanted her to understand. Somehow it seemed important. Somehow it seemed to him, in his gut, that she *would*. In a strange way, though she was merely a girl child, she was like him, he thought. Through all her young, vulnerable seasons, she had learned to be independent, taking care of herself.

That would end soon. Some sun, she would be able to enjoy the care, the warmth, the security that a good warrior would provide, a warrior who would stay by her side.

He looked at her more closely. For a moment, he thought he saw something of what that nameless future man would know. Her long, blue-black hair whipped free in the wind, streaming and unfettered behind her. He saw eyes so deep and midnight blue that they could pierce a man's soul. Her posture was loose limbed, ageless, delicately balanced, as though she were ready to fly. But then he blinked, and he saw that she really was only a child after all.

She crumbled to the ground beside his pony, all the fire gone from her. Twelic turned away because he found he could not bear the sound of her forlorn, little-girl sobs.

11

WHEN THE HASOTOIN reached the hillocks overlooking the council place, Looking Glass felt the last of his hope drain away.

The lodges of Lawyer's people and some other *xayxayx*-named headmen hugged the river. White Bird's people, Old Joseph's, Toolhoolhoolzote's and Huishuis Kute's swelled up over the rises on the other side. Brown, windswept grass spread out between the two camps, an unprecedented, uncrossable breach given the newfound Christianity of one group.

Dark Moon came up behind the others, trudging numbly along behind the herd. When the Hasotoin drew their ponies in, she hesitated as well, standing first on one foot then the other to try to ease the hurt in her soles. She leaned up against one of Twelic's mares, but she would not dare presume to ride her, not now.

Her throat began hurting again and she swallowed hard. She would not cry. Never, she vowed, would she cry again. Only not feeling, not letting anyone too close to her heart, would help her survive what would happen to her now.

She focused dully on the council place as the band rode down into it. The white men, camped near the forefront, watched closely as the Hasotoin approached.

"They have all come in, then," observed a junior officer, grinning widely. "A good sign, wouldn't you say?"

The Commissioner of Indian Affairs looked at him incredulously. It occurred to him that a man would have to be dead not to feel the simmering resentment glaring forth from all those black eyes. He was about to ask this tribe to cede most of their lands for the benefit of white men who had stolen from them, attacked them, and blatantly ignored the rights the government had awarded them in 1855. What was more, they knew it.

"Colonel Henrison," he barked. "Take six companies of your volunteers to that stretch of grass there between their huts. Drill in that location until I instruct you otherwise."

"You expect trouble?" the junior officer asked avidly.

"God bless us, I hope not. Perhaps a show of force will intimidate and influence them."

Perhaps, but the commissioner doubted it. Suddenly, the suggestions he had received from the local settlers did not seem so heinous after all. He wondered if they were not the best hope, in the end.

The newspaper in Lewiston, the town that had burgeoned up around the boat landing, had urged its readers to occupy and cultivate those lands they wished to own, simply claiming squatter's rights over the Nez Percé. A Boise, Idaho, editor had suggested shipments of blankets infected with smallpox, guaranteeing that they would be distributed to those areas that needed to be cleared out for white settlement. Pernicious, yes, but at the moment the commissioner wondered if the Indians would be removed from these rich mining lands in any other way.

Twelic watched as Looking Glass moved off toward the talking spot. Frustration clawed in him that he could not be there, could not listen in this time. But he was no longer a boy, and his presence would surely be chastised.

Then Looking Glass paused and glanced back at him.

"My son and my nephew, you should come as well."

Twelic felt his heart thump in surprise. He looked at Young Looking Glass. His cousin shrugged and began following.

None of the other men were invited? Not Tenku or Four Goose or his own respected father? Twelic finally moved after them, but his head felt fuzzy with disbelief.

When they reached the council site, he saw that Old Joseph had brought his sons as well. Alokot, the youngest, looked as confounded as Twelic felt, but Young Joseph maintained the same intent, vaguely supercilious expression his father wore.

The other headmen came, Lawyer and his comrades arriving last. The Lapwai bands spoke heartily and happily with the *xayxayx* in their own twangy, alien tongue. Twelic felt his skin crawl.

"Do you see now? Do you understand?" his uncle asked him.

Twelic's eyes narrowed as he surveyed the scene. "None of the old ones are present," he mused, "except for Lawyer's men."

"That is because Lawyer has no foresight. He sees things only as they are now. He cannot dream."

Twelic looked back at him sharply. "You have dreamed then, uncle?"

"My spirit guide showed me this council and told me that our people would be torn by it. The future will be different, and the future is for the young."

Twelic felt his bowels run weak with a sensation like fear. "You are saying this treaty will reach beyond you?"

"There will be no treaty, but what happens here this sun will torment our people long after my bones are cold."

The others made themselves comfortable, and Twelic sat pensively as well. A man dressed in *xayxayx* finery stepped forward to begin speaking. One of Lawyer's cronies translated.

"We are here to ask your cooperation and assistance with a problem that is troublesome to us all," the white man began. "It has become increasingly difficult of late for our divergent peoples to live in this same small pocket of country. We are here to find a peaceable solution to this matter. We are here to avert war." He paused to allow the implied threat to settle in, but there was no perceptible reaction from the headmen.

"I have a suggestion that will at first strike you as unmanageable. I beg you, however, to consider it with open hearts, knowing that I, and the Great Father in Washington, want only what is best for our red children. We do not presume to rob you, but to protect you. We do not intend to destroy you, but to make strong, capable men of your youngsters, that they might embrace the Lord God and learn to live by white ways. It is your strongest hope for the future, I assure you.

"The Great Father in Washington has many soldiers, like those you see working even now over in that field. He has more soldiers than you have men, women, and children combined. You cannot hope to win a fight against us, and you cannot protect yourself from us without government assistance.

"If all our white men come here, to your land, in an unorganized way, your children will be killed, your stock will continue to be stolen. The Great Father in Washington wishes to set aside a place for you so that these men cannot hurt you.

"I would therefore suggest that you bring all your bands here, to this valley, to live with your friend Lawyer and his people. We will mark this land off as your reservation, and you have my solemn word that no white men will be permitted here to molest you upon it."

The commissioner stepped back, and Old Joseph stood casually. "What do you propose to do with our country when we are gone from it?"

The commissioner looked momentarily nonplussed. "It would be declared open to settlement so that the white men there will not feel forced to fight you for a claim."

"There are no white men in my land."

"Not yet. But there will be. There are more white men than—"

Old Joseph cut him off with a dismissive wave of his hand. "Yes, you have said that. I would like to make sure I understand the rest of what you are proposing.

"You ask me to give up my beautiful Valley of the Winding Waters, to give it to your kind. Then I should move onto a country not claimed by my fathers. If I do this, you will respect my rights there."

The commissioner nodded cautiously.

"Perhaps you can tell me also why I should not find such a promise preposterous. Your man Stee-vuns said these same words to me eight circles of seasons ago. He told me then that if I signed his paper talk then, he would not allow any white men in Nimipu country. I signed. But now, as I look about, I see white men all over. Can you tell me why I should believe your words when the words of the last treaty man were lies?''

Toolhoolhoolzote got to his feet arrogantly. ''There will be no new treaty, white man. We will stay with the old one. We are here to insist that your last paper words be honored.''

''That is not possible!'' the commissioner argued when he understood the translator. ''My government is in no position to take such action. The miners, the settlers, are already here. We certainly cannot demand that they go again.''

Old Joseph raised a brow. ''Why?''

There was no answer.

''Then,'' Old Joseph finished succinctly, ''we have nothing to talk about.''

He turned away. Lawyer jumped to his feet to block his path.

''They will give us gold!'' he protested. ''They will give us schools and shops and fences and plowed lands! Think before you refuse all these things!''

''And where, old friend, would *you* have to move to in order to receive these presents?''

Lawyer looked confused. ''My country is already part of the reservation they are suggesting.''

''Ah, so you would have *me* move so that you can receive white gold. Yes, I can see why you find this new treaty so appealing.''

Old Joseph shook his head, and looked back to the white men, simply speaking the response that was on his comrades' faces.

''No.''

The headmen met again when darkness came, this time at White Bird's fire. It was banked low, to avoid drawing attention, although the moon was high and most of the *xayxayx* slept.

''Our strongest enemies are among our own numbers,'' Looking Glass observed.

There was an upheaval of voices, but no one truly argued with him. The men gathered were *tiwats* and leaders; they had strong *wyakin* guides. Each of them knew as deeply and certainly as Looking Glass that his words were true.

"We cannot hope to survive these white men if we do not stand united," Looking Glass went on. "We cannot hope to gain any satisfaction from that slick-talking co-mish-un-er as long as we are at odds with each other. Some of us think he speaks true. Most of us hear his lies. I fear that while he finds one open heart among us, he will not hear the greater, louder voice of our denial."

"Lawyer robs our strength," Toolhoolhoolzote snarled, unafraid to speak the charge aloud. "He stands alone in embracing those *xayxayx* words."

"No!" Lawyer argued heatedly. "There are the headmen Jason and Timothy as well. They know that our strength depends upon grasping the white man's hand."

"You take the white man's hand because you can no longer dream," White Bird said tiredly, and Lawyer flushed.

How had they guessed? He had taken pains, great pains, to hide that truth. Hearing it spoken aloud made his fear come back, mushrooming inside him, just when he had thought it assuaged by the white man's gold.

"I think Tahmahnewes is punishing you for taking the white man's hand!" Huishuis Kute charged angrily. "He has taken *wyakin* away."

"Brother," Old Joseph tried, "perhaps if you spoke to your *wyakin* and begged his forgiveness, he would return to you."

Looking Glass cleared his throat. "Will you relent?" he asked Lawyer.

Lawyer pushed his chin out and hoped it did not tremble. "To turn away from the white men is to see our people die."

"So be it." Looking Glass sighed and surveyed the council. "Who here will vote for Lawyer's new treaty?"

Only Timothy and Jason raised their hands.

"Then I see no help for it. We are now two tribes."

There were gasps and shouts, but again, no one truly argued. Looking Glass got to his feet.

"We, the Dreamers, will not sign your *xayxayx* treaty," he told Lawyer. "We cannot. It is unconscionable. We will tell your co-mish-un-er this with the new sun. We will tell him that if he does not stand by that old treaty, then we will protect our lands ourselves. But we will not give our countries to the white men and receive only lies and misery in return."

His shoulders drooped sadly. "I am sorry, brother. From now on, you are not one of us. From now on, you are on your own."

The keening of the women began with the first glow of the new sun. Word spread among them like a prairie fire, growing hotter and more painful with each breath of the wind.

Broken Bird found her brother as he was leaving his hearth to go to the talking place. "It is true then?" she demanded.

Looking Glass nodded. "Yes, but it changes nothing for us. Those treaty bands are the ones who will suffer for it."

"The squaws will suffer," she said harshly. "They always do."

"They will still have their buffalo, their camas prairies, and their fish. How can you call that bad?"

"They will not have their kin!"

Looking Glass scowled. "They have a choice," he said finally, evenly. "They can give up their homes and live on Lawyer's res-er-va-shun. They can plant things in Mother Earth's bosom, and watch Father Sun shine on the gold they have earned. Or they can reap with pleasure the rich gifts Tahmahnewes gives them freely. They can trust their *wyakin* spirits to stand guard over their souls." He looked back at the council place. "Lawyer is a white man now," he mused. "What are you?"

"I am Nimipu." She could not even bring herself to hesitate, no matter how much she mourned for those who would be destroyed by the *xayxayx*, for foolishly trusting them and taking up their ways.

Looking Glass nodded and began moving on again.

"What of the orphan?" she called out behind him. "What side will she live on?"

She was sure he had forgotten the girl with all this other trouble, but her brother surprised her.

"Old Joseph's wife will take her," he said, glancing back. "She will go to the Kahmuenem people. That is the best I could do."

The best? It was an auspicious home at the hearth of a headman. Broken Bird gave a shout of laughter even as her heart cracked anew at the loss.

She went to find the little one. Looking Glass trod heavily to the talking spot and watched the commissioner, seated at a table with his papers.

"My Hasotoin will not be part of your treaty," he said when the white man looked up. "I am Looking Glass, and I will not sign."

He stepped back, detaching himself from the proceedings. After a moment, Toolhoolhoolzote, White Bird, and Old Joseph approached the table as well.

"There will be no new treaty," Toolhoolhoolzote reiterated.

"I am with my brothers," White Bird said. "If these white men are not removed, if you do not honor your old words, then we will protect ourselves."

He and Toolhoolhoolzote went back to their camps. Lawyer arrived just as Old Joseph declined to sign as well.

The Kahmuenem headman joined Looking Glass outside the cleared circle, and Lawyer spoke earnestly to the commissioner in halting *xayxayx* words.

"We are separate now," he tried to explain. "They will not help you, but I wish to remain friends with your people."

"*None* of them will sign?" exclaimed the junior officer. "Good Lord, that's better than half the tribe!"

"Two thirds," the man called Henrison corrected darkly.

The commissioner slammed his palm down upon the treaty papers. "Damn it! I cannot allow this! How shall I tell six thousand settlers that they must leave the area?"

Lawyer thumbed his chest. "I have a way. How many marks—" He motioned across the papers. "How many of those must you have?"

The commissioner gave a bark of frustrated laughter. "How

many important men are there? Chiefs and subchiefs and the like?''

''Eighteen chiefs signed the 1855 pact,'' the junior officer answered authoritatively. ''Add to that their subordinates—''

''How many men do you have with you?'' the commissioner demanded of Lawyer. The Lapwai headman flashed his palms five times. ''Fifty ought to do it,'' he mused.

''Give or take a few,'' agreed the junior officer.

Henrison sucked his breath in. ''Good God, that's perfidy!''

''Gather up your men,'' the commissioner instructed Lawyer. ''Bring them to me.''

When it was done, he folded the treaty papers carefully and slid them into his breast pocket. His smile was grim. ''I thank all of you for your cooperation.''

''In a pig's eye!'' Henrison snapped. ''That treaty will go out to the world as the concurrent agreement of the tribe! In reality, it's nothing more than the agreement of one band. And that Lawyer chief knows enough English to be fully aware of it!''

''Let's hope so,'' the commissioner agreed. ''If Lawyer knows what he has signed, that makes it a valid pact. Considering that we have just successfully reclaimed three quarters of the land we gave them in that '55 treaty, I hardly think we ought to be splitting hairs, gentlemen.''

''Tell that to those gents there. Tell them that your Lawyer just signed away their homelands.''

He pointed to Old Joseph and Looking Glass. The headmen watched on woodenly, not understanding a word that was said. Both, however, felt the truth in their bones.

Dark Moon watched the tall man with the arrogant nose as he came toward his hearth. He looked very, very angry, and her heart thundered so hard she felt faint.

He did not want a babe killer to live with him either.

She skittered around behind Broken Bird as he drew close. The midwife caught her shoulder and pulled her gently back, though she stumbled and struggled.

The beak-nosed man held a strange bunch of papers, white

bound in black. He slammed the thing again and again against the earth as she watched. She squealed and jumped so badly she careened back into the midwife.

Arenoth watched her normally gentle, placid husband in amazement. "It went badly, then," she said finally.

"I do not know what happened," Old Joseph admitted, the anger rushing out of him, leaving him very, very tired. "I did not sign."

"But Lawyer did?" asked his wife.

The headman nodded. "My heart tells me he has somehow lied."

He thought of the way the commissioner had smiled at the end, and he kicked his Bible into the fire pit. The banked embers there caught it, and it ignited to flame. Arenoth gasped.

He had carried that book with him for twelve circles of seasons, since the missionaries had come and told him about their God. He had never betrayed his *wyakin,* but he had embraced the *xayxayx* medicine with equal fervor, for it spoke of generosity and kindness, things he believed in.

Now Old Joseph knew that the white men lied. No longer could he trust their God.

"We should go home," he murmured. "We must get back to Kahmuenem and guard what is ours."

Arenoth nodded and began turning away, then her gaze fell on Broken Bird and the Hasotoin orphan. At once, she remembered them, and why they were here.

"Oh, child," she whispered, thinking of the fright her husband must have given her.

Broken Bird gave her another little push and turned away before she could cry openly. Dark Moon felt the cool air at her back where the woman's warmth had been a moment ago, and she whipped around.

No, no, no, no!

She flinched away from the hand Arenoth reached out to her in comfort. The Hasotoin were already mounting. Dark Moon ran to the spot where their camp had been, barren now of anything but flat, crushed grass.

"Please," she moaned. "Please." But no one heard her.

They were going. They truly were going to leave this place without her.

Broken Bird and Culmuh, Twelic and Young Looking Glass, were the last to go. She cried out with all the terror in her soul, for the one she could bear losing least of all.

"Twelic! No!"

There was no answer.

Part Two

Part Two

12

Part Two

12

Wallowa valley, 1863

DAWN WAS STILL a breath away, and the white, swollen moon waited for it, hanging low over blue-gray mountains. Dark Moon turned about slowly, looking at it all. Feathers of mist floated through the valley, trapped by the peaks. They swirled over Lake Wallowa, its waters perfectly, placidly still, like the magic mirror that had given Looking Glass his name.

"This happens before every snow season," Old Joseph said from behind her. "The water is still warm from the last sun, but by dawn the air is chilled. That is when the mists come."

Dark Moon gasped and whirled about at his voice. The headman was standing at the first door to the Kahmuenem longhouse, his robe about his shoulders, his hair wild from sleep. In all her eight snows, Looking Glass had hardly ever spoken to her. She was not sure what this man expected from her now.

"I . . . I never saw it happen before," she ventured finally.

"That is because you rise too late. The new sun will burn it off."

She flinched, sure he was reprimanding her. He had not even raised his voice since she had come to his valley, but Wahlitits had left her alone for long periods of time as well, and Twelic had always been kind to her until the end.

Her heart spasmed suddenly. She could not let herself think about him, because his betrayal made her want to cry. *How could he have turned her out like that? How could he have ridden away?*

"I always leave my bedding before anyone else stirs," Old Joseph continued. "Even in the other seasons, the dawn always brings magic. It is a good way to leave sleep and start working." He began walking toward the lake. "Come, I will show you my special place."

Dark Moon gaped at his retreating back, then moved warily, obediently, after him.

He lowered himself to a rock ledge overhanging the water. A swell of ground there hid them from the village. She hugged herself, watching him, knowing that if he hurt her now, no other would see. But he only patted the rock beside him.

Dark Moon hesitated, then sat, keeping a careful distance between them.

"I have been thinking that you need some kind of work," he went on. "Work makes the body hard and agile, and it soothes the mind." He paused, studying the mists as they began to fade. "What should your work be, do you think? Looking Glass tells me that you are very good with ponies."

"No!" Her throat constricted. She looked down at her hands, the hands that had marked Twelic's foal's legs, that had seen her banished from the Hasotoin band.

"I . . . cannot care for ponies anymore," she whispered wretchedly.

Old Joseph shrugged. "Perhaps not, but I would like to see for myself."

Dark Moon stared at him.

"There are not very many ponies here now, so we will have to wait until the spring to find out. But when they come back from the hills, my herd will be yours to care for."

She could not let that happen! She scrambled to her feet again, shaking her head in denial. "I would hurt one!"

Old Joseph watched her calmly, not sure he understood, but wise enough to respect her fear. "If you do, then it will be my fault for asking you to touch them. I will remember that I have done so, and I will not blame you."

She could not believe such a thing.

"Since spring is several moons away, we must find something for you to do until then. I think one chore should be for you to come here with me, to this rock, with every sun-coming.'' Learn peace, child, he thought. Learn that Tahmah-newes truly is kind and generous with His simple gifts.

He stood as sounds from the village began to reach them, and turned away, leaving her.

When he was gone, Dark Moon sat on the ledge again, trembling.

13

Keh-khee-tahl, Moon of First Harvest, 1867

THE SPECKLED COLT came off the ground, hooves pointed down, his spine bowed angrily. Old Joseph smiled faintly from his summer hearth as Dark Moon tumbled off his back and landed, limbs sprawled, in the grass behind him.

The headman's youngest son grinned. "Mother has finally found her daughter," Alokot observed, tongue in cheek.

"And she is a good girl," Arenoth admonished as she strung fish up to dry.

"Good? Yes," Alokot agreed. "She is very good with a pony, and she is growing quite excellent with a bow. Are those the things a squaw should know?"

In the distance, Dark Moon sat up, her sleek black hair spilling over her shoulders. She did not like to braid it, and Arenoth had finally given up trying to persuade her. This girl would never look like the others. Now, in her twelfth spring, she was ripe and leggy and long. She moved with a pony's own grace, and there was the matter of her strange, indigo eyes as well. She truly was a beautiful girl.

As Arenoth watched, the *tiwats*'s son, a promising young warrior named Earth Sound, hurried to her side to help her to her feet. Arenoth was close enough to see the startled-doe look come over her. If Earth Sound stayed too long, Dark Moon would run back into the summer lodge, Arenoth knew.

"Go to her, please," she said to her son.

Alokot scowled. "You cannot protect her forever. Earth Sound would not hurt her."

"She still does not know that, and I will protect her as long as she is mine to protect."

Alokot shrugged and walked over to where the colt stood, sides heaving. "I think that pony is afraid to back up because he does not know what is behind him," he observed.

Dark Moon nodded cautiously, politely ignoring Earth Sound.

"Maybe you should talk to him in that pony way you have," Alokot went on, "so he knows he can trust you."

Dark Moon twitched as though someone had slapped her. She did not think anyone knew about her pony talk. The Hasotoin had ridiculed her mercilessly about that.

But these people were not Hasotoin. Slowly, carefully, she let her breath out. These people had never hurt her, and somehow she had managed not to mark any of Old Joseph's pony babes while she had been here. No one had died either, though she could scarcely believe it.

She eyed both warriors, then she went around to the back of the colt. She scratched the dock of his tail and murmured to him until he began to relax, then she whinnied. Her gaze darted again to Alokot and Earth Sound, but they only watched, bemused, as the pony snaked his neck around to look at her.

She forgot the warriors. "There, it is fine, do you see?" she crooned to her animal friend. "I stand right here, and I do not fall off the earth. Come back, little stallion, come back to where I stand."

Gently, she took up the reins again, pulling on the leather where it looped through his mouth. The animal took one tentative step backward, then another.

She looked up at Alokot with that rare expression that made his belly squirm. Suddenly, her eyes were big and bright and alive, and a grin split her face.

"How do you do that?" Earth Sound burst out, looking between her and the colt.

The fire went out of Dark Moon abruptly and her gaze turned wary. "I . . . I do not know exactly. It just happens."

"But you must show me!"

She retreated a step. "No. I cannot. I am sorry."

"I will bring you something back from buffalo country," he cajoled.

As Twelic had brought her things back, Dark Moon thought bitterly. She closed her eyes against that memory.

"You will go east then this season?" she asked Alokot. "We will not go to First Fruits with the other bands?"

It had been four circles of seasons since the Hasotoin had thrown her out. In all that time, Old Joseph had persistently remained in his valleys, watching for *xayxayx* miners. His young men traveled to the buffalo ranges to earn their stature. Oh, Spirit Chief, she did not want to leave this place of autumn mists and safety, not even for the moon or two it would take to collect salmon and roots!

Blessedly, Alokot nodded. "The women will stay here for the season. I will lead a few men to Crow country to get meat and robes for the winter."

"I will bring you a robe anyway," Earth Sound persisted, "whether you teach me to talk to the horses or not."

Dark Moon's relief at being able to stay in Old Joseph's country recoiled abruptly inside her.

"I . . . thank you." She would not argue with him. If he wanted to give her a robe, she would have to accept it.

Earth Sound was stronger than she was, with a warrior's own power, and even looking at him seemed to make the burning hurt begin again in her most private parts. She fought the urge to rub herself there.

She could not forget Wahlitits.

She could not make Earth Sound angry.

She could not be run out of this place.

Oh, please, Tahmahnewes, do not let that happen.

Old Joseph did not go east with his sons and his warriors. In a secret part of her heart, Dark Moon was very glad.

She found him at his summer place with the dawn, just after the others had ridden out. It was much like the rock overhang at the Wallowa valley where the Kahmuenem people spent their snow seasons. But in these warm moons, they traveled to their Imnaha valley, and the old headman greeted the dawn at the river.

Old Joseph knew she was there without turning about. "What questions do you have for me this morning?" he asked.

"How can I get an elk?"

He raised his brows at her as she came to sit beside him. "What would a squaw want with such a beast?"

"Their hides make the best moccasins."

"Yes, that is true. But who would you make moccasins for?"

"Alokot. He has taught me much, and I would like to make a kill of my own while he is gone and give him a present."

"Squaws usually give moccasins to one they would like to take as mate."

She stiffened against a deep thud of her heart. Broken Bird and Twelic had insisted that she mate as well . . . at the end, right before they had sent her away.

"Is that . . ." She paused and licked her lips carefully. "Is that what you would have me do, then?" she asked.

"Not unless you wish to."

"I will never wish that," she answered fervently.

"Well, then." Old Joseph thought a moment. "I think perhaps you should make Alokot something else, something besides moccasins. He would like to claim a girl who lives with Huishuis Kute's people. Her name is Wetatonmi. I am almost sure Wetatonmi will give him moccasins this season. I will take you to get a doe instead, and you can make him a medicine pouch."

"That . . . that would be good." But she was disappointed. An elk would have been such a brave, fine kill.

The dawn was strong now. She got to her feet, and heard the headman grunt softly behind her as he did the same. Then, from the other side of the hill, there came a sudden commotion.

Dark Moon went still, her eyes darting back to Old Joseph. "Is it those miners?"

She knew he feared them, and that seemed good enough cause for her to dread them as well. But when they hurried

back around the crest, there were no white-skins in the valley.
Instead, the warriors who had remained behind surged about
a lone pony, a rangy beast carrying an ugly little man. The
squaws hung back, clutching their babes protectively as they
watched the procession.

"Ah, I have heard of this one," Old Joseph mused.

He greeted the visitor at the council fire near his summer
lodge. When the man dismounted, Dark Moon saw that he was
even uglier than she had first thought. He was so short he
barely came to her chin, and he had an odd lump on his back.
She started to go around him to the herd, but when she passed
him, he looked up at her with his tiny, black eyes.

She took a stumbling step backward again. *Go away,* she
thought. But then she realized that she did not truly want him
to. In some odd way, she was drawn to him. She shook her
head, feeling dazed.

Who was he?

He was not Nimipu; she had been surrounded by those people all her snows, and this man was different. Finally, he
turned away, and her breath seemed to come back.

She squatted down where she stood.

Old Joseph gave the stranger a pipe. They smoked for a
while, and then he told the warriors that the visitor was Smoholla.

Smoholla. Dark Moon shook her head. It meant nothing to
her. She did not know the name.

"I am here to remind you of the old ways," Smoholla said,
and oh, his voice! It was gravelly and rough, and it made her
skin feel ticklish.

"I am a prophet. I have been to see all your people, to tell
you something very important. Your Tahmahnewes has spoken
to me! I have come to pass on His message."

There was an uncomfortable, startled stir among the warriors. Many of them sat to listen.

"You will all die if you forget how your grandfathers
lived," Smoholla went on. "That is what your Great Spirit
Chief wants me to tell you. You must remember the time when
the Nimipu lived only in longhouses, and in the summer, in

teasel-thatched huts. Look about you! What do you see? Buffalo-hide lodges! Where are all your young men? Are they at the river, fishing? No! They have gone over the mountains, to some other peoples' country, to take the great, shaggy beasts that are not their own!''

Dark Moon scowled. She could not think what was so wrong with that. The Kahmuenem still had their longhouse in the Wallowa valley, although many families, especially those led by the younger men, had pitched private, taut-skinned lodges at the outskirts of the village. Once, she remembered, everyone *had* lived together, but in these last few seasons, the warriors had begun saying that the buffalo peoples' way was better.

''Tahmahnewes wants that to change,'' the prophet went on. ''It is not the Nimipu way, and you must remain Nimipu and strong if you are to survive. You are unique from those other people. Your strengths are your own.''

A roar of outrage went through the people. Smoholla shouted above it.

''Listen to me, Kahmuenem people! I speak true! I have already died and gone to the afterworld. It was there that I met your Great Spirit Chief, there that He appointed me to return to you. Tahmahnewes is most bitterly opposed to the *xayxayx* ways, and He urges you to push them from your hearts.''

''You should talk to Lawyer's people!'' someone shouted angrily.

''Tahmahnewes knows what that Lawyer is doing, and he will curse his people for their mining and farming. He says that young men should never work in such a way. Men who work cannot dream, and wisdom comes to us through dreams. If your people do not cling to their old truths, you will surely be destroyed as well.''

''Who would destroy us?'' a warrior demanded arrogantly.

''The *xayxayx*. Men who believe in their own way.''

The council erupted anew with shouts at the prophet. Dark Moon stood again, unsteadily.

She could not truly bring herself to fear the *xayxayx*. Old

Joseph said they were dangerous, but she had known far worse enemies in her twelve snows. No, the prophet's message regarding them was not what made her heart lurch.

Wisdom comes to us through dreams.

Did you dream out there, little one?

Bah! A child of five snows cannot dream!

Suddenly, she understood what it was about Smoholla that had bothered her. She looked back at him and found his eyes steady and hard on hers. She gave a startled little cry.

He knew.

She was sure that he knew the Hasotoin had thrown her out, and that he knew why.

The prophet stayed for two more suns. He did not look at her again, but he did not have to. Whenever he was close, Dark Moon felt terror rock through her.

Had Tahmahnewes sent him to remind her of her evil so that she did not harm these Kahmuenem people who had cared for her? She had to know, but each time she decided that, her belly shrank into itself. If she was as bad as the Hasotoin had said, then she would have to leave the Kahmuenem as well.

She did not know if she could bear it.

She hardened her jaw and pushed to her feet, away from Arenoth's hearth. She found the prophet near his big, ugly pony, getting ready to mount. He looked over his shoulder to find her.

"I thought you would seek me out."

"Why?" The word blurted from her, though she already knew.

"You want to know if you can dream."

"I want to know if I already have!" What had happened to her during Twelic's *wyakin* search? And, oh, Tahmahnewes, had she truly killed that Hasotoin babe long ago?

The prophet only shook his head. Disappointment made her feel dizzy. He did not know, after all.

"They said I do it without knowing," she whispered.

The prophet shrugged. "Have you been denied your *wyakin*?"

"No!" Her eyes flashed up to him again. "I have never been sent for one!"

"Then you do not know yet if Tahmahnewes would scorn you." He looked at her more closely. "The people fear your power, do they? They think it is evil?"

"Yes . . . no." She finally nodded wretchedly.

"It is only evil if it does not come from Tahmahnewes. The Great Spirit Chief grants only goodness and strength. Wait to see if you find a *wyakin*, child. If one is denied you, then you know they speak true."

She could not wait that long! It had taken so much courage just to approach him now!

Smoholla read her dismay. His twisted face creased deeper in thought.

He was not a charlatan, though he knew many said that he was. He was guilty only of using his powers to sell his own personal beliefs. He had, from the first, sensed a kindred spirit in this child, perhaps a spirit stronger than any he had yet encountered. It was worth cultivating, he thought. It would not do to have her fear herself.

"Since you are young, since Tahmahnewes has not actually denied you a *wyakin* yet, it might be possible for you to dream without one. But if you do, that would not tell you if the vision was sent by your Great Spirit Chief or by some evil spirit monster," he cautioned.

Her heart leaped. She did not care. It was better to know something than to know nothing at all.

"You should find a safe place, somewhere where your fear will not block you from relinquishing your grip on this world," he went on. "You should be hungry and tired, as a child is when he seeks his *wyakin*. Sit quietly, and close out all smells and sounds. Go deeper and deeper into your mind. Be careful not to grow impatient. If an image should finally appear before you, follow it with your soul, wherever it may take you."

Those were all the things she had done when Twelic had

gone on his vision quest, when she had built the imaginary fire in her mind. She shuddered.

She would do it again.

She had to try.

14

ALOKOT HAD NOT yet returned from his long hunt, but Old Joseph had taken some food from the water. Eels sizzled over Arenoth's cook fire, long, smoking sausages of their meat mixed with wild onions and herbs and stuffed back into their skin.

Arenoth worked a piece free from the spitting stick and used her *xayxayx* knife to cut it into portions. She pushed a piece toward the orphan.

Dark Moon would not meet her eyes. "I . . . no," she declined politely. "Your husband will be hungry. He should have it."

"There is enough here for everyone," Arenoth countered.

"I am not hungry," she murmured, and felt shamed for the lie. Her gut twisted emptily.

Arenoth knew it was useless. Still, she would have argued anyway if Dark Moon had not cleared her throat to say something more.

"I would like to sleep outside this night."

Arenoth looked helplessly to her husband. His expression was resigned. "I see no harm in that," the headman said finally.

Dark Moon pushed to her feet and hurried from the buffalo lodge. Arenoth watched her moccasins retreat beneath the rolled-up flap. She turned to her husband angrily.

"Why?" she demanded. "You know what she would do!"

"And it must be done," Old Joseph answered.

"She is starving herself to see if she can find a dream. What did that old pretender Smoholla say to her?"

"He encouraged her, I think."

"She is too young! If she were ready, you would have sent her for her *wyakin*!"

"No."

Old Joseph put down his sausage and shook his head. "Think, wife. Think of the fear that still hides behind her eyes. If I were to send her for her *wyakin* now, though she is old enough, her terror would keep her from finding one. She would be ruined. This way is better. It is something she has found the courage to do on her own."

"She will dream." Arenoth breathed.

"Yes. And it will be a good dream. When it happens, perhaps Tahmahnewes will finally let her leave the past behind."

Dark Moon decided she would go to the ponies. *Find somewhere safe,* the prophet had said. Even more than the Kahmuenem valleys, the herd was the safest place she had ever known.

The animals nickered to her when she reached them. Mares nudged her with their soft noses and she stroked them absently, looking about for the best spot.

Finally, she sat down where she stood. The moon was just beginning to come up. She thought it might be a good idea to concentrate on that as well. For good or for bad, it had been her first name giver, after all.

She stared at it determinedly, not blinking, then she began to wonder.

What *had* happened to it the night it had gone away? Had it just suddenly blinked out? For the first time she wished she had dared to ask someone. The ponies rustled and munched, and she fought an urge to look about at them. The wind was still vaguely chilled with spring and it tickled over her skin, raising gooseflesh. She hugged herself, then grimaced and dropped her arms back to her sides.

Sit quietly, and close out all smells and sounds.

But, oh, it was hard to ignore her hunger!

She had not eaten for four suns. It made her feel weak, but she battled sleep, keeping her eyes wide until they felt grainy and dry.

The moon floated higher.

The pony sounds seemed quieter.

Close it out.

Suddenly, a sour badness filled her belly. *The moon was shrinking.* Oh, sweet Tahmahnewes, the moon was going away!

She kept staring, and realized that she knew what to do, knew it without remembering Smoholla's words. Fear screamed up in her again, telling her to stop. She did not *want* to dream! She wanted to learn that she was not strong enough to do it without a *wyakin*, that she could never have hurt anyone! But now a black moon was covering the real one, and though she willed it desperately, she could not push it away.

The dark hole in the sky kept growing, and she felt herself falling, spinning into its blackness. . . .

Suddenly, there was no sky, no moon at all.

Her heart pounded, faster and faster, because there were no ponies here inside the dark moon either; there were only woods, thick and sheltering. She looked about wildly, and she knew the place. *She had come here with Alokot.* These were the hills that hugged the Imnaha valley.

Her fear shivered away. She was safe here, knew all the hidden nooks and caverns. Alokot had shown them to her.

She was not cold anymore.

A patched coat of winter hair hugged her warmly, and the smells were glorious too, so much sharper than she had ever known them to be. The new spring green was pungent and strong. Beneath it, musty and furtive, were other smells, like the moldy leaves and mulch that had lain under the snow all winter. There was something else, too. She twitched her nose, searching for it. It was something elusive, something frightful. . . .

The feral scent of cat.

She was not herself anymore. Her blood rushed with instinctual danger, with bestial panic that was not her own. *Run.* Yes, that was what she had to do, before the cat slinked out of the brush and crashed down upon her, before he laid open her flesh with lethal claws. Her feet went faster and faster, cloven hooves pounding. She had to go to the trail.

Pain creased through her head. She could not know about a trail. She was just an animal . . . something big and strong, with heavy, precarious weight upon her head.

An elk. She was in an elk, but some of her own knowledge remained.

She would go to the trail.

She guided herself out from the deepest woods, toward the edge of the Imnaha swale. Danger there. Alokot said to be careful at that spot. Her heart thundered as she neared it, but something in her throbbed with exhilaration as well.

She saw it ahead, the place where the trees fell away, as though beyond it lay a clear path. She raced there, and then the land dived off into a creek bed of rocks and steep, slippery sand.

The elk screamed. His limbs splayed, digging, scrambling for traction to stop, *stop, stop. . . .*

The sound of his cry tore through her head, burned her own throat. Her heart thudded with his, banging in her chest, and then there was nothing, only air, and they were falling.

She was losing him, losing the strong, fine animal who had sheltered her. She felt the agony of his knowledge of his own death, and she wept with it even as the hurt came.

Finally, there was blackness as the dark moon consumed her. No trees, no fear, no ponies . . .

She sank into that place until the pictures in her mind let her go.

The new sun touched her face gently, nudging her awake. Dark Moon sat up, something dark and constant pounding behind her eyes.

The ponies moved about her. She was still in the herd, safe . . . and then she remembered, and she knew she would never be safe again.

Oh, sweet Tahmahnewes, she had dreamed.

A terrible, mewling sound came up her throat. She clapped a hand over her mouth and staggered upright, and the Imnaha valley swirled about her. A pony came to her, sensing her distress, standing close. She leaned against it, fighting for strength.

Maybe it was not true.

But it was; she knew it. It was only a matter of looking to be sure.

For a wild moment, she thought of just going back to the camp. No one knew what she had done, so she would not even have to lie. She could just pretend nothing had happened out here, that she still did not know she could dream without a *wyakin*.

She could . . . but the truth would always be a vicious little animal in her gut now. *She* knew. And because she did, she had to go find the elk in the swale.

An elk. She gave a wild little laugh. She had gotten her kill after all. Something inside her had done it, something bad and stubborn that had not listened to Old Joseph about the moccasins, even though she knew he was wise. It had happened that way with the rattlesnake, too, long ago. She was sure now. Something bad inside her must have wanted to kill that boy.

She gathered the pony's mane to pull herself up onto its back. They rode out of the valley, into the hills. The dream was clear in her memory, mocking her. She went straight to the precipice and dismounted a good distance from the drop so that the pony would not wander over it by accident.

She walked closer with feet that dragged. The elk was there.

He lay in the bottom of the creek bed, and for one horrible moment, their eyes met. They recognized each other; she felt it with a jolt that went all the way down inside her. She gave another small cry and slid down to his side.

He did not struggle away from her, but only watched her, waiting. His front legs were bent at unnatural angles beneath him. She fumbled for her knife, drew it gently across his neck, and put him out of his misery.

She would have to take him back to Old Joseph and admit what she had done. She could not offend his *cewcew*, his ghost, by wasting the flesh he had given.

She worked grimly, her face hard and expressionless as she butchered the carcass. She took with her the best parts of the meat, and left the rest buried and protected beneath some rocks.

The sun grew hot and high. When she reached the lodges, she found Old Joseph sitting quietly at his cold outside firepit. She dismounted at his feet, laying the elk meat carefully before him.

Oh, Tahmahnewes, she could not look at him! He had been so good and true to her, but she was what the Hasotoin had said, and now he would know that she could hurt him.

Her voice came out strangled. "I . . . am . . . sorry."

The headman was quiet for a long time. "For feeding us? For bringing us meat in this time when the game is just returning to Imnaha? I had no luck with my own hunt on the last sun. Where did you find this?"

Her heart hurtled up into her throat. Did he not see? Did he not understand? *Why was he not angry?*

"I dreamed!" she whispered. "I killed him."

He sniffed at the meat. "You got your elk. Arenoth can help you tan the hide and you can save it for moccasins for some other time."

"I dreamed I was in him," she burst out, "and that I led him to die! And when I went to look, there he was!"

"You called him. Like your grandfather, you can speak to animals and fill them with your soul."

She nodded desperately.

"So do you think now that perhaps you called that rattlesnake to Looking Glass's band?"

"I will go," she managed. "I will not hurt you."

"Listen to me!"

His voice was harsher than she had heard it since the time he had torn up his Bible. Dark Moon flinched and took an involuntary step back.

"I do not think you called that rattlesnake," he went on. "I was not there, but I have heard all the stories about that time.

That was an evil thing, and sometimes animals move without being called. That snake could have come there all by himself, or perhaps another spirit monster called him. But I do not think that spirit monster was yours."

"But—"

"No one can ever know all about the past, but what you have done now is a good thing, not evil. Our people are hungry and tired of eating fish while we wait for Alokot to return. You have brought us meat, and they will be grateful. I will send a warrior out right away to get the rest of the carcass."

Her mouth went dry and she stared at him.

"I do not want you to leave us," he went on. "My heart would hurt to see you go. I think, instead, you should go now for your *wyakin*. Find out more about this power you have. Let Tahmahnewes show you how He would like you to use it."

Her *wyakin?* A whole new fear came to grip her.

They said her grandfather was magic, that he had very powerful blood. But Strong Cub's life moved within her also. What if Tahmahnewes denied her?

But she knew what would happen. If she did not find a spirit protector, it would be all the same in the end. Even the Kahmuenem would hate her.

"No," she groaned.

"Tahmahnewes will not deny you," Old Joseph said kindly, and he prayed that he was right.

Dark Moon stared at him, her heart beating hard. She felt trapped and helpless. She could not disappoint him. If he thought she should try, then she would have to do it.

Her chin came up as she made a vow silently to herself. If she did not dream this most important dream, at least she would be sure that a spirit monster had given her her magic. She would not wait for it to get away from her again, to kill or to mark something else. If she had no *wyakin*, she would leave them.

She turned away carefully, then she paused. "Did . . . did the moon go away last night?" she whispered.

Joseph hesitated. "No."

She flinched as though he had struck her.

15

WHEN OLD JOSEPH finally decided upon the moment she should go, Dark Moon had begun hoping, against all reason, that he had forgotten.

A moon passed, and the suns grew hotter and longer, draining the color from the sky and the grasses. She had to drive the ponies farther down the river to get good water. Earth Sound's father, the *tiwats* Burned Tree, asked her to take his mares as well; she was painstakingly careful with those, never touching them, making sure she was never, ever hungry or tired when she was near them.

As the animals splashed languidly through the shallow water, she pulled herself up on a rock to watch them and wait. When Old Joseph spoke from behind her, she jumped.

"Leave them, child. I will watch over them and send them back to the valley when they are sated."

A painful stillness settled over her. She nodded without looking at him and slid down so that her feet touched the earth again. Now that he had finally said the words, there was none of the terror she had expected. There was nothing inside her but numb inevitability.

Old Joseph watched her face and felt as though he were sending a doe to slaughter.

In his heart, he still did not fear that the Great Spirit Chief would forsake her. It was her courage that left him uncertain. The few children he had known to fail at this were those timid creatures who thought more of the shame of no *wyakin* than of the glorious horizons Tahmahnewes offered them. This one had known more shame than most.

He thought of stopping her after all, but she had already stripped out of her doeskin and raised her arms to the sky. Her long, sleek hair spilled down her back as she closed her eyes as though in prayer, then she slowly, slowly, she lowered her hands again.

Spirit Chief, she is one of yours, sprung from your very heart. Protect her.

Old Joseph had to believe that He would, but suddenly, he knew that if he was wrong, he would not see her again.

His old heart ached with trepidation.

Dark Moon wondered detachedly if she could do this without her ponies. She heard one whinny to her, loud and shrill, as she left them, and she fought the urge to look back. Perhaps it was telling her that its spirit would travel with her, but she did not dare believe it was so.

She found a path into the hills and followed it upward, hesitating only briefly when she crossed over the game trail where she had flown with the elk. Then the icy sense of doom settled more deeply in her gut and she went on.

She stopped at the peak of the highest hill just as dusk fell. She found what she needed to start a fire in the thickening darkness, working without conscious thought. When the orange glow flickered, battling back the shadows, she looked around, taking stock of her surroundings. She had paused here instinctively, but now she saw that it was a good place, a rocky ledge partially sheltered by firs and evergreens.

She crossed her legs carefully beneath her and sat, resting her hands on her thighs.

The moon did not draw her in this time, though she focused on it, willing it until her heart felt sick. By dawn her muscles throbbed in protest at her stillness. The sun came up, its first rays warming her as they shafted through the trees behind her. Then it came full over her head and began baking down on her until her tongue felt dry and thick in her mouth.

As night fell again, a rock seemed to settle in her belly

where she was supposed to feel nothing but hunger. She tried very, very hard not to think about the stones that bit into her bare buttocks, or the flies that nibbled on her flesh. Still, she found herself wishing that she had swept the ground clean before she had sat, and fought the urge to wriggle away from the itchy little gnats.

She was failing.

She decided, without much emotion, that she would stay here through four more suns. If she did not dream by then, she would drink some water. Then she would call an animal to her evil hearth and feast on the flesh Tahmahnewes did not mean for her nourishment.

On the third night, the moon did not even come. It was as though even her first name giver had abandoned her now that she truly needed it.

Her belly squeezed against its own emptiness and her eyes ached to close. Knowing it was useless to fight it any longer, she shuddered and let her head drop. It was over. Sweet Tahmahnewes, there would be no dream.

Behind her closed lids, she found the moon.

She thought she cried out, but her parched, swollen tongue would allow no true sound. She stared, stunned, into the milky whiteness and watched it turn dark again, watched pictures fill its crater. *Her ponies.* They had come with her, standing by her, after all!

Her heart skittered, then pounded. The herd ran, galloping hard. But the vision was wrong . . . these were not all Nimipu ponies. Some of the coveted spotted ponies surged among them, but most were solid black and blood red, bigger and stronger. They thundered past her, and her head whipped back and forth, back and forth, as she watched them.

Behind her came the sounds of war.

She knew them with gut instinct, the cracks of the gunfire, the screams of pain. Then a sleek, black mare ran close to her. She was near enough to touch, near enough that she could see the soft, glistening red inside her nostrils and smell the musk of her sweat. Her long, black mane streamed out behind her.

Come into me. Run with me.

Suddenly, Dark Moon's legs felt stronger and faster than her own. They were hard hoofed and pounding. She fell into the mare as she had gone into the elk, and together they raced on.

To the Safe Place.

She did not know what it was, or where it lay, and that made her scowl. Then she realized that it did not matter. It would be a good place where Mother Earth would no longer tremble beneath her feet with the agony of war.

They stopped running, but still she was inside the pony. She felt the wind lift her forelock, and she looked around, nostrils flaring. The feeling of peace grew deeper and more pervasive in her heart.

She could not hear the gunfire any longer.

No one screamed.

Snow fell, buffering sound. The elk was back, watching her calmly from a copse, alive again, not part of her any longer. With a shuddering, falling sensation, she felt herself drop back into her own heart. She went to the elk and touched him.

She had killed him once, but he was not afraid of her now.

She walked to a creek, its surface cracked and crusted with ice. A fish was there beneath the frozen surface, swimming languidly, waiting, trapped, for man to take him.

All around, people—Nimipu people—looked back at her, ragged, tired, but smiling.

This time she did not wake gently.

She found herself cuddled into a bed of cool pine needles and she opened her eyes abruptly. Then she bolted upright, her heart pounding.

She remembered her ponies, remembered that they had come with her after all. She looked about sharply, more than half expecting to find them still there, grazing with the black mare.

But there were no solid-colored ponies in the Nimipu herds, not really. Dark Moon shook her head, and saw now, in the sunlight, that she was near a mountain creek. She made her way unsteadily toward it.

No ice. No fish, either. But the memory remained etched

and clear in her mind. A *wyakin.*

She waited for a jolt of elation and triumph, but there was only respite, a lingering feeling of rest. She sank to her knees and drank deeply.

"Thank you," she whispered to Tahmahnewes, but only the quiet sounds of the forest responded.

She was not evil.

Perhaps she had been, once, but now the Spirit Chief had smiled on her.

The relief was so unexpected, so debilitating, that she curled up against the bank and did what she had vowed never to do again.

She cried.

When she reached the village again, another sun was falling. Her insect bites itched furiously now, and her skin was nicked and marked with scabs where she had scratched. She rubbed herself as she went to Old Joseph's summer hearth.

Alokot had returned.

She smiled shyly at him in greeting, then turned her eyes to Young Joseph, who looked back at her with his brows high. Earth Sound was there as well, and his father. Their talk fell silent.

Finally, Arenoth cleared her throat. "Will we have the Weekwetset now?"

Old Joseph's heart grieved for the sweet, reserved child who was gone from them, but he rejoiced for the new, steady look in her eyes.

"Yes," he said quietly. "Start cooking. It is time."

Dark Moon dug her fingers into her hair to scratch her scalp. Arenoth hurried with a robe to cover her.

"Go off with you now. Go to the river and wash. I have much to do to get ready."

"Wait," said old Burned Tree. "I have something for those scratches, something to make the itch go away. I will bring it from my hearth."

Dark Moon watched him shuffle off to his lodge close by, bemused at the kindness. Then she looked back at Old Joseph.

There was so much she wanted to ask him! But she could not speak anything of her vision until it was her time to dance. Finally, gripping the little leather bag of Burned Tree's salve, she went off to the water.

Before long, the smells of food began reaching her, fawn and fish and wild tubers. There was the newer, heavier aroma of the buffalo, too. She scrubbed her hair clean as her belly cramped fiercely, and stroked Burned Tree's creamy concoction over herself. She lifted her arm to sniff it more closely. It smelled of lupine and some kind of grass, a sweet, clinging odor.

She did not think she had ever smelled *good* before.

For a moment, her good fortune shook her. Suddenly, she was afraid to go back to the camp. Perhaps it would all vanish, like a dream. Perhaps her *dream* had been a dream, perhaps none of this had truly happened at all. . . .

She came out of the river copse and hesitated. Those who looked her way smiled fleetingly before going back to their work. They had done that every sun since she had come to this place, and she knew their kindnesses this sun were not truly unique. *She* was different. She no longer felt shamed or awkward because she did not feel she deserved their amity.

She shivered. That was perhaps the most precious gift she had ever known.

Arenoth had dug three whole fire pits, and over each of them sizzled pieces of Alokot's kills. Antelope and other meats were spitted among the buffalo.

The woman looked up when Dark Moon approached. She passed her the gall of a deer.

"My husband had a good hunt this sun as well, here in the hills. This is a special time for you. He says you should have this."

Dark Moon gaped at the morsel. Never, ever had she been granted a taste of this choice piece. She had not even taken it from her own elk; she had been too distraught to think of it.

She placed the soft green meat gingerly on her tongue and gave a little groan of pleasure. Arenoth laughed.

"There is one more thing before you go to dance. Come inside."

Dark Moon followed her hesitantly. There could be nothing more than this.

She was wrong.

A pale yellow dress lay over a pile of parfleches. She gasped, reached out to touch it, then snatched her hand back. It could not be for her. She had never owned anything so beautiful, had never worn anything but the remnants of other peoples' hides.

This was of the finest doeskin, with a ring of elk teeth about the neck. She knew immediately that those were from her own kill, and there were sturdy elkskin moccasins as well. Her eyes went wide as she looked at Arenoth.

"I did not use all of it," the woman explained. "There is plenty more elkskin if you would like to make moccasins for someone else. That was a big animal, a prime kill."

Dark Moon nodded dumbly.

"If you like, we could put some of that fur you brought with you down the sides of them," Arenoth went on.

The fur? The only piece she had left after healing Twelic's foal was that from the first whole hare he had ever given her. She had never shown it to anyone, but sometimes, late at night, she took it out to stroke it.

She had always meant to throw the piece in the river, hurling Twelic's memory away just as he had cast her out. Now she found herself mutely digging through her little pile of belongings to find it again.

She squatted down and laid the skin across Arenoth's lap.

The crack of gunfire, the screams of pain . . .

Suddenly, she gasped and pulled her hand away.

"What is it?" Arenoth looked up quizzically.

The *wyakin* memory faded in her mind, and she could not speak of it yet anyway. "I . . . I am not very good at sewing," she managed.

"I am not good enough either, not to get it done before you must dance. We need extra help." Arenoth stuck her head out her door flap and hooted.

A moment later some others crowded in, carrying sinews and bone needles and *xayxayx* awls. Dark Moon watched in amazement as the rabbit fur was deftly sliced. Needles flew as it was stitched into place, then the squaws slipped the dress over her head and watched with critical approval as she tied the moccasins onto her feet.

"I . . . thank you," she whispered as they filed out again. Arenoth pressed pieces of buffalo meat into their hands as they walked.

She went outside the lodge, hugging herself. The night was deep and dark now, and already some of the children had danced. Old Joseph appeared at her side as the last one departed from the ritual circle of fires.

"Go ahead, child. Tell them what you have seen, but remember to save some details that only you should know."

Her heart clenched suddenly, and she looked up at him.

She knew her name. It had come to her as she had rested and regained her strength before she had started back down the hill. Then it had sounded glorious; now, suddenly, it seemed arrogant, impossible. How could one such as she claim a name like the one she had thought of?

Old Joseph nudged her shoulder. "If Tahmahnewes whispered it to you, then it is right," he said. She was not the first child to doubt the goodness of her revelation.

Dark Moon stumbled into the circle. All about the camp, the people quieted to watch her.

She felt like a pretender in all the wonderful finery Arenoth had made for her. She knew what they were thinking, oh, she did! They remembered the vanishing moon as well, and the fate that had sent her to them. No matter what Old Joseph said, they were ready to mock any sort of dream that would come to the daughter spawn of a man with no magic.

They were waiting. She forced herself to sing.

Her voice came out stilted and self-conscious, sounding scarcely like her own. *Do not think of them. Pretend you are alone.* She heard Old Joseph speak as though he stood just beside her. Her eyes flew up and she found him outside the fires, watching with his face full of pride.

He was proud of *her*.

Her voice came stronger, and suddenly, her vision was real and alive before her eyes again. She sang of the black pony and the rumbles of war.

The *tiwats'* drums beat louder and louder. They filled her head and she moved with them, thumping her heels down and whirling about. She felt herself move like the cat who had stalked her elk, and it was easy, it was so *easy* now, each motion flowing into the next of its own accord. She closed her eyes and let the rhythm take her.

When it came time to tell her new name, Old Joseph already knew it was a dance few of the Kahmuenem would ever forget.

Dark Moon sang it out, then stopped to look out at the people, her breasts rising and falling from exertion.

"Kiye Kipi," she said again, more quietly. Oh, Tahmah-newes, it was the most wonderful thing she had ever had to call her own! "Kiye Kipi! I am She Who Runs with the Animals!"

That was her destiny. Of all the Great Spirit Chief's beasts, it was the horses who had come to her in her most vital, testing dream. Her beloved ponies were her *wyakin*.

They were the lifeblood of the People, and she was to be their pony wife.

16

Lah-te-tahl, Moon of First Blossoming
of Flowers, 1871

THE HERD CAME down from the Wallowa foothills, a surging, stampeding line of them, five and six deep. Kiye Kipi watched them crest the nearest hill, then disappear as the trail dipped down behind a ridge. A moment later, they galloped into the valley, red and brown, their white spotted rumps winking in the sun.

The warriors who had worked to round up the animals appeared on the hill behind them. Alokot and Earth Sound reined in and watched Kiye Kipi ride to the corrals. The spring-fresh wind toyed with her hair so that it floated and danced behind her. She rode without reins or saddle, her doeskin hiked up, her hands resting on strong, tawny thighs. She seemed to guide the pony subliminally; when they moved, they moved as one.

She glanced up at them, her strange eyes flashing almost violet in the sun, then they shifted quickly away again.

"How is a woman like her to wed?" Earth Sound complained. "How can she give a care to babes and a hearth when everyone presses their ponies upon her?"

"It is what Tahmahnewes asks of her."

Alokot knew it was not her responsibilities that kept her from meeting Earth Sound's determined advances. It was something else, some lingering hurt or betrayal that had not yet set her free. Until it did, Alokot did not think any warrior would ever entice her from his father's lodge.

* * *

Though the suns were warm, the nights were still bitter with cold. Kiye Kipi saw Old Joseph shiver, and she pushed more wood into Arenoth's fire.

"Is that better?" She was very glad that the Kahmuenem no longer used their old longhouse, no matter what that prophet had said long ago. These buffalo-skin lodges were much less drafty; the heat from the hearths could easily pervade them.

Old Joseph nodded and rubbed his hands together. They made a dry, swish-swish sound that was familiar to her and comforting.

"That Burned Tree should be more careful with his medicine," he complained. "His last Weekwetset did not work very well. This robe season is lasting forever."

Kiye Kipi felt her heart cringe. He was forgetting what season it was again.

"Soon, grandfather," she answered gently. "With the next moon it will be time for the grass to come up again."

She took heart when he cocked his head to the side at some distant sound. "That will be Alokot and Wetatonmi," he announced. "They will eat with us tonight."

Kiye Kipi grinned at the door flap. She could not detect anyone approaching over the sound of the wind.

She looked to Arenoth. "Is it true? Why do they come here?"

"Alokot would like to speak with you."

She guessed he was probably concerned about the game that had been so elusive this season. Old Joseph blamed it on the *xayxayx,* but so far none of those men had appeared in their valleys.

She was glad to see Alokot all the same, and she liked Wetatonmi, too. She looked up at the other girl, wishing, not for the first time, that she could somehow be like her. Wetatonmi had seen nineteen snows. She was of strong blood, was niece to Huishuis Kute. She had delicate, fine features unlike the arresting cheekbones and wide eyes that Kiye Kipi knew she possessed. She was small while Kiye Kipi stood as tall as many warriors. But more than anything, her manner was easy and warm. As Kiye Kipi watched, the girl kept her hand on her husband's strong, muscled forearm, pushing her body close to his warmth.

Something funny moved inside her at the sight. She looked away.

Young Joseph arrived as well and nodded greetings to all of them before settling on the other side of his father. Arenoth found strips of the dried buffalo left over from last hunting season. The meat usually lasted well through the time when they changed valleys, although it was almost gone now, despite their having conserved it carefully.

Alokot looked at Kiye Kipi as he took his share. "Did you have luck today?" he asked.

She shook her head, feeling that low, deep twinge that always came when it seemed as though she had failed. "I dreamed, but the antelope are still far up the mountains and I could not get into them. Perhaps I will do better when we get to Imnaha. When will we go?"

"Before this moon passes. Then I will take a party east immediately, over the big mountains to the open ground."

He seemed to exchange a look with his father. Kiye Kipi caught it and frowned.

"But there is a problem with that as well," he went on. "In the last few warm seasons, there have been less and less buffalo there, just as the game in our own country seems to be dwindling. The Crow and the Sioux say the *xayxayx* are scaring the herds off from their land also. If we do not get more meat on this trip, next robe season will be even hungrier than this one has been."

Another worm of shame wriggled in her belly. The peoples' hunger was her fault, she thought, for not being able to call the deer and the elk closer.

She thought again that her power was not as strong as everyone believed it was. She was still so unsure of what she could and could not do, and of the unruly nature of her magic. Her hands clenched into fists, then slowly relaxed again.

"You could help," Alokot said.

"Oh, I have tried!" she burst out. "I cannot reach them when they are far!"

Young Joseph looked up and spoke for the first time. "Perhaps you should travel closer to them," he suggested.

She looked uncertainly at Alokot again.

"I need you to go over the mountains with me," he said, "to try to call the buffalo. Even one small herd would feed our band all through the next several seasons."

Her heart lurched. *Over the mountains?*

Only once in the last four circles of seasons had the Kahmuenem migrated from their homelands. A large contingent had finally traveled north to Tolo Lake two summers ago. She had begged Old Joseph and Arenoth to allow her to stay behind with the elders to care and hunt for them. They had relented at her desperate fear, and she had remained at Imnaha.

She looked about, and did not think anyone was going to relent this time. She felt sick. They were finally going to make her leave the valleys.

"You can see that it is something our people need badly," Old Joseph said, "and you are our animal caller. I think of your welfare also. It is not enough for you to possess special power. You know what you are, what you have come from, and you must do more to prove yourself than most."

Arenoth gasped at his harshness, but he continued relentlessly. "Your magic is good, your *wyakin* is a strong one, but you must have the experience to use them wisely. You should have the respect of others if you are to continue to thrive and grow after I am gone."

"Gone?" She choked on the word and her eyes widened. Oh, sweet *Tahmahnewes*, what was he saying?

"I am old," he reminded her wearily. "I can no longer see. I am getting near to the time when our Great Spirit Chief will call me."

"No," she breathed. She knew she would not be able to bear such a thing.

"Those who have gone over the mountains are the most respected of all," Old Joseph went on implacably. "If you go, you will have no trouble when I am no longer here to protect you.''

He felt as he had when he had sent her for her *wyakin,* as though he were somehow directing a doe to its slaughter. Kiye Kipi continued to shake her head slowly, dazedly, in denial.

"If you are that ill, you need me here," she managed.

"I am going," Alokot said bluntly.

She looked at him. He met her eyes steadily, and there were no lies there. He was the band's first warrior, often forceful and unswerving in his ideas, but his love for his father was true. He would not go east if he truly felt that there was any chance Old Joseph would not survive the summer.

She was trapped.

"What of those hunting colts you bred?" Old Joseph asked, changing tactics. There were several of them resulting from the time when she had taken over the care of some of the warriors' ponies. They would be doing their first hunting on this trip, and then it would be decided if they should be gelded or permitted to breed on.

"Would you sit back now and trust someone else's opinion as to whether or not they should be culled from the breeding stock?" he asked.

"Alokot would not lie to me," she managed. "He would tell me true how they worked."

"Many warriors are prejudiced against them because they are not very flashy," Alokot reminded her. "My opinion matters only with my own herd."

Like a wolf with its prey, he backed off to circle around behind her and nip at her heels. "Your magic could be invaluable in a buffalo hunt, when we are faced with so many dangerous beasts. You can talk to the ponies. You can guide them so they and their riders do not get hurt."

"I am going this trip," Wetatonmi urged quietly. "Please think about it. It would be nice to have the companionship of a friend."

Friend?

Kiye Kipi's heart stuttered at that. Wetatonmi's quiet entreaty touched her deep in a spot that not even Old Joseph had been able to reach.

Friend.

How glorious it would be to possess such a thing!

She wanted to please them, all of them, even the quiet, thoughtful Young Joseph. She shook her head again, but something else, something entirely different, came out of her mouth.

"I . . . I will try."

17

WHEN THE SUN came that they were to leave, Kiye Kipi could no longer remember why she had ever promised such a thing.

She huddled in her robe while the dawn winds buffeted Arenoth's lodge. How could she run with animals she had never even seen? She knew the buffalo were huge, shaggy beasts, but when she tried to envision them in her mind, no true picture came. She moaned and rolled over in her bedding, hiding her face from her own fear.

These people believed in her, but oh, Tahmahnewes, what if she was not all they thought she was?

The air was still cool, but sweat trickled down the back of her neck. She pushed her bedding away and went outside.

Old Burned Tree was there. She began to step around him, thinking he was waiting for Old Joseph, but he stopped her.

"There is something I would give you." He pulled forward a dappled gray pony who stood behind him. "She is a gift for helping that mare of mine survive her breech birth."

Kiye Kipi gaped at him. She could not accept such a thing. The *tiwats* had done almost all of that work himself, showing her how to reach inside and turn the babe about.

"What use have I for a good hunting horse?" he went on. "I am busy with my medicine. My son provides for me. If you do not take her, I will just trade her away." Burned Tree would take to the western lands this season the mares that the warriors wished to cull. Kiye Kipi knew he would not get much for the gray filly, because the Umatillas and the Yakimas liked the traditional Nimipu ponies with their dark, glistening coats and the spatters of white on their rumps. This pony was another of the first she had bred, short and strong and long-winded but not very colorful.

"You cannot hunt and call buffalo without a mount of your own," Burned Tree pointed out.

Her heart clenched at that reminder. She looked about, and found Alokot's warriors working to leave. Her head began hurting.

She went back into the lodge as Old Joseph and Arenoth were rising. Grimly, she gathered up those possessions she called her own. Her hand hovered for a moment over the old fire starter that Twelic had given her, then she swallowed carefully and put it into a parfleche. She pushed a bag of horse medicine in on top of it, then she sat back on her heels, confused. She did not truly know what was expected of her, or what she needed to take.

"Here is some salmon jerky to keep your belly warm until you find game," Arenoth said from beside her. Kiye Kipi looked up, startled, then reached out to take the food as well.

"You will need that bow that I made for you, and your sleeping robe," Old Joseph suggested.

"Yes." She gathered them and went outside again, clutching her supplies against her breasts. A handful of squaws were going as well, those who did not yet have any babes. Everyone talked brightly, circling restlessly, waiting for Alokot to give the word to ride out. Wetatonmi looked over at her and grinned. Slowly, stiffly, Kiye Kipi found Burned Tree's dappled filly and mounted as well.

Her hands tightened around the reins like claws. She gave a sigh of helplessness and looked back at the Imnaha camp one last time.

Old Joseph smiled encouragingly from outside his lodge. Fear shafted through her heart, then trembled away. She waited, but in spite of her worries, no true instinct told her that she would not see him alive again. She let her eyes coast over the valley. A deep and hurtful pain came alive inside her then, like a small, vicious animal trying to fight free of her gut.

She knew, somehow, that she would never see this sweet, sheltering place in just the same way again.

She dreamed without meaning to when they had been out for four suns.

She sat bolt upright in her robe as dawn turned the sky to pink, panic closing her throat so that she could barely breathe. She had been as delicately strung as a bow string since they had left Imnaha. She had slept little and had eaten even less, and now it had happened again, but, like the elk vision, this dream had been good.

This dream. She did not want to think of any others yet to come.

Wetatonmi stirred close by. They were huddled in a copse with only their robes for protection, for they had stopped just long enough to rest.

"What is it?" Wetatonmi asked sleepily, and Alokot came awake at his wife's voice.

"Antelope," she answered hoarsely. "North of here. Before the ponies sweat from galloping, we will find them."

Immediately, Alokot called out to the others. They began moving, and Earth Sound came to them.

"Why did you not bring them to us?" he asked.

"It does not matter," Alokot said. "They are not far."

Within moments they were astride again, riding north. As the ponies began to blow from exertion, she recognized a stream she had seen in her mind. "East," she said to Alokot, riding beside her. "We must follow this water east."

The party swerved and, after another long ride, went up on a rise. Below them, a small knot of tawny color moved by the water where it wound around.

"Ah!" One of the squaws gasped in delight. Immediately, the closest buck lifted his head. His rack came up haughtily and his nose quivered at their scent.

Alokot swore darkly beneath his breath and Kiye Kipi swal-

lowed a groan. Sensing the danger, the buck spun on his back
legs and ran.

The whole herd erupted after him. Alokot shrilled a cry, and
the warriors surged forward as well. Though they notched their
bows, Kiye Kipi saw the hopelessness in their eyes, the hunger
in the thin sets of their mouths. Slowly, surely, she watched
the antelope pull ahead of them.

Then the antelope began tiring.

Kiye Kipi felt her heart give a little kick. Her eyes widened
and she looked for Alokot in the crowd. He howled again and
leaped from his war pony onto one of the colts she had bred.

Oh, fly! Please fly!

Did the pony hear her? She could not know, could not feel
her way inside him. He was not fast, but he kept on, his hooves
tearing up grass as Alokot's war pony began struggling, falling
farther and farther behind.

Suddenly, impulsively, she kicked her own little filly and
pulled free the bow Old Joseph had made her. Ahead of her,
she heard the others shouting, and then more and more of the
warriors changed ponies. The wind whipped her hair and stung
her eyes. She dropped her reins to shoot, leaning into the filly
with her legs.

Her arrow flew, then another and another hissed through the
air around her. The antelope began dropping, first one, then
more and more. The hunting ponies surged past them easily,
and the warriors whipped around again to return to the slaughter. Earth Sound stood up on his own mount and screamed,
raising his bow high.

Far back near the rise, the squaws and the other warriors
remained, watching them. But those with her strong little hunting ponies leaped to the ground, laughing, retrieving their arrows. Kiye Kipi watched, a trembling goodness working up
from her belly.

*It had worked. Everything she had thought about those po-
nies had been right.*

Alokot ran up beside her and pulled her off her filly. She
swayed unsteadily, adrenaline throbbing at her temples. She

gripped her pony's mane as something hard and ticklish worked in her throat.

She wrapped her arms around her pony's neck and, for the first time in her life, she laughed until it hurt.

It took the party several more suns to dry and pack up the fruits of their kill. Kiye Kipi borrowed one of Wetatonmi's ponies to help carry her own bounty, for many warriors gave her pieces and hides in gratitude for her dream. She could not look at the stuff without feeling bemused.

They rode on, keeping south below the Salmon River at Alokot's urging. He did not want to encounter any white-skins.

When she first saw the Bitterroot Mountains, her jaw dropped at their vastness. How would they ever get over them?

"Have you done this before?" she blurted, looking to where Wetatonmi rode beside her. The other girl gave a delighted laugh.

"No, friend. You are different. Most squaws do not get to see the open country unless they go with their husbands. Even if I had not met Alokot, I think I might have wed just to get this chance."

Kiye Kipi's heart kicked in surprise. "You would have gone to someone, let him do . . . do that to you, just for this?" She colored fiercely as soon as she asked the question. Wetatonmi looked at her for a moment before she understood.

"Not just anyone. Someone kind and strong . . ." She trailed off, then grinned sheepishly. "Someone just like Alokot, I suppose."

Kiye Kipi shook her head. She could not imagine such a thing.

Wetatonmi thought for a moment. "I have heard what that warrior did to you long ago. That was not mating."

Kiye Kipi jerked. "It was like the ponies," she said flatly.

"Yes. Ponies rut. Men cherish. There is a difference."

Kiye Kipi looked away from her, out toward the mountains again, a memory of pain rekindling deep inside where Wahlitits had hurt her. What was in a man's heart could not change the feeling of skin when it tore. Of that, at least, she was very, very sure.

The pass over the Bitterroots was lined on one side with rugged chasms and sheer drops that made her head spin when she looked over them. They led their ponies carefully by hand along the narrow trail. Kiye Kipi kept her back hard against the rock wall behind her, her palms damp and her heart skipping.

"How much farther?" she gasped.

Wetatonmi did not look as if she were enjoying herself so much any more, either. "Alokot says there is a good place to camp at the top."

"And going down?"

Wetatonmi gave a tight little laugh. "I suppose I will think about that when I get there."

The farther they went, the more her breath felt trapped in her throat. Fear kept it there . . . and something else. Her skin felt shivery as she looked out at the immense, tree-tangled canyon below them.

It was beautiful, she thought in awe. It was a place she could never even have dreamed of.

Near dusk, they came to a place where the trail opened up into a tiny glade. Water, cold and clear, caught orange in the last sun as it splashed over a pinnacle of rock high above their heads. The place was barely large enough for all of them and their ponies, but they roasted pieces of the antelope over one big fire, and found nooks and crannies of privacy to put their sleeping robes. The air was thin and sharp and tangy, and her belly felt good as she crouched down beside the fire with Wetatonmi.

Hunger did not disturb her very much; once it had been a part of her every sun. It was this ache of fullness that was new to her. There had been food enough in the Wallowa until recently, but she had always nibbled, afraid to sate herself, because she still could not believe it would last. But this meat . . . this meat was *hers*.

Having earned it gave her a glorious sense of . . . well, freedom, she decided. It was a kind of self-reliance she had not even known as a scavenging child, for even then she had been dependent upon others' castoffs. She reached to slice more from the spit she shared with the other squaw, then she realized the warriors had gone rigidly silent.

She looked to them, curious. Alokot crouched stiffly in the firelight. His face made her blood feel suddenly cold. "What is it?"

She was the first to speak, and her voice sounded strident and strange in the night quiet. Alokot hissed at her.

"Hush. Go to your ponies. Make no noise."

Mutely, the squaws did as they were told.

Finally, Kiye Kipi heard it as well, a scraping, scrabbling sound from the trail behind them. She whipped around to look that way, her hair lifting from her nape.

Bear.

She shook her head, confused. She had no reason to think such a thing, and yet she could *smell* the beast's matted, damp fur, could feel its voice rumble in her heart. She hurried to her dappled filly and swung up onto her back, but as the other squaws started ahead on the new trail, she stayed, waiting, struggling.

Not bear. No, something else, something that made her heart thunder and reminded her of a dream . . . a dream she could not quite grasp.

The murky smells and images faded as newcomers rode into the glade. The warriors began shouting greetings, snapping her attention back.

It was another Nimipu hunting party.

Wahlitits.

She stared at him, her food pushing up in her throat again, bringing nausea. She wrenched her gaze away to look at the others.

There, on a snorting, spotted stallion, rode Twelic.

18

TWELIC DISMOUNTED, AND the warriors came together with back-slapping camaraderie. Kiye Kipi sat frozen, watching him, a maelstrom of emotion tearing through her heart. A very, very old gladness swelled in her. Once it had been so easy to greet him. Now that good feeling cracked with a pain so sharp, so sudden, it brought her breath back in a harsh gasp.

In the end, he had walked away when she had needed him most.

Twelic's eyes moved past Alokot to assess the squaws who were returning to the glade. He knew they were all mated, but that did not prevent him from appreciating the graceful way a woman rode, or the feminine warmth and smells of them. His grin stretched, then he looked to see one who had not joined the others, who sat separate and apart on a strange solid-colored pony.

He knew her. Recognition taunted him from some deep, secret part of his soul. Then he understood, and his breath shot out of him as if a pony had kicked him in the chest.

She reminded him of the dream he had had that had made him a warrior.

Her hair was unbraided, streaming straight to her waist, and she sat as though she were part of the pony beneath her. But that *wyakin* horse had been black, and this one was an ugly, mottled gray. The vision pony had melted into a woman who was strong and knowing, but this was a girl with staggering heat in her eyes.

He drew closer, and saw that those eyes shone almost blue in the firelight. He gave a sudden bark of laughter, the tension leaving him.

"Screamer."

Tahmahnewes, how long had it been? Long enough that she was no longer an urchin child, wide eyed with deep, haunting fear. The seasons had passed so rapidly that many had gone by since he had wondered how she fared. Never had he consciously considered that she would have grown by now.

Grown and mated. Clearly, if she was here, one of these warriors was her husband.

"Go away," she bit out venomously.

His eyes opened wider. "Why?"

Because you were not my friend, though I trusted you only. Because you were not my savior, though I would have given to you anything at all.

She could not tell him that. Now, so many seasons later, she was wiser than that babe child he had scorned. If you let anyone too close to your heart, it bled.

She hid her heart. It was, she knew, the safest way.

"Why did you bring him?" she asked instead, bringing her chin up to angle it at Wahlitits.

"That has not changed," he mused, looking back at the warrior. "He still has no coups, and now my uncle grows afraid that his desperation will somehow harm the band. He asked me to take him with me this season, to give him a chance."

"He deserves no chance." Oh, how the hatred hurt her throat! It was a new sensation for her, bitter and choking.

"Then Tahmahnewes will see that he fails," Twelic answered mildly.

To him, it was as simple as that. She got a hard, grim hold on herself, and her gaze moved over the other Hasotoin warriors.

He saw her recognize the ones called Swan Necklace and Thunder Dance. Once they had been boys who had tripped her and mocked her and pulled on her hair.

"They will not know you unless they are told who you

are,'' Twelic pointed out. "They remember a scruffy babe in torn hides, but your husband provides well for you." The dress she wore was adorned with elk's teeth and deer claw bells. That was the work of a successful hunter, no small feat in this time of lean prey.

He was surprised again when her mouth went even tighter. "I have no mate," she snapped. "I am Kiye Kipi now. I came because I call for the hunt."

Kiye Kipi? *She Who Runs with the Animals.* Something jolted deep within him again, that same *wyakin* memory taunting him.

He shook it off. "There, then." He forced some jauntiness into his tone. "If Wahlitits gives you trouble, you can call a buffalo to come sit on him."

She flinched. He still thought she was evil, that she would hurt people.

Then she looked at Wahlitits's mean, narrow face, and she thought of a huge, hairy beast squatting over him. For the second time in a few special suns, she laughed.

Twelic looked up at her again, startled. In all those seasons she had lived with them, he could not ever remember hearing her laughter. It was a rough-sweet sound, vaguely throaty, and it made his blood quicken.

The reaction startled him clear down to his toes.

He reached a hand out to help her dismount. "Come back to the camp. I think it will scare the last of the sense out of him when he knows you have found your power. Maybe he will even tuck his tail between his legs and go home."

Kiye Kipi looked at his hand. Then she did what she knew she should have done a thousand seasons ago. She ignored the warmth, the lure, of his friendship. She swung one long, bare leg over her pony's neck and dropped to the ground herself.

She followed him back toward the Hasotoin, and with each step she took, her chin came up unconsciously, almost defiantly. Twelic found the reflex made him feel strange again.

So much of her looked the same, but there was so much he did not know at all.

*   *   *

The hunting parties crowded around the leaping communal fire until long after the moon began to drop. Even the women remained, murmuring and laughing quietly among themselves. There would be no hard work with the new dawn; it was unlikely they would meet game on this rugged pass, and all that would be expected of them was to ride out after the warriors.

Kiye Kipi sat between Wetatonmi and Twelic, burrowed deep in her robe to ward off the night chill. Though she tried to listen to what the squaws said, her gaze wandered back to Twelic.

He sat, shoulders vaguely hunched as he shared some of their antelope. Except for the two narrow braids that ran down each side of his face, his hair was free and tangled and turning wavy in the mountain damp. His black eyes were sharp in their thoughtfulness as he listened to the others; they moved quickly to each warrior as he spoke. His nose was as strong as it had been when he was a boy. But he was not at all pretty anymore.

There was something hard and arrogant about the man he had become, she thought. His cheekbones were still strong and attractive, and his mouth looked gentle enough to nuzzle a babe. But now there was a gouged scar beneath his left eye, a rugged set to his jaw. He reminded her of a lone wolf, she thought suddenly, lean, independent, and hungry.

He glanced her way and grinned, and something about *that* was different as well, so different that her skin felt suddenly hot and she pushed her robe back.

Her heart was beating strangely. She reached across Wetatonmi and took the squaws' water pouch, drinking deeply.

Twelic looked to Alokot. "I think we should all hunt together on this trip."

Alokot raised a brow. "Why? What do you have that we need so much we should share our meat?"

Twelic laughed. "It is not what we have, my friend. It is what *you* have—an animal caller." The warriors grinned at his bald honesty. "Have a heart, brother," he urged. "The Hasotoin are hungry as well."

Alokot thought about it. The Nimipu dreamers were one,

after all. "Perhaps we should ask our caller," he allowed. "If you agree, Kiye Kipi, then we will do this."

Kiye Kipi started, coming back to the conversation as she felt all their eyes move to her. She looked at Alokot, aghast. He knew what these men remembered her to be. How could he make her responsible for a decision that would keep them together or make them go?

She looked warily around at the Hasotoin, but she did not see what she thought she would find.

Gradually, recognition and awareness dawned on their faces as they studied her more closely. But there were no barks of ridicule when they remembered her, no taunts or mockery. She saw fear flash briefly in some eyes, but more than anything, there was the same hunger she had seen on the Kahmuenem warriors' faces when she had led them to the antelope.

Once they had tormented her, but somehow, she knew they would not dare hurt her now, not on this trip. They would not speculate about the magic that allowed her to commune with the beasts. They would tolerate her because they needed her.

She felt her throat close with another burst of unexpected anger. She was not sure she liked the sensation at all.

In the end, she could not deny them. She thought of their babes at home near the Kooskooskia, wailing with empty bellies, and she let out her breath.

"Yes," she managed. "That would be . . . good."

Besides, she thought with a tight little grimace, there was always the possibility that she would not be able to do what they expected of her.

She felt the weight of another heavy gaze and looked up again. Now, finally, Wahlitits recognized her as well. His jaw dropped before he closed his mouth again so suddenly he gave a little grunt of pain.

And you, I will have a buffalo sit on you, just as Twelic said!

It seemed as though the mean little thought flashed from her mind into his own, for the warrior colored suddenly and hotly. He forgot what he had been saying to the man beside him. She saw his thoughts shatter and his tongue stumble.

Still, she could not stop staring at him, could not stop remembering the hurt . . . dry, arcing through her, his meanness making her bleed.

Conversation faltered as others followed her gaze. Finally, someone cleared his throat and spoke in strained jest.

"Watch where you step, Wahlitits, or she will get you!"

"I do not fear her! I never feared her!" he burst out angrily. Before anyone could react, he launched himself to his feet and stalked away. There was silence for a moment, then laughter followed him, mocking him.

Their journey down the pass was slower and less organized than their ascent, due largely to the increased size of their party. Ponies stumbled, their footing breathtakingly precarious.

Twelic watched Kiye Kipi with more curiosity than he found he was comfortable with.

It was clear that she was afraid. Every muscle in her body seemed as hard as stone. She kept her eyes on the chasm that fell away below her, her sleek hair tucked behind her ears so that it would not obstruct her vision even for one deadly moment. But still, she moved on without flinching.

He looked at her neat, fur-trimmed moccasins. *Slide, step . . . slide, step . . .* Not once did they hesitate.

What a woman you have become, Screamer, he thought. He realized that fear had probably once been so integral a part of her life that perhaps now she would only recognize its absence. It did not shake or trouble her.

He admired her courage.

"Do not look down," he suggested suddenly.

Kiye Kipi started a bit; somehow, he had passed the woman behind her and had come up on her tail.

"We are almost to the bottom now," he went on. "Soon, we will be gathered around our fires again, and you can torment Wahlitits some more. Think of that, and it will keep your mind off the sheer drop."

"I did not mean to cause him shame." Her voice was grim and tight.

"It should have been satisfying nonetheless."

"No."

How could she tell him? She found herself struggling to try, against all her better instincts.

"There is no way to take back what he did to me. Hurting him cannot bring my old life back."

Twelic was startled. "Do you want that?" he asked.

"You ask me too late," she snapped.

Suddenly, the betrayal was as big and alive inside her again as when she had screamed his name over the prairie, hearing silence, only silence, in return. She looked back at him, forgetting the danger that lurked beside the trail.

"Why?" she demanded angrily. "Why could you not have saved me? *You* could have stopped them from sending me away!"

His thoughts reeled. "Do you hate the Kahmuenem so much?"

"No! I . . ." She trailed off, confused, all the heat flickering and fading abruptly inside her. Hate Old Joseph? Arenoth?

"No," she answered lamely. "But I did not want to go."

"You were a child then. Surely you can see now how good the change was for you."

She could not let him get close again, and it was happening insidiously. She was talking of things she had kept buried in her heart, and somehow they looked different when she brought them out of their long-kept darkness and into the light of the sun.

Carefully, deliberately, she changed the subject. "What do you think of to keep from looking down?" she asked.

He gave a bark of the laughter she had once loved so much. "Adventures." It was what he had always wanted.

"You have them now."

"Yes."

He did not add that he also remembered rollicking in Cloud Singer's bedding, that that was the best diversion of all. Young Looking Glass had claimed the squaw, but he had lost her again. Twelic could imagine why. Cloud Singer was not one for lazy, passive lovemaking.

There were other squaws he remembered as well, one in

nearly every band he visited regularly. But while they were sweet and warm and accommodating, there was always a frantic edge in them, as though they barely restrained themselves from digging claws into his flesh and trying to hang on to him. Cloud Singer was a shrewd, selfish woman, and she took all from him she could get without suffering under the need to give anything in return.

His gaze slid sideways to Kiye Kipi. For a strange moment, he wondered if perhaps she would understand the lure of such freedom when even most men could not appreciate it. He had thought once that leaving the Hasotoin would allow her to sink sweetly and gently into a warrior's care. Now, suddenly, he could see that she would not easily give up the independence she had learned so long ago, either.

"Tell me about these buffalo," she said suddenly, and he found he was oddly grateful for the change in conversation.

"They travel together," he answered, dragging his thoughts back, "in herds far larger than the elk and the antelope. And they can be dangerous. Despite their size, they are very fast, and this is their rutting season. That makes the bulls unpredictable. Just as you get your spear in one, he is as likely to turn back and gore your pony as he is to die."

She shuddered. Did Alokot think she could somehow prevent that?

She looked up the trail to the Hasotoin warriors ahead. They needed her now, but what would they do if she failed? She looked at Wahlitits again, and knew he would be the cruelest of all.

Then her eyes shot back to Swan Necklace. He took the trail just behind Wahlitits, and suddenly her vision swam crazily, smearing the images of both warriors. *Do not look down!* But she was not looking down; this was something else, something terrible and crazy. As she stared, her eyes came clear again, and this time both men had blood on their hands.

"Ah!" The cry came out of her as she felt herself sway. The canyon below her spun. Twelic felt his heart cram into his throat as she staggered.

He dropped the lead of his pony and grabbed her. He

dragged her hard under his arm and pushed back against the rock wall behind them.

"You looked!" He was furious that she had defied his advice.

Kiye Kipi struggled away from him. Suddenly, being so close to him was as unbearable as what she had seen. Heat . . . the *heat* of him was warm across her shoulders, down her side. She brought her elbow up hard into his ribs to make him let her go.

He grunted and stared at her as though she had grown horns.

"I looked nowhere!" she snapped, then she felt confused. She *had* looked—but not into the canyon. She had been watching the Hasotoin warriors.

Fearfully, she glanced that way again. Everything was normal now. Wahlitits and Swan Necklace walked beside each other, heads close in conversation. Their hands were tight around their own leads.

No blood, not now. But something strange cramped her belly just the same.

"What is it?" Twelic muttered. He was still disgruntled, but she could not help that.

"Are they friends?" she demanded.

"Who?"

"Wahlitits and Swan Necklace."

Twelic shrugged. It was true that Swan Necklace had not become the warrior he had hoped he would be, despite his physical talents and the chances Twelic had given him. In many ways, he was like Wahlitits, impatient and reckless. But Twelic had noticed no particular bond between the two men.

Kiye Kipi felt suddenly cold at his expression. It told her everything she needed to know.

"Watch them, please," she said more quietly. "I think they will bring death to someone. I think together they will bring the trouble your uncle fears."

Twelic stared at her. "What kind of magic do you have, Screamer?"

She flinched at his use of that name from so long ago. It reminded her again of safety, of security, a lone voice of shelter in the storm that had once been her life. This time, it broke something inside her. She heard herself admitting what she had told no one before, not even Old Joseph.

"I do not know. Oh, Twelic, sometimes I still do not know!"

19

THEY CAME DOWN into the Bitterroot valley as the sun settled below the peaks at their backs. The prairie was pitched in blue-gray gloom, and it took Kiye Kipi's breath away as surely as the canyons behind them. She had never seen so much *emptiness* before. It was broken only by what she thought was a smudge of more mountains on the far horizon. In its own way, it was beautiful.

"Is there water?" she asked as Twelic came up beside her.

"Of course."

"How do we find it?" There were no deciduous trees anywhere, only grass as far as the eye could see.

"Those of us who have been here before know where it is."

Some of her old awe for him stirred in her belly. *Dangerous, dangerous.* But she could not seem to stop it.

"How do you remember?" she asked. "Everything looks the same."

"A warrior remembers." He swung up on his spotted stallion. "And this warrior will race you to the horizon, beating you even with a head start."

The *horizon*? She gaped at him, then she understood. They would run until their ponies steamed in the cooling air. It was a game . . . a race.

But why would he want to race with *her*?

"If you stand there much longer, I will call it a forfeit," he challenged.

Her eyes snapped up to him again. "If we ride to the horizon, *you* will forfeit," she warned.

He barked a sound of disbelief and began trotting. Suddenly, Kiye Kipi grinned a secret smile.

She pulled herself up onto the gray filly. Twelic was far ahead of her now, but that was all right. She put her heels to her pony and the little horse surged into a smooth, slow run.

On and on they went, until the wind ripped the laughter from her throat and hurled it back over her shoulder. Oh, this felt good! She did not think she had ever done anything for the sheer joy of it before; she was not sure many squaws ever did. For the first time in her life, she actively envied the warriors . . . but envy, too, was a burden, difficult to struggle with when she felt so free.

She shook her head so that her hair streamed out behind her, and tilted her face up into the air. Twelic twisted around to gape at her. The ugly little pony she rode kept gaining on him, on his spotted stallion that was the best of Looking Glass's breeding.

This could not be happening.

He circled around again, back toward the others. As he passed them, he heard many of the Kahmuenem laughing and hooting and shouting wagers. And the Hasotoin warriors were meeting them.

Tahmahnewes, he could not lose this race to a squaw!

Her people were shouting encouragement to her. He did not like her expression as she came abreast of him.

"What do I win?" she called out.

"You have not won yet!"

"The horizon is that way!"

She gave that throaty laugh again as she passed him. She *had* won. He could not drive his stallion any harder, any longer. This woman—*the Screamer*—had beat him on the ugliest little pony he had ever seen.

But in that moment, it was almost impossible to remember that she was a child he had once spit milk into.

He reined in, and the Kahmuenem howled and shouted.

He looked after her as she, too, pulled her pony in, sharply and suddenly enough that the filly reared magnificently in the dying light. Then she trotted back toward him, winded, laughing, her breasts rising and falling.

The fascination that speared through him astounded him so much it very nearly unseated him.

They found water and made camp. A handful of their cook fires spattered the prairie, red and orange embers glowing in the night. Crickets screeched, and from somewhere far away, Kiye Kipi heard a coyote howling.

"The ponies are my *wyakin,*" she explained quietly. "I just . . . know them."

Across the fire she shared with Alokot and Wetatonmi, she saw a muscle twitch in Twelic's jaw. "Solid-colored ones," he murmured. "Unlike anything the People have ever bred before." It seemed like he was talking to a memory, not to her.

"Their color was a mistake," she said, then she pushed impulsively to her feet. "Come. I will show you."

She moved long. legged through the tall grass to where the horses grazed. He watched her a moment, then he got up and followed.

Kiyi Kipe found the pony she was looking for and slung an arm around his neck to lead him back. "Look at his eyes, his face."

Those were different as well, Twelic saw. The pony's eyes were big and dark and set further apart than usual. The strong bone just beneath his eyes was vaguely dented.

"Four summers ago, at the time when I found my *wyakin,* Alokot's warriors came back from this open country with a pony that looked much like this one," she went on. "His muzzle was smaller and this spot below his eyes was deeper. He was little and old and white-gray. His teeth were yellow and long. The warrior who captured him was going to geld him.

"Then we went back to Wallowa for the snow season. That trip always tires the herd, and by the time we got near Wallowa, we were moving slowly. But I saw that this white pony showed no weariness despite his age. Old Joseph traded the warrior for him and we put him with some of his mares.''

She frowned briefly. ''I let him cover the ones who were strong and long-winded like he was, but not always prettiest. All his babes came out like this, dull colored instead of spotted. Still, Old Joseph did not geld all of them, and I asked many of the warriors to breed to those colts. They did, and now we have these hunting ponies that can run forever.''

Twelic gave a small, crooked grin. ''At least there is a practical explanation for my shame.''

Kiye Kipi felt her belly twist. ''I . . . I am sorry about that.''

''Do not be.'' Still, she would not look up. Her head was bent, black hair glistening in the moonlight.

A startlingly deep instinct—something almost like fear— told him not to touch her. But he could not be cautious; it was not his way. He reached and tipped her chin up.

He felt the shudder work all the way through her. Her eyes came up sharply and she took a stumbling step back.

He remembered the way she had reacted to his touch on the trail, and anger flared in him again at such unprecedented, inexplicable rejection. Then, suddenly, he understood; he remembered Wahlitits.

Tahmahnewes, *those scars were still with her.* Was *that* why she had not wed? Had no other man seen the truth and calmed the terror inside her with kindness and finesse? But he knew as soon as he wondered that it would not be that easy, not with this one. It was not just a matter of a mongrel warrior violating her. What Wahlitits had done to her was cloaked among so many other cruelties, layered with loneliness and hunger and the scorn of too many others.

It would not be easy for her to forget. He did not think she would let many men meet the challenge.

Deliberately, he let his hand drop away. ''What have you to feel sorry for?'' he went on. ''I challenged you foolishly, and you met the dare. That is good cunning, something warriors are praised for.''

''I am not a warrior,'' she said simply.

A corner of his mouth lifted. ''No, but a man would be a

fool to turn away from you because you are shrewd as well as beautiful.''

Beautiful? She gaped at him, but he seemed not to notice.

''I lost that race,'' he pointed out, ''and it was fair. What should I pay you?''

Her head swam. ''There is nothing I want or need.''

Oh, there is, Screamer, but you do not know it, and I am not the one to give it to you.

The thought jolted him.

He knew then what it was about her that disturbed him, why some instinct had told him not to touch her. She was not like other women, and she was not like Cloud Singer. She would not sink her claws into him; somehow he knew that she would be content merely to revel in any pleasure he might give her. But she would demand something in return, without knowing it, without meaning to.

This woman could make him love, could make his blood heat with challenge and intrigue as well as physical desire. Even more than the tradition and propriety of a wife, he knew suddenly that that would be the most dangerous snare of all. It would change everything.

Abruptly, he stepped away from her. ''The hide of my first kill is yours,'' he said shortly.

He had always been generous with her, but this stunned her. ''No!'' She shook her head. ''I have no way to carry it! I brought only one pony, and I have already borrowed a pack animal from Wetatonmi.''

''Then I will find you another of those funny-looking stallions when I go to Sioux country over the next mountains. I will bring you the blood to make more of the ponies that have bested me, and I will make sure this one has beautiful color as well.''

In the end, that was the fairest price of all, he thought, the best—and only—thing he dared to give her.

Kiye Kipi watched him go, her heart chugging.

At first, she did not understand the liquid-warm feeling that filled her, that made it feel as though she were floating over the wild grasses the others rode through. Sometimes Weta-tonmi rode beside her, and made her laugh in shocked surprise with her observations of the Hasotoin warriors. Sometimes Twelic came to talk to her. Sometimes she galloped alone. She could breathe so very freely in this open land where the sunsets turned the plains to fire.

Finally, disbelievingly, she realized that she was *happy*. It was nothing more or less than that.

But the longer they rode, the more she realized that the warriors were not pleased. By the fifth sun after they left the Bitterroot pass, even Alokot looked grim. They had seen no buffalo. They had not even found sign.

Finally, they came to a place where the land undulated enough to hide their traveling lodges and ponies from a watering hole. Alokot and Twelic rode together, talking, then Alokot raised a hand to signal to the others to stop.

"We will camp here for a little while," he announced when they caught up and crowded around him. "This looks like a good hole. We will see if anything comes here." If there was game, any kind of game, it would appear at this lush spot.

"Why does your animal caller not bring them to us?" a Hasotoin man demanded. Kiye Kipi felt her heart lurch.

"I feel nothing here," she admitted.

It was the one nagging truth itching at the pit of her stomach. She still did not know if she was unable to dream the buffalo because she could not picture them, or if it was more than that. She had been filled with so many good things lately that she had not tried very hard to think of game.

When the next sun came, she would put all her heart into it, she vowed. She would leave the camp and try to make herself dream.

She helped Wetatonmi pull her shelter into place as darkness settled, but she shook her head when her friend would have helped her carry her own packs inside.

"No. I will stay out here tonight." One thing she knew for sure; when she slept inside, her magic could not even get away from her and seek out game on its own. She was still frightened of having that happen again, but she thought now that maybe it was worth the risk. Alokot and Twelic looked so troubled.

She took her robe to a place near the meager rise and curled up there without joining the others for any of the antelope. She watched their fires for a long time; their voices were subdued, not as they had been. Finally, despite their droning murmur, she slept.

She woke to the sun on her face, and ants crawling through the travel dust on her skin. She sat up and brushed them off, but still she itched.

The camp was asleep. She crawled up to the top of the rise and peeked over. Game drank at dawn, but there was nothing at the hole.

She knew then that it was not just her magic that was not working. *Where were the animals?* Had Old Joseph's dreaded *xayxayx* done this, created this dearth? They had seen no white-skinned men on their journey. It seemed impossible.

She scowled and rubbed her forehead. Her hand came away grimy. First she would wash, she thought. Then, when she felt clean and good and relaxed, she would ride to some spot far from the others and see if she could dream.

She studied the creek from her high vantage point. It was best if she went downstream; that way if any game did come, they would not pick up her taste on the water they drank. She left her robe and wandered down the other side of the hill.

The creek was shallow and thick with sediment, but it was cool enough with mountain runoff to make her teeth chatter. She sank into it, doeskin and all, and sighed. She wished she had some of old Burned Tree's balm; the ants had bitten her and the stuff smelled so good.

She peeled her dress from her skin, yanked it over her head and hurled it to the bank. It landed with a soggy, squashy sound.

Closing her eyes in enjoyment, she lay back. The water was barely deep enough for her to float, but it cradled her. Finally, she scrubbed the bottom sand against her scalp and scraped it over her skin as well. She rolled over onto her stomach, drew her knees under her and swished her hands busily through her hair until the grains floated out.

Twelic knew, in that moment, that it had been a mistake to follow her.

Even his pony went rigid beneath him, feeling his tension, his sudden, uncharacteristic panic. She was a squaw, just another young squaw, naked and languid in the water. He had seen many that way. He had watched the long, delicate curves of their spines as they bent over, had run his hands and his mouth there, had cupped the fullness of their breasts and had felt their delighted laughter vibrate against his skin.

This was different.

A treacherous ache of arousal began to squirm through his body again. *No.* He fought it, half turned away. He had meant only to tease her, to take her doeskin back to the camp and play a prank. Impulsive of him, and stupid. If he stayed here a moment longer, he knew he could lose himself in her.

She came up suddenly, flinging her hair back, and turned around. Her panicked squeal pierced the quiet when she saw him. She jolted to her feet, water streaming down her belly, and the sight of her seemed to slice something open inside him.

Curse her, why had she grown, why had she come here to this spot, why had she become the woman she was?

"Go away!" she gasped, and then she remembered herself, dropping again so hard the water sprayed up around her. He thought she had bitten her tongue, because a pained, surprised look came to her eyes.

He could not help himself. He laughed.

Fury washed over her, reddening her skin, making her eyes flash. Relief was sweet and rushing through him. It made her seem younger, easier, a girl not unlike his own sister.

Recklessly, he leaned low off his pony and scooped up the sodden ball of her dress. "Yes, I will do that. I will go."

"No!"

She came up again before he could even straighten on his mount. Reflexively, he pulled his reins around and spun his pony. He heard her gasp again as she understood what he intended, but he had not gambled on the quickness of her long legs. A moment later, before he could goad the pony into moving, he heard the violent splash of water again and her hands dug into his calf.

"Give it back!"

She was strong; Tahmahnewes, she was strong! He was unprepared, felt her grip pulling him down. His startled pony skittered sideways, in the opposite direction, unseating him. Impulsively, he transferred her dress to his other hand, keeping it out of her reach as he hit the ground.

She would not win this one.

Then he knew that she already had.

She was not his sister. She was long and lean and stunningly beautiful with fire in her eyes. He landed with a grunt and she sprawled naked beside him, his weight throwing her own balance off. Wanting screamed up in him again, just as hot as her temper, more wild and untamed than anything he had grappled with before.

Kiye Kipi saw the change in his eyes.

Terror staggered through her. His hot, probing gaze slid over her breasts, her ribs, to the soft tufts of hair at the top of her thighs. It was just like before.

It would hurt. It would hurt so terribly, and now she knew that afterward, she would never, ever be able to make things right again.

"No," she breathed. "Oh, please . . ." She scrambled away from him, crablike, covering herself.

"Wait."

Tahmahnewes, what was he doing? She went still, her heart thrumming, her eyes huge. Twelic closed his own and knew it was too late. It had been too late since he had followed her here, since he had not turned away at first glance.

"You are lithe and beautiful," he went on quietly. "You should never, ever be ashamed of that."

She gave a little groan. "Do not hurt me."

"Do you think that is all there is to this?" Of course she did. But if he never gave her anything again, he could give her the precious gift of knowing she was wrong.

He would take no pleasure for himself. His jaw hardened

with that resolve, and with the already unconscionable pain of restraint. His blood roared. He did not think he had ever wanted anyone more, and he knew would never take less.

"Let me show you."

"No."

He pushed against her shoulder. She was stiff, fragile, ready to break. When he put his hand against her heart to feel it scrambling, she flinched and the color drained from her face.

"You must trust me." He knew better now than to ask if he had ever hurt her. All he could do was vow that he would not do so again.

She saw that in his eyes. He was Twelic. Perhaps he had once broken her heart, but he had never, ever, done harm to her flesh. That she could trust. That she could believe in.

Trembling, she lay back as it seemed he wanted her to do. She watched him, her eyes huge.

His hand moved from her heart to her breast. She gasped, but Wahlitits had never touched her there. There were no memories there, only the smooth roughness of his palm, covering her, closing over her. Then his thumb stroked over her nipple, and something strange, something *wild*, leaped inside her.

"Yes. It is like a bird, beating its wings in your heart, trying to get out."

He understood. How could he understand?

"This will be better."

His hand slid down her ribs, almost tickling her, but not quite. Oh, his touch slid between her thighs, and she jolted. But then he bent to her, closing his mouth over her nipple where his hand had been before.

Kiye Kipi groaned, a long, shuddering sound that she could not recognize. It felt . . . it felt *good*.

His tongue—*his tongue*—laved over her nipple as his fingers probed. Sensation swam through her, hot, pooling low in her belly. She wanted . . . something. She cried out in frustration, because there could not possibly be more.

There was.

He pushed her thighs apart. She clamped them closed again,

trapping his fingers, and shook her head, but his touch did not hurt. His fingers slid and pressed and roamed, and the hot feeling curled up in her, as though it would explode.

"I want nothing from you." Oh, it hurt him to say it. "Just know that a man's touch does not have to be painful, demeaning."

She swallowed dryly, watching him.

"Do I hurt you?"

"N-no." What hurt was the wanting, the tightening feeling inside her. She thought if it did not release her somehow, she would die.

"Then let your legs fall apart. Relax, and it will feel better."

She shuddered and slowly, awkwardly, did as he asked.

Time seemed to hang as interminably still as the sun baking down on them. It was agonizing in its sweetness and shamelessness as she lay open to his gaze. She could not do this! How could she do this? Running, hiding, had always been her strongest protection. She could not bear to look at him as he stripped that instinct from her as well as her modesty. She could feel his gaze on her bare breasts, on her exposed, secret flesh. It was warm and tingling, like a caress.

His finger slid deep inside her, then out again, and his thumb rubbed. The heat inside her whirled tighter and tighter, hotter and hotter. She groaned and dug her nails into the grass. It could not go on. She could not bear it, she thought wildly, and then the sun burst.

It seemed to explode over her, raining white-yellow fire down on her skin. She heard a voice not her own gasp from her. "Oh!"

"It was dry when he touched you, a rubbing pain like hot sand inside you."

She groaned.

"Now you see. It was not like this."

He moved his hand and trailed a finger up her belly. It left a little path of dampness. So different. She shook her head, feeling it swim as the heat, the tension, throbbed out of her again.

"How . . . do you know these things?" she whispered.

He knew women. And he knew that what he had just given her, he would never give to another again. There was, after all, an ironic fidelity in chastity.

He pushed away from her abruptly. Already, too late, the heat in his blood died to embers; already, something unsettled and panicked began to move in his gut.

What had he done?

"Where do you go?" she cried. He was on his pony when she sat up, feeling dazed.

"Somewhere out there, there is a deer, an antelope, some meat to fill our bellies. I must find it." *I must go, put space between us, before I forget everything I need and everything you deserve.* Oh, yes, she could undo him. She was too sweet, too innocent . . . too different.

"But—" she began.

"Finish washing, Screamer," he interrupted. "There is work to be done this sun."

He left her, but she only lay back in the grass again, her heart thrumming.

20

IT WAS A long time before she returned to the camp. Twelic was back. Wherever he had gone, he had had no luck. The squaws were idling, not cutting up kills. He sat talking to Alokot, and when she wandered down off the rise, he looked up at her with a careful smile before he went back to his conversation.

What had that been back there?

She thought she understood with her head, but her heart skittered away from what seemed impossible. No matter what he had said all those seasons ago, had he decided he wanted to mate with her after all?

She waited for the old terror to fill her at the thought, but she knew, oh, yes, she knew now, that it would not be a bad thing with Twelic. All their nights would be filled with that hot, wild feeling he had brought to her beside the water. They could race the wind with every sun, because she could help him hunt.

She hugged herself, feeling shivery even in the relentless prairie heat. Never, ever, had she thought such a thing could happen to her, that she could be someone's mate, perhaps even have little babes. But it seemed possible now, it truly did!

Her head spun with plans, with decisions. She knew what she had to do now. She had to find those beasts, the buffalo. She had to show Twelic that she *could* travel with him, that she could be useful. Then he would surely ask her to return to the Hasotoin with him.

She could go home again.

For a moment, something cringed inside her at the thought of leaving Old Joseph. But he would understand, she knew he would. Even he had spoken of her mating.

She gathered up her robe where she had left it beside the rise and went to where the two warriors talked.

"I may be gone for a while," she announced when they looked up at her. "I am going to find those buffalo now."

Alokot scowled out at the windswept prairie. "Do you think it will do any good here? We were just talking of moving on, over the next mountains."

She nodded with far more confidence than she felt. "I am sure I can find something."

"She should try," Twelic agreed. His response was too quick. It was almost as though . . . as though he were eager for her to go.

Her heart gave a kick and she looked at him sharply.

"If we move on," he explained, "we should at least do it because we know there is nothing here."

That was it; of course that was all he was concerned with, this strange, pervasive dearth of animals.

"There is something here," she said fervently. "There must be."

She hurried out to the herd, her belly rumbling. She had already missed two meals now, and that was good. She would not have to waste much time fasting. Briefly, she wished she could be like Looking Glass or Old Joseph—it seemed all they had to do was close their eyes for a vision to leap before them. But they were powerful headmen, and she was only a squaw.

She swung up onto her dappled pony and started out, crossing the creek before doubt took her. How would she ever find more water for a safe place to wait? She could not have her filly starving for moisture while she looked.

Let the filly take you to it.

She started a bit as the advice filled her head, but it left her feeling strong and confident and encouraged again. Her *wyakin*. Yes, of course, she would let her *wyakin* lead her.

She gave the pony her head. They went on until the sun

dropped, the filly following her nose. They reached a creek that was scarcely more than a rivulet bubbling over some stones, but it was enough for the pony. She dismounted and spread her robe on the ground, then she sat down upon it to wait.

Finally, the moon appeared, low and swollen and yellow. She stared into it determinedly. Oh, this was so important. It was, she realized, the most important dream she had ever asked for. Just when she thought she could bear it no more, the moon darkened. *Her ponies.* Their image came to her as they always did and her breath moaned out of her unconsciously, gratefully, as she went to them in her mind.

The wonderful sound of their hoofbeats filled her head, thundering, trembling the earth. Their feet tore up the thick, wild grass, running on and on. . . .

But there were no buffalo.

Where were they?

She felt the vision begin to tremble away from her. *No!* She had to find them, *had* to. She was with her ponies, and that was good, but they did not hurl her into the heart of one of the beasts this time. They just kept galloping, moving.

Fear clawed at her, then she understood. *They were taking her somewhere.* Not *into* the beasts this time, but *to* them.

Breath rushed into her again and she relaxed. Details sharpened in her mind's eye. She saw a strange hill, flat on the top, too steep to run up. It was a lonely, disruptive hump on the prairie, rising on the far side of a tumbling river. There by the water was a scrawny knot of trees.

The sky was golden and blue beyond it. Sunrise. The ponies galloped around it, and then she saw.

The beasts were hunchbacked and matted, and their scent came to her on the wind, gamy and ripe. They nosed muddy water at a place where the grasslands were spongy and wet. Then the vision shattered. Kiye Kipi gave a little cry of gladness and curled into herself on the robe.

Her head hurt, and her pulse was dangerously fast, skittering. The dream left her as all of them did, drained, addled, craving rest. Oh, how she wanted to sleep. But she could not do that, not this time.

She had to take this dream back to Twelic.

She shook her head groggily, then she struggled to her feet again. The prairie dipped and swayed about her. Slowly, she made her way to the water. She splashed it on her face and guzzled thirstily, then she made the little nickering sound in her throat. The dappled filly came to her, standing close.

''Thank you,'' she managed, and pulled herself up onto her back.

She had to hurry. That strange lump of land had felt very far away. And the camp . . . that was a good ride from here as well. Before she could fully straighten up, she put her heels to the filly. They began running in the easy, ground-eating lope the special pony could maintain forever.

Still, dawn came back before they reached the camp.

Her hurrying hoofbeats brought the warriors out of their lodges, groggy but ready with their weapons.

''I found them!'' she cried, and suddenly, everyone was moving. The squaws came out as well, and there were shouts of excitement. Where was Twelic? She could not find him, though she longed to see his face when he realized her success, wanted it with a fierce, proud intensity that was unlike anything she had known before.

Alokot came to her instead.

''We must hurry,'' she told him. ''They are far to the north of here.''

She did not know how she knew that, but she did. She dropped to the ground and worked fast to help Wetatonmi break down her lodge. The camp was quickly packed up again, and the party rode out.

She finally found Twelic at the front of the crowd. She hurried to catch up with him, feeling suddenly shy.

''You could not call them closer?'' he asked tensely.

Her jaw dropped, and it felt as though her belly would sink clear to her toes. It had not even occurred to her to try. She had just been so glad to have found them.

She had not proved herself yet after all.

She began studying the horizon, afraid she would miss some sign she had dreamed of, something that would lead her to the right place. *Had* it been north? Now that she thought about it, there was no true reason to believe that was so. Doubt squirmed inside her. If she changed her directions now, what would everyone think?

But she knew; of course she knew. The warriors would have second thoughts about following her. They would wonder about her magic.

Twelic would wonder about her magic.

When the sun went high, her filly finally began tiring. Alokot saw and motioned impatiently to one of his own hunting ponies. Reluctantly, she left Twelic to ride close to it and change mounts.

She did not feel his eyes on her. He watched her gather her legs beneath her, long and lean and brown, and jump like the wind onto the other pony. Her throat tightened. No, she was not like other squaws, all of them riding so demurely behind their men. He thought of touching her again, of igniting all that wild heat inside her that had just begun to burn.

But that was for another man, one who could bear being consumed and burdened by her fire.

They reached the place where she had dreamed her vision before Kiye Kipi realized where they were. "Wait!" she cried, panicked, as they splashed across the shallow water.

Alokot reined in to turn about and look at her.

"East now." She thought about it. Yes, east. The sun had been coming up behind that funny hill. Of that, at least, she was sure.

But dark fell again, and still they had not found it.

"We should make camp," one of the Hasotoin grumbled. "Who knows how far she will take us?"

Cold numbed her inside. There was doubt in his tone.

She twisted around on her pony to see that it was Swan Necklace who had spoken. Somehow, instinctively, that seemed even more dangerous. "If we stop now, we could lose them," she answered tightly. "When I saw them, it was dawn."

"Which dawn?" another Hasotoin demanded.

Her head began hurting. Oh, she was losing them.

Then Twelic's voice came sharp from beside her. She jumped and looked at him, gratitude filling her so abruptly she felt faint. He would save her. He always saved her . . . almost.

"If it was this past dawn," he pointed out, "then they are far ahead of us and we need to keep going to catch up."

He was their leader, and they obeyed him. The Hasotoin party rode on, though both Wahlitits and Swan Necklace looked disgruntled. Kiye Kipi knew, with a feeling like a knife in her belly, that Wahlitits was praying she would fail if only because he was too lazy and tired to keep riding.

She could not let it happen.

Near dawn, they splashed down into a river, deep enough that the current made their weary ponies pull and stagger. Alokot reined in on the other side.

"We must stop, Kiye Kipi." He said it quietly, as though it pained him. "This is the Big Hole. We have come far. We need to rest, to think about this."

She nodded dully, and looked around. Suddenly, her heart staggered.

There, downriver, was a scraggly knot of trees.

They had to be the ones, had to be! She had seen no others on this whole vast grassland. She pulled Alokot's hunting pony around hard, her eyes wild, searching the horizon.

"There!"

Alokot looked sharply the way she pointed. The lingering darkness had disoriented her at first, but the black of the southeast horizon was irregular, lumping up against the paler, thick gray of the sky.

"That is a butte," Alokot said slowly.

Did he think she thought it was the buffalo? Her tension shattered into little pieces inside her, making her gasp with laughter, with release.

"Yes," she managed. "And beyond it, there is a marsh hole, and that is where I saw the buffalo drinking."

Twelic came up behind her. Even in the darkness, he was close enough that she saw the avid light come into his eyes.

They reminded her of a wildcat who had scented prey. Something good shuddered back into life inside her. This, the hunt, was what he hungered for, and, thank Tahmahnewes, somehow she had managed to give it to him.

"We should go as far as the butte," he suggested. "I can crawl up to the top and see if they are here. If they are not, I can find their tracks. Either way, we can rest, and move in on them when the sun comes strong again."

The Hasotoin were silent.

The squaws were weary, shrugging.

They went quietly to the butte. The buffalo had left. Twelic came sliding back down the slope without any cautionary quiet, but he was grinning as the others dismounted.

"You must have seen them this past dawn," he said. "They have traveled on."

It made sense, but she had been afraid to say so before. She had dreamed them last night.

"They have grazed and trampled down a wide swath," he went on, "heading north again. There must be many of them."

"A hundred for each man here," she said absently. She could smell them. She tilted her head back, her nose into the breeze, and thought perhaps it was the sweetest odor that had ever come to her nostrils.

Twelic sniffed too, and then he gave a quiet hoot. Suddenly, he forgot all the reasons he had not to touch her. He grabbed her, spinning her around so that she almost cried out.

"Ah, Screamer, you are good to have along."

He let her go again to get his sleeping robe. For a long while, Kiye Kipi only stood clutching hers, thinking dizzily of the way his strong arms had felt around her.

You are good to have along.

Oh, how she loved him.

She had loved him forever, and now, finally and truly, he would be hers.

THE AIR THUNDERED with sound, and Mother Earth trembled as Kiye Kipi watched the hunt. Nothing in her dreams could have prepared her for this.

It had not taken them long to find the buffalo. They had crept up quietly on their trail with the first true sun, then the warriors had spread out to surround them. At a signal from Twelic on one side, and Alokot on the other, they had rushed in upon the herd, whooping and galloping.

Now they chased the beasts through a churning cloud of dust. As the melee stormed farther and farther away from her, huge, furry carcasses began littering its wake.

"Come," said Wetatonmi, and Kiye Kipi pulled her eyes reluctantly away. "Bless Tahmahnewes, there is much work to be done now."

The other squaw rode to the first fallen cow, but Kiye Kipi stayed astride, her gaze going back to the hunt.

"Do you hunger to be over there with them?" Wetatonmi asked suddenly.

Kiye Kipi's jaw dropped at such a thought. Then something moved in her belly, something impatient and edgy.

Yes.

She wanted to be strong enough to hunt those animals; she wanted any excuse to join the furor. She was not content waiting back here, sweating and toiling beneath the hot sun with the other squaws.

She sighed and dropped to the ground beside Wetatonmi,

pulling her knife free instead. It was hot, grisly work. The cow's blood crusted on their arms and hands in the blazing sun as they took the hide. Gnats and flies hovered over the dead beast, then swarmed to investigate the women. Kiye Kipi dragged the back of her hand over her forehead to stop the sweat from sliding into her eyes.

They pinned the skin out, flesh side down, with pickets from the parfleche Wetatonmi carried. "Arenoth says we can come back to these after dusk. They will not dry hard and useless as long as we get to them before the next sun."

Kiye Kipi nodded and helped drag her knife through the meat of the huge, fatty belly. A damp stench wafted up to them as the innards spilled. Wetatonmi caught a handful of gut and tugged it out.

"This will have to go to the water to be washed out. Then we can use it to carry the fat and the blood home."

Hooves and horns were set aside to be boiled, and slabs of the meat were cut and piled high. They had moved on to the next bull before the warriors came back, galloping hard and singing.

She saw Twelic at the head of the bunch. Her heart lifted and she stood away from the work to watch him.

"This coyote would have seen his life end," Alokot crowed, swinging to the ground.

"I trust coyote's luck," Twelic laughed.

"What happened?" Kiye Kipi demanded.

"He rode between a cow and her calf for a double kill, one with his spear, the other with his rifle." Alokot was shaking his head, but it was clear that he had enjoyed the spectacle. "I have been east several times now, and I have never seen anything like that."

"That is because you never saw the Sioux and Cheyenne hunt."

Alokot scowled briefly. "No. I have never gone that far." But, he thought, the way the buffalo were thinning, he would get there soon enough.

Kiye Kipi still gaped at Twelic. "Why would you do such a thing?" she asked.

She thought of all the hungry babes back in Nimipu land. She expected him to mention them, but instead, a hard gleam came to his eyes as he looked into hers.

"Because if I did not, I would always wonder if I could."

Her belly moved. Yes, she understood that. Hadn't she sought her first elk dream for much the same reason?

Twelic put his foot against one of the fallen buffalo, bracing himself to tug the spear free. He let it fall into the grass, marking another man's kill.

Kiye Kipi gaped as she realized he would help.

"You do squaw's work on these trips?" she asked.

Twelic shrugged. "The carcasses stretch as far as the eye can see. It makes more sense to help you work your way up the trail than for each man to ride about, looking for his own kills." Besides, he thought, more hands would make this work go more quickly, and then he would be packed and on his way again.

They labored as the sun fell and the moon rose. Kiye Kipi thought helplessly that they would never finish, but when she lugged another long rope of gut back from a water hole, she saw fires leaping brightly. She found Wetatonmi and Alokot and Twelic at one of them, and dropped with a grunt of weariness, uncaring of the cold, damp tangle of entrails that spilled over her lap.

"Now what?" she asked, tying her hair in a knot to get it off her hot, sticky neck.

Twelic held out a long bone, its core thick with coagulated marrow. "Now we feast, Screamer. Now, thanks to you, we feast."

She looked at him, relieved. The last of the work would keep, she thought.

She reached to take the bone from him, but he motioned to her to tilt her head back instead. She eyed him hesitantly for a moment, then probed the core with her tongue. The warm ooze melted deliciously into her mouth.

"That, too, is something a man can do with a woman," he whispered before he could stop himself. "Some sun you will know that as well."

Her eyes widened and something began tightening again deep inside her. "Oh!" she whispered. "Yes . . . please."

Twelic's eyes narrowed, then he laughed, a hoarse sound that did not sound much like his own voice.

Her shoulders throbbed dully with the ache of exertion. The tender skin on the inside of her thighs felt chafed and raw from so much riding, but oh, it was good to be happy.

They worked through all the next sun until the kills were broken down enough to be carried home. Then the Hasotoin hunters, and even many of the Kahmuenem, began bringing her pieces. Her dream had been true, and no man had been injured or lost. Even the ponies had come out of it unscathed.

By the time the cook fires were once again crackling and snapping in the darkness, the pile beside Kiye Kipi had grown to staggering proportions. She spitted some of the better pieces to eat with Wetatonmi and Alokot, but still her mind reeled at the thought of getting it all back to Imnaha. She was almost glad that Wahlitits and Swan Necklace and Twelic had not given her anything.

Her gaze moved to Twelic. This night, for the first time since the bands had joined together, he sat with his own men. He spoke to them heatedly as they gathered around him.

"When will we move on?" she asked, wondering aloud.

Alokot's eyes came up to her, though he still leaned over his meat. "With the new sun," he said, chewing.

She gnawed on her lip. That was well, she decided. They were about half a moon's ride from Nimipu country.

Surely, by then, Twelic would ask her to go home to the Hasotoin.

The sound of the stirring camp poked and prodded its way into her sleep with the next dawn. Finally, reluctantly, Kiye Kipi sat up.

Her gaze fell first upon the Hasotoin, on the far side of the camp. She frowned. Their meat was all loaded, and Twelic was mounted, shouting orders to his men, who still roamed about.

Her gaze snapped to Alokot. He was bent over a pony's hoof, inspecting it critically, but he showed no true haste to have his party packed and ready to leave with Twelic.

Something was wrong.

She scrambled out from beneath her robe, her eyes flashing between the two bands.

"What is it?" Wetatonmi asked, alarmed.

"Where do the Hasotoin go?"

The other squaw relaxed. "I heard Twelic say they will keep on, over the next mountains. As long as he is this far east, he would like to raid for ponies."

I will find you another of those funny-looking stallions when I go on to Sioux country.

But she had not thought he meant now, this season.

She did not want it! She wanted to ride back to Nimipu territory with him, wanted him to talk to her in that warm, secret way he had. Oh, Tahmahnewes, she wanted him to claim her!

She looked at him again, her gut rolling. Perhaps he meant to take her with him to that farther place. But he was already astride, and he had not awakened her.

She began moving toward him. Thunder Dance was standing close beside him.

"And what of the Kahmuenem animal caller?" she heard him ask, and her heart lurched. "Must we listen to the moans and sighs of one of your sated women all the way to the far plains and back?"

Twelic's answering grin was like a hunting knife laying open her heart.

"I have no wish to make you jealous, friend. She will stay."

Thunder Dance swung up on his own pony. "My own women have no complaints."

"You do not have women. You have a wife."

"It has its advantages. There is something warm waiting for me at home."

"Ah, but there is something *hot* waiting for me in the *Lam-tama* village. Cloud Singer will be there, ready and hungry.

Or perhaps I will visit the Pikunanmu. I have not seen Little
Doe for quite a while now.''

Kiye Kipi took a staggering step backward.

He swung his pony around and saw her.

Cloud Singer? Little Doe?

She did not know who they were, but she knew, suddenly,
what they were not. They would not be the orphan spawn of
a man with no *wyakin*. They would never have been babe
killers.

Oh, Tahmahnewes, how could she ever have forgotten that?
She flinched and took another step away from him.

''Screamer, wait. I wanted to gift you before I go.''

There was a hide lying across his lap. She had not noticed
it before. She could not bear to touch it, to take it.

Once again, because she was a fool, because she had trusted
him, she would have to watch him go, and this time it hurt
worse, so much worse, than before.

She turned on her heel and fled. She heard his hoofbeats
behind her, then his voice cracked out and she stumbled as it
cut into her.

''Wait!'' he snapped again.

She whirled back to face him. ''I want nothing from you!''

''You have earned it.''

The anger started slowly, a burning sensation in her chest.
Oh, yes, she was stupid, but she was no longer a child. He
had fooled her twice now, but this time he was not taking
anything from her that she could not live without.

''I have more than I need,'' she spat. ''Give it to one of the
squaws who keep you hot.''

His eyes narrowed. ''I have more than enough to give
them.''

''Then one will enjoy more than the others.''

''Then that one will believe she means more.''

''Such a squaw would be stupid.'' She waited, her eyes
snapping, for him to deny it.

''Yes,'' he answered quietly.

She closed her eyes. Wetatonmi was wrong. Men did not
cherish. They were like rutting ponies after all.

"I took nothing for myself when I touched you," he erupted suddenly. "I promised even less." He knew it was true, and hated the guilt, the regret that tightened inside him anyway.

She looked at him again miserably, and he had to look away. He would not doubt his choices now, after all these seasons! Curse her for making him think of it.

"Do you try to convince yourself?" she demanded.

She saw him flinch, and felt nothing. In place of her heart was something that felt like a cold, hard stone.

He turned away. She did not call after him.

There was nothing left inside her to cry with, after all.

22

THE IMNAHA VALLEY looked different when they returned, but somehow she had known from the beginning that it would. It did not seem safe, secretive, protective any longer.

Kiye Kipi stayed for a moment on the slope of the hills, watching as the others rode down. A haze shrouded the sun, turning the light yellow-gray. It hung over the people, making their faces seem wan.

The woman worked desultorily. Though the hunters were triumphant, their smiles of greeting were thin. Kiye Kipi knew then that something was wrong, something more than her heart feeling as cold and empty as death.

Old Joseph.

He was not out and about to welcome them. She looked about wildly, but she could not see Arenoth either. Young Joseph came out of their lodge instead, his eyes dark and serious.

No, no, no!

She drove her heels hard into her filly and caught up with Alokot. She was suddenly blazingly angry.

"You said he would last the summer! *You lied!*"

Young Joseph approached, looking up at them. "He is not gone."

"What then?"

"He fails. He waits for you."

But Kiyi Kipe knew he did not mean her. She was not really kin, after all.

She backed her pony up blindly, whipping around. She needed him now, her kind, old friend, but he would want his children, the flesh of his flesh.

She galloped to the river where she had greeted the sun with him so many times. No one seemed to notice her go.

She curled up on the bank to nurse the fear and the grief that clawed at her, but still she could not cry.

It was dark when Arenoth found her.

"Come, daughter, it is time."

Kiye Kipi looked around at her. "He is gone," she managed.

But Arenoth shook her head. "No. He wants to see you as well."

"Why?"

"Would you deny him because you are not of the very same blood?"

Deny him? She laughed a taut, crazy sound. How could she deny one who had treated her with more truth and kindness than anyone she had ever known? He had believed in her, and never, not once, had he hurt her.

However would she go on without him?

She stumbled to her feet to follow the woman back to the camp. Young Joseph and Alokot were still in the lodge. She stepped quietly up behind them, knowing Old Joseph could not see her.

But his ears were still as keen as the winter wind.

"What do you fear, child? Losing me, or feeling your heart bleed again?"

She gasped at his voice, and at the truth in it. Her eyes burned hot, and her throat closed.

Alokot and Young Joseph stepped aside for her. *She did not want to see him.* She could not watch him go!

Oh, yes, she was a coward, but he had given her courage, had shown her the way to survive. She owed it to him to be brave.

She inched closer, and her heart bled.

His flesh was shrunken and shriveled. Death had nibbled on

him determinedly while she had been away.

What if she had not gone?

"My body is returning to my Mother Earth," he said quietly, "and my spirit is going very soon to see the Great Spirit Chief. It is time."

She flinched and dropped to her knees beside him, and took his beloved hand in her own. He smiled and moved his mouth, working for his voice.

"You are my daughter," he rasped finally. "Now listen well, all of you. I do not have much time.

"When I am gone, think of your country. Always remember that your father never sold his land, and that his bones lie here. You must stop your ears whenever you are asked to sign a treaty selling your home. A few seasons more, and the white men will be all around you. They have their eyes on this land. My children, never forget my dying words. Never sell the bones of your father and mother. That is my last wish."

"Do not speak of that now," she gasped.

"I must. It is all that is left.

"Go now, and take my heart with you. I would be alone with my wife."

Strong hands pulled her up from behind. Alokot. She turned into him blindly, and let him guide her outside.

For a long time, they stood silently beside the lodge in the night breeze. It felt as cold as the afterworld that would rob them.

Kiye Kipi made a choking sound.

"He was already gone," Alokot said, and his voice was strangled. "The spirits were already taking him. That was why he said that, why he talked crazy."

"No," said Young Joesph. "I do not think that is it."

"There has been no mention of treaties for many seasons," Alokot argued stubbornly.

"There will be," Kiye Kipi whispered. "He knows."

She startled herself, and looked to both of them, haunted. But she knew, oh, yes, she knew that if Old Joseph had been with the spirits, then he had seen something no other of them saw, some truth they did not yet know.

Arenoth gave a pitched scream from the lodge behind them. Kiye Kipi flinched and cried out as it turned into a keening howl of mourning.

He did not even know of the kills they had made. He did not even know she had done well.

She had not meant to love again. She was not sure she could bear it.

She sat where she stood, giving in to hard, dry sobs. It was all she could give him, but she gave it with the last soft, sweet part of her heart.

Later, as the sun came again, she helped Arenoth bathe and dress him in the clothes he had loved best. They rubbed river chalk over his leggings so the leather gleamed white in the sun. They streaked his solemn, still face with red paint, and ran an even line of it down the part of his hair.

Her hands shook but she kept working, pausing only when Arenoth moaned. Then she gripped herself harder, and went on.

Nothing hurt forever. Broken bones knit together again, and wounds scabbed over, and the memories of the heart grew pale and weak. She would not forget, no, never that, but she knew that this pain would fade to a scar, too. All her pains had.

When it was done, Arenoth went to the water to rub mud over herself. She slashed at her doeskin and her braids with her knife, her cries haunting the camp, screeching then dying in horror.

When she came back and threw her braids into the fire, the people began saying good-bye.

The stench of burning hair bit into the breeze. Kiye Kipi fought to keep herself from gagging, moving behind Alokot and Young Joseph, Earth Sound, and Burned Tree as they carried Old Joseph into the hills. Some of the boys had already dug a hole there for him, and they had piled rocks high to mark the spot and keep the animals from his remains. Arenoth began wailing again as the men lowered him, his head to the east, where the sun gave new birth.

"Wait!" Kiye Kipi cried suddenly. Alokot looked back at her.

She was not truly one of them; she could not forget that. But he had loved her unlike her own faceless kin. She ran back to the village, rummaging in the hides she had brought back from the hunt.

She found what she was looking for, a perfect doeskin from the antelope kill. She hurried back to the hill, silently handing it to the men.

"Please. I . . . please."

Alokot nodded. Somehow he understood.

They wrapped the old man in it. It was her gift, but first it had been his gift to her, her magic and this Kahmuenem world that had been pushed upon her, tearing her apart, then somehow leaving her whole and strong.

She swallowed back the keening that built in her own throat. *Good-bye.* Oh, Tahmahnewes, she was always saying good-bye.

She did not want to see them throw his bow and trinkets in upon him. She could not bear to hear the screams of his favorite ponies as they died. She went back to the fire where Arenoth's braids had turned to ashes, the fire he had sat at so many times.

"I will remember," she whispered. "Oh, friend, whatever you saw, I will remember your warning. I will not let them come here. I will not let them touch your bones."

Burned Tree had not performed the Pasapukitse yet; he had not blown Old Joseph's ghost away. She felt him close, and knew he heard her, and she was not afraid.

She spent seven suns in the sweat lodge to purify her blood from the taint of his death. Burned Tree badgered her into observing the cautionary tradition. When she came out, Alokot was waiting for her.

"We must talk."

She shrugged, nodded, and followed him back to his lodge. The air held an undercurrent of coolness, of autumn watching with hungry eyes from the hills. She shivered it off and began to duck inside, but Alokot turned in to his brother's lodge instead.

Of course. Quiet, intelligent Joseph would take responsibility for the Kahmuenem now, as it had always been known he would. Briefly, she looked at the other cowhide tepee, Arenoth's old one, sitting alone against the hills now.

A single stab of pain pierced her heart, then she moved to Joseph's lodge flap and ducked inside.

All the kin were there, Wetatonmi and Alokot and Joseph's own two wives, though she knew them with only the same polite distance that marked her relationship with their mate. She nodded greetings to them and sat.

Though it was Joseph's lodge, Joseph's council, Alokot began.

"Earth Sound has asked for you."

A pulse scrambled at her throat, but her voice was calm. "No."

"He is a good warrior," said Joseph. "Next to my own brother, he is the best this band has to offer. Would you leave us and go to another?"

"No. I would stay."

He nodded, and she was surprised to see that he looked relieved. He had never really spoken aloud of his faith in her magic.

"Your father showed me that I can call," she went on. "I would remain and feed his Kahmuenem. It is all I can give him for now."

Joseph seemed to think for a long time, staring into the fire. "Is there another beside Earth Sound you would choose for your mate?"

Her heart clenched so suddenly, so tightly, the pain robbed her breath. She shook her head mutely. *It will heal. It will go away.*

Joseph tried again. "My mother will come to my lodge now. There is no longer a hearth for you. I am a headman. I do not travel much now. You are kin to my kin, and I would keep you, but I cannot support four women very well."

"Come with us," Wetatonmi said impulsively. "I would

like you to be Alokot's wife with me.''

Kiye Kipi's heart made a strange little movement beneath her breast. She thought that if she could weep, perhaps she would do so now.

''That . . . is kind,'' she managed, ''but I cannot.''

How could she tell them? She looked at Alokot.

He was the Kahmuenem war leader, as handsome and graceful as a cougar. He was beloved of everyone for his unjudgmental kindness and his strength. If anything ever happened to his brother, he would be chief. Becoming his second woman would be an honor she could not believe she deserved, just as being first wife to Earth Sound would be a strong place.

She thought instead of hot sun and cold water, and strong, sure hands on her open flesh.

It was dry when he touched you, a rubbing pain like hot sand inside you. It was not like this.

No more. Never again. There were worse pains than flesh tearing. There was the hurt of being a fool.

Her chin came up and she looked around at all of them. ''Do you think I need a warrior to hunt for me?'' she asked. ''If I want to eat, I can call a doe to my fire. Even now, I have enough meat for the winter, gifted to me when we went east. I can live alone, and that is what I would choose for myself.''

They exchanged looks, and she knew they were struggling. She wondered if such a thing were truly unprecedented. She guessed from Joseph's appalled face that it was.

She stood quietly, showing them that she had said all she would or could. In the end, Joseph could decree as he chose. She knew that, and prayed as she waited.

Finally, blessedly, he nodded. They needed to keep her too much to deny her.

Arenoth found her voice. ''Bring those hides you were gifted with, and I can help you make a lodge of your own.''

23

Ah-la-tah-mahl, Hard Moon to Build a Fire, 1873

COLD FINGERS OF winter air sneaked up from beneath her lodge cover. They insinuated themselves in her spare, neat space, reaching down beneath her robe, and Kiye Kipi finally pushed her bedding aside.

She poked her nose past the door flap. The Wallowa village was silent and still in the snow. She had to go into the hills in spite of it. An aged mare of Old Joseph's would be heavy in foal by now, and she wanted her in the corral when she pushed her babe out.

Every other season, the mare had come back on her own when her time was close. Kiye Kipi's belly squirmed that she had not yet done so this winter.

Please do not leave us yet. She was the last, strong bond she had with the old headman. She was not yet ready to let her go.

She shivered and went back to drag a stick through the embers of her fire. The coals underneath settled again with a fresh, orange glow. She laid more wood against them and found her teasel comb, then she dragged her robe over her shoulders again, flipped her hair out on top of it, and brought the ends around her waist to tug the knots free.

"Pony Wife." The small voice bleated through the door flap.

"Come," she answered.

A girl child entered, too small and skinny, with big eyes. She shivered badly beneath her wet, woolen blanket. Her family did not have many horses. Her name was Dirty Dove, and her father had died hunting with a weak *wyakin*. Her mother had come back to the Kahmuenem, her kin, only to find that her brother was overburdened providing for his own family, and her father had gone on to the afterworld as well.

"Bring yourself closer," Kiye Kipi said quietly. "Get warm."

Dirty Dove looked horrified at the thought of intruding upon her hearth. "I do not think there is time," she said finally. "There is a pony babe in the woods, alone. I saw him when I was getting wood."

Kiye Kipi felt her heart kick.

"What does he look like?"

"Red with white spots."

Yes, that would be the old mare's babe. If he was alone, she was down. Kiye Kipi shrugged out from beneath her robe.

"I need you to stay here," she said. "I am going to bring this pony babe back to the lodge."

"Inside?" Dirty Dove looked about, wide-eyed. Kiye Kipi smiled.

"He has no mother to keep him warm from the snow." And he has probably not yet nursed, she thought. He would be weak.

"Cover up with my robe," she said, ducking out. "Those *xayxayx* blankets are so useless they are silly." She could not imagine how the white-skins could be such tenacious intruders as to survive the Nimipu cold moons in them and little else.

The cold, wet wind groaned over her. It was still heavy with snow, and she knew that before long it would make her very bones ache. She put her head into the gusts and began walking out of the valley anyway. Dirty Dove needed the warmth more than she did.

She saw him right away, a blood-bay spot on the white-crusted hills, standing on wobbly legs. He looked as though he would run when she approached, but she knew he did not yet possess the strength or the agility to do so.

He had been born this past night; she saw that right away

and her heart leaped with hope. Perhaps his mare was not yet dead after all.

She whinnied to him, inching closer, then she crooned in her own tongue. Finally, he came to her cautiously to whiffle his nose over her skin.

"There, now." She wrapped her fist around his short little tail, and her other arm around his neck. Struggling with his unwilling gait, she pushed him back toward the camp.

Dirty Dove was waiting in her lodge, still looking bemused. "Oh!" she cried when she saw the pony babe. Though he was tiny, the lodge did not offer him much room to wobble about.

"Now I will give him some medicine," Kiye Kipi explained. "And I would like to go find his mother. Can you stay a little while longer and watch over him?"

Dirty Dove nodded hard, then looked up at her shyly. "I would like to be a pony wife when I grow."

"Tahmahnewes decides what *wyakins* we should have," Kiye Kipi replied absently, digging through her horse medicine. When she looked up, the girl looked shattered.

"But perhaps He will reward you for helping me with this pony this sun," she went on.

"Does He do that?" Dirty Dove asked breathlessly.

"Yes, I think so," she admitted, "but do not tell Burned Tree I said it. He believes otherwise, but before I ever thought I would have a *wyakin* at all, I helped with ponies, and look what has happened."

Dirty Dove nodded raptly, watching as Kiye Kipi hugged the foal again and pushed some weed paste down his throat.

"There, now he will be quiet for a while. If it wears off before I come back, you must sit gently on his shoulder to keep him down. He cannot hurt himself in here, but I like these lodge hides as they are."

Dirty Dove giggled, looking as though she startled even herself with the sound.

Kiye Kipi went outside again, to the next lodge, and called for Wetatonmi. "I need a robe," she said when her friend poked her head out. "And something of Old Joseph's, please."

Wetatonmi raised a brow, but did not ask questions before she disappeared back inside. Alokot returned with her, carrying a thick buffalo blanket and a blunt-handled riding crop his mother had given him from his father's possessions.

The pair watched her go, Wetatonmi smiling, Alokot frowning. Wetatonmi knocked him in the ribs with her elbow.

"Do not fret so. She is fine."

"It is strange, such a beautiful woman choosing to live alone without a man. This is her eighteenth snow. She is very nearly too old to change her mind about mating." No matter what she had said after their father's death, Alokot had always assumed she would do just that. "How can a squaw be happy that way?"

Wetatonmi shrugged. "She is not."

"You talk circles." He scowled.

They watched her call her pony. Kiye Kipi mounted with an easy confidence, a dignity, that reminded him of a warrior he knew.

Alokot frowned again, thinking suddenly of Twelic of the Hasotoin.

He wondered again what had happened between them all those seasons ago in a land far away. Something had; he had guessed it from the time they had both disappeared one sun-drenched morning. He was equally sure that his serene wife knew what it was.

"For some women, satisfaction is more important than happiness," Wetatonmi went on, "and love is the only true danger their hearts cannot bear."

He raised a brow at her. "Danger? Do I put you at risk?"

She laughed easily. "Oh, yes, my love, you do."

"What do you fear?" he demanded.

"That you will not be here when this babe comes. I think he will be born at the end of the summer moons, and you are not always home from your travels by then."

"Who will?" He looked at her blankly.

"I am with child." He was a warrior, and he loved fiercely and well, but she knew he had not really noticed the vague change in her shape. She laughed again at his astounded expression.

"Come inside. I will show you."

Kiye Kipi rode into the hills, Wetatonmi's blanket snug about her shoulders, Old Joseph's crop secure in her belt. Occasionally, she reached a wind-chapped hand to it and stroked it gently.

She still did not have complete control over her magic. Even now, after so many seasons, it sneaked up on her sometimes when her defenses were down. She dreamed in her sleep when she was troubled or very, very tired. Sometimes she thought she would never be able to stop that from happening, but at least she had finally learned how to call more accurately a dream upon command, even when there was no moon.

It helped, she had learned, to have some piece, some tangible link, to join her with whatever it was she was calling . . . the hoof of a doe, the antler of an elk. In this case, because the mare had belonged to Old Joseph, she wrapped her hand around the small, precious proof of his memory as she dismounted.

"I will find her, friend," she vowed. Even if the pony was dead, it seemed somehow important that she pray her into the afterworld.

She stood in the snow and looked about. The mare could be anywhere. The hills and mountains were immense, their sheltered valleys endless. Who knew where the mare had finally lain down?

She sat on the damp, white blanket and laid the crop on her lap. She kept her hand tight about it, closed her eyes, and waited.

When her hair had gone as crusty and white as the country, the carved wood seemed to grow warm, then hot, beneath her touch.

Behind her eyes, colors blended and swirled and began throbbing into coherency.

When she had finally stopped feeling the cold, when it had sunk so deeply into her that it became a part of her, she found the pony. A moan of disbelief wrenched unconsciously from her throat. There was nothing in the Wallowa like the place she saw. How had the mare gone so far? Then she knew, with a jolt, with the small, still conscious part of her mind. The pony was old and sore-limbed and heavy with her babe. She had not gone far; she had been heading for home.

Kiye Kipi's moan escalated into a growl of fury. The vision fled into the wind with her voice. She blinked as she looked around, her sight clearing, her head hurting. But this time, her belly hurt worse, tight and clenching in on itself.

She had to get back to Joseph and tell him.

The mare had been trying to come back to the village, but she had stumbled into some other part of the valley instead. She had seen her, her butchered flesh bleeding red into the snow. No beast had gotten to her, no hungry wolf with feral teeth. Kiye Kipi could have stood that, could have borne it. That was the natural way of things.

Xayxayx were not.

She pulled herself back onto her own mare, her heart thundering, her skin crawling. She had seen the pony, and she had seen a lodge, and somehow, impossibly, that lodge had been in this Kahmuenem valley.

"You are sure?" Joseph asked, but there was no doubt in his voice, only a rare, deep anger. Kiye Kipi clutched Weta-tonmi's blanket about her, her belly twisting.

"How did the pony babe get away?" he went on, musing aloud.

"I did not see that part, nor do I know these *xayxayx* ways. But I think . . . they would have shooed him off to die in the cold. He has no meat on him. He was of no use to their gnawing, empty guts."

Wetatonmi and Alokot had rushed into the lodge as well, and now Wetatonmi gasped, horrified. "Why not just cut his throat then? Let him die quickly and kindly?"

"Because they are white men," Alokot snapped.

"Where?" Joseph asked her. "The Wallowa is vast."

Kiye Kipi bit her lip. "Close to the hills somewhere. They

are using them to block the worst of the winds from their lodge. I would guess the place is north of here, by the way the snow was falling.''

Joseph and Alokot exchanged looks. ''Was there water?'' Joseph asked.

''A frozen creek behind their shelter.'' She struggled to remember more than that, but she could not. Her horror at the vision had driven her out of it too quickly for her to recall myriad little details.

''I think I know where they are,'' said Alokot.

Joseph nodded. ''Yes. Yellow Snake Swale.''

Kiye Kipi understood. It was a fertile grazing area where the ponies often went when they were free in the hills during the cold moons. Tough, dry grass could often be found there even beneath the snows. The place was the northernmost, easternmost part of Kahmuenem country, the land that most closely touched Toolhoolhoolzote's country.

And Toolhoolhoolzote had been fighting the *xayxayx* invasion for a very long time.

Her blood chilled. ''Would that *tiwats* headman have sent them into our country?''

Alokot's eyes narrowed. ''He is strong, but he can be a selfish, hard man. I do not think he would care where those white-skins moved on to, as long as he drove them out of his own land.''

Joseph, ever peaceable, shook his head. ''We have no proof of that. We cannot talk ill of him. His Pikunanmu are Dreamer kin.''

And my kin, Kiye Kipi thought with a bitter jolt. No, she had no true blood kin, only these people who were dear and closest to her heart.

''Perhaps these *xayxayx* wandered here of their own accord,'' Wetatonmi ventured.

''That is possible too,'' Alokot allowed. Tahmahnewes knew their numbers had grown enough over the seasons; they spawned like mongrels, he thought viciously. But none had trespassed upon Kahmuenem land until now.

He thought of his father's dying words, the ones their pony

wife had always insisted were a truth of the future. He glanced unintentionally at Kiye Kipi, and realized that she was remembering, too.

"What can we do?" she asked. *They had promised.* They had promised Old Joseph that no white-skins would come here to his land!

"It does no good to speak to their agent man," Joseph answered. "Five *xayxayx* possess far more influence than five hundred Nimipu. Our father learned that."

"Perhaps it is time to kill the ones who dare to come here," Alokot said tightly.

"And in doing so declare war against all their nation?"

"Surely you cannot mean to let them stay!" Kiye Kipi gasped.

"No," Joseph said quietly. "I mean to remove them myself."

"How?"

"Reason."

"And if that does not work?" Alokot demanded.

"Then we will see, brother. I think talking to them will be only the start."

They left camp with the next sun, Joseph and Burned Tree, Alokot, and a contingent of ten warriors. The women watched from their lodges as the men gathered their ponies. Their eyes were wide. They had known hunger, had seen war parties lost to Shoshone, had grieved and buried their dearest dead. They had survived it all, yet Kiye Kipi saw now that these *xayxayx* in their country was a problem that mystified and frightened them as nothing else could.

A babe, feeling his mother's tension, began to wail. Kiye Kipi made a decision and went to Joseph.

"I would join you."

He raised a brow. "Your magic is not necessary on this trip."

"Look at the women of your people," she pleaded. "Their men will go off to encounter an unpredictable enemy they are not permitted to fight in any usual way. Who knows how much their husbands will tell them when they return? You know warriors do that; they shield the mothers of their babes, and they do not always notice the things women care about. Let me go so that they have one of their own to bring back to them what they need to know.''

He looked at the women, and she thought of Old Joseph. She had to go. She had promised him. Her pulse skipped as she waited for an answer.

Dirty Dove brought her pony to her. Kiye Kipi took the reins and wondered what Joseph would do if she simply mounted.

She wanted to go on this mission. She *needed* to, for her own heart.

She pushed one last time. "Perhaps they have some of our other ponies as well," she pointed out. "I would not like to see a good stud used for food."

"No," Joseph agreed flatly, and finally nodded. She smiled, but she did not thank him.

She swung up on her mare, and the party headed north. It would be a long ride, and she saw that many, many of them rode the long-winded ponies she had bred. She rode to the front, beside Joseph and Alokot, to help lead the way. They thought her vision had come from Yellow Snake Swale, but she would not be sure until she saw the terrain herself.

They came upon it at the end of the sun, and there were three lodges there.

Three? She looked at the men. But she knew this was it, because the nearest shelter looked the same. The others were farther up in the hills; that was how she had missed them.

The wind and the snow had assaulted the spot where the mare had died, whipping the bloody crystals about, covering them with fresh white. Still, she could see it, a vague, red-brown shadow flung over the land in front of that first *xayxayx* lodge.

A keening sound of fury worked up in her throat. She had been right. There were a handful of other ponies in a corral against the hills, and they were Nimipu.

She jerked her mare toward them. Earth Sound was beside her in a moment.

"What do you do?" he demanded.

She turned on him, a fierce heat burning in her eyes. "They will not have them," she breathed. "What makes them believe they can steal because their skin is white?"

"Wait," Alokot snapped. "Do not upset things before Joseph talks."

She looked back, and her heart thumped harder. A soldier came out of the lodge to meet them.

A soldier in Kahmuenem? *What was happening here?*

There were others, too: one of those trapper men she remembered seeing at the council long ago who talked two tongues, two women dressed in their flimsy, whipping *xayxayx* skirts. Five men stood clutching rifles like those the warriors possessed. But these did not gleam dully like the ones the Nimipu polished and rubbed so lovingly. These caught the struggling sun and winked with it; she knew without being told that they were new and strong.

She had known hatred for Wahlitits, but now loathing filled her throat with a whole different ferocity. What were these people? They had taken her ponies, helped themselves to Nimipu land, and now they were armed as though to kill for it!

The soldier talked, and the trapper man translated into a garbled version of the Nimipu tongue. Kiye Kipi had to struggle to understand him.

"You have saved us a trip," he said. "We were on our way to your camp to meet with your people."

Joseph nudged his pony closer. "I hope you would tell us that you have come to remove these men."

Both the soldier and the trapper looked nonplussed. "We're here to tell you that the time has come to move onto the reservation. Your horses are trespassing on these settlers' land."

Trespassing? Kiye Kipi choked. They had *taken* them!

"It is your white men who are trespassing," Joseph pointed out calmly. "We have come to instruct them to go."

"*You* must go."

Her head started pounding. What impossible thing were they

saying? She had never known such atrocious arrogance before.

"No Indians are supposed to be in this country," the soldier reminded them. "You are not to interfere with its settlement. There was a treaty to that effect in '63."

"That was not our treaty. Our father did not sign."

"It was signed, and it is valid," the soldier said stubbornly. "I have a copy of it here."

"It does not pertain to our land. This is Kahmuenem, and Kahmuenem is ours."

The soldier began to look apoplectic. "I have been sent to instruct you that your people should join Lawyer on the reservation by April the first. We have been lenient with you so far because no one has wished to settle here. Now that has changed."

"I will not give you my father's land," Joseph said, turning away.

"April the first!" the soldier shouted after him. Kiye Kipi did not understand his words, but she knew the threat in them, and she saw Joseph did as well.

"I will be there," he answered grimly in his own tongue.

Kiye Kipi gave a small sound of anguish as they rode away from her trapped ponies. There was no help for it. The *xayxayx* men were guarding the corral now with their shiny new guns.

THE MEN TRAVELED to Lapwai with the next moon. No one offered any argument this time when Kiye Kipi rode with them.

The council place was much as she remembered it, but the wooden white-skin lodges were more numerous now, raping more of the land. They crawled over the prairie like ugly, weathered, gray insects.

Unbidden, Kiye Kipi thought of Twelic again when she saw it. She thought of the restless wind that he chased so hungrily. In that moment, if only for that moment, she understood. She felt trapped here, as though she could not fully get her breath. Joseph sat on his blanket, with Alokot and Burned Tree flanking him, but she could not sit. Her blood seemed to itch as it moved through her.

She especially did not like the white-skin who began the talk. He was not a soldier, she decided. He wore black *xayxayx* clothing, slender and tight against his tall, angular frame. His eyes were dark and somehow too bright. As he watched her come up to stand behind the others, her heart seemed to leap in a tangle of fear and anger. His gaze was bad.

"Where are the rest of your people?" he began without preamble, his eyes moving over the small knot of Kahmuenem warriors. Not even a foolish white-skin could mistake them for an entire band, and another man, nearly red skinned, looked smug as he translated.

"They remain in our home," Joseph replied blandly.

"Your home is here now. Beginning today."

"No. It is not."

"I have orders from the Great Chief in Washington that you should come onto the reservation now. Enough years have passed for you to prepare."

Joseph shrugged. "There is only one Great Chief, and he dwells in the sky. He has told me nothing like that."

Kiye Kipi's mouth twitched in a grin. She had lived beside this man for seasons, had followed him through the last few. She had always respected his remote intelligence, but now something strong and proud leaped in her breast at his smooth, relentless logic as well.

"*I* am telling you," the man answered, then he added pompously, "My name is Monteith. I'm your agent. I have the authority."

"You think your white chiefs give you authority," Joseph argued. "But they have no right to come here and take our country. The Kahmuenem have never accepted any presents from your government."

"Lawyer has," Monteith snapped.

"That is Lawyer. He cannot sell my land. It has always belonged to my people. It came unclouded from our fathers, and we will defend it as long as a drop of Nimipu blood warms the hearts of our men."

"You're saying you'll fight, then?" He looked avid, Kiye Kipi thought, feeling her blood chill. He looked as though he wanted to fight. Perhaps that was the way of these *xayxayx* men, too.

"I am saying," Joseph answered patiently, "that we will defend it. We will not leave it.

"You say that Lawyer gave it to you. I am telling you that he has deceived you. He is separate from our people, no longer part of the Nimipu Dreamers. You have your treaty with him, not with us, and as such it does not affect our Kahmuenem country. If ever we owned it, we own it still, for my father never sold it.

"Suppose a white man should come to me and say, 'Joseph, I like your horses, and I want to buy them.' I say to him, 'No, my horses suit me, I will not sell them.' Then he goes to my neighbor, and he says to him, 'Joseph has got some good horses. I want to buy them, but he refuses to sell.' My neighbor answers, 'Pay me the money, and I will sell you Joseph's horses.' The white man returns to me and says, 'Joseph, I have bought your horses, and you must let me have them.' If ever we sold our lands to the government, that is the shameful way in which they were bought. Is that the way your people do things? Is that the way they deal with each other?''

Monteith's jaw went hard and his face reddened, but another man, standing close to him, looked thoughtful. Finally, a wry smile touched that one's mouth.

"It is difficult to argue with that," he observed quietly.

He looked to Joseph. "I don't suppose it would affect your opinion to know that Agent Monteith wishes to support you here at Lapwai until your people learn our ways? That it is in the best interest of you and your children to learn to adjust? As you have been told before, we cannot keep the white men from coming here, no matter what others have promised you long ago. You will have to learn to live among them."

Joseph cocked his head. "Who are you?"

"Commissioner Odeneal. I am in charge of Indian Affairs."

"You have authority over this other man, then?"

Odeneal nodded, looking at Monteith, and the agent's face reddened.

"Then perhaps you will explain to him that we do not need his help. My people have plenty, and we are content and happy if you will leave us alone. I will tell you something that might help you. Your reservation is too small for all the Nimipu and their stock. You would be better off keeping your presents. I do not know how Toolhoolhoolzote and White Bird fare, but my Kahmuenem can go to town near here and pay for all we need. We have plenty of horses to sell, and we will not have any help from you. We are free now. We can go where we please, and that is the way we will remain." He stood again with aristocratic composure. "Our fathers were born in Kahmuenem. There they died. There are their graves. We will never leave them."

Kiye Kipi watched the men called Monteith and Odeneal put their heads together. Her heart kicked a bit when Odeneal looked up again.

"Your agent feels that the strongest deterrent to you remaining in your own country is that you Dreamers seriously interfere with his efforts to civilize Lawyer's treaty Indians."

Joseph shrugged. "We no longer have anything to do with that band."

"Be that as it may, your men travel to buffalo country, and Agent Monteith says this creates a stir among the stabilized Indians to return to a nomadic way of life."

Joseph gave him a chastising look, as though he were a small child. "Of course it does. Is not freedom of movement a natural urge among all men?"

"What are you saying?" Monteith asked angrily.

"I am telling you that we would not have this problem if your white men had not given in to that same urge. Their own wanderlust has led them from your country into mine."

To Kiye Kipi's amazement, the more important man laughed. Huge guffaws took him as he shook his head from side to side. Finally, he cleared his throat.

"Should you ever get tired of leading your tribe, Mr. Joseph, I am sure we can find a place for you among the Washington bureaucracy.

"You present several good arguments," Odeneal went on, then he looked to Monteith. "The truth of the matter remains that only a few settlers live anywhere near the Wallowa valley. Am I correct?"

"They have first rights to it," Monteith answered, tight-lipped.

"That is a gray area, at best." Odeneal thought. "I am willing to recommend that they not be allowed to encroach any farther. We can set aside this Kahmuenem place for Joseph's band."

"You're letting him win, sir!" Monteith burst out.

"Is there a problem with that?"

"He's an *Indian*!"

"So he is. Mr. Joseph, would this solution appeal to you?"

Joseph watched him evenly. "I want my land. I do not wish to be confined upon it, beholden to white authority."

"Well, that may be a little more difficult to arrange. However, we can start by marking your country off as your own. Thank you for your time. If you'll wait just a moment longer, I'll bring papers back for you to sign."

The warriors waited for Odeneal to come back while the sun grew low. Kiye Kipi hugged herself in the freshening twilight wind, and her gaze moved to the *xayxayx* corral. Joseph had promised that the Nimipu would fight for their country. Sweet Tahmahnewes, what if it came to that? Her belly flopped over.

If it came to that, she thought, then their ponies would have to take the People to the Safe Place.

She jerked as though someone had slapped her. It had been so long since she had thought of her whole *wyakin* dream, of the secret part she had never told anyone! Slowly, almost of their own volition, her feet took her to the *xayxayx* horses.

The soldiers there eyed her distrustfully. She was startled at their mean gazes, then, in spite of herself, she laughed. What did they think? Only white-skins claimed things that did not belong to them.

One soldier rushed at her suddenly, trying to grab her arm. She jerked it back, out of his range, and managed to hook one moccasin over the lowest fence wrung. She snarled at him as her eyes swept the corral hungrily. *What?* She did not truly know what it was she was looking for. It was just that some instinct told her only that she needed to know if these ponies were better than hers.

The soldier man toppled her, his hands hard and grasping in her hair. Hurt tugged over her scalp and her skin itched dirtily at his touch. She turned on him viciously.

"Do not touch me with your thieving hands!"

He seemed frightened enough that she was startled. Did he fear *her*? It did not matter. In that short glimpse, she had found what she needed to know.

25

"HOW MANY DID we lose to them?" Alokot asked her.

Kiye Kipi looked at him, then she shook her head sadly and glanced ahead to the herd they were driving toward Imnaha.

"Four hands."

She knew it could have been worse. The Kahmuenem herds numbered in the thousands, and twenty ponies was not a significant loss, at least not to anyone but herself, but her heart twisted in grief for the ones who were gone.

When she remembered Lapwai, she knew fear as well. The Nimipu herds were the Peoples' strength.

She looked to Alokot again. "I would like to speak in a council," she said abruptly. "Could I do such a thing?"

His handsome jaw dropped. "Is it about the ponies?" he managed finally.

"Yes."

"I will ask Joseph."

She nodded, knowing she had to be satisfied with that. "When are you going to buffalo country?"

"As soon as we settle in at Imnaha. With tomorrow's sun, or perhaps with the next one."

"Then I should speak to the warriors tonight."

He frowned at her thoughtfully before he nodded.

Joseph sent for her as the moon rose. She had been standing in front of her lodge, her hands clasped tightly in front of her as she watched his outside fire. She willed him to bend,

silently pleading with him to call her. Then she saw a boy
leave the men who had gathered there and move toward her
lodge.

At once, her heart quailed. *What was she doing?*

She could not ever remember a woman talking in council
before. How could she stand in front of all those hard-eyed
warriors and presume to tell them what to do? But she had to,
because the truth in her heart would not go away. Perhaps they
would raise brows and snap doubts at her, but she was not an
unwanted orphan anymore. She was their pony wife and she
had never failed them.

She followed the boy warrior to the council fire, then she
felt another jolt. The orange light hurled fearful shadows at
the men's faces, over their strong noses and pensive expres-
sions. Even Alokot looked somehow cruel and forbidding.

She brought her chin up and measured them with her strange
indigo eyes. "I have come to tell you that I think we must
make more ugly ponies."

Her announcement was greeted by an uproarious sound of
disbelief.

"Have the others served you well so far?" she demanded
with more confidence than she felt.

"We have all we need to hunt with!" someone shouted.

"We would not use them for hunting," she answered. "We
would use them for fighting."

She had thought and thought, and had planned those words
carefully. There was nothing more vital to their interests than
the coups of war.

She thought again of the big, rangy ponies she had glimpsed
so briefly at Lapwai. She looked at Joseph. "You told those
xayxayx at the fort that we will defend this land as long as
Nimipu blood warms our hearts. If that ever happens, many
of the ponies we have now are unprepared for the challenge."

There came another great crescendo of outrage. "It is true!"
she shouted, to be heard above them. "When we went to Lapwai, I saw things about the white-skin horses that disturb me.

"Listen," she urged, and finally they did, though many still seemed disgruntled. "The first thing I noticed is that they are fed seeds as well as grass."

"That is not new," someone argued. "We have always known that."

"But have you thought how it would keep them from chasing our ponies? Their horses will not last long away from their corrals and this strange diet. When a pony is fed something new—even different grass—he will usually become quite ill in his belly. You have seen it happen, when they roll and roll in pain. I have thought a great deal about this. If the *xayxayx* were to chase us, they would have to carry their special pony seeds with them, and how much of this could they pack? Or they would have to keep stopping to change their horses for fresh ones. That would keep them from catching us."

"Our warriors do not run," someone growled.

"Every man here has family."

She thought of her *wyakin* dream again. There had indeed been fighting, but the women and the babes had fled on the ponies.

She went on more stubbornly. "I also saw that those white-skin horses wear some strange metal on their feet. I do not know why anyone would want to do this to an animal's hooves. Perhaps there is some advantage that I cannot see. But I know one thing—those ponies would have a very hard time climbing through our Nimipu mountains. Tahmahnewes made our ponies' hooves tough and tractable to handle this country. Those *xayxayx* ponies will slip and slide to their deaths, I think."

"All this is true," said Alokot, "but what has it to do with making more ugly horses?"

She bit her lip. "If there is fighting, I think our ponies are stronger than theirs in those ways I have just said. But there is one other thing that troubles me. The *xayxayx* horses come in all shapes and colors. They are not inbred like ours are, and they appear quite hardy. They have very deep chests and strong legs. In close fighting, on flat land, they could be stronger.

"We use the same choice stallions again and again when

we breed. Sometimes they are even put with their daughters and mothers. We use the ones with the best colors, and the studs that I have made for hunting ponies, and sometimes we cross them together. Some are beautiful, and some are long winded, but all of them are small. We need to make some war mounts with those long legs that the *xayxayx* horses have, and with the same deep chests. I think you should go over the farthest mountains when you go east this season, and bring back some big, strong ponies regardless of their color.''

Joseph cleared his throat. ''It would hurt our trading badly. We need spotted ponies for wealth.''

''No.'' She shook her head. ''I have thought of that, and I am not saying we should use our spotted mares and studs for this effort. It takes a whole circle of seasons for a mare to birth a babe. If we used the colorful mares to make the war ponies, then I agree that our trade herds would suffer in number. The ones with the silver stars and blankets should breed together, I think. What I am asking for are *new* ponies, so we have more foals dropping next season than we have ever had before. I would cross them only with the hunting stock.''

She waited for arguments, but she knew there was no true disadvantage to her theory, and her blood pumped.

Finally, one warrior nodded. ''I will try it. I see no harm in it.''

Another agreed. ''If our hunting mares are heavy with babes over the snow season, it does not matter. We do not use them much then anyway.''

Someone else laughed. ''If it does not work, we can feed them seeds, paint their hooves silver, and trade them to the *xayxayx*.''

She had done it. She had talked them into it.

''Remember,'' she cautioned, ''the ones you bring back should have those long legs and they should measure far from their withers to their chests. That is the important thing, or this will not work.''

''They should be ugly,'' someone agreed, and there was more laughter. Only Earth Sound spoke with a distinct lack of humor.

"You will not be going east with us then, to help choose these ponies yourself?"

Her heart thumped. "No," she answered quietly. "I think I am needed more here."

"What could be more important than leading us to the buffalo?" he demanded.

Those squat little white-skin cabins in Yellow Snake. No other but she could make sure no more ponies fell to them. Only she could see them without going among those men who had settled there.

"I can dream from here," she explained. "I will do it before you go, and tell you where I think the buffalo can be found." She had done it before, the last two seasons since her only ride to the east.

Was she being a coward? For a moment, she struggled with herself, remembering an icy cold creek and the sun baking down upon it, as warm as the hands of the man who had touched her.

She could not go back to that place.

"I will dream tonight," she promised Alokot. "I will tell you what I see in the morning."

The hunters were already mounted when she sought him out. The sun was new in the valley, pale and yellow as it could only be early in the season. Kiye Kipi left the hills and walked back into the camp, the cool wind tickling her skin. She felt cold both inside and out.

She stopped beside Alokot's pony. "You will have to go over the farthest mountains anyway," she said quietly. "That is where you will find the buffalo, as well as the ponies I need."

His jaw tightened in concern. "You say they are in Sioux country?"

"What is left of them," she answered. "There are none left in the Big Hole valley at all."

The hunters stayed away through the whole long, hot season. Panic clawed in her belly whenever she thought of how

far away the *xayxayx* had driven the quarry. Wetatonmi badgered her about it, wanting to know what was keeping them.

They walked toward the herd through the high grass. It
swished about them, thick and golden with the late summer
sun. Insects droned from within its tangles, and the land
smelled dry and dusty and warm.

"Alokot will not be back before this babe pushes out, will
he?" Wetatonmi demanded.

Kiye Kipi looked at her friend's belly, so big and swollen
now. "I do not know," she admitted. "I know pony babes,
but not much about real ones."

"Swinging Tree says I am close."

That midwife was never wrong, Kiye Kipi knew, but she
only shrugged.

"My husband is not close," Wetatonmi went on.

"No, I do not think so."

"You do not know real babes, but you know why our men
are gone so long, and it is not just because you asked them to
bring back those ponies."

Kiye Kipi chewed her lip and sat down in the grass. "We
can watch from here," she said finally.

"For the hunters?"

"No." She would not talk about that. The warriors would
have to ride far, but she was sure they would find the buffalo.
They had to. She did not want to alarm the others before it
was necessary.

"I want to see if any of these mares have not gotten caught
with babes yet," she said instead.

She had bred the spotted ponies among each other, just as
she had promised Joseph she would. Now she watched them
graze, her critical gaze singling out hundreds upon hundreds
of them, then moving on. She found only a few who appeared
not to have taken.

"How can you tell?" Wetatonmi asked.

"They still tease the stallions. Watch."

Most of the mares pinned their ears and bared their teeth
when the males approached them. They were full as Tahmahnewes intended them to be, and had no more use for the studs'

courting rituals. If only we could be the same way, she thought. If only we could stop wanting what we do not need.

Do not think about it. Do not.

She recoiled from the memories and pointed to a younger filly who was flagging her tail at a stallion and winking her vulva. "That one is empty. She still tries to lure him. Perhaps she was not yet mature enough to mate at the beginning of the season."

She stood again, whistling to her own mare. Now it was a simple matter of cutting the barren ones from the herd. She would put them in the corral with a stallion, confining them all so that they could not be distracted from their purpose. Those who were just cantankerous would be overpowered by the male's superior strength. She shuddered at that, but there was no help for it. Some would just not take, no matter what, and they would be traded away next season.

Her gray mare came to her and she pulled herself up on her, riding into the herd. Then her eyes went to the eastern horizon, and she went still.

"What is it?" Wetatonmi demanded.

"They return." The hunters were back, and it had not taken them all that long after all.

Wetatonmi squealed a sound of relief and delight. She pushed her cumbersome weight to her feet again and began running toward the men in a slow, trundling gait. Kiye Kipi followed more closely, searching, studying them. . . .

They drove many riderless ponies. And at least some of them carried meat.

They would have at least one more season then, another cold time before their bellies cramped with too much emptiness.

The other squaws dropped their work to crowd together at the edge of camp. Boys ran out onto the plain, and the younger babes squealed at their mothers' obvious excitement. The women called provocative greetings to their mates, and the men laughed as they got closer.

Kiye Kipi's eyes left the fruits of their hunting. Suddenly, she was far more interested in the ponies they had brought.

She rode to them, grinning as she cut those animals away who did not carry burdens.

They were coarse, rangy beasts. The warriors watched her, their brows raised dubiously. Kiye Kipi laughed. To her, they were strong and beautiful.

She drove them into another corral to wait for the hunting ponies that would breed them, then she turned back. The rest of the work could wait until after the excitement of this feast. Her own belly growled hungrily in anticipation; it had not truly felt full all summer. Then her eyes fell on Alokot.

He led an unencumbered pony of his own, but this one reared and plunged angrily at the other end of his rope. Suddenly, her heart beat so hard with premonition she felt faint.

She slid weakly to the ground again, eyeing him.

The pony was a stallion, and not like the others. He was not big or rough looking in his strength. His eyes were sharp and intelligent and full of fire, and he was black, solid black, glistening in the sun as though that orb had somehow touched the night. He was as small boned as the first white-gray one she had used long ago to start making the hunting ponies, the one she had told Twelic about.

Alokot rode to her and handed her the rope.

"I . . . no. He is yours," she protested, but she knew it was not true.

"We saw a Hasotoin party in Sioux country," Alokot said, watching her closely. "The warrior Twelic sent this one back for you. He says it is as he once promised, and that you would understand."

Her heart began feeling sick.

She wanted to turn away from the stallion, to scorn him, wanted it with every thudding beat of her pulse. But she could not. Because suddenly her *wyakin* dream was back with her again, those long-neglected pieces of it that belonged to her alone. She knew, in her heart, that he would sire that black mare. With the other big ponies the warriors had brought back, he would make the babes that were what she was looking for, babes that would grow up to best any animal the *xayxayx* could produce.

He knew. Somehow, Twelic knew her wyakin *dream.*

She cursed him and hated him, and felt her heart roll over with a longing she needed desperately to forget.

He did not want her. He wanted the wind.

She had finally learned peace. Why would he not let her forget the sunshine?

26

Khoy-tsahl, Moon of the Blueback Salmon, 1875

SHE HAD NOT smelled the pervasive odor of baking salmon in so long it seemed almost strange to her, like a memory of something that had not really happened.

Kiye Kipi put her face into the wind as she stood at the edge of the big communal camp. It carried the aromas of hundreds of cook fires where the fish were tucked into beds of embers, but there was a lingering odor of sickness in the air as well. Many of the People suffered from runny bowels and cramping guts. Burned Tree said it was because they were no longer eating the rich, heavy meat they had gotten so used to over the last seasons.

But there was no more meat.

She heard an elder groan wretchedly, and she shivered with a cold feeling. There had been no buffalo last season, and this summer Alokot had not even gone to the grasslands. Unlike the Sioux and the Crow who claimed that country, the Nez Percé hunters were not familiar enough with the distant prairie to ferret out the few herds that were left. Nor were the plains peoples willing to share any longer. Any attempts at hunting lately had been met with war.

Kiye Kipi stood on tiptoe to look about at all the other bands that had gathered, returning to the lakes for sustenance. Did they remember that old prophet Smoholla? He had warned them once that badness would happen if they abandoned their own ways.

She pushed the trouble from her mind and tossed her hair

back over her shoulders with a shake of her head. She went out toward the herd. She kept her eyes straight ahead as she trod the crushed-grass path of many other feet, but no one whispered about her or threw taunts at her this time. Those who knew her would not dare to speculate over anything but perhaps the wonder that she had seen twenty snows and had never mated. Few of the other bands would remember her, she thought. She was just another strange face to them; the Dreamers had not all gathered together in a very long time, and many who were children then had been forgotten.

The ponies jostled around her, and she pushed through them to those that belonged to the Kahmuenem. They were not difficult to spot; among them were hundreds of sleek, black yearlings.

Kiye Kipi thought fleetingly of the stallion who had sired them all. She had left that haughty, unruly beast back at Imnaha. She had never warmed to him; each glance into his intelligent eyes remained a piercing memory of stupid innocence and hope. She thought that he somehow knew that she both hated him and admired him . . . much like the warrior who had taunted her by sending him.

Where was Twelic?

She closed her eyes and fought the urge to look around again. The Hasotoin had not arrived yet, but he would be with them this season. Somehow, she was sure of it.

She wished again, more than anything, that she had not come to this place with the rest of the Kahmuenem.

A black filly nudged her; she sighed and looped her arm about the pony's neck. She had come because of these new yearlings, and she would stay until she saw her work done.

She rubbed her forehead against the pony's, and a strange shimmy of fear and elation worked through her. She had known, from the moment she had helped to birth this one, that she was the mare in her *wyakin* vision. She had known it as soon as she looked into her big, dark eyes.

"Pony Wife?"

Kiye Kipi started and stepped away, scanning the falling darkness to find the person who had called her. A young warrior moved into the herd, lanky and tall, perhaps of sixteen or seventeen snows. He grinned shyly yet somehow rakishly when he reached her.

"They said you were beautiful and that you could be found here."

Kiye Kipi felt her skin heat. *A man would be a fool to turn away from you because you are shrewd as well as beautiful.*

She must stop thinking of him!

She looked more closely at the youth. "Who are you?"

"Seven Knives, of the Pikunanmu."

Her heart gave a little kick. *Toolhoolhoolzote's people.* Her mother's people, her own.

"What do you want with me?"

"Our *tiwats* headman would see you."

"He has never wished to see me before," she snapped.

Seven Knives looked baffled. She shook her head, her long hair swimming at her waist.

"Never mind. Go away."

She moved back toward the camp path. He called out from behind her.

"But—I cannot! He has heard of these black colts you breed! He has sent me to get you, to bring several of them to his camp to trade."

The colts. Of course he would have heard of them. Many had sent word to the Wallowa that they wanted some, and the Kahmuenem warriors had entrusted her to trade a portion of them away. Their blood would have to be added to the other bands' herds judiciously; she would have to tell the warriors how to breed them to get the war horses they coveted.

She had never considered that Toolhoolhoolzote himself might want some.

Did he even know who she was?

"You can tell your headman to meet me here with the first sun tomorrow," she answered levelly. "Then I will show him whatever ponies he wishes to see."

"He would see them now."

"That is not possible."

Seven Knives's jaw dropped incredulously. "You would defy him?"

She would, for her ponies . . . and for herself. Suddenly, something cold filled her, something hard and angry and strong that had been waiting twenty snows for this time. She had thought often of meeting with Twelic again on this prairie, but she had given no thought to this man who was her grandfather. Now he would call her, finally, when she no longer needed him.

She no longer needed either of them, she reminded herself.

Her chin came up. "The colts' worth is in their speed and strength and endurance," she told the warrior. "I will not run them in this darkness for him to see those gifts. It would be dangerous for them. Please tell your *tiwats* to meet me at the dawn."

She watched the sun come again through her smoke hole. The sky turned indigo-gray, then smoky blue, as dawn came.

Would he come? Would he actually obey her impertinent dictate and come to her?

He would if he wanted the ponies. She knew little enough of Toolhoolhoolzote, but she had heard that he did not like anyone to have anything that he himself did not possess.

So finally, finally, she would meet him. Her belly rolled over with a sick feeling, and she got up.

Suddenly, from the lodge closest to hers, came the muffled squall of a babe crying. It was Wetatonmi's new boy child, Little Mole. She closed her eyes. Her life was good and full and burgeoning now. Nothing Toolhoolhoolzote might say or do could hurt her.

She brushed her hair, splashing lukewarm water on her face and scrubbing herself with it until she felt good and fresh. Then she shook our her best doeskin, the one with the elks' teeth, and slipped it over her head. The teeth were the same ones from her twelfth summer, though the soft, tanned hide had changed innumerable times.

She went outside, looked toward the herd, and saw that Toolhoolhoolzote waited for her.

She curled her hands into fists. As she drew closer to him, she saw with a jolt that he did not have good eyes. They contained more than just anger at the affront she had shown him. This was a man who had a strong thirst for power; to him, it was more precious than any kin or any of the goodness Tahmahnewes showered upon His People. In defying him, she had usurped that.

"You have much pride for a squaw who needs to sell ponies," he snapped when she reached him. "I should chastise you."

His voice was dry and scratchy, and she realized his age for the first time. He was an immense man, as big and as wide as two, but with muscle, not fat. In spite of that, he had probably seen close to sixty snow seasons.

"But you will not," she answered quietly. "You need something from me now."

"Now?" His big face creased angrily.

He did not know.

"I am Vixen's daughter."

His eyes narrowed at the name of his kin. Then she supposed he remembered the babe that woman had borne, because he moved suddenly closer to inspect her.

"You?"

"You need not fear. I do not wish to return to your hearth."

He drew himself up. She did the same.

"Your mother did not respect her elders, either," he growled.

"I respected Old Joseph greatly. He raised me."

"You lie. Vixen and her mongrel mate went to the Hasotoin."

"Then how is it that I am Kahmuenem?"

A shrewd light touched his eyes. "You are Pikunanmu."

She tried to swallow the bitter laughter that welled in her throat, but it escaped until it got healthier, big enough to hurt her chest.

Pikunanmu. No. Nor was she Hasotoin either; her heart had belonged to those people, but she had never truly been accepted among them. For the first time, she understood Broken

Bird's gift in sending her away, and her heart felt so good and full with it, it almost hurt.

"They say you have great power," Toolhoolhoolzote mused. "I have heard that it is so strong it sometimes gets away from you when you sleep."

So strong? Now, finally, his words struck deep within her. Her eyes flew up to him again.

Was he saying it was a *good* thing that she dreamed when she did not mean to?

He would not placate her with something like that; he would resent it.

He was the strongest caller of all of them. He would know.

So strong. So strong that it pulled away from her when she did not expect it, strong enough that she did not always have to hunt for it. Her pulse began scrambling hard. She felt her last, deepest fear lift from her, float free of her chest, and oh, how she could breathe, how good she felt without it!

"That is true," she managed. "Yes, that sometimes happens."

"The Pikunanmu would be a mighty band if you joined with me. We are kin. We should guide our people together."

"No." She walked into the herd, leaving him. The ponies nickered to her.

She looked at her black filly. *Run.*

The pony plunged and reared, then began to gallop.

It was easy; oh, it was so easy now, at least with that one special foal! Soon they were all following the black filly, all the yearlings, bucking, surging, flying across the land. Her heart pumped fiercely with the beauty, the strength of them.

She turned back to the old *tiwats*. "You may have five of them because you are a headman. You are wrong. I do not *need* to sell them. Every man wants one, so there must be enough to go around, enough that their blood will blend through all the Nimipu bands."

Toolhoolhoolzote was silent for a long time, then he seemed to ignore what she had said, what she had done.

"You do not wish to work with me at my hearth?" he demanded.

"I wanted your hearth once, your shelter. Now I would be cold there."

"I ask you to come back." She saw that he could not truly believe she was denying him.

"No," she answered. "You ask me to give you the benefit of my ponies and my magic. There is a difference."

His gaze turned furious, his face mottled. "Your mother was a fool as well. She could have had power, but she made all the wrong choices."

"Then I am not like her. I have made the right one."

She turned back and whistled to the ponies. They broke to a canter, swung around, and returned to the rest of the herd.

"I am sorry I cannot help you." And she was, vaguely. She had heard that Toolhoolhoolzote had fine mares. It would have been good for some of the black ponies to go there.

"I will take the five of them," he snarled.

Surprised, she looked to him and waited.

He picked them out, thrusting a gnarly finger at each of those he would choose. Whatever else he was, he was pony-wise and covetous. He would not spurn the chance to own these beasts, and he opted for the best of them.

"I want five of their babes each," she said. "That is what I will trade for, and an additional bearskin for that last one." He was the strongest colt of the lot, almost as good as his sire.

"You will have those things," Toolhoolhoolzote said tightly. "And a curse upon your head for spurning your kin."

Once again, she surprised herself by laughing. "I think that curse landed upon me twenty snows ago, *tiwats*. I have already survived it more than you could know."

Kiye Kipi went to the ponies early again the next sun. Several more warriors had asked to see the blacks.

"Five foals in exchange?" one asked. "Your price is high."

"Ask our headmen. They are worth it." White Bird and Huishuis Kute had taken some by now as well.

"We will talk about this and return to your hearth later."

She nodded amicably. She knew they would give her what she wanted . . . if there were any ponies left to trade for. Soon they would all be gone and she could finally go home, back to the Imnaha. Suddenly, she felt very, very tired.

She turned away just as a churning cloud of movement and dust caught her eye on the horizon. She went still, staring, her breath half in her chest and half out.

It could be the Hasotoin arriving.

For a moment, she dared to hope that she was wrong. The hot wind buffeted her, insects tickled her bare ankles, and her black filly came to nudge her with her soft nose. Still, she stood unmoving until the new band got closer. She could not pick out the gnarled Old Looking Glass riding at the front of them. Perhaps she was mistaken. Then the sun glinted off a piece of mirror, and she knew that she was not.

Young Looking Glass wore the magic piece now.

So his father was gone as well.

She felt no grief. She had never truly known him, despite living so close to his hearth. Her gaze moved past his son with his weak chin and fallow eyes, and staggered over Culmuh and Broken Bird. So old now! Still, she searched, not wanting to, unable to help herself.

Twelic came in over a far hill, away from the others, and her throat tightened. Of course. He would have peeled off from the band to hunt.

He galloped closer.

He was everything she remembered, arrogant, lean, and strong. His chest was bare in the heat, his hair whipping free and tangled in the wind. Nothing had changed, except perhaps that she had. Her heart squeezed once, hard, within her, then it went as perfectly still and cold as the snows that came each winter to blanket Wallowa.

No more. Never again. She would not let him touch her heart again.

She turned away, and Twelic felt his own breath break harshly from his chest as she went.

She walked with one arm looped gently around the neck of a black pony, and she looked both proud and lonely in a way that was uniquely hers. Desire and panic clamored up in him again at the *sense* of her. He reined in, jolted by her rude withdrawal, then he understood.

He had lost her finally, had lost the childlike devotion and wide-eyed trust, and all the warmth of the woman. His peace offering of the stallion had not made any difference.

He still could not understand his compulsion to send it to her, except that for some reason, as soon as he had seen him, he had remembered his promise to her, his wager . . . except that the hurt in her eyes, as he had left her on that distant prairie, had refused to leave him through all the seasons.

He thought he heard Tahmahnewes laughing.

The black pony went with her, catching his attention again. His eyes moved to it and riveted upon it as it tossed its head, its long, black mane streaming.

Suddenly, he lost his breath completely.

Perhaps he had known it from the moment he had promised her that horse, from the first time he had wanted her so inexplicably and in so many unwelcomed ways. Perhaps he had always known, from the time he had dreamed of war and ponies running.

The black mare.

Her serene pride.

The truth crashed through him like thunder. This orphan woman he had not been able to forget was indeed his *wyakin* squaw, after all.

27

It DID NOT take Cloud Singer long to find Twelic. When darkness fell and he still had not approached the Lamtama camp, she draped her pride over herself like a rich buffalo blanket and went to the Hasotoin hearths instead.

She found him sharing the headman's fire with his cousin, the mate she had discarded. Young Looking Glass's new wife moved about, filling horn bowls with water for them, pulling planks of salmon from her fire.

That did not bother Cloud Singer. If she had hurt Young Looking Glass by throwing him away, then it was his pain, not hers. She had quickly grown bored with him, tired of waiting for his father to die so that she might be a headman's wife. She had been unable to tolerate the long, cold nights when he would rather sleep than come to her bedding, and the facile conversation at his hearth.

Twelic offered far more promise, and during the short time she had spent with the Hasotoin, her fascination with him had been rekindled. He was one warrior she had never truly been able to lure. Even now, he was hers only after a fashion.

She knew he kept other squaws in other camps, yet he always came back to her, season after season, bringing trinkets and robes when he had been gone too long. She was sure that when he finally did choose a mate, he would come to her.

She stood beside him now until he looked up and acknowledged her.

"I greet you, friend," she said softly. "I thought you would visit my father by now."

Twelic looked away from her again, back to Looking Glass. "I will try to come there later," he said finally.

Later? Something was wrong.

He always burned to be with her, at least when she was close enough to make his body start wanting her. Confused, she lowered herself prettily to sit beside him.

His strong jaw hardened. "This is not a good place for you, Cloud Singer."

Belatedly, she noticed that Looking Glass would not turn his gaze her way. His wife had stopped working to grip her knife with white knuckles and stare at her. Cloud Singer shrugged. Their reaction could not be helped. She could not leave now, not with any measure of dignity.

"I have missed you. The snow has melted since I saw you last."

"I went to the grasslands early in the spring."

She was surprised. "None of our warriors tried for buffalo this season."

"Most warriors give up too easily."

"Did you find any?"

He had not, but he tangled with some Sioux and had brought back pemmican and ponies enough that the trip had not been wasted. "They are there," he answered noncommittally.

She shrugged and touched her fingertip to the small area of ruddy skin that showed where his breechclout fell away from the top of his leggings.

He did not react.

Always before she had been able to raise gooseflesh there with one provocative touch. She looked sharply at his face again. His eyes were trained across the big camp now. She followed his gaze, and at first could not believe what she was seeing.

He was watching another woman, here, now, while she was right beside him.

"Who is she?" she spat, all thoughts of dignity suddenly forgotten.

The squaw was as tall as most men, and that should have made her ungainly, but it did not. She worked with easy, fluid gestures to load an ugly white pony and rope an even stranger black yearling to its side. As Cloud Singer watched, the woman looked over her shoulder at a warrior and flashed him a fleeting, dazzling smile. She sent him away when he would have helped her, and somehow, that threatened Cloud Singer most of all, more than her exotic beauty and the long, sleek hair that fell unfettered to her waist, even more than the hold she seemed to have on Twelic's concentration.

"Who is she?" she demanded again.

To her shock, Twelic laughed, a deep, strained sound she could scarcely recognize.

She was a babe he had saved from starving, he thought. She was a girl-woman who had loved him once. She was a dream of his future. Even in turning away from him, she would not let him go.

"She is the pony wife," he answered.

To both Cloud Singer and himself, that said it all now.

Kiye Kipi pulled her saddle tight with hands that were as tense as claws, but her eyes were calm as she finished and looked around for Joseph and Alokot.

They were at the headman's fire. All the kin were there, delicately pulling sweet, pink salmon meat from its fragile bones. Now and again a peal of laughter rose from their hearth.

She went to them and squatted beside Joseph. "I am leaving now," she said quietly. "I would like to go home."

Joseph looked at her, as slack-jawed as she thought it was possible for him to be.

"It is dark. What is the rush?" Arenoth asked.

Her heart made a funny movement beneath her breast, and it took all her will not to look around at the Hasotoin fires again. "All the foals are traded," she answered.

"That is no reason to go riding off into the night!" Weta-tonmi protested, lifting Little Mole to her breast.

Oh, it is. Kiye Kipi stood again. "I have my bow and some

fish. I will be safely back to Imnaha before tomorrow's darkness.''

''I will find Earth Sound to go with you.'' Alokot began rising, looking around for the warrior.

''No!''

She did not think she could bear that just now, another warrior watching her, using any opportunity to push close to her, to touch her grazingly with hot hands. She wanted to be alone, where memories could not reach her.

The snow in her heart had thawed. Now it was filled with a clamoring panic to get away from Twelic.

Even so, they were not going to let her go alone, she saw. ''I will take Dirty Dove,'' she tried, compromising.

Finally, Joseph shrugged, though he scowled.

''Some sun I will listen to your bidding, and you will think my head addled,'' she teased. She touched him gently on the shoulder, and he smiled faintly.

She turned away. Her gaze fell on her mounts, grazing not far from the lodges, and her heart staggered suddenly.

Twelic stood by her black filly, watching her.

Why? Curse him, why had he sought her out now? She had been so close to escaping!

Suddenly, anger boiled through her. He thought he could weaken her again, soften her, make her talk to him and shiver. He thought he could reach her again and make her want, but he did not know.

She crossed to him with long, irate strides.

''You waste your time here. I am leaving,'' she snapped. She swung up onto her white mare and wrenched her reins around.

''Did I hurt you so badly?'' he asked quietly.

Oh, how arrogant of him! He would take even her pride away from her, make it sound as though she feared him. She twisted back to him, her eyes on fire.

Twelic felt his throat constrict. No, she was not a girl any longer. She was older, ageless. She was stronger and wiser. Everything about her said that she would not allow herself to be hurt anymore.

"I need to speak with you," he tried, putting his hand on the black filly's withers as though to hold her.

"Of what?" Kiye Kipi spat. "To tell me how these past seasons have treated you? To tell me how full and rich your life has been since you turned away from me?" Once again, she felt him reaching past her defenses, pulling to light all the old hurts and regrets she had kept hidden. "I was a child then. *Why did you need to play with me when you had so many others?*"

"I was not playing." Of that, at least, he was very, very sure.

She made a sound of disbelief that scratched at his heart.

He had not meant to come here, knew it was best if he let her go. It would have been seasons before he saw her again. By then, perhaps, it would go away, the new, sudden conviction that this once idolizing girl, this fire-eyed woman, was somehow part of his spirit. But as he looked at her again, he knew with a sick-sweet drop of his gut that that would not happen, not if he waited a thousand snows.

"I did not play with you," he repeated, and his own voice was hot now with frustration. "I wanted you, knowing it was wrong for both of us. Your innocence, your need . . ." He trailed off, his eyes narrowing. "You pushed me past everything I knew to be right."

"*I* did?" she choked.

"You let me touch you."

"*I trusted you!*"

"And I protected you enough to walk away!" Tahmahnewes, did she think it had been easy for him?

"Why?"

He did not know. He could not remember anymore.

Once it had seemed so important, the certainty that if he got too close to her, the heat of her would consume him. Once he had told himself that he had been protecting her from loving him, even as he knew he was protecting himself.

Now it could not matter anymore that she was perhaps the one woman who could make him need beyond all reason. "Where did you get her?" he asked. "I must know."

Kiye Kipi felt her mind spin. It took her a long heartbeat to understand what he was talking about.

"You sent her," she said flatly, looking at the black filly.

"No. I sent a stallion."

"And I put him with this white hunting pony I ride now." *The one who flew past you on the prairie when I was young and my heart was full. Do you remember, Twelic? Do you remember?*

Her spine straightened with the memory. "She is by that stallion, and out of this mare."

He had known it, of course, but he had needed to hear it. He had needed to be sure.

"Yes, that is how fate works," he said quietly. "She won him for you, and now you have your *wyakin* from her."

How did he know?

Once again, the urge to run filled her, banging against her chest. "I cannot . . ." She broke off, licking dry lips. "I cannot speak of that."

"Your face tells me all I need to know."

"Why do you care?" she asked. "It is nothing to you!"

Oh, but it was. He simply could not tell her yet, did not have the courage, did not know how fully their fates were intertwined. "Tell me your dream," he said instead.

She looked at him incredulously. "No!"

"You have already sung of it in front of the Kahmuenem."

"I kept the part with this pony for myself."

He was not surprised, only frustrated. "Then keep another small part from me, but tell me about this pony."

She could keep the Safe Place. No one at all knew about that. She had told Old Joseph's people only about the fighting and the Nimipu herds.

She looked away from him. She wanted to tell him, oh, she did! Against all reason, the urge to share with him was strong as ever.

He knew about her *wyakin*. Somehow, in some small measure, he did.

"She . . . took me through fighting," she said carefully.

"And there was peace and respite after that."

Her heart jolted. *Had they dreamed the same?*

It was more danger than she could bear, more shattering than she could comprehend. She pulled the white mare around again, dragging the black filly along.

"You cannot run from it, Screamer." *Nor can I.*

She *could* run, she would. She would leave this place, and leave him far.

She took several trotting steps before a scream fractured the night air, coming from somewhere near his Hasotoin camp. They both turned about sharply, and Kiye Kipi knew, somehow, that that singular sound would trap her as completely and irrevocably as her *wyakin* dream.

"Give me your pony," he snapped.

She recoiled at the demand, at the obedience it required. She did not want to know what that sound had been, and heard herself answer, "She can carry both of us."

She tugged away the line that held her to the black filly. He hesitated a moment, then he swung himself up behind her. For once, she did not feel the heat of him as he pressed close against her back.

That scream.

She put her heels to the mare, and they loped past the fires and around the lodges, back toward the Hasotoin camp.

A man was laid out flat in the grass beside Wahlitits's lodge. *Wahlitits.* Everything bad in her life seemed to come back to him.

Crimson blood seeped and spread across the buckskin shirt the man wore. The mongrel warrior, Wahlitits, leaned over him, and for a wild moment she was sure that he had killed him. Then she reined in and Twelic went to the ground.

"Eagle Robe," he said tightly. "Wahlitits's father."

She remembered him now.

Not even the cruel coward Wahlitis would kill his own father.

She dropped to the ground as well, her knees feeling weak. She stood helplessly as Twelic hunkered over him. Looking Glass and his friends crowded close as well, and the throng pushed her backward.

"What has happened?" she heard Twelic demand, and somehow she knew before Eagle Robe answered.

"*Xayxayx* . . . tearing up land not far from here, building . . . something . . . a lodge."

Another white-skin lodge in Nimipu land. Her belly began to feel sick.

"He says . . . Lawyer gave . . . this prairie as well. That it is the white man's now," Eagle Robe went on. "I tried to scare his ponies off. He took my gun and . . . he shot me for it."

A woman keened. Wahlitits roared a sound of fury, then his voice was joined by others, outraged bellows and violent oaths. The warriors jostled among each other, not only Hasotoin and the Kahmuenem who had followed her, but now White Bird's men and Toolhoolhoolzote's as well.

The white-skins had killed before, in those headmen's countries. She had heard Old Looking Glass and Old Joseph speak of it. But this was the camas prairie. It was a place that fed all the People. It *had* to feed them now that the buffalo were gone. Surely Lawyer would not have given it.

But he had; somehow she knew he had, as surely as he had tried to give the Kahmuenem land that had never been his to give. And the *xayxayx*, the wretched *xayxayx*, had taken it. They had killed to prove their claim to it.

She knew Eagle Robe had died. His voice had fallen silent, and the sounds of grief and fear and rage were all around her now. She turned away. Twelic's voice stopped her.

He left the throng to come up behind her.

"We will talk more later."

"No. I am leaving now."

He was quiet for a long time. "I know that," he said finally. "But I will see you again soon."

Not many seasons would pass this time after all. He looked back at Eagle Robe and across the camp to where her black filly waited for her, and he knew, with a draining feeling of both foreboding and excitement, that his *wyakin* was about to unfold.

Kiye Kipi nodded. She knew her own would as well, and it filled her with more terror than even she had ever known.

Part Three

28

THE SNOWS WERE a memory at Wallowa for another season. The herd ponies were corralled for their journey to Imnaha, and the warhorses and hunting ponies waited, laden, in the camp. Kiye Kipi studied her own two mares, then she lightened the load on the old white one and added it to her stronger, younger *wyakin* pony. She stepped back and eyed them critically one last time.

If they had to run ahead of those white-skin horses . . .

She gnawed her lip, troubled, then she turned away to scan the camp. She knew the women got tired of her admonitions to leave behind everything they would not urgently need at Imnaha, but she would remind them one more time. She felt responsible for their safety now, and she did not know when that safety might depend upon their ponies' endurance.

Wetatonmi was lashing her last parfleche to Little Mole's tiny saddle. "I will take that one," she offered, moving to her. "Is it important?"

Wetatonmi glanced up at her. "It contains Alokot's stone chisels for sharpening his knives and his spear."

No, that could not be left behind. Kiye Kipi took it in her own arms.

"Little Mole's pony is strong enough," Wetatonmi protested. "You made it."

Kiye Kipi gave a fleeting smile. The gelding had been her birthing gift to the babe, another breeding out of her white-gray mare. She had matched her with the littlest stud she could find, and had created a pony small enough to be managed well by a boy of three snows. She had never tried such a thing before, breeding for diminutive size, and she was pleased with the result.

She ran her free hand appreciatively down the pony's mane.

"Perhaps it is not too late for you," Wetatonmi blurted. "Perhaps some sun you will have your own wee one to make a pony for."

Kiye Kipi's eyes clouded over, hiding everything behind them. Immediately, Wetatonmi cursed her thoughtlessness.

"It is too late," Kiye Kipi answered softly. "I have seen twenty-two snows."

"I birthed this one at that same age."

"You have a mate. I neither want nor need one of those."

Still, Wetatonmi saw her look across to Eagle Robe almost whimsically. That warrior had finally given up on her and had taken a wife from the Lamtama.

"Do you regret it?" Wetatonmi asked, curious in spite of herself.

Kiye Kipi looked north toward the mountains. "I cannot. Tahmahnewes chooses."

He had chosen from the night He had sent her with a strange, vanishing moon, she thought. Now there were *xayxayx* on the other side of those peaks, filling the land and threatening every breath of air the Spirit Chief had given. There was a warrior beyond those mountains as well, lean as a camp wolf, hot eyed as a rogue bear. He was her future; she knew that now. Not babes, not a mate, just a man who could make her blood heat with one strong, calloused hand, a man who would never love a woman as Earth Sound loved his wife.

She turned away from Wetatonmi. "I think Joseph is ready now," she said flatly. "We should go."

The trip to Imnaha always took the better part of two suns. The strong ponies and the warriors would have made it in half that time, but the elders were slow and cantankerous, lagging behind, chewing twigs behind seamed lips. Kiye Kipi watched them impatiently, something she had rarely done before.

These would be the first they would lose. . . .

She shook the nagging thought away, taking comfort in the sleek, black ponies that surged ahead of her. There were enough of them now. If need be, they could carry nearly all of the Kahmuenem to Imnaha and beyond.

Imnaha . . . Suddenly, with that thought, she knew, and her pulse began throbbing in the slow, sick way of dread.

Why had she not thought of it before?

Oh, sweet Spirit Chief, that was why this whole snow season had passed without any more trouble from the *xayxayx*! Some said the white-skins were keeping their word to stay out of the Wallowa, but she knew in her gut that that was not it. She had scanned and scanned for them in her dreams, but she had failed to find them because they would not go to Wallowa.

They would sneak into the more fertile, higher ground of the other Kahmuenem valley instead.

She put her heels to her black pony and dashed to the men, making one pony rear and his rider spit angrily at her craziness. "Stop!" she cried to Alokot and Joseph. "Please, you must stop everyone right now!"

But it was too late. They were already upon the place. The women were riding in twos and threes into a narrow gorge between the hills that would spill them out into the valley.

Suddenly, one of them gave a startled cry. Then the wails and keens began, frightened and confused. Their ponies began crashing into each other as some turned about to retreat, rearing and spilling tiny babe-riders as the first squaws to reach the valley began to saw on their reins, backing up.

"What is it?" Joseph demanded, but Alokot was already gone, his war pony galloping to the gorge, his handsome face going dark with fury.

Joseph followed him without waiting for an answer. She knew he understood. There was only one enemy who would do this. No Shoshone or Blackfoot or Sioux would simply creep in and settle that which was not theirs. They would fight for it, meet the warriors with their weapons, as the Spirit Chief meant it to be. They would be conquerors or they would be vanquished, but they would not be thieves.

Dirty Dove careened wildly to her side. "What is happening?" she cried.

"Go to the gorge!" Kiye Kipi shouted. "Help those babes get out of there before more get hurt!"

She hauled her own pony about and raced to the elders, cutting them off amid startled complaints and raucous questions. She turned them away from the pass and scattered the herd as well, frightening them into bolting back the way they had come. Then she returned to the gorge, because she knew but had to see, because she had seen but had to know.

Many of the women there were still trying to get out, sobbing and shouting. She saw Wetatonmi clutching Little Mole, his pony gone now, lost somewhere in the confusion. Kiye Kipi dodged all of them, her black filly skidding down into the valley, hooves planted.

It was over.

She froze there, feeling sick and stunned. Her sanctuary, the place where she had learned strength and goodness, had been savaged. Never again would she watch the sun rise blue and golden over these hills where she had found her *wyakin*; never again would she see the water glitter in its light.

White-skin lodges—*so many of them*—crawled over the land, rich wood turned gray from the snows. And the trees, oh, the trees! Ugly, butchered stumps thrust up from the earth at the edges of the glade, bleeding their white-green sap of life. The stench was horrible, wafting to her, gagging her. Refuse and excrement clogged the water, spoiling the banks. She had come to know it now, this unique, white-skins' smell.

And the soldiers . . .

They moved about, blue coated, arrogant with their shiny weapons. They blocked Alokot and his warriors from the *xay-xayx* settlers, keeping them back from their own land.

She had thought she was ready for it, waiting.

She thought of Old Joseph and the way they had failed him. *"Nooooo!"*

Joseph did not sit on his blanket this time to council with the white men. He stood, tall and imposing, nose to nose with the soldier who seemed to lead them.

"You trespass!" he charged furiously. "Your man Odeneal gave his word that this country would remain ours."

"Odeneal?" The white soldier chief scowled about at his subordinates, clearly confused.

"He was in charge of Indian Affairs a few years back," someone offered.

"Ah, him." The soldier chief turned again to Joseph. "He's gone now, uh . . . not with our government any longer."

Joseph's eyes narrowed as the explanation was translated. "I have papers he signed."

"The president repealed them."

"By whose authority?"

The white man's eyes bugged. "Well, he's the *president*. I don't suppose he needs any."

Kiye Kipi saw another man approach, coming busily from the *xayxayx* lodges. She fought back a gasp as she remembered him.

Mon-teeth. The agent.

"Odeneal set the *Wallowa* aside for you," he snapped when he reached them. "This is different country, not that that has any bearing on the matter any longer. The governor of Idaho has helped me persuade Washington of the senselessness of such an arrangement. The settlers want this country, and we have a treaty preceding Odeneal's pact. It is impossible for me to govern all of you when you're on different plots of land. You must go to Lapwai now."

Alokot brought up his rifle. "I am tired of trying to tell them that our father signed nothing. There is another way."

Kiye Kipi's heart froze, but Alokot did not shoot. The soldier chief pushed past Monteith to stand in front of the agent.

"Now, look here," he said placatingly. "Let's try to handle this like civilized men."

"Civilized men do not steal," Alokot snarled.

"Nothing's been stolen. No one is leaving you without land holdings. Parcels have been set aside for you at Lapwai. You can grow those roots you like so much, and other things, too— corn and melons, all manner of sustenance for your people.

General Oliver Otis Howard waits there for you even now, to allot these places to you and to all the other chiefs in a fair, equitable manner.''

"I know nothing of this How-erd," Joseph said flatly.

"He's the most important man we have out here in this territory," the soldier chief explained urgently. "He's been sent to expedite this matter, and he's not entirely unsympathetic toward your plight. He's a good Christian man. He's already addressed the Secretary of War on your behalf. I was present at the dictation of that letter. He told him that it is a great mistake to take your little valley from you. He urged Congress to buy out the white men's claims to it per that last treaty. Unfortunately, you must see Congress's point of view. It puts a marked strain upon the government's finances to do so, and upon their sources of manpower to keep soldiers out here to protect you from the white men wanting to come in. General Howard is first and foremost a soldier, and he must enforce Congress's will. That is why he has sent us to inform you of this change.''

He stopped, breathless. Joseph turned away without answering.

"What do you do?" Alokot demanded, watching carefully between his brother and the soldier chief.

Joseph looked around for the ancient Burned Tree. "Take the women and the elders back to Wallowa," he ordered Alokot. "We know they are safe enough there."

"And the rest of us?" pressed Alokot.

"We will go on to Lapwai. I would speak with this Howerd.''

29

Night fell over the *xayxayx* fort as hard and as quickly as death. It pitched their spreading, wooden lodges into blue-black gloom. Thick yellow light from their lanterns made round circles on the earth at their planked doors, but the dull glow could not push back the darkness.

Kiye Kipi studied the place pensively from the concealing shadows. No longer could she see the corral, though she stood near the building where the council with Odeneal had once taken place. The compound was immense now as the white-skins laid sole claim even to this country that Lawyer had so stupidly shared with them. She could not see the other Dreamer camps either, but she knew they were all around. Looking Glass, White Bird, Huishuis Kute and Toolhoolhoolzote had all encountered troops in their countries as well this last moon. They had come here as angrily as Joseph had, to try again, yet again, to tell these obstinate men that neither they nor their fathers had ever signed Lawyer's treaty.

This time, they would fail. There would be no man like Odeneal to listen to them with open ears. Kiye Kipi did not think, in that spot deep inside herself where she felt things, that this How-erd would be as reasonable as the headmen hoped.

"Have you seen him yet?"

She sucked her breath in and whipped around. Twelic stood in another patch of shadows behind her.

She knew he spoke of How-erd.

She gave a quick shake of her head, and her stance turned carefully aloof. Her indigo eyes became guarded and flat, reflecting back the murky light of the lanterns.

Watching her change, he knew, as he always knew, that he should have stayed away. He should have granted them both that measure of peace. But she was like a flame calling to a moth. He had known she would be here, and he had been compelled to find her.

"I have heard that he embraces their *xayxayx* god," he went on, coming to hunker down near where she stood.

She would not sit beside him. She would not.

"We will see with the new sun," she answered stiffly.

"It alarms me," he continued. "Their god is one who breathes fire. That is what Old Looking Glass said."

"Old Looking Glass is gone now."

"And I fear we all will suffer for it."

She started even as he did, as he heard his own voice confiding in her as though she were a warrior. But he knew he would not say such a thing even to another man. It disturbed him even more deeply to know that he would tell her what he would tell no other.

Oh, yes, she was beginning to touch him in many ways.

"I have strong doubts about the son's leadership," he went on, scowling. "This is not a time for ineffectual headmen, and young Looking Glass has always hidden from trouble. I think he senses my doubts, my disapproval. He feeds me at his hearth even as he tries to undermine me. I am a thorn in his hide."

Kiye Kipi could not help herself. She laughed.

A thorn? Oh, yes, he would be that. Had thoughts of him not nettled her now for seasons?

The rich, throaty sound of her voice moved over Twelic's skin, as inviting as the wind. He stood quickly to face her again, his hands tightening at his sides as he fought the urge to touch her. He knew now that she did not want that any more than he did.

"Looking Glass will learn soon enough that you cannot be shaken free," she managed finally. She stepped back from him, keeping space between them. "Go back to your lodge, Twelic. Your squaws wait for you. There will be time enough for worry in the morning."

There was no accusation in her voice now, only dreary acceptance of what he was, of what he thought he had wanted long ago. He watched her move into the darkness.

"And you? Who waits for you?" he asked. Had she finally gone to another?

Kiye Kipi did not answer him. She stiffened briefly, her steps faltering, but she kept going until the night swallowed her.

Only then, when he could not see, did she lean briefly against the side of a *xayxayx* building and swallow back all the old regrets that she still tried so desperately to forget.

How-erd had only one arm.

When she saw it, Kiye Kipi felt her throat tighten painfully. It was a battle scar that spoke of courage and a relentless, undaunted will to win. She did not know anything of *xayxayx* shamans, but even if they were exceptionally powerful healers, only a man's own heart could save him from such a grotesque, bleeding injury.

Or perhaps his god had done it, the one that breathed fire.

She watched him stride to the front of one of his buildings, his eyes moving over the headmen and the warriors and the people gathered. He had face hair, and that trait of these men always made her skin crawl. Then Mon-teeth appeared, coming up beside the general-soldier, and her heart thudded so hard she forgot everything else.

He seemed so satisfied this time.

His grin was wide and arrogant. Though Joseph stood again to face him, he did not even look at him.

"Now I'm able to give you Dreamers your orders with the full cooperation and support of my government," he smirked. "You must come in, and there is no getting out of it. You can go pick up all your horses and the remainder of your people, but then you must come on the reservation. I have land for all of you. General Howard and his troops will remain on the premises to see that you comply.''

Joseph gave a soul-deep sigh. ''I do not know how to get our position across to men who do not have ears to hear. My father did not sell our land in your treaty. We took no presents, and we will not leave our country, no matter what your president decrees. You must take your people out of the Imnaha.''

How-erd used his single hand to stroke his face hair. ''There's no need for you to repeat yourself, sir. This will be the last council between your headmen and ourselves pertaining to this matter. There'll be no more debate about who did or did not sign the '63 treaty. The time has come to enforce it, one way or another. Mr. Monteith is right. You must come on to the reservation immediately.''

The translation was garbled, thick-tongued. Kiye Kipi frowned, missing much of it. She read How-erd's tone instead, and she felt sick.

Perhaps that soldier chief at Imnaha had spoken true. Perhaps this man had once stood on their behalf. But she did not think he was kind or good or truehearted. Now his jaw was set obstinately and his voice was flat.

''My advice to you is that you support the proposals of our government before hostilities break out,'' he went on.

Toolhoolhoolzote rose to stand beside Joseph. ''I want to know by what right you order me about,'' he demanded. ''The Spirit Chief made this world as it is. He made a part of it for us to live upon. I do not see where you get your authority to say that we shall not live where he placed us.''

How-erd's eyes moved to him, hot and narrowed. ''Who are you, sir?''

Toolhoolhoolzote drew his immense body up. ''I am shaman and headman both. I know what Tahmahnewes wants for my people, and your orders are not it.''

''He's one of the chief Dreamers,'' Monteith spat, ''one of the ones behind this hocus-pocus about work interfering with a good trance. It's pagan,'' he added deliberately, knowing Howard's extreme Christian faith. ''I promise you, sir, that once I have them on the reservation, I will abolish these customs.''

Dutifully, the translator repeated. Kiye Kipi's breath came out of her as though he had driven a fist into her gut.

"You cannot!" she cried, and all eyes came around to her. She flushed hot and stepped back, but her heart still pounded. Abolish Tahmahnewes?

How-erd looked at her, then his gaze shot back to Tool-hoolhoolzote. "You are inciting the others, sir. It will not be tolerated."

"Tolerated by whom? Who are you to ask us here to talk, then tell me I should not? Are you the Great Spirit? Did you make the world? Did you make the sun? Did you make the rivers to run for us to drink? Did you make the grass to grow? Did you do all these things that you can talk to us as though we were boys?"

How-erd's face got ruddy with frustration and anger. "I am only attempting to give peace and prosperity to your people by following my orders from Washington to place you on a reserve."

Toolhoolhoolzote thrust his chin out arrogantly. "What person at your Wash-ing-tone pretends to divide the land and put me on it?"

"I am that man, sir! I stand here for the President of the United States, and there is no 'spirit,' great or small, that will hinder me!"

"Then you must wrestle me to the ground and drag me there! Tell your men to bring their guns, because my warriors are stronger!"

An escalating roar came up from the Pikunanmu men. Kiye Kipi looked around at them, her heart staggering.

"I am warning you, sir!" How-erd bellowed.

Toolhoolhoolzote sneered. "I do not fear you, and I will not obey you, for you are not greater than I."

Kiye Kipi saw the last of How-erd's temper pull away from him. It went violently, turning his cheeks livid and his mouth small. He whipped around to face his soldiers.

"Take this man to the guardhouse. We will accomplish nothing while he interferes."

From somewhere far back in the throng, a Pikunanmu

woman keened. The soldiers came on, pushing through the People, making the squaws scatter in terror. When the warriors moved to block their women from the *xayxayx,* the white men brought their guns up, their deadly silver gleaming. More screams fractured the air, and a Pikunanmu man howled in fury. The soldiers swarmed over Toolhoolhoolzote, taking both of his arms, hauling him off.

"No," Kiye Kipi breathed. "No!" She could not believe this was happening!

She did not like Toolhoolhoolzote. But Tahmahnewes, he was a headman, a *tiwats* of the greatest renown! A grudging respect swelled her chest as he went with the soldiers. He did not fight them. He did not wrest his arms away, although she thought that with his strength, perhaps he might have done so. Though his men shouted and shoved at the soldiers, he maintained a burning, furious dignity as he went away.

Then his eyes found hers.

She flinched, astounded at the message in them. He was doing this at least in part because of her. He was doing it because if he tried to overpower these men and failed, the price would be high.

His people would wonder why he had not used his magic.

They would wonder why he had not used his brutish strength.

They would turn away from a *tiwats* who had been conquered, and they would look to his animal-caller granddaughter, a woman who shared his blood and his power, who made ponies that could win.

She did not want his following! She wanted only for these white men, these soldiers, to leave them alone.

"*No!*" This time she screamed it, in fury and helplessness. The men heard her and roared louder.

"Good God, sir!" Monteith shouted, his arrogance gone now, his fear clear on his face. "What have you done?"

Howard looked at him stonily.

"You need not worry, Mr. Monteith. We have the upper hand. Their medicine man is out of the way, and Joseph will soon see the sense in what I propose. Once he comes in, I'm sure the others will follow his example."

Monteith looked round-eyed at the Kahmuenem headmen. "Why him? What makes you so sure?"

"He is their backbone, the brains behind their bravado. He is the only one of them who has ever managed to negotiate even a temporary victory from Washington."

Monteith gaped at him. "And you think he will simply obey now because you tell him to?"

"Not at all. He will return to his Wallowa, I expect, but I have positioned more troops there while he is occupied here. We have taken control of both of his valleys now. He will go back there, but he will not be permitted to resettle. Soon he will see that Lapwai is his only choice."

Kiye Kipi did not know what to say to the grieving women.

They watched her from their fires, their eyes pleading that it was not true, that it could not happen, that their beloved Kahmuenem could not be taken from them. Their babes sensed their fear and wailed ceaselessly. At Joseph's fire, men shouted.

Finally, she pushed to her feet and trudged there.

"We cannot make war upon them," she heard Joseph declare, and she stumbled.

What was he saying? Let the *xayxayx* take Imnaha?

Alokot shot to his feet, his face livid, trembling with a rage so unprecedented it frightened her. "You forget our father's dying wish!" he spat. "Do you step into his moccasins to fail him?"

Breaths hissed out of the warriors. They fell silent, stunned by this fracture of their leaders' unity.

Joseph shook his head. "I do not forget," he said into the eerie quiet. "I know that he would never see his people slaughtered."

"Only a coward would give his country, his father's bones, without a fight!" Alokot snarled.

"I am not afraid to fight, but there is one thing more precious to me than Nimipu land. I must protect our children."

"They will not be our children if we surrender the freedom

that is their legacy! They will be *xayxayx* children, thieves!"

"They will die if we resist. How-erd has promised war. You heard him."

"Then I say let there be war. I will meet their rifles with my own."

Alokot stalked away, and Kiye Kipi tried to choke back a distraught sound. But she was not quick enough; it escaped her, strangled and lost. Joseph looked to her sharply.

"And what have you to say, Pony Wife? What do our women tell you?"

Her heart lurched.

She took a step backward, away from him, shaking her head. She could not talk at this council. This was not like the ponies. Hatred blazed from too many eyes; frustration and fury made the warriors' faces look murderous and grotesque.

Then she remembered the women, back near her own fire.

Their faces had been worse! They were the innocents here, the ones who would suffer, the ones who would bleed unless someone saved them. This raucous male anger was as deadly to their welfare as the *xayxayx.*

"We must go," she heard herself say.

There was another roar of outrage, but now she stepped into it, her heart thudding. "No! No!" she shouted. "Not here to Lapwai. I think we must go somewhere far."

Suddenly, all her old instincts boiled up in her. An old, old terror strangled her throat at Joseph's plan. She could not, *would not,* come to live at this white-skin place! Mon-teeth would take away her magic. He would try to take away Tah-mahnewes. She could not go back to that, to life in a bad place, resigned to poverty, to ignominy, to the shame that came with the loss of all hope.

No! Mon-teeth would not take it all away from her again!

Her chin came up and her spine straightened. "If you come here, I do not want to follow you," she said to Joseph. Voices barked in support, then fell quiet again as she looked around at the warriors. "But I think you are crazy, as well. I cannot in good conscience sanction the deaths of our women, our babes. Think of them! They are yours to protect! I think you should lead them to safety.''

"There is no safety," someone snarled. "The *xayxayx* must be destroyed. They are everywhere now."

"No," she answered quietly. "They are not." *They are not at the Safe Place.*

But she could not tell them that, no matter how sure she was; she could not share so much of her *wyakin* dream. "I have made ponies that can carry us as far and as long as we wish to go," she said instead. "If we cannot bow to the whiteskins, and we cannot fight them, then we must never let them catch us. Decide what you will, but that is my choice. I say we should flee."

She turned away, leaving them to their arguments, to their shouts and frustration. So many stood angrily behind Alokot, and that scared her. But she knew the women would vacillate between her stand and Joseph's.

She closed her eyes and shuddered. They did not want their babes to die. As Joseph had said, the children were more precious than anything, even the land. But, oh, the land!

It was late when both Joseph and Alokot returned to the hearth she shared with Joseph's wives. There was a strained civility between them, but they sat shoulder to shoulder now.

"What will happen?" she asked quietly.

Alokot's jaw hardened. "We will make preparations to come in to this place."

Her heart shuddered. *She could not go on to the Safe Place alone.* She needed one of them, either of them, to see her side! She cursed the blood that made her a woman, that let them ignore her even as they asked what she thought.

"I am not saying that we will stay here," Alokot went on. "I have agreed only to support my brother for the next thirty suns. That is how long How-erd has given us to come in. We will go home for the ponies and the women, then we will camp at Tolo Lake near the end of the moon. From there, we will decide where to go."

She nodded warily, her heart settling a bit. Time . . . to plan and to council and resolve this thing, to bring the Kahmuenem people together again as one. It was enough for now.

It had to be.

She stood, weariness seeping so deeply into her bones they hurt. Then, from somewhere close, she heard the rolling thump of hoofbeats, and her blood ran intuitively cold again.

Alokot stood, his eyes searching the darkness until he found the single rider. "It is Burned Tree," he said flatly.

No more. Oh, please, Tahmahnewes, no more trouble!

But Kiye Kipi knew as soon as she saw the shaman's haggard face that there was. He rode recklessly to the fire, his pony staggering, his own legs unsteady from age and exhaustion as he dropped to the ground. Oh, yes, there was more. Something had happened at Wallowa.

Wetatonmi and Little Mole were there. She had taken her babe back there to keep him clear of the trouble!

"What?" she demanded before anyone else could speak. "Tell us!"

"Soldiers!" Burned Tree gasped. "We returned to the winter valley, and they are there as well."

Her knees folded.

She sat down again hard, her head swimming, barely hearing as the old man went on. His seamed face shone in the firelight. She looked away because she could not bear to see, but the image remained and horror bloomed for its implications.

The *tiwats* was weeping.

She understood the fullness of it then. Somehow, impossibly, all of Kahmuenem was lost to them. *Gone.* It did not matter if they ran or fought or came to Lapwai. Somehow, they had already lost. The *xayxayx* had finally wrested their country away.

"I have left the women there," Burned Tree went on wretchedly, "because I did not know where else to take them. But the blue-coats will not even let them pitch their lodges against the rain. And they have taken our ponies."

Kiye Kipi's eyes snapped up again.

The ponies.

The black stallion, the herds, her *wyakin*. The only slim,

precious hope the Nimipu had left.

She screamed a sound of such rage and betrayal that even Joseph jumped. She came to her feet again, clawing through her parfleches for her bridle.

"Stop!" Alokot snarled. "What do you do?"

"They will not have them," she breathed. "If they take the horses . . . oh, sweet Tahmahnewes, if they steal the ponies, I will kill every cursed *xayxayx* myself!"

30

DAWN BROUGHT THICK, clinging fog.

Alokot stepped out of it into the Hasotoin camp, his eyes searching the people who had begun to move about there. Twelic saw him as he ducked out from Looking Glass's lodge, and he knew.

The Screamer. Kiye Kipi.

"What has happened to her?" he heard himself demand.

For a gut-tightening moment, he cursed the *wyakin* and the instincts that tied him to her. He had problems of his own. His eyes felt grainy and raw from the long night behind him. He had smoked bowls and bowls of weed with his cousin, but he had not been able to sway Looking Glass from his chosen course. *That* was his responsibility, the Hasotoin women and the babes and the elders that their headman would lead off to certain slaughter.

Then Alokot answered. "She left while we slept, to go back to Wallowa. I tried to stop her, but she can be as unrestrainable as the wind."

Twelic felt his heart move strangely in his chest. Word of the Kahmuenem's trouble had spread among the camps as the moon rose. "And she is alone."

"Yes. They have her ponies." Anyone who knew her would understand.

"Our Kahmuenem will leave with the first full light to go back there," he went on, "but she is on her black mare and I doubt we will catch her. I cannot leave my warriors and ride ahead, because I do not trust what they might do in my absence now. I have promised my brother that there will be no fighting until the end of the moon, when we talk further.''

Twelic nodded noncommittally.

''I ask your assistance for another reason, friend. My wife and child are there.''

Suddenly, Twelic's eyes grew hot. ''You have brothers closer to your hearth,'' he demanded. ''Why me?''

But they both knew. Kiye Kipi had come from the Hasotoin to the Kahmuenem, and she had tied them together. Because of her, they had hunted the buffalo together. She would not listen to Earth Sound or any of Alokot's warriors, but perhaps she would listen to Twelic. And if she did not, if she went on anyway . . .

''If Kiye Kipi finds trouble, Wetatonmi will leap to her assistance,'' Alokot said grimly. ''I will ride easier with my responsibilities if I know a strong warrior is there to protect them.''

Twelic's mouth twisted into a look that was half grimace, half smile. He had never really had a choice, after all.

He turned to his lodge for his weapons and bridle, but Alokot stopped him.

''You should take my new war colt. She made it, and you know how good those blacks are. It is fast enough and long-winded enough to catch her mare.''

''No.'' Adrenaline was already tightening his muscles. ''I will catch her. I know the land better than she does, and I trust my own pony.''

Alokot nodded. If there was trouble, Twelic wanted the mount he had always relied upon, the one that knew his heart and his commands. He was perhaps the only elite warrior Alokot knew who, for some reason, had not embraced Kiye Kipi's strong new ponies.

He turned back to his own camp, then paused thoughtfully. A woman was coming out of the swirling fog now. Somehow he knew that she had been standing there for some time, listening.

He wondered if he should wait, if perhaps Twelic would

change his mind because of her. Then he looked back and saw the look in that warrior's eyes.

No. No squaw, no soldier, no spirit monster would keep him from Kiye Kipi now.

Brazenly, nearly crazed with disbelief, Cloud Singer clawed her fingers around his war pony's bridle.

"What is she to you?" she screeched. "Why would you leave your Hasotoin now to go to her?"

Twelic dragged his reins back angrily, and the pony reared away from her grip, nearly pulling her off her feet. "She was Hasotoin once," he snapped. That, he thought, and so much more.

"She is hard and wild, not like a woman at all! She needs no man!"

He very nearly smiled as he pulled his pony around. "She does not think she needs a man, and that is why I must go to her."

He galloped off. Cloud Singer watched him, her pulse thunderous.

She had tolerated sharing him with other squaws because she was a headman's daughter. She was above their sweet, mewling ways, and they changed like the sun anyway. No sooner did they try to claim him than they lost him. Twelic always came back to her in the end.

The others were no threat to her, but there had never been an animal caller before.

Again, something about this one drove panic deep in her heart. Cloud Singer knew, instinctively, that Kiye Kipi did not try to hold Twelic. His fascination with her ran too deep.

A sense of doom prickled along her skin. This one was her equal. In this one, she had met her match.

She turned back to her father's camp, her eyes narrowing with thought. Twelic was gone now, but he would come back. And when he did, she would best her, this pony wife. She would think of something, somehow, to put her out of Twelic's mind.

*   *   *

When Kiye Kipi first heard the distant sound of hoofbeats, muted as a heartbeat in the thick air, she thought that Alokot had caught up with her. She pulled her mare in, her breath coming a little easier. She had left the camp despite his advice because there was nothing else she could do, but she was not fool enough to be glad she was going alone.

She waited for him to draw closer, then, suddenly, fear shafted through her. Perhaps it was not Alokot at all. Perhaps she would meet one of the white-skins here. They were all over, in White Bird's camp and Toolhoolhoolzote's, in both Kahmuenem valleys. They were everywhere.

She dragged her bow off her back, her hands fumbling for an arrow. Sweet Tahmahnewes, could she put one into a man, no matter what his skin or his crimes?

She felt sick. She did not know.

She dragged her pony around, her gaze probing the mist for somewhere to hide. She could see nothing; no sun had come yet to burn the fog off. Still, she was close to Wallowa now, and she knew the land. She thumped her legs hard against the mare's ribs and smacked her bow down on her rump. They lunged toward a place where she thought she would find a swale.

Water trickled over rocks at the deepest part of it. A handful of deciduous trees clogged the banks. She dropped down off her pony onto shaky legs and led her into the copse even as the hoofbeats grew louder.

It was not the gait of one of her blacks. She knew that sound, steady and rhythmic. This pony's beat was clumsy with exhaustion.

She squatted, her heart thundering, and tried again to notch an arrow. Then he rode into view, and her breath snagged.

"You?" she squeaked.

Twelic pulled his own pony in, looking around at the sound of her voice. "Where are you?" he demanded.

She stepped out of the swale, watching him, her bow finally aimed and ready. "If you come to stop me, go back."

"You are Tahmahnewes's own fool!"

She lowered the weapon angrily, feeling somehow betrayed.

"Do you think I would do this if I had a choice?" she spat. She turned back to her mare and swung onto her back. "You of all people know what these ponies mean to us!"

She had put her heels back to her mare again. Before he could breathe, she was galloping off, back toward Wallowa.

He whipped his own weary horse into running.

The brave animal struggled, sides heaving. Even if he caught her, he would not be able to stay abreast of her, Twelic knew. Nor could he let her go on alone.

A true, unprecedented fear twisted his gut at the thought. Suddenly, her death was a more shattering possibility than the loss of the Kahmuenem herd.

He knew then that that was why he had come after her, not because of any *wyakin* or rage against these men who would invade them, not out of brotherhood to Alokot. He had left his Hasotoin because he loved her. Perhaps he had wanted her with a man's desire from the time she had raced past him on a distant prairie, but he knew he had lost a young boy's heart to her when he had spit milk into her for the first time.

The realization made him desperate, violent. As soon as he pulled close enough to her, he reached across and snagged her reins out of her hands.

She howled in fury as her black veered around, crashing into his own mount. The ponies came together with the sickly, thudding sound of sweaty flesh meeting flesh. Then they were toppling backward, falling, as the ponies reared up and struggled away.

Never, ever, would he have treated another squaw in such a manner. But this one was undaunted.

She shot back up again almost as soon as she hit the ground. His hand lashed out, grabbing her ankle, and she fell, the breath bursting from her in a soft grunt. He scrambled to her, dropping his weight on top of her, pinning her down.

"Curse you with every spirit monster there is!" she grated. "Curse you for doing this when I would save them!"

"And I would save you from yourself!"

He caught her wrists in his larger hand, holding them hard to the ground over her head. She arched her back to buck him off, and then she went very still.

Her eyes heated with another kind of fire.

Do not remember! Oh, Tahmahnewes, she did not dare, because the danger in that was almost as terrifying as the thought of what might happen to her ponies if she did not get back to Wallowa. But it was like before.

Sweet Spirit Chief, it was just like before.

The smell of him was suddenly close and sweetly familiar, filling her head with smoke and tallow and leather. There was something else, too, something that was indescribably him, and she shuddered with it. On the buffalo prairie, it had been sun drenched. Now it was damp and close and private.

She squeezed her eyes shut. She could not remember, because then the pain of what she would never have would become unbearable.

"Get away from me!" She had meant it to come out as a command; instead it was a plea. She writhed again, desperately. Even when she looked away from him, she could still feel him, his body so heavy and solid against her. His chest pressed against her breasts made them throb. His hand was calloused and relentless where it gripped hers, as it had been when she had lain naked and shameless beside him so many seasons ago.

Touch me.

She felt her neck, her face, even her chest go hot with mortification. She *wanted* him to do that again, wanted it with an ache that terrified her.

She could not hate him when every breath she took was filled with him.

"Please!" she hissed again.

"Vow to me that you will not run," he gasped.

"N-no." She shook her head. "I will not go."

He trusted her because he had to.

He saw the awareness in her eyes and knew she was remembering, and the sweet yearning before she had closed them was more than he could bear. He felt himself harden with pounding necessity, heard his blood roar in his ears, and he jerked his hands away as though she had burned him.

He could not grapple with this now. There were *xayxayx* in Wallowa.

She scrambled away from him when he released her, but she only squatted a short distance away in the fog, watching him warily. Twelic took a measured breath, feeling shaken.

"I am not telling you that you cannot go home," he said carefully. "I am saying that you cannot do it alone."

Her eyes narrowed. "Then come with me."

"I cannot keep the pace you ride at," he admitted. "Your pony will not be able to either, not for much longer."

Her eyes went to them, standing off in the distance, noses hanging. Steam rose from their heated flesh, mingling with the mist. She gave a little keening sound of frustration.

She could not hurt her pony.

"We do not know what we will find there," he went on. "This How-erd is like no enemy I have met before. He is sneaky and determined and dangerous. We should wait here for the Kahmuenem to catch up with us. They left right behind me. We will have power in numbers."

"No!" Her eyes came around to him again. "I cannot wait that long. Burned Tree is with them, and several others who will slow them down."

He bit back an oath. He would have to compromise, though it was something he was not accustomed to doing.

"Then we will keep going," he said grimly, "but we will walk our ponies until they recover." Perhaps, if he could keep her to a slow pace, Alokot would reach them after all.

It was, she supposed, the best she could hope for. At least she would be *moving*. And she did not dare fight him, did not dare give him the opportunity to grapple with her and touch her again.

That was the strongest motivator of all.

She stood, her legs cramping with exhaustion. "Let us walk, then."

Alokot did not find them before they reached the place. They came in at the top of the hills, and even Twelic's heart staggered at what they saw.

Blue-coat soldiers moved over the trampled grasses, guns in their hands. There was something cocky and sure about the way they walked now, sure about the way they lounged near the lodge tents they had erected to one side of the glade. The squaws and the elders did not have such protection from the elements. The keening sound of their fear chilled him as deep as his bones. Their voices wailed in the air as they huddled together in small knots on the ground, robes pulled over their heads as much to guard them from the eyes of their tormentors as to keep the damp mists away.

Their mounts were crammed into the corral. They milled white-eyed and panicked there, their loads falling dangerously askew as they reared and kicked and thrashed at their confinement. Even as he watched, one went down as larger horses crashed into it.

He would have clapped his hand over her eyes to stop her from seeing, but he knew she would have fought him. Kiye Kipi moaned beside him, and the sound was even worse to him than the voices of loss and fear below.

"They have only the ones your people were riding," he pointed out flatly.

"I . . ." She struggled to remain calm. "I turned the herd about at Imnaha, stampeding them back this way. I think they might have found the hills." *Please let that be so.*

He nodded. It could not matter yet. Before they looked for the others, they would have to free the ones that were trapped.

He took a strong breath as adrenaline began to squirm in his gut. It heated his blood, chasing his heart. *Now.* He brought his rifle up, threw his head back, and a war cry screamed up from his throat.

Kiye Kipi's heart jumped. What was he doing?

Even as she turned to him in disbelief, he was gone, his stallion plunging down the slope. Below them, soldiers whipped about, taking aim, running and bumping into each other in panic. They would shoot him! *They would kill him for this as surely as they stole and lied and schemed!*

"*Nooooo!*"

He reached the valley and looked back at her. She could feel his eyes probing even as he galloped recklessly toward the white-skins. *What?* What did he want of her? Then she understood, and something fierce and strong and wild exploded in her as well.

For an eternal moment, Twelic thought that he should have instructed her before he leaped into action. Somehow, he had thought she would know instinctively what he was doing. But she was a woman; she could not know, not really.

Then he saw that she did . . . she did.

She put her legs to her *wyakin* mare and it began sliding, scrambling down the path his own stallion had left. Then she was in the valley and she leaped to the ground, hiking her doeskin up high, running, running. The white-skins did not see her. Twelic screamed again, brandishing his weapon at them, keeping their attention on himself.

Kiye Kipi reached the corral, her breath burning. For a desperate moment, she did not think her hands would work. She fought with the gate, rattling it violently, biting back a scream of her own. The *xayxayx* must not notice her. That was why Twelic was acting so crazy, to keep their attention off her.

The wood finally scraped back, splintering tiny pieces into her palms. She did not feel the pain.

She stepped back, howling at the ponies inside without using her voice. *They did not hear her!* She could not reach into them without dreaming first! Stupid, stupid . . . then she remembered the way she had always made them run before.

She spun back to her black mare, waiting at the edge of the valley. *Call them! Fly!*

Her *wyakin* mare shrilled a wild whinny. Then she crashed back up the hill, and the others began to follow, lunging free through the gate, storming by. Now, finally, she screamed her own sound, one of jubilation and triumph.

Where was Twelic?

The white-skins had not shot him. They turned away from him now, mouths agape as they watched the trapped ponies flee. He whipped his stallion into a gallop again before they could locate her in the churning tide. Kiye Kipi began running again, fast, in the direction he was going.

She felt his strong arm catch her about the waist, hurtling her upward. She scissored her leg over his pony's neck and landed in front of him with a thud that clacked her teeth together. Then they careened into the herd, racing among them, chasing after the black mare, who stood quivering and proud now at the top of the hills.

She felt something rumble at her back and looked over her shoulder at him, incredulous.

Twelic was laughing.

A tense, high-pitched giggle tightened her throat as well. "We . . . bested them!" she gasped.

"Yes."

They fought well together.

She was as crazy, as daring, as he was.

Somehow, though it worried him, he found that he was not surprised.

31

THEY DROVE THE ponies into a chasm between the hills. Kiye Kipi moved among them, running her hands over their legs, standing on tiptoe to whisper soft nonsense into their ears.

Twelic squatted at the rocky edge of the hole, watching her, scowling. He did not know what to do about her.

She moved like the breeze, flitting here and there, her hair streaming like black rain. He fought the urge to bury his hands in it, to pull her to him. For the first time he realized that loving her again now would not be like touching her the first time. She would not lie still and shivering and accepting beneath his hands. Now, he thought she would be as hungry for pleasure as he; she would roll with him like no squaw he had ever known, giving as unrestrainably as she took.

Something deep inside him coiled, hot and wanting that.

He knew that if she reminded him of the breeze now, then the breeze could gather itself without warning into a cruel, violent wind. And the wind had always moaned his name.

Suddenly, she went still, cocking her head. He listened, stiffening as well. The sound of hoofbeats came to them, then a girl burst over the precipice behind him, riding a small, brown gelding and clutching a toddler between her thighs.

"They have come!" Dirty Dove cried out, riding down to them. Twelic felt his gut cramp.

"Who?" he asked sharply.

The girl looked at him, wary and shy. "Our warriors are back."

Twelic felt his adrenaline fade into a strange emptiness. It was time to go back to his Hasotoin then.

"We are going to Tolo Lake," Kiye Kipi said quietly. "You can ride with us that far. I would not see you go back hungry and alone."

His eyes got hard at the way she knew his thoughts. But then, it was the same instinct that had let them save the ponies.

She did not look at him. She took the wee one from the girl's arms, hefting the child's strong, sturdy little weight against her hip. Twelic's heart squirmed again at the sight of her holding the child.

She deserved that, he thought suddenly. She should have wee ones of her own.

But he did not want that life, had never wanted it. If he had a woman and babes depending upon him, he would not be willing to die.

"Where is Wetatonmi?" he heard Kiye Kipi ask. "Why has she sent this little man with you?"

"She is afraid the white-skins would take him," the girl answered.

"*Take* him? Take a babe?"

"They would take everything else," Twelic snapped, "ponies and land, even Tahmahnewes himself."

"The people are moving out of the valley now," Dirty Dove went on. "Joseph guides them. Alokot and some others are coming here to help you find the rest of the ponies." She hesitated shyly, throwing a quick look at Twelic again. "You were both wonderful, rescuing them like that."

It *had* been wonderful, Kiye Kipi thought. The coup made her blood feel good and hot and strong.

She set the toddler reluctantly on his feet, already missing the warm softness of his little body, knowing, once again, that she was needed and meant for other things. "Watch over him, please," she said to Dirty Dove, then she stepped away from them, gathered herself, and shrilled a loud whinny into the soft, damp quiet.

From a long way off, a stallion answered.

Twelic knew without being told that it was the black he had given her.

They combed the ridges and ravines until the sun went down, searching through the upland meadows and the bushy creek bottoms of Kahmuenem. Several stallions led their mares in at her calls, but Kiye Kipi's heart grew heavier and colder as twilight encroached. She did not have all of them, and there was so little time to dream to search out the remainder. She saw that in Alokot's eyes as he and Twelic rode into a culvert below her.

They drove no ponies ahead of them this time. She goaded her mare again and rode down to meet them.

"I need another sun," she pleaded. "I have never been able to get them all together this quickly!" Tahmahnewes, there were thousands of them!

But Alokot shook his head. "We must go."

"No!" Her heart moved with desperation, with anger. "I am missing hundreds!"

Alokot's mouth set grimly. "It cannot be helped."

She looked to Twelic, begging in spite of her pride. "Help me," she whispered. "Stay with me."

He could not do it for her. He looked away, unaccustomed to this sort of frustration. Alokot spared him an answer.

"You cannot stay, Kiye Kipi. None of us can. How-erd's soldiers think we have left for Lapwai. That is good. They are appeased. We need to keep them that way until we decide what to do next."

Oh, Spirit Chief, she knew there was sense in what he said. Her heart bled as she turned her mare away. "Then I would at least look in on the valley camp before I go."

"Our people are gone from there," Alokot said sharply. "It will only make you hurt."

Her chin came up. "My heart has hurt before."

It was her last chance to find them. The stallions knew it was spring. Perhaps those who were still out would return to the place where their instincts told them they belonged now, where their people were waiting to take them to Imnaha.

Only they would not be going to Imnaha, not this time.

She choked back a cry of grief and rode away. After a few moments, she heard them follow.

By the time they reached the peaks overlooking the old Wallowa camp, night was quickly settling in. The *xayxayx* had built fires, their orange-red light throwing eerie shadows over the place that had once been Kahmuenem.

Beloved Kahmuenem. Kiye Kipi moaned. Once again, there were still some Nimipu ponies in the corral below them.

The tears she had been unable to give to anyone else, she finally gave to them and this homeland. They scalded her eyes, sliding hot and silently down her face as she stared.

The soldier tents had spread, even in the short time she had been in the hills. The *xayxayx* rummaged through the discarded possessions the squaws had left behind in their haste. Greedy white hands tore through parfleches for anything usable, then they threw the empty, seasoned leathers into the flames.

How many buffalo had gone down to make them? How many grueling hours of sweat and work, searching and dreaming?

She swallowed, cleared her throat, and whinnied.

Below them, the valley filled with nasal *xayxayx* curses. A hard, thin smile took her mouth. The soldiers were alarmed, suspecting that a horse had not made the sound at all. But she meant them no harm, not now, not yet. She only said good-bye to the five strong, stout hunting ponies in the corral.

There was no way she could get to them. If they had been roaming free, she might have had her mare call them. But she could not go down there and fling the gate open yet again.

She began to turn away when a pitiful, thin whinny answered hers. It was not from one of the ponies inside the fence. She snapped back, her eyes searching. Then her heart clenched in fury one more time.

A tiny black foal, separated from his mother, stumbled out from the thick growth at the edge of the valley below them. He craned his long neck around, calling again, searching desperately for the voice that had called. The soldiers saw him and rushed for him, hooting and laughing. Even as the little one tried to fight his way free, the white-skins wrestled him back into their camp, roping his thin legs out from beneath him. He landed hard, with another pitiful, bleating cry.

"You will not win, *xayxayx*," she vowed, choking. "As Tahmahnewes is my witness, you may win this battle now, but you will not win the war."

They rode through the long night, catching up with Joseph and the herd just as the moon rose. Still they pushed on, not even the old ones complaining. Kiye Kipi knew that their bones had to ache, but everyone wanted to put space between themselves and the white-skins. They needed to find a sweet, familiar place where they could rest and weep and grieve.

Twelic left with the dawn.

She knew he would branch off before he did it, knew by the way the moonlight played over the muscles of his shoulders, clenched now and anxious. His deep, dark eyes began roving. For the first time she consciously thought that this trouble touched his Hasotoin as well. The man Mon-teeth had told all the bands to come in, even if How-erd had sent more soldiers only to Kahmuenem.

Emotion welled up from somewhere so deep inside her she nearly cried out with it. He had left his own people to help her, to give her a precious gift she would not ever be able to repay. He had given her some of her ponies back, the animals that were her magic and their peoples' salvation.

That was something perhaps more dear than the love she had not been able to earn from him.

She would not cry again.

Her heart was so raw. She brought her chin up and got a shaky grip on herself.

"Thank you, friend," she managed.

He looked around at her sharply. If only for this moment, for this one time, the careful distance was gone from her tone. It stripped too many of his own defenses away from him.

He nodded bluntly. "I must go back."

"Yes."

"Tell Alokot I am glad his wife and child are safe."

She knew he had not come for that reason, but she did not dare speculate about what the truth might be.

"I will," she said quietly.

He turned his pony about, heading north again, toward Lapwai.

"Wait!"

He reined in, waiting for her to go on, his long hair lifting in the wind that called to him. What was she doing?

It was craziness, desperate, dangerous craziness. But with most of her ponies safe and surging on ahead of them, she could not hate him. She wanted to, with every fiber of her being, but all that would come to her was the vicious truth that she was not sure she would ever see him alive again. The threat of war was so sure now, sizzling like meat over flames.

Yearning came back, filling her suddenly. *Just once.* She knew she would never go to another man. In some perverse way, she was tied to this one. She would never have his heart, but oh, she wanted to let herself love him, just once before she turned away. A true woman's need rose in her, to touch him the way he had once touched her. She wanted it all, just once, to have the memory to take with her through all the lonely suns ahead. She wanted it now, before it was too late, but in the end she only shook her head.

She was not sure she would walk away from it whole.

"Nothing," she whispered. She was sure he would not be able to hear her, but his voice came back.

"It is best this way," he said quietly.

Of course it was.

Just as the sun came high again, another startled, frightened cry broke from the people ahead of her. How she was learning to hate that sound!

Kiye Kipi rode to the front of the throng, to the place where Joseph and Alokot had stopped on the west bank of the Snake River. The water was an angry, yellow flood, swollen with spring rains and melting snows from the mountain slopes. As they watched, tree limbs and animal carcasses broke the churning surface, spinning, then disappearing again as foam swallowed them.

They had not reached this place quickly enough.

A few suns ago, it would have been crossable. But the river was treacherous in this moon, rampaging suddenly, defying anyone to breach it.

How-erd had given them only thirty suns. She knew the Snake would stay this way well into the summer moons.

She stopped to lick her lips. "What do we do?"

A nerve twitched at Joseph's throat. "We must go over."

"It would be easier to hold our guns to our breasts," Alokot snapped.

"Tell me of a choice, brother."

Earth Sound had been hovering close by, and now he approached them. "Troops from Wallowa are behind us, less than half a sun's ride."

Kiye Kipi's heart spasmed. *Why?* Why were the blue-coats following them? They were doing what they wanted, heading in the general direction of Lawyer's country! The *xayxayx* could not know they were truly going to Tolo, that they would stop there just before they got to the reserve. And what did it matter if they did? They could wait anywhere they liked—except Kahmuenem—until the moon was over.

Then she understood. How-erd was shrewd and calculating, just as Twelic had said. His warriors would not give the Kahmuenem any opportunity to go another way, would not let them consider turning about to fight. Their babes and women were with them. If they stopped, the white-skins would greet them with guns.

The water boiled by at their feet, swirling and taunting them with more of the pieces of life it had claimed.

"Our every alternative is on the other side," Joseph said grimly. She knew it was true, and suddenly, she knew something else as well.

That Safe Place was northeast, somewhere beyond this water.

"Joseph is right," she heard herself say. "I think we must keep going."

Alokot turned on her, still angry and frustrated. "Then tell us, Pony Wife, how we are to do it. Are your blacks and your hunting ponies strong enough to cross this?"

She could not be positive, but she thought perhaps they were. "I do not know what else to do but have them try it."

"We have thousands of spotted ponies as well," he snapped. "What of them? What of our families and their lodges, what of the elders and the dogs?"

She left them and rode closer to the bank. The roar was deafening, mocking her. *It was not possible.* Too many would die. Unless . . .

She looked back at the squaws, staring wide-eyed at her. "Your lodge skins!" she cried. "Unroll them quickly, please!"

She went back to the men. "This is what I think we must do," she began to explain.

They listened, Alokot narrow eyed, Joseph and Earth Sound grim. Gradually, other warriors began crowding around to hear her. She knew they would accept her plan if only because there was no other alternative.

Please, please let those blacks be strong enough. She saw in their eyes that her warhorses would have to prove their worth beyond all doubt now . . . or Mon-teeth would win.

It would begin slipping through her fingers like sand again, all the acceptance and the respect of belonging, of being needed. If her ponies failed, she would be more alone than she had ever been before, because even she would not be able to bear her own company.

She dropped to the ground to help the squaws lash the skins into rafts. She worked quickly, grimly, not allowing her hands to shake. She looked up only once, at Dirty Dove waiting nearby.

"More ropes!"

The girl looked miserable. "There are no more."

"Then reins, leads, anything that will tie."

Dirty Dove ran off and came back a moment later, laden with the things. Then she, too, hunkered down to strap the squaws' packs onto the lodge covers. They thrust their knives through the corners, punching holes, pulling the ends of the straps through until there were four of them to each raft, winding into the grass like snakes.

Kiye Kipi stood again, feeling all eyes upon her, some of them hopeful, some pleading, some dubious. "The elders and all but the youngest babes can hold on to the sides of these things."

"And what of the rest of us?" someone demanded.

"We will go over in shifts."

Old Joseph, oh, friend, pray for me.

"You . . . the warriors, should go first, in case something . . . goes wrong." She squared her jaw, making her voice hard through sheer dint of will. "Take the rafts with the packs first. Tow them across with the ropes. Then bring them back for the wee ones and the elders, and lastly come for the women."

"No pony can do that! That is three trips!"

"Four." She thought they would probably have to drive the spotted herd across, as well.

Joseph looked at her. "You are sure about this?"

She gave him a horrible smile. "No."

A dark, voluminous cloud moved over the sun, throwing them into shadow. She shivered at the omen, and looked at Alokot, at Earth Sound. "Go, please."

The warriors mounted, gathering up the raft ropes. In squares of four, they hoisted them off the ground and moved down into the water.

The legs of the first pony were wrenched aside, out from under him, by the river's monstrous force. He floundered, and someone screamed. Then the rest of the war ponies splashed in. The violent current caught them as well, sweeping them downstream, tumbling one pony over so that his legs flailed wildly above the foam.

Kiye Kipi moaned. She had sent them to their deaths.

Then the toppled pony came upright again, struggling gamely, his rider still clinging impossibly to his back and gasping. They were so far down the river now, but they were doing it, they were making it! She prayed again, her hands balling into fists.

Alokot came out on the far bank. His black staggered up, finding purchase with his front hooves, his back legs thrusting, kicking, scrambling. Then he was on land again, and another warrior came up, and another. The rafts lurched and scraped onto the sand.

Another sound echoed out over the thunder of the water. It was a howl of jubilation, and it came from her own throat.

Kiye Kipi ran down to the bank again. "The elders now!" she screamed across. "Come back! Come back for the elders and the babes!"

The warriors unloaded the packs, taking up the rafts again. This time they crossed more easily, so much less encumbered. The ponies were not terrified this time; they were becoming inured.

"Yes," she breathed. "Yes."

When the old ones and the babes were safe on the far bank, the warriors came back one more time. This time the spare raft ropes were used to tie the tiniest babes onto their mothers' backs. The squaws began to climb up behind their men.

"No!"

They looked around at her, startled.

"You ask too much of them," she explained.

Her ponies had proven their worth, and her heart swelled with love and gratitude for them. She wanted to wrap her arms around their glossy wet necks and weep. But it was not over yet. Their sides heaved; their nostrils flared hard, showing crimson red inside.

More clouds moved over the sun.

"We must not ask them to carry any more weight this time than they have to," she went on. "I think the women will have to ride over by themselves."

A few shook their heads in fear and desperation. Then We-tatonmi pushed past Alokot and leaped astride his black. "We saw how the men did it," she snapped. "Are we cowards? If we are, then we should go back to Wallowa now and let those white-skins destroy us!"

Kiye Kipi found her eyes, her heart in her own. *Thank you, friend.*

Dirty Dove went to a pony as well, and then all the women were mounting, following their example. Little Mole was already on the far bank; he had been old enough to hold on to one of the rafts. Wetatonmi took a suckling child from a squaw who had just given birth, one who was barely strong enough to get herself across.

"We are ready now," she said.

"What of you?" Dirty Dove asked Kiye Kipi.

She waited with the dismounted warriors, glancing back to the spotted herd that the boys held farther back on the prairie. "I will come last," she said quietly.

The women began struggling across, some screaming, their babes wailing, most holding on grimly as the water crashed over them. One fell off and fought frantically for the far bank until a friend caught her doeskin dress and hauled her along. But they made it . . . they made it.

Wetatonmi and Dirty Dove turned the ponies about one last time, driving them back so that they could goad on the rest of the herd.

They staggered down into the raging water even as the sky finally opened up above them. Kiye Kipi gasped as the sudden downpour drenched her and thunder rumbled across the sky. Her blood went cold, and she looked up at the thick, churning clouds.

Tahmahnewes was warning her.

He did not have to. She looked back at the blacks again, her heart chugging as they finally reached the close bank. Many stumbled and fell with exhaustion, their sides heaving, their eyes white and rolling.

She keened a sound of despair. She would kill them if she pushed them further.

She ran to them, tormenting them into rising again. They staggered up. "Make them walk!" she cried to Wetatonmi and Dirty Dove, and some of the warriors came to help, slowly leading the beasts back and forth until their breath quieted. She looked grimly to Alokot.

"We will have to wait out this storm," she said.

The warrior backhanded streaming water out of his eyes.

Her own hair was plastered flat to her head, her cheeks. She looked to the people on the far bank; she could scarcely make them out in the teeming rain.

"By then the blacks should have recovered," she went on. "Where are those soldiers?"

Alokot's gaze measured her. "I do not think it matters any longer."

"Why?" She gaped at him, not understanding, then she followed his eyes to the blacks again.

"For the first time, I truly believe we can beat these white-skins at whatever game they play," he mused quietly.

"No other tribe ever has," Joseph said flatly, riding up to them. "It is why so many of our elders struggled so hard against this fight."

"No other people have had these ponies," Alokot pointed out.

The three exchanged looks, and something wild leaped in Kiye Kipi's heart. Oh, yes, the Nimipu were different. Somehow, she felt it now, too. The blacks' strength was unbreachable, and with them the Nimipu could run from this assault unlike any other native people before them. But it was more than that, she realized. It was Joseph, so shrewd, his wisdom and tenacity tempering the ferocity of his warriors. It was men like Alokot and Twelic, as intelligent and thoughtful as they were brave.

And it was the women.

It was Wetatonmi and Dirty Dove, courageous in their own right, willing to suffer and strive to survive. Once again, Kiye Kipi felt like crying. But now they were good tears, born of something treacherous, something like hope.

"We can do this," she breathed. "These white-skins will not have us."

Even Joseph's eyes looked suddenly clearer. Alokot nodded and grinned savagely.

"Yes. If they force us to fight, I think we can win."

32

THE HARD EDGE of their confidence lasted as long as the storm.

The rain sheeted down and the warriors paced the bank, studying the river as though they could tame it with their angry eyes. Kiye Kipi helped Wetatonmi and Dirty Dove restore the ponies, while the boys sat slouched atop their mounts on the prairie, watching over the rest of the herd.

Kiye Kipi looked back to them idly and saw one youth straighten abruptly. *The soldiers were coming.*

Her heart squeezed in panic. Surely How-erd's men would not shoot at them for simply stopping to rest their mounts! But then, she could not be sure what these men were capable of anymore.

"We have trouble!" the boy cried, galloping back to them. Alokot swore vicious oaths at the blue-coats as he swung up onto his warhorse.

"No! No!" the young warrior argued. "The soldiers remain farther back, watching us with their tube-glasses that catch the light. The ones who chase us now are those *xayxayx* who have come to live in our valleys!"

The settlers? Why? They had gotten the land; the Indians were gone.

Then she understood. They saw their chance to take the spoils now, as well. They wanted everything; they wanted it all.

"Do the soldiers stop them?" she cried. "Do they just look on?"

A whooping, yowling sound answered her. The rain was easing, and the white-skins' voices carried clearly. She whipped about again. The settlers were stampeding the spotted herd.

Rage swept through her. "No!"

Her *wyakin* mare whinnied loudly. The other blacks responded in spite of their exhaustion, stomping, rearing, throwing their heads where they were held near the water. The boys tried mightily to stop the others from bolting, but they plunged now as well, beginning to gallop, and they were not weary. In their startled fear, they turned for home.

Kiye Kipi flung herself, belly first, onto the back of her mare. Alokot swept past her, then Earth Sound and the others. But oh, Spirit Chief, their war ponies were struggling so, still exhausted from the river! She passed them again easily.

Ahead of her, the boys managed to turn the bulk of the herd around, but hundreds more still swarmed for Kahmuenem. The white-skins chased them, laughing and hooting, flapping their hats and shirts and shooting their guns into the air.

Hoofbeats were coming up hard behind her. She twisted about incredulously. She could not think what animal would be strong enough to run so fast after being tortured by the river.

It was the stallion, the black that Twelic had given her.

He carried no man; he had thrown his rider. His gait was as thunderous as her heartbeat as he came up beside her, and she veered her mare that way to head him off before he could pass. But he was crazed now, and he did not swerve. She felt the ponies come together with a sickening lurch, hooves flailing as her own mare reared.

Pain twisted up her thigh where her knee was caught between them. Then her mare was going down, and she was thrown from her back. She hit the ground hard and came up on her knees, gasping, hurt shooting through her.

The black stallion went on.

Her mare heaved herself to her feet again, her eyes white-wild, looking after the ponies who still ran. *She would lose her!* She would surely lose her, too, if she could not call the herd back with her mind!

She screamed at them desperately, silently, clutching fistfuls of grass. Agony creased through her with the effort. Her mare reared up again, pummeling the air with her front hooves. Kiye Kipi saw their gaits breaking, saw the herd crashing as some of them turned into each other in confusion. A few mares split off, but it was not enough. She could not reach them!

If only she could throw herself into a dream!

But she could not, had never been able to do that, no matter what Toolhoolhoolzote had said about her magic. Her truest power lay in the deepest, darkest place of her soul. Perhaps it was strong enough to escape when she slept, but she was not sleeping now, and she still could not hurl her way into these real beasts. Only her own mare truly responded, whinnying a shrill sound of torment as her heart told her to run, and her mistress's magic held her.

Kiye Kipi threw her head back and gave an inconsolable wail. Alokot reached her and dismounted, hauling her to her feet again. Her eyes came away from the lost ponies and focused on him helplessly.

"I . . . could not do it," she moaned.

"You have the black's sons, his daughters. They will breed on. The *xayxayx* mostly took the spotted ones, and they are good for little now but trading. I do not think we will be doing that this summer."

It did not matter. They were her peoples' wealth, her beloved responsibility, and they were gone.

It did not even matter that she had lost a hated, coveted piece of Twelic. She looked back at the storm of ponies, small but still riotous on the horizon. What mattered was that finally, the *xayxayx* had taken too much.

Hatred made her throat ache. She looked up to the sky and made a vow to Tahmahnewes.

Oh, yes, the Nimipu would win this fight! They would do it because of Joseph and the warriors, because of the women and the black ponies that remained. But they would do it also because she would take this power that Tahmahnewes had given her and hone it to unprecedented strength. Her jaw hardened and her eyes blazed. She would protect her people against this thieving, unconscionable enemy, or she would die trying.

She knew what she had to do. She had to find a way to jump right into the living flesh of the animals that were her spirit guides.

Fear tightened her belly. She was not sure it was something any animal caller had accomplished before.

She turned away from Alokot, and her voice was strange and flat when she spoke again.

"Come. We have a river to cross."

The other Dreamer bands were at Tolo Lake as well.

The Kahmuenem reached the place at dawn, the strong riders reining in to wait for the stragglers. Kiye Kipi shrugged to unstick her stiff, drying doeskin from her back. All around her, the women looked on, cold, wet, and dispirited.

She moved among them, touching a hand here, managing a smile there. "Put up your lodges," she said quietly. "We will eat, rest, and then we will all feel better."

"The lodge covers have holes in them from the rafts," someone murmured, as though it were too much of a task to think what to do about it.

"Better that snakes crawl in than the *xayxayx*," she pointed out.

The squaws dismounted and began to work. Kiye Kipi rode her mare out to where the boys had stopped with the herd.

Fresh hatred and pain clenched her heart. She thought the band had probably left for Imnaha with nearly three thousand ponies, but that had been nearly a lifetime ago. Perhaps twenty-five hundred were left now. The white-skins would feast well this winter season, she thought viciously. They would ride a few animals as strong as her own.

The sun was hot and high by the time she had rubbed the ponies down lovingly with fresh grass. She spent the rest of the daylight tending to those with strained muscles and wounds. Finally, she returned her medicines to her parfleches and trudged back to the camp. The people were settled now, their voices dull and empty as they talked amongst each other.

She dropped her parfleches near Wetatonmi's lodge. Her own hide cover lay in a wet, mangled heap nearby. There would be time enough to fix it later. Now she left the Kahmuenem to wander through the other camps.

She paused, hovered, listened, at every headman's fire, then she moved on again. The air felt hot, restless. Hatred for the *xayxayx* seemed to burn like banked embers in every man's eyes. The warriors continued to speak for fighting back against the white-skins who would cheat them and dictate to them as though they were gods. The elders and headmen fretted over the impossible price of war.

Old men, can you not see? The price of peace would be so much greater! The *xayxayx* took ponies, land, everything!

She found herself near the Hasotoin fire before she knew she was going there. She stepped back quickly into the shadows that dusk brought, her heart coming alive again, moving strangely. Stupid, stupid . . . She did not want to see Twelic. She still felt vulnerable to him after his recent kindness; there was an ache in her where her belly should have been.

He stood beside the council fire, at Looking Glass's back. For a long time, she watched him unobserved, his rigid stance, his arrogant jaw. His hair fell loose and wavy over his shoulders except for his braids, and the firelight played on the smooth, naked skin of his chest. Something shuddered deep inside her.

She watched his face, so perfectly handsome once, so rough and hard now with its scars and its anger. She wondered idly how she must look to him these suns, now that there was nothing left in her of the child. Was her fear on her face? Did it make her look as gaunt as he did?

Did he still think she was beautiful?

She ran her fingers unconsciously through her tangled hair just as he became aware of her. His eyes flashed up abruptly and he left the council, his stride long and hard as he crossed to her. She took one instinctive step back, then she waited for him.

Her enemy, her friend, her only true lover . . . *what was he?* Could she just be his friend when she wanted him so?

She was taller than many warriors, but she met this one eye to eye. She gazed at him levelly.

"What has happened to you since I left?" he demanded. They did not need greetings anymore.

Startled, Kiye Kipi followed his eyes down her doeskin. The hem was rent, the side torn from where she had gotten trapped between the stallion and her mare. A livid, purple bruise was beginning to swell at her knee.

Now that she was aware of it, it ached again, but she only shrugged. "They took more ponies. I tried to stop them."

New anger flared in his eyes. "I should have stayed with you longer."

Her spine straightened. "There was nothing anyone could have done."

Her implication was clear. If she could not have saved the herd, then he certainly could not have done it. Twelic felt a jolt of irritation, followed by impossible amusement.

"So be it, Pony Wife. How arrogant of me to think that I, a mere warrior, could have made a difference."

She very nearly smiled. Her heart was too heavy. She shrugged again instead.

"What have you done for that wound?"

"Done?" Surprised, she glanced down at her knee again. "It is not a wound, only a hurt in the flesh. No bone is broken, no blood escapes."

"You will not be able to walk on it in the morning."

She looked at him incredulously. "Why not?"

"It will grow stiff over night, like an unfleshed hide."

"Oh." She nodded. "Then I will put that balm on it that I use on the ponies' muscles when they work too hard."

"That will help. But you should keep the blood moving through it as well."

Before she knew he would touch her again, he went down on one knee. His hands were strong, hard, kneading. His touch was the single memory that could undo the last of her caution, her sanity.

"No." She stepped back quickly. *Not again. Not now.*

"Quiet," he muttered irritably, holding her.

His fingers worked and pain screamed suddenly up into her thigh again. For a moment, it cleared her head and she gasped. Then the warmth began to pool in her gut, liquid and swelling, wanting with a whole different kind of ache.

Oh, curse him! It was the one thing she could not bear . . . the unquenchable yearning of every woman's desire, when she was not and never would be his woman.

"Stop!" This time she wrenched away from him hard.

He looked up at her, one brow raised idly, but his own belly tightened at her reaction. It was the same one she had given him near Wallowa. Still she wanted, no matter what her flashing eyes said, no matter what the set of her shoulders conveyed.

"You remember."

Dangerous. He was playing with fire. It tantalized him, caught at him. But he had to know, even if he could not think what to do about it.

He straightened slowly, still watching her. Kiye Kipi flushed and looked back at the council fire. There had been just enough male arrogance in his voice to make her hate him again.

"What happens here?" she asked, her voice strangled.

Finally, he looked as well. "If the other headmen are cowards, then this Hasotoin leader is a fool," he snapped, his thoughts coming back to the trouble.

"Looking Glass would fight the *xayxayx*?" she asked, surprised.

It did not seem in his character, and indeed, Twelic shook his head.

"No. When the rest of you go to Lapwai, he will crawl off on his belly to hide."

Her heart thumped. "Where? There is no place safe anymore . . . not in Nimipu land."

"I cannot get him to see that. He would go home."

She was almost sure there would be soldiers on the Kooskooskia, too. If they were not there yet, they soon would be.

"The blue-coats will find him there!" she protested.

"Yes. And only their god knows what they will do to our women, our babes. I have heard stories of the Cheyenne, the Navajo . . ." He trailed off.

"You would worry over that? You?"

His eyes swerved to her angrily. "What sort of man do you think I am, Screamer? Do you think I have no heart? I have a care for the weak. I saved you once, when you were young."

Her heart kicked. Yes, in some ways he had.

And in some ways, he had broken her so that she would never, truly be whole.

"Looking Glass thinks if he does what he has always done, if he hides from this trouble, then he will avoid it again," he went on. "That will not happen this time. Even if he remains quiet and unobtrusive in our homeland, I think How-erd's blue-coats will ferret him out."

Yet she knew that that was what many warriors wanted, to return to their homes and meet the soldiers when they came to try to force them away. "What do *you* want?" she asked curiously.

"To get the women and babes to that place of peace I dreamed of, and then I would turn back and kill them all."

She jolted. She had never told him how clearly she had dreamed of that Safe Place. Now it frightened her even more than his touch to know how clearly it had come to him as well.

She began to back up, but he snagged her arm, holding her. His touch—still hot and hard—made her tremble.

"You know it is there," he said.

She nodded, her breath feeling short.

"And you will take the People to it," he went on.

"My Kahmuenem perhaps. Your Hasotoin will die if Looking Glass has his way."

She felt his hand tighten. "No. Not all of us. My dream saw you carry our people to safety."

Oh, Tahmahnewes, they could not speak of this again! It seemed so dangerous, so profane, and yet she looked back at him, placing her own hand over his. Perhaps this was what she had come for, this reassurance that only he could give her, because his dream, his future were somehow bound to hers.

"You said . . ." She trailed off, swallowing carefully. "You said the rest of us would go to Lapwai. Do you believe that?"

"You will intend to."

"But we will not make it?"

"No."

She did not doubt that. There was too much rage in the warriors' eyes. And yet . . .

"It cannot be a bad thing," she said. "We both dreamed of it as good. We both went to this Safe Place."

He was too quiet for too long. "No, Screamer. I saw *you* go there. I never saw that land at all."

It took several heartbeats for the full impact of his words to reach her. *I never saw that land at all.*

But she had been so sure . . .

With him, it would be a haven. Without him, exile. The possibility froze the blood inside her. *She could not lose him.* She knew, suddenly, that she could not go on without him. Like the wind, though she could not see it or hold it in her hand, she always knew he was there.

Tahmahnewes, still she loved him.

She began to inch away from him again, shaking her head in denial. Then a shout came from somewhere nearby, and she whirled around, looking for the trouble.

"What now?" Twelic snarled. The sound had come from within the Hasotoin camp.

She understood suddenly, instinctively. The vision bloomed in her mind's eye again, a dream she had had that was not truly a dream at all. She remembered the mountain pass over the Bitterroots, walking beside Twelic . . . Wahlitits and Swan Necklace with blood on their hands.

Her heart began pounding sickly. Wahlitits was astride, trotting toward them, his face twisted with shame and anger and frustration. She realized that he had been riding about, trying to incite the warriors even more. He was one to want war without considering anyone but himself, anything but the coup he so desperately needed.

He had scattered an elder's drying salmon. The fish was flattened to mush in the mud; his pony's hooves were caked with the stringy pink pulp. Behind him, the old squaw waved her knife angrily.

"You play so brave!" she shouted. "All you do is rob my belly! If you are so strong, why is it that you have not even avenged your father's death by now? Coward! *Coward!* We have no use for your kind now!"

"No." Kiye Kipi heard her own voice moan from her. She did not care for the warrior's pride. As his mouth began to pinch, she knew only that his anger meant danger. It had always meant danger, to her, and now to everyone else.

Twelic caught her, holding her back when she would have run to him. She fought him as Wahlitits began calling to the other men.

Too many would listen to him now.

"Follow me! It is time! We will kill them all!" he shouted. "Those who would act while the true cowards of our people suffer, come with me! I will avenge my father! I will avenge the land. I will avenge it all!"

"No!" She shouted it this time, and Twelic shook her. She twisted around to look at him.

"You must stop him," she gasped. "Do you remember? Blood on their hands . . ."

"He has no courage, no strength," he answered tightly. "He will do nothing but talk about it. That is all he has ever done."

"No." She shook her head wildly. "Not this time."

She looked back to see Swan Necklace joining him, and she knew.

This time Wahlitits would get his coup, and it would bring fighting to the Nimipu whether they were ready for it or not.

33

WAHLITITS RETURNED FOURTEEN suns later.

It was near dawn, and the last of the Keh-khee-tahl moon was thin and falling. Still, many in the big Tolo camp were awake. Some squaws worked to dry fish as though the food stores could save them. Still others rested pensively outside their lodges.

Kiye Kipi sat with Wetatonmi, Little Mole dozing on her lap. Wetatonmi was packing and unpacking parfleches, moving this item there, tossing another thing aside.

"Perhaps it will not come to fighting," Kiye Kipi said quietly. But she did not believe it, and neither did her friend. The other squaw shrugged stiffly, and Kiye Kipi looked up at the slivered moon again, feeling cold.

The time How-erd had given them was up.

The sky was a dusky pink-blue when Alokot returned to the fire. "It is decided," he said flatly. "Joseph will go in."

Kiye Kipi felt her head begin to spin. One of Joseph's wives gave a little keening cry.

"And you, husband?" Wetatonmi demanded.

"I cannot. I promised our father."

Wetatonmi began gathering her parfleches a final time.

"You will go with Joseph," Alokot said, and his wife turned on him with more ferocity than Kiye Kipi had ever seen in her before.

"Never! I will put my knife to my throat first. My place is with you."

Alokot's face mottled. "Our child—"

"Will not be raised by *xayxayx* ways and a fire-breathing god!" she vowed. "Not as long as there is breath in my body!"

Kiye Kipi gathered the sleeping toddler in her arms and stood as well. "You say you think we can survive this," she reminded Alokot. "Stand behind your words, brother. Let us fight. I would try." She knew he would not deny her. They would need her; those who fought back would require her magic, her ponies. That was what her *wyakin* had told her.

Twelic had dreamed it that way, too. She looked around at the Hasotoin fires, a quick, darting glance, unable to stop herself.

She could not see him there. It seemed an omen.

Alokot opened his mouth to argue further when a war cry shattered the preternatural calm. They all snapped about to look the way she did. The cry had come from the Hasotoin camp again.

She had known this would happen, too, though few of the others, even Twelic, believed it yet. Now they would see. Wahlitits had finally gotten his coup.

He came into the lake camp at a gallop, Swan Necklace beside him, his other new comrades trailing. Oh, Tahmah-newes, yes, there was blood on his hands, not as she had seen it once before, but black and drying in the new light. He thrust his gun at the sky, hooting, and there was something wild on his face, something crazed.

She pushed Little Mole back at his mother and began running to the Hasotoin camp, the others following her. As they passed his fire, Joseph lunged to his feet as well, then stood there as still as stone. Looking Glass was one of the few who had been sleeping. He came out of his lodge, groggy, his hair tangled. But Toolhoolhoolzote, White Bird, and Huishuis Kute came to the Hasotoin camp, and their warriors followed them, yelling, shoving past each other to get close to the commotion.

"I am the first man brave enough to strike back against these mongrels!" Wahlitits crowed. His grin made his narrow face look like that of a spirit monster, then it was gone from her line of sight as the warriors dragged him from his mount. He went down thinking they heralded him, then his scream chilled her blood. The warriors began pummeling him.

Sweet Tahmahnewes, what was happening to them, to all of them?

Joseph's voice boomed out, and Kiye Kipi stumbled about to see that he had left his fire to join them. She had never heard him bellow before, not in all the seasons she had known him.

"You are not brave! Your stupidity stinks like a dead, rotting beast!"

The crowd quieted, staring at him, stunned.

"See what you have done?" he roared on. "The babes, the elders, the women no longer have the choice of seeking sanctuary! You have destroyed them!"

Blood and saliva trickled from one corner of Wahlitits's mouth as he stood again, swaying unsteadily. "Those who would go to Lapwai . . . are the cowards," he insisted.

"No," said White Bird more quietly. "Tahmahnewes never meant that women and children should have to fight to prove their worth, and a man who forces them to do so has none."

The beginnings of fear, of understanding, touched Wahlitits's face too late. His eyes began darting around at all of them, searching for someone who would back him, but even his own men were retreating now before the headmen's wrath.

"For more seasons than you have lived, our leaders have resisted spilling white blood," White Bird went on. "Now, for the first time in Nimipu history, you, a mongrel warrior, have defied all that wisdom. You have done it on your own, without council. What do you think How-erd will do now? He will send soldiers here for us. You, one man, have declared war upon his *xayxayx*. You have done it for all of us, even those of us who would not fight. You are no better than the whiteskins, to make our choices for us!"

The warriors began roaring again.

"I curse you." White Bird spat angrily. "I banish you forever from my hearth."

A wail of disbelief broke from Wahlitits. "I have coups!"

he screeched. "Fifteen white-skins have died! You were going to fight anyway! You were!"

The women began weeping. Kiye Kipi turned to the one closest to her and hugged her clumsily. She knew terror, but she knew a dull, dazed sense of acceptance, too.

Now they would have to run.

Skeletal lodge frames thrust up from Mother Earth, naked in the new sun as it rose higher. Squaws shouted, packing frantically, while the headmen met at White Bird's fire. Their elite warriors pressed close about them.

Kiye Kipi's gaze moved between them and the women, then she pushed her way past the warriors to the council. She could not, would not, wait at her pony like a docile, mindless squaw. She simply could not do it anymore.

As always, and without surprise, she found herself beside Twelic.

His gaze moved to her fleetingly, then turned to the headmen again. She felt the heat of fury coming off Twelic's skin so intensely that it seemed he touched her without truly doing so. Then his fingers closed over her own.

She jolted and started to pull away . . . but no. There was no threat in his touch, just cohesion, strength, comfort. She needed that now more than she needed to stay safe from him.

She held on to him as Joseph looked to her and gave a short nod.

"Our pony wife has said we should run. I do not think we have a choice now."

"She is a woman." Toolhoolhoolzote sneered, and oh, his hatred when he looked at her! It slapped at her like a physical blow. She would have staggered back but for the fact that Twelic held her.

"I will not abide by her words," the *tiwats* went on. "She calls animals. Who is she to lead men?"

Huishuis Kute looked around as though he could spot her. He was a thin, ugly man, but she found that she did not dislike him. There was something intelligent about his eyes.

"I do not know of her," he answered, "but if that is what

she has said, then her sense is good. What else can we do? If we go on to Lapwai, I do not trust what How-erd might do now. We should find someplace safe, a spot where we can protect our women, and wait for him. Then he will have to come to us, and we can try to talk this thing out. We can tell him it was only one warrior, a crazy one, and that his actions do not speak for us all. Maybe then he will accept our women at Lapwai.''

"We have tried to tell him that Lawyer did not speak for us!'' someone shouted. "He has no ears!''

"That is why I think we should be cautious,'' Huishuis Kute agreed. "We must keep ahead of the *xayxayx* until we can get our families to safety. Then we can try to talk to him.''

"There is a protected place in my country,'' said old White Bird, "a canyon named after my father. I invite you all to come there. It is deep, a good place for defense. We can put our women inside it. The soldiers will not be able to get down to them without passing our warriors on the slopes first. They would have to appear on open ground, high above the defile, in plain view of our weapons.''

Voices escalated in agreement. Kiye Kipi let her breath out in a hiss, and Twelic looked at her sharply.

"It will not work,'' she said, strangled. "I did not dream of this White Bird Canyon. I know that is not the place.''

Twelic's eyes told her that he did not believe their flight would end there either, but then went dark and unreadable.

"Be . . . safe, Screamer.''

It sounded so lame, so much less than what he intended. He pulled his hand away abruptly, struggling with something inside himself, something as strong and vicious as any white-skinned enemy. *How could he let her go there?* He wondered for the first time if he would lose her at the canyon, if the place they had dreamed of was only Tahmahnewes's afterworld. He wondered if he would spend the rest of his suns wondering if he could have said good-bye to the wind, defying everything he was, to give himself to the sweet heat she promised.

Horror bloomed in her eyes as she understood. "Your people are still going back to the Kooskooskia!'' she breathed.

He looked deliberately at the headmen again. ''My cousin will not be swayed, not even by this.''

The council began breaking up. She did not see Toolhool-hoolzote lunge to his feet in fury, but Twelic did.

''Be careful of that one who is your grandfather,'' he mused. ''He is a formidable enemy.''

She spared Toolhoolhoolzote a glance, then came back to him.

''You do not have to stay with Looking Glass!'' But she knew as soon as she said the words that they were crazy.

He only gave her a measuring glance and turned away. The *xayxayx* would do what he himself could not. They would keep him from her, give back to him the only life he craved. The Hasotoin would be fighting now.

Perhaps there was peace in that after all.

The ride to White Bird Canyon took less than half a sun, even with the lagging elders and the camp encumbrances. The Dreamer bands reached it as the sun went low again, pitching the chasm into premature darkness.

Kiye Kipi stayed up on the ridge, watching as the others descended, her ponies teeming down the hills. Her eyes searched over the place, looking for assurance it could not give.

She knew nothing of fighting.

Twelic, where are you now?

Panic closed her throat. She needed him! She could not do this alone! Their dreams had been the same; they were supposed to be together now. She needed to see this place through his eyes, but she had only her own, and that scared her.

The Tolo feeder river ran through the canyon's cavernous depths, snaking out of sight behind a ridge to the south. She thought that might be a good place to protect her ponies, but would the *xayxayx* come that way? She did not know and her head hurt. Cottonwoods snarled together there, then gave way to barren, undulating land that swelled more and more as it stretched out. The higher slopes were scattered with pines and alder brush, patched with thickets. Perhaps the warriors could hide there.

All around her, on the high ground, the sweet grass of summer rippled in the last golden light of the sun. She twisted around on her mount to look out at that, too. A distant, well-trodden path made a dark crease on the prairie. She followed it with her eyes, guessing that it led back to Lapwai.

A *xayxayx* road . . . in the heart of White Bird's land, land that had never been given. It was so wrong!

Would they come that way, How-erd's incessant, righteous bastards?

Her gut twisted. If they did, they would have no trouble finding them. The Nimipu had crossed over that same trail. Thousands upon thousands of their ponies had left a different kind of track, torn grasses, fresh droppings still steaming. Mother Earth was gouged and torn from their travois poles. She did not know fighting, but she knew that that was not good.

She started down into the canyon. If the white-skins came, they would come slowly. She remembered that, had always believed it, had worked against it. They would be traveling on their seed-fed, silver-hooved ponies.

If they came, at least they would not be on the Kooskooskia.

All that was left now was to wait. She felt cold all the way to her bones.

34

THEY CAME IN the night like *cewcew* ghosts.

Kiye Kipi lay wide-eyed and wakeful in her bedding. Beyond the tattered hide of her lodge wall, she heard the wolves howling their songs to each other. Crickets screeched. They were good sounds, peaceful sounds . . . and then came the furtive step of a moccasin.

She sat up, feeling as if a thousand insects crawled on her skin, then she moved to her door flap to peer out. Earth Sound went past on careful, whispering feet, keeping to the shadows. His best skills were in tracking, in stealth, in melting into places where no man could see him. Joseph had sent him to watch over that treacherous *xayxayx* trail from Lapwai.

She hissed a sound, and he looked back, startled, then he ducked into her lodge. He held himself careful and distant from her now, never truly meeting her eyes. Renewed sadness flickered in her, for him, for herself, but there were more important things to think of now.

"Tell me," she urged.

"They come from the north."

She closed her eyes and breathed again. She would be able to hide the herd behind the southern ridge after all.

She got to her feet and began gathering some parfleches and her bow. "It took them long," she whispered. Five suns, longer than any of them had expected. "What of their ponies?"

"Staggering as you once said they would be," the warrior

allowed. "They have come far. I recognize some of the soldiers from Wallowa."

Her heart kicked a little. "So this How-erd is fallible."

Finally, he looked at her, heat in his eyes. "Yes, I think so.
He put many of his men in our valleys, expecting trouble to
come from us. For some reason, he has his eyes set on Joseph.
Wahlitits's trouble near his reservation seems to have surprised
him."

"So he has had to rush all his soldiers here to come after
us now."

"Yes. They do not look as though they have slept, and their
mounts are heavily laden. They rest in a camp up on the grasslands. I think they are waiting for dawn."

She nodded with a bitter, knowing smile. Dawn would not
be enough time for them to recover, not with that forced
march.

"Tell Joseph that I will take all the herds down the river,"
she said. "Tell Alokot that if there is fighting, I will send him
fresh ponies if they are needed."

She ducked outside, keeping to the shadows as he had. Now
that it was upon them, her heart felt calm, cold. Her hands did
not tremble as she laid her quiver against her back.

She was ready.

*Curse them, Tahmahnewes. Please let us stop them before
they take it all.*

The first sun came into the canyon in streams of pale yel-
low-white. Kiye Kipi watched from the riverbank. Her ponies
surrounded her, nudging her now and then in curiosity.

There was a forced normalcy in the squaws' brittle movements, but if white-skins were watching, she did not think they
would notice anything amiss. *Were they watching?* Did they
have sentinels, too? How many mistakes would this How-erd
make?

The sun began to rise full above the chasm, and still his
xayxayx did not attack. Something treacherous began to move
in her belly, something almost like hope.

A handful of warriors began to surround Alokot. The

women returned to their lodges, keeping their little ones and their riding ponies close. The other men moved around the swelling rises, talking idly, but they all had their weapons in their hands.

Then one of Joseph's wives gave Alokot a swatch of whitened doeskin. He tied it to the end of his spear, knotting it with his teeth, then he leaped upon his black and rode up the precipice to greet the *xayxayx*.

Kiye Kipi hald her breath. Her heart slugged once, twice, against her ribs as she waited.

Silence.

She let her air out slowly. Perhaps How-erd would see reason after all. Perhaps he would listen to Alokot's words about Wahlitits. She dared to believe that for one more quiet, fragile heartbeat, then the cracking sound of a gun splintered the air.

She screamed without meaning to, and came to her feet. All around her, the warriors who remained in the chasm dived for cover. They went into the trees, crouched behind bushes, pulled piles of rocks about themselves. She gaped at the places they had been, disbelieving. She could not see any of them now at all.

Quiet fell again, eerie and strange, too encompassing. The only sounds in the Canyon were the heavy rustlings of hides falling as the squaws began frantically tearing down their lodges.

What was happening up there?

When a war cry finally screamed out from above, it raised the hair on her nape. More gunfire sounded suddenly, rattling into the silence. Alokot crashed over the ridge behind her, his pony plunging, then crabbing and scrambling over the ridges to the east side of the canyon.

"They come!" he shouted.

"Did you tell them?" she screamed.

"They shot first, so I will lead them down here!"

His warriors came behind him. Kiye Kipi called for her mare, catching her from the ponies who were beginning to mill in panic around her.

She pulled herself up on her, a bullet whining through the

air over her head. She could not help herself. She yipped again, ducking instinctively, then she saw Wetatonmi and Dirty Dove break from the crowd of women and run toward her.

"No! Go back!" she screamed. The *xayxayx* were beginning to come down behind her. Brush rattled and cracked there, but Dirty Dove planted her palms on the rump of a hunting pony and hurtled herself astride. Wetatonmi caught another black.

"What do you do?" Kiye Kipi cried. "Where is your babe?"

"Joseph's wife has him. The women will flee, and Joseph will lead them." Wetatonmi's eyes came around to her, blazing with courage, daring her to argue with her. "I can help. I have had enough of this thieving, murdering offal. Now, finally, we have war."

Kiye Kipi felt it, too, a lurch of her heart, a rush of adrenaline. *Now finally war.* The *xayxayx* would take no more from them, and oh, yes, it was a good feeling, one of anger and strength and pride.

Another bullet exploded in the ground nearby, hurling up clods of Mother Earth. Kiye Kipi wrenched her mare around and galloped into the river. She heard them follow her, driving the straggling ponies, but most of the herd crashed willingly after her *wyakin* mare. They ran for the concealing rise at the far side of the canyon as the full force of the white-skins came down.

The warriors were ready.

They swarmed up from hiding to meet them, the resentment and hatred of seasons guiding their arrows and their bullets. Finally, finally, they could fight back.

There were howls of surprise and pain from the *xayxayx* behind her. She twisted around once, briefly, to watch the first of them fall.

Yes!

Up ahead, Joseph led the squaws out through the southern part of the canyon. Then they reached that place of safety as well, and she threw her head back and gave her own fierce howl of satisfaction. Beside her, Wetatonmi laughed.

Kiye Kipi looked for Dirty Dove. "Take all but the blacks, and follow Joseph!" she shouted.

The girl scowled stubbornly, unwilling to leave.

"Go!" she yelled again. "That is as important as anything else we will do here. Save them!"

The girl began cutting out the spotted herd. Kiye Kipi swung to the ground. "We will take these others to the warriors as they are needed!" she called to Wetatonmi.

They crawled back to the edge of the bluff on their bellies, peering around.

It was slaughter.

Horror swelled up in her throat, the thick, closing press of nausea. Wetatonmi keened, but neither wept. The *xayxayx* were dying.

Their ponies were staggering, foaming. Some collapsed, their eyes rolling, as their riders were driven from their backs. There were soldiers and settlers, all manner of white men, jowls quivering behind their face hair, eyes bugging in shock. Still the warriors' heads bobbed up from hiding. Arrows hissed and hit their marks with moist, meaty thuds that made Kiye Kipi gag again. Bullets tore through flesh, red blood spattered, and the *xayxayx* continued to fall.

The warriors ducked down again, reloading, renotching, and pressed on.

They had made a protective line between the soldiers and the camp. Alokot and his Kahmuenem took the center. Another warrior she knew vaguely—Two Moons—led White Bird's Lamtama on one end of the line. Toolhoolhoolzote came on with his Pikunanmu warriors from the other side.

She knew another fleeting moment of respect for him, grudging, yet somehow hot. He was as old as the moon, but he was still as strong as four men, and he fought with more fury than most for the shame he had suffered at How-erd's hands. Even as a *xayxayx* rider passed too close to him, the old *tiwats* lunged up from concealment and dragged him to the ground.

Kiye Kipi looked away. She did not want to see what he did to him.

The other white-skins had stopped coming on. She started to howl again in triumph, then her heart hitched.

They had reached a little rise of ground, the last hillock before the valley of the camp. A soldier chief moved among them, shouting, blowing on a little metal horn. At first she did not understand, then she saw that they were trying to dig in for their own protected assault.

She looked wildly for Alokot, for the other leaders, to warn them. The canyon was thick with smoke, acrid and burning her eyes. The air thundered with the din of rifles and war cries. *She could not find them!*

Those white-skins could not be allowed to organize. She knew it with an instinct that roared up inside her. She scrambled to her feet again.

"What do you do?" Wetatonmi cried.

She did not know, not exactly. Then it came to her, as certainly as the seasons following one behind the other.

She had to get into their ponies. She had to scatter them and distract the white-eyes.

She could not do that! She had already tried before and failed! Except . . . these ponies were not like the ones that had escaped her, fleeing ahead of her magic at the river. These were not fresh and strong. They were staggering from exhaustion, moving only when they were beaten into it by desperate white hands.

Her eyes narrowed on them, her heart slugging. The soldiers flailed at them, trying to move them. The whites of their eyes caught the sun. The metal of their *xayxayx* bridles sawed at their mouths, making them gape as though in silent screams.

They were weakened, near collapse, and she thought that maybe, maybe, she could get into them because of that.

She focused on them fiercely, screaming danger into their minds. A new desperation wailed up in her, not one of loss this time but of rage, and that was different, too. She hurled fear at them with all of her soul.

And barely, barely reached them.

She felt it, felt their own exhaustion crash over her, become a part of her, making her sway. *Run. Danger. Go, go, go!* Her eyes drifted closed, and she had to force them open again as she heard Wetatonmi cry out.

Her friend was watching her, mouth agape, as though she did not know her. Then her eyes went to the *xayxayx* ponies and she grinned.

Kiye Kipi followed her gaze. The white-skin mounts were unmanageable, rearing, straining against the control of their riders. Blue-coats were thrown. Others dismounted, hanging on to their reins. The debilitated ponies dragged them.

She had done it!

The warriors saw the confusion erupt in the white-skin trenches, and they roared and screamed their way into it. Two Moons charged at the ones now afoot. They dropped their reins and fled in panic as his men converged upon the swell of land they had tried to claim. She saw Alokot rise up from his spot of concealment, his Kahmuenem appearing all around him, and then the two warrior forces opened a furious crossfire on the soldiers who remained.

Kiye Kipi called for her *wyakin* mare.

"Do our men need ponies?" Wetatonmi gasped doubtfully.

"No." But the blacks would still win this fight, once and for all.

She did not think of dying. The possibility tickled at the back of her head, then was gone like a wink of summer lightning. It did not matter. She would die at Lapwai anyway if Mon-teeth took her magic away; she knew it as deep as her soul. Better here, better striving, better to bring these wretched men down with her as she fell.

She dragged herself up onto her pony. Wetatonmi screamed, and she saw the closest warriors look around at her, but it was too late to stop. The white-skins saw her, taking aim at her in that quick lull of Nimipu fire. She flattened herself against her mare's neck, goaded her hard, and they flew into the fight.

The other blacks followed, stampeding. The heat of her intent rushed through them like prairie fire. It touched her pony, and that beast screamed it to the others. The herd raced wildly through the warrior line.

Alokot's stunned and furious face flashed in and out of her

vision as she passed him. "Follow me!" she screamed.

Oh, Tahmahnewes, he did not understand, did not hear her! *Twelic would know what she intended.* But Twelic was gone from her now, and she could not stop, could not go back, could not tell Alokot what she needed.

The herd stormed over the place Two Moons's men had reclaimed, boiling furiously toward the white-skin forces beyond it.

Behind her, she heard Alokot's voice raised in a war cry. Finally, he understood.

His warriors fell in behind her thundering ponies, grabbing up mounts of their own, swinging astride in full gallop. They swarmed over the last of the *xayxayx* who stared, horrified and disbelieving, at the raging tide of horseflesh coming toward them. Behind her, protected by the herd now, the warriors brought still more white-skins down as they were able to ride right through their ranks. Her mare screamed at the others again, and they swept around, back toward the safety of the bluff.

Here and there, a white-skin pony staggered into the stampede, getting caught up in it and carried along. Ahead of her, Wetatonmi came to her feet, howling a war cry of her own.

Kiye Kipi reached her, sliding off. Wetatonmi caught her, bracing her weight when she would have fallen, still howling and laughing in gasps of breath.

"We . . . did it! Oh, friend, look what . . . you have done! *Look!*"

The last of the *xayxayx* had pressed back up into the ridges to avoid being trampled. Their brothers lay bleeding their last lifeblood into White Bird's soil, the land they had tried to steal by lies. She saw Two Moons follow another knot of them to the Lapwai road, gunning them down.

"Yes," she whispered. "Oh, yes."

The Nimipu had triumphed.

35

THE SUN BAKED down on death.

Kiye Kipi flinched and looked up at the white-blue sky as the first turkey vulture gave its chilling call. She left her place behind the ridge and moved into the camp again on legs that were still unsteady.

Most of the warriors had ridden out to find Joseph and the women. Wetatonmi was gone now as well, and she had taken the ponies. But Alokot and Two Moons remained, and some of their men. They worked to help their wounded brothers onto ponies.

One warrior held his forearm, and blood dripped through his fingers, but he was grinning. Two more men were prone, groaning, and another sat holding his head in his hands, pressing his palms against a pain there. Four of them. *Four wounded.*

But almost ten times that number of white-fleshed bodies were forage for the death birds.

Kiye Kipi looked about at them all, her mouth twisting in a horrible grimace that was almost a smile. She did not see How-erd among them, and she did not think he had come here. But, oh, how she wished she could see his face when he learned of this furious Nimipu victory!

You will not take us, sol-jer, not without a fight.

She swallowed back her gorge at the blood-heavy wind and went to the nearest *xayxayx* body. Nausea swept up from her belly again, making her tongue curl. He smelled of death, and old sweat and urine. She thought of a treaty that no one had signed, and a dead pony's blood in the snow, and she put her foot under the man's shoulder to push him over.

His gun was beneath him. She kneeled, sweat beading on her forehead, and cut his ammunition from his waist. Then she gathered everything up before she could vomit.

Those settlers had taught her about the spoils of conquest, after all.

Joseph had moved the People to the Salmon River.

Kiye Kipi returned there with the warriors as the moon came up. There was a mood of fierce celebration in the camp that brought goosebumps to her skin, and for a moment she only stood and looked about at it all. Fires leaped orange in the night. Men hooted and strutted around them as they told of their coups. The headmen sat more quietly at a hearth they shared together, but they looked no less satisfied. They gestured at each other, their fingers stabbing the air, laughing.

Finally, she pulled a cumbersome *xayxayx* blanket from the back of her pony and spilled it on the ground. Wetatonmi and Joseph's wives and a handful of others crowded around to see it.

"What is in there?" someone asked.

"It is the next fight."

Several of them started as though she had struck them, but then their eyes settled. The Nimipu had had a strong, amazing coup, and it had ignited even the squaws with the will to fight back. It had happened because of the People's strengths: the headmen's thoughtful preparedness, the warriors' pent-up fury, and because of her ponies. But no one believed that How-erd would give up because of it. He would be back, and he would not underestimate them again.

She squatted and began sorting through the items on the blanket. There was the ammunition, the dead white-skin's rifle that she had taken, and odd bits of food and utensils from their abandoned grassland camp. The warriors had cleared the canyon of all the *xayxayx* weapons, and even the herd had swelled a bit with thirty or more of their ponies. The People had greatly replenished their supplies with all the things that would allow them to run on.

She tucked her hair behind her ears and stood again, smiling faintly at that. Then she noticed another squaw watching her from outside the fire shadows.

Venom burned in the woman's eyes. *Why?*

"Do you need something from me?" Kiye Kipi asked carefully.

"Toolhoolhoolzote is right," the woman spat, coming forward. "You are no warrior, but perhaps it is good that you think you are. Warriors die."

Wetatonmi and the other squaws gasped. Kiye Kipi felt her heart thump as she tried to understand. "Are you one of that *tiwats*'s people? Are you Pikunanmu?"

"I am White Bird's daughter. I am Lamtama, and when you are gone, I will still be here. You think you can lure him with your strength, but know this, Pony Wife. A warrior will not be held by someone who is just another man."

Understanding came to her in a sickening rush. She knew where she had seen this squaw now. She had been hovering around Twelic at Tolo, and seasons ago at the camas prairie. She had heard her name once like a *xayxayx* bullet in her heart.

Cloud Singer.

The woman's words hit their target, shredding something inside her. She flinched before she could stop herself, stepping back, but worse than the taunt was the truth in it. He had touched this woman. He had loved her in a way he would never love an orphan of the moon, because such an orphan could never be like other squaws.

She no longer knew how to be. She no longer wanted to be. She would not ever be the kind of woman Twelic sought.

She girded herself, fighting a strangled sensation in her throat. Hurt was not new to her. She had no need to strike back. No word, no argument, could dispel the bleakness of what was.

"Then you have nothing to fear, do you?" she countered quietly.

She looked down at the blanket again, at Wetatonmi and

Joseph's wives all crouched there, their faces upturned, their
eyes watching her miserably. She managed a thin laugh for
their sake.

"You may take what you like of these things, except for
the rifle. That gun is mine."

She left them to go to the headmen's fire. As she passed
one of the Lamtama hearths, a warrior of Cloud Singer's people stood and hooted at her. He did a dance of her startling
coup with the ponies, and his brothers shouted their praise.
Her pulse stuttered again, then steadied. *Just another man.* So
be it. If that was what she was, then the Nimipu needed every
man they could claim.

She forced a grin at the warrior, straightened her spine, and
went on.

Alokot and Two Moons and some of the Pikunanmu men
were with the headmen. She felt Toolhoolhoolzote's eyes burn
into her as she squatted among them. Alokot gave her a
crooked smile. She had not spoken to him since the fight.

"I thought first of killing you myself," he said. "Now I
suppose I should herald you."

A funny feeling coiled in her belly, almost warm, not quite
comfortable. No matter what Cloud Singer had said, this was
a new kind of acceptance, and it gave her a strange satisfaction.

"It was a crazy thing to do," Joseph chastised mildly. "The
others have told me of it."

Huishuis Kute chuckled. "And you wish you could have
been there to see it."

Kiye Kipi lifted one shoulder carefully. "I could think of
no other way to stop the fighting while those *xayxayx* were
still beaten. I did not trust them not to reorganize and get their
strength back."

"Half of them were dead by then," a Pikunanmu scoffed
indignantly.

"And all of our warriors lived," she countered. "I wanted
to keep it that way." She looked across the flames to Burned
Tree, and the *tiwats* nodded.

"Yes, the wounded will recover," he told her.

She breathed a little easier. Those two on the ground had looked bad.

"What do we do now?" she asked Joseph.

There was a short, pensive silence, then old White Bird addressed her directly.

"We have decided that we must go to buffalo country."

Toolhoolhoolzote snarled a sound that scraped at her bones.

Joseph went on, "It is this Nimipu land that How-erd wants for his people. Perhaps if we leave it to him, he will let us alone."

Her heart contracted, and hot loss swept through her again. *Leave it to him.* But they had done that, truly, suns and suns ago.

Now they would have to find safety. Now the People would have to start over, but they would not do it at that cursed Lapwai.

"Once we are over the Bitterroots, How-erd will think that we do not mean to fight him," Alokot said. "Perhaps he will stop chasing us then. We can leave the women and children in safety there, and come back here to fight for what is ours."

Kiye Kipi nodded thoughtfully, but she had been to buffalo country, and she did not think that that was the Safe Place. Still, she could see no sense in telling them so. Tahmahnewes, she just wasn't sure. She would have to see more of that land, she decided. She would have to look at it again, and then she would know.

She rubbed her temples where an ache was building after the long, violent upheaval. She needed to sleep. She got to her feet, then paused as something else struck her. She looked sharply at Alokot again.

"The Bitterroots?" she squeaked. How would she ever get all the ponies over that treacherous pass?

He cocked a brow at her, then he understood. "There are two ways over that range."

"See?" sneered Toolhoolhoolzote. "She knows of little but her own self-worth. And you would follow her?"

"No one follows her," Joseph said calmly. "I merely chew upon her advice sometimes. She dreams."

"And we fight behind her ponies." Huishuis Kute laughed again.

"We took the southern pass that season you went with us to the buffalo range," Alokot explained. "Because of the women and the herds, we will take the northern route this time. It is not quite so bad. Also, the Crows live north, and we need their sanctuary, their permission to settle there, even temporarily."

North was good, she thought. She could not shake the feeling that the Safe Place was there, somewhere.

She turned away, then the sound of hoofbeats made her tense again. They all looked up warily, and saw a rider approach.

From the Kooskooskia?

She felt as though her very blood were draining out of her. But she had known; of course she had known. Even as they had left Tolo, her heart had been sure that she had not seen the last of Twelic. She had not truly bled for his loss because she had never doubted that the *xayxayx* would drive him back to her. Now it would happen. She felt a kick of something like anticipation, then dread settled in, deep and pervasive, making her head hurt even more.

"I bring word from the Hasotoin. We need your help," the man gasped when he reached their fire.

Joseph stood, nodding, waiting for him to go on.

"The *xayxayx* have found us."

The People packed up again with the dawn. Kiye Kipi worked with Wetatonmi, her gaze darting again and again to Joseph's shelter. His wives had saved her lodge cover from White Bird Canyon. She was impatient to get it from them, to be astride and moving on.

She had slept beneath the stars last night, thinking, her heart squirming, but she had not dreamed. She had tried, oh, she had, clutching a fire starter that was old and cracked and warping from too much damp and too many seasons. But she had seen nothing of the distant Kooskooskia, only the face of a warrior that was not really a dream at all. She knew only what that Hasotoin messenger had told them.

The blue-coats had swarmed over Looking Glass's people at dawn, and they had not been ready, had not been waiting for it. The squaws had fled, abandoning their possessions and their lodges. They had lost nearly a thousand ponies.

Always the ponies. Oh, yes, the white-skins wanted them.

Anger made her hands tighten like claws over one of Wetatonmi's parfleches. She made a strangled sound in her throat, and her friend looked to her, startled.

After a moment, her gaze cleared knowingly. "Do you fret for that warrior? He lives. The messenger said that a babe and a boy were killed."

Kiye Kipi gave a bitter, high-pitched laugh. Wetatonmi did not understand after all. She did not fear for Twelic. He would be there to greet her when the Dreamer bands found him.

He would be there to welcome Cloud Singer as well, and she wondered how she would bear watching that, sun after sun, until this was over.

"What warrior?" she asked deliberately.

Wetatonmi's jaw dropped. "The one who is named for the wind."

"He is nothing to me. Barely a friend."

"But out on the buffalo prairie—"

"On that prairie I learned that no man should claim me."

She closed her eyes briefly. She could not forget that, not because of Cloud Singer, not ever again.

She snatched up her rifle, and the new strength and solace that it gave her. "I must find Joseph. I must speak to him."

She moved to his lodge although it was still quiet, unwilling to wait any longer. She called out for the headman, and one of his wives poked her nose past the flap, motioning her inside.

Joseph was gathering his weapons, little used now but still lovingly tended and strong. He looked up at her with an arched brow.

"We must not go straight to find Looking Glass," she blurted. "How-erd will be expecting that."

He straightened slowly. "The Hasotoin wait for us in the

Clearwater Mountains. They cannot move on without us. They do not have enough mounts.''

''Can their men hunt?'' she demanded.

''I imagine so.''

''Then they will not starve. And they are hidden. They are as safe, perhaps safer, than we are.''

She took a deep breath. ''How-erd must know that we will go to them. I think he will have sol-jers waiting for us.''

Joseph's eyes widened, then narrowed. His wives stood watching pensively, one chewing on a knuckle.

''How-erd is a keen adversary,'' he said finally.

Kiye Kipi nodded. ''Though he has faults, I do not think he possesses many.''

''Is that the reason for your caution?''

Her heart lurched. Like Wetatonmi, did he think she considered Twelic? It was true enough that she was not eager to find him. There was a part of her heart that was as cowardly as Looking Glass, a part that shuddered at the thought of seeing her life tangled together with his now as their *wyakins* seemed to have decided. But she would not ever base her peoples' safety upon that.

She began to protest, then she realized that Joseph was only asking if she had dreamed.

''I . . . nothing has come to me,'' she admitted, flushing. ''But I thought much last night when I should have been sleeping.''

He almost smiled. She realized then that he had not slept either. The folds of his eyes were drooping, his face haggard.

''So be it.'' He stood again and went outside.

She followed, and he waved the other headmen around him. All but Toolhoolhoolzote came.

''We should not leave an obvious trail to where we are going,'' he announced. ''I think first we should cross back to the west side of the Salmon. If How-erd's soldiers come after us again, then we can recross to the east and put that water between us.''

''It is beginning to swell!'' someone protested.

''And How-erd will have an even more difficult time

crossing it than we will," Kiye Kipi put in earnestly. "We know how, but it will slow him down." *And then what?* She did not know, but it was a start.

There were a few nods, then Huishuis Kute made a deep harrumph in his throat. "We should try it."

He waved a hand to the people. They began mounting, ready to ride on to find the Hasotoin.

36

THEY USED THE black ponies to cross the water as they had done at the mighty Snake, but this time the sun shone warmly down on them. This river tugged and teased at the ponies, but they were stronger.

As soon as they reached the west bank, Earth Sound took his warriors out ahead. The rest of the Dreamers traveled more slowly, wandering and gossiping from band to band. But Alokot rode up on the hills, his sharp eyes watching the country, and Two Moons stayed behind with some of his men.

The People rode through the sun, and then they camped again. A sense of euphoria began to take the squaws the longer they went on without trouble, but Kiye Kipi's rigid back ached with tension. They thought it would be easy now, she realized, trying to shrug away the hurt. They thought they would go on this way straight through the Bitterroots to safety. But she could not stop wondering where How-erd was.

Was he still at Lapwai, ordering his men about Nimipu country like some far-reaching god? No, she could not believe that. She thought of his empty sleeve, and she shuddered. She knew that he would appear somewhere, soon, among his soldiers.

She slept fitfully beneath the stars again, unwilling to settle in too deeply, too comfortably. When the sun returned, Earth Sound came back, and she knew she had been right.

His hoofbeats were fast and anxious. She sat up, shivering, as dawn tried to warm the night chill. The warrior rode to

Joseph's lodge and she kicked her robe away to follow him.

"It is as you warned us," Earth Sound said tightly when the headman came out. "They are looking for us."

Her heart skipped, but Joseph seemed calm, resigned. "Where?" he asked.

"There are two parties, and if we cross over the water again, we will be right between them."

White Bird came up, yawning, scratching his hair.

"One camps on the horizon east of here," Earth Sound went on. "There are smokes near the Kooskooskia Mountains."

"Looking Glass?" Huishuis Kute wondered, joining them.

"Not unless he is camping in the valley, in plain sight."

No, Kiye Kipi thought. That would not be. Twelic would bow to his cousin's stupidity only so much, like a sapling bending in the wind but never breaking. Even if he were one of the Hasotoin warriors who had been wounded, he would have a voice to speak, to argue.

And, oh, yes, he would argue.

She almost smiled, but her mouth felt tight. Her pulse was beginning to pound at her temples.

"What of the other party?" Joseph asked.

"They approach from Lapwai with wagons and ponies."

That would be their seeds and supplies, Kiye Kipi thought. Suddenly, her heart lurched.

"Then there is a third party," she gasped. How-erd. It must be How-erd. *But where?*

They all looked around at her. She licked her lips.

"Those wagons must be going to men who need them," she pointed out.

Huishuis Kute's eyes widened, then he nodded thoughtfully. "They could be heading for those men camped near the Koos-kooskia's Clearwater Mountains," he observed.

"Either way," Joseph said, "if we cross this river again, Earth Sound is right. We will be between them."

A hard swell of warrior voices agreed with him.

"Better to foil them," Alokot snapped, "than to run from them with our tails tucked. Let us go."

''We cannot find Looking Glass by doing anything else,'' Earth Sound reminded them.

The enormity of that settled slowly upon the women. Some of them moaned; others pressed closer to grope for their men. The warriors looked about, the first doubt, the first panic showing in their strong faces. They would have to move directly across the route of the wagon soldiers to reach that troublesome headman, then they would have to cross the open prairie in plain sight of those camped near the mountains, heading virtually toward them.

The men could fight their way across. There was not a man who was not avid to do so. But again, always again, there were the babes, the elders, the squaws.

And the ponies.

Kiye Kipi looked out to where the herd grazed, her heart tightening. She would have to take them under the noses of these soldiers as well, and oh, Tahmahnewes, they would surely try again to wrest them from her!

Unless . . .

She whipped around to look at Joseph again. ''A decoy?'' she wondered. ''Could that work?''

The men went quiet, studying her.

''Yes!'' The idea was stronger now, and she went on. ''The warriors can meet the soldiers and divert them. I can lead the women and the ponies through when it happens.''

She squatted in the dirt, reaching to snag a stick from the nearest hearth. ''See here,'' she said, drawing. ''We can rush right across the path of the wagon soldiers and go into the mountains straight north. We can travel to Looking Glass *behind* those camped by the foothills. Are there trails through those Clearwaters?''

Someone grunted noncommittally, but Huishuis Kute nodded. Joseph scowled.

''That would mean a blatant attack upon the *xayxayx*,'' he argued. ''We have never done that before. At White Bird Canyon, the soldiers struck us first. We only defended ourselves. If we go to buffalo country with honor, with care, then we can speak to How-erd, perhaps even to his president chief, once our women are safe. We can go to them with our shoulders straight and our heads high, knowing that we have done no wrong, and demand our land back. I do not want to leave a trail of white bodies.''

''They would leave a trail of red,'' someone snapped.

''They care not for right or wrong, only for the land they can claim!''

The air exploded in a cacophony of voices. Men yelled, and the headmen shouted louder to be heard above them. The women pressed close to Kiye Kipi, pleading with her for something she could not give, hands reaching out to pluck at her doeskin.

''How far away are these parties?'' Joseph demanded over the uproar.

''Half a sun's ride, each of them,'' Earth Sound reported.

''Then we have some time to talk about this.''

He led the headmen back to his hearth for another council. Kiye Kipi watched them go, her heart pounding to hear what would be said. Then the squaws blocked her line of sight so that she had to stand on tiptoe to look over them.

She came back down again slowly, and gave a small, helpless sound.

She was not so much a man after all. Her heart bled for the women's fear, not so different from this scrambling panic of her own. They needed her now, for something the men could not give them. They needed comfort.

She closed her eyes, steadying herself, then bent to scoop up a wailing child. She slipped her arm through another squaw's.

''Come,'' she said quietly. ''Whatever they decide, we will be moving somewhere soon. Let us pack, let us get ready.'' She managed a thin smile. ''We will all be fine. This will not stop us. Did we not escape from the canyon?''

They quieted. Sweet Tahmahnewes, they believed her.

Alokot found her before they had even finished bringing down Wetatonmi's lodge. She jolted to her feet again, watching his face for some clue, but for a long time he only looked at his wife, his child.

"Watch for the first dust of a scuffle on both sides," he said finally. "We will send two parties, one to the wagon soldiers, another to those camping. When they are both engaged, you and Joseph can rush the others on to the mountains."

The squaws began bustling. But when they would have mounted, Kiye Kipi cried out to them. "No!"

Joseph came to her. His face was so grim, so troubled! She knew he had not reconciled himself to this decision. It so went against his thoughtful, sagacious nature. Her heart moved for him, but it thrummed heatedly as well. She realized that she wanted this to succeed as badly as the People needed it to.

"Remember those little tube glasses the soldiers carry," she said more quietly.

The headman scowled. "Yes. Perhaps they are watching us."

"If they see us getting ready to ride out, they could guess what we are up to."

The men were leaving, a massive knot of them traveling through the grasses. The *xayxayx* would certainly see them coming, and would perhaps even be ready to engage them. But that was good; it would keep their thoughts off the women until it was too late to stop their mad dash.

At least, that was the way she prayed it would happen.

Joseph looked around at his wives.

"At the first sign of fighting, *then* we will leap upon our ponies and go. For now, we wait," Kiye Kipi said.

They began spreading the word to the others. Kiye Kipi turned away, and bumped squarely into Dirty Dove.

"You can help me drive the herd," she said, and the girl's face brightened with the kind of excitement only a child could know now. She could not bear to look at the girl.

They moved into the herd of ponies, waiting there, watching the warriors fade into a smaller and smaller shadow on the horizon. Kiye Kipi called her mare close and dug her fingers into her mane as they waited.

"I would be just like you," Dirty Dove vowed suddenly.

Kiye Kipi started and looked back at her.

Oh, no, child, not that, never that. Unbidden, she thought of Twelic again. She thought of his touch and the heat in his eyes, the way he understood, always understood, but without loving, without caring. She thought of cold nights alone, with only dreams to warm her, and of the smooth, cool feeling of the gun in her hand.

Just another man.

She closed her eyes weakly against all of it. "There is so much more," she managed. "So much one like me can never know."

Dirty Dove was undaunted. "If I cannot go for my *wyakin* this summer, then I will at least learn. I will be *something* when it is over."

"Yes," Kiye Kipi agreed. "Something, I suppose." *If it is ever over.*

She looked back at the prairie. A distant bullet popped quietly there. It sounded so innocent from this far, but her heart hurtled into her throat, her hand tightened on her gun, and her adrenaline started to course.

She leaped onto her *wyakin* black and she did not, could not, think of Twelic anymore. There were only the women, the ponies, and an unconscionable enemy who would destroy them all.

"What the holy hell . . ."

The volunteer trailed off, dropping down beside Captain Perry behind their breastworks of wagons. He was a veteran of the War Between the States, had not actively fought in years, and was more than a little rattled now. Perry cursed the man whose idea it had been to press civilians into service for this campaign.

An arrow hissed by over their heads, and Perry ducked this time, almost too late.

"See there!" the volunteer cried. "That's what I mean! That weren't meant to hit you, sir!"

"No," Perry snapped. "It was intended to keep me pinned

down.'' And it was working. Though his men returned the
Indians' fire, they could not get out to offer any substantial
counterattack.

An enlisted man crawled up to them on his belly. ''Now
they've got the cavalry over by the mountains, sir!''

Perry straightened up again to take a look through his spyglass. Dust and smoke did indeed belch up from a spot near
the hills.

''Think Titelman made it,'' the volunteer asked, ''or they
got him holed up somewhere as well?''

''It doesn't matter,'' Perry bit out.

He was beginning to understand what was happening here.
The cavalry was trapped; his own men had been reduced to
fighting in self-defense. Even if Titelman made it back to civilization for reinforcements, they would most likely be met by
the Nez Percé as they came in. Every one of the government
forces would be held in check, immobilized until something
happened. What? What were they planning, and how many
fighting bucks did they have? At the moment, divided as they
were, he could not tell.

''Yo!'' cried the volunteer, leaning up over the wagon
again. ''Getta look at this!''

Perry focused his glass again, then he swore colorfully. Off
on the grasslands there rose another churning cloud of dust.
now. Their families, of course. The remaining exiles were
dashing across the prairie with their women and ponies, and
there was not a damned thing he could do about it. They drew
closer and closer to the Clearwater Mountains, where they
would disappear like termites into wood.

A grudging respect worked in his stomach. *That* was what
these bucks had been waiting for. Even as he watched, some
of them began splitting off, retreating back toward their
squaws.

The volunteer was gaping at them. ''We goin' after them,
sir?''

Perry brought the glass down with an angry snap of his
wrist. ''What for?'' he countered irritably. ''By the time we
manage to break through here, they'll be so hidden in those

mountains we'll never find them. And we have no way of enlisting the cavalry, of springing them free to assist us. It's quite possible we'd be outnumbered."

"Oh, boy," the enlisted man muttered. He had his own spyglass out, and was looking through it.

"What now?" Perry snarled.

"Titelman came back with reinforcements, all right. Now some big old buck has them fighting for their lives, too!"

Still more of them. Perry turned away.

"Aren't we going to relieve them?" the enlisted man demanded.

"There are times when discretion is the better part of valor. General Howard will locate us shortly. He'll want these wagons. We'll leave it to him to decide the next move."

The enlisted man protested. "He's still trying to get back across the Salmon where they loop-de-looped around!"

Perry settled into glum silence. They all knew that by the time Howard reached them, the Indians would be gone and Titelman's reinforcements would most likely be dead.

"Hell, I was over in Kansas Territory for a while," the enlisted man complained. "Those Cheyenne would as soon take your scalp as look at you. We could fight them. They'd just swarm at you, and the devil take the hindmost. But these aren't like any Indians I've ever met before."

"No," Perry answered. "They are not."

He had learned *that* when he had barely escaped White Bird Canyon. The Nez Percé had met his men there like a battalion of West Point soldiers; their strategies had not been dissimilar. Only Custer's slaughter the year before had been more devastating, had taken more of a complete toll. Perry was of the firm opinion that Custer had been a pompous fool, and those Sioux had been lucky. But that was not the case with this tribe.

The Nez Percé were tactical, intelligent. One of them, at least, was showing the markings of a brilliant military mind. General Howard remained convinced that it was Joseph.

Perry zoomed in on the fleeing caravan one last time, finding a handsome, hook-nosed man riding at the front of them. He could think of no reason to argue Howard's point, none at all.

It was going to be a very long war.

Kiye Kipi reined in and watched as the ponies swam over the hillock, a glistening sea of sweat-dark red and black and brown. Their stars and blankets winked in and out of the sun that speckled through the trees overhead. Their hooves tore up the forest floor, filling the air with a musty, fetid smell. But it was not entirely unpleasant, and she laughed, tilting her head back to breathe it in.

Behind her, there was only silence. *No soldiers.* They had done it!

Joseph and the squaws had gone on ahead to find Looking Glass, but she and Dirty Dove, Burned Tree, and a few other elders remained behind to keep the herd from straying off the pass. She kicked her mare again and moved after them before a new smell came to her nostrils, one that made her elation begin to shimmy inside her.

Cook fires.

She pulled off the trail as Dirty Dove cut the ponies around, steering them down the last incline into a valley on the far side of the range. From the top of the rise, she looked down upon the people camped below.

The Hasotoin . . . and the rest of the Dreamers.

Some were mourning the babe and the boy who had been killed. Their keens were faint and subdued as they moved about, helping the new arrivals to settle. But the Pikunanmu people were louder, and her heart ached.

Had they lost warriors in this last fight?

She goaded her mare and plunged down the slope, riding toward them without a thought for Toolhoolhoolzote, wanting only to know what had happened. Stupid, stupid . . . she had not considered that warriors might fall in her plan. She had only been concerned with the women, the elders, the babes, and the ponies. A horrible guilt engulfed her, closing her throat . . . and then she saw Twelic.

She pulled her mare back in midstride, not intending to, her eyes wide. Cloud Singer was moving toward him, and her heart clenched tight enough to make her breath burst painfully from her throat again. She did not want to see this, did not want to know, yet she stared like a doe caught in the line of an arrow, watching it fly toward her heart.

The squaw reached him, flipped back one braid, tilted her head appealingly to the side as she smiled. Twelic put a hand on each of her shoulders and nodded, saying something she was too far away to hear.

Kiye Kipi jerked her eyes away.

She did not know envy, had never grappled with it before. Even when she had squatted, hungry and alone, far from Hasotoin hearths, even then she had never wanted to take from one of those bellies to fill her own. She had longed to share, but not to rob. She had ached to belong, not to oust someone else. Even when she had first heard Cloud Singer's name, she had not thought to hate her, had only bled because she was not like her.

Now jealousy filled her, hot and rancid in her belly. And it hurt, oh, Tahmahnewes, it hurt. It made her throat and her eyes burn.

She went to the Pikunanmu and dismounted, unnaturally stiff and clumsy.

"What has happened?" she asked a warrior.

His gaze moved to her guardedly, then he recognized her.

"We held both *xayxayx* parties well enough, but then a third one appeared to assist them."

She gasped. "How-erd?"

"No. We still do not know where that one is. This was a blue-coat returning with some settlers to attack our flanks and move us off. Our *tiwats* noticed their approach and took some warriors to stop them."

"And . . . they died?"

"No. Only one elder fell. He insisted upon riding with Toolhoolhoolzote, though he was old and no longer quick. He said it was better to die fighting these white-skins than to fall running from them like a woman."

Kiye Kipi flinched. Toolhoolhoolzote and his cronies had not expected the women to survive her flight.

But they had. They had all come through.

She nodded, her chin coming up, and turned away. Twelic was behind her.

She gasped, startled, and looked about for Cloud Singer. That squaw was nowhere to be found now, but he was standing close, his eyes hot and moving over her as though searching for something. She found herself doing the same thing, her gaze roaming his strong, hard face and the solid, muscled expanse of his chest, the way it tapered down to the thin edge of the buckskin leggings and breechclout he wore.

He was not harmed. She swallowed dryly.

"I greet you again"—his mouth quirked in half a smile— "how many coups later?"

Cloud Singer possessed a delicate beauty. She, Kiye Kipi, had coups. She did not think she could speak without choking.

"I thank you," he went on.

"For what?"

"You brought the People here to save my imbecile cousin."

"I did not do that," she managed shortly. "I had no part in the fighting."

"Not this time. I hear you were very active at White Bird." The dark, sun-touched skin around his eyes finally crinkled as he smiled outright. "I will have to watch my back while you are around, that you do not best me and steal away with my followers."

She recoiled as though he had slapped her.

The woman in her wanted to touch him, to wrap her arms around his neck and hold on. She wanted his comfort and strength, just for a moment, just long enough to forget the stiffening white bodies in White Bird and the old Pikunanmu warrior who was gone. She almost swayed with the need; now that he was close, it threatened to well up and swallow her. Instead, she took another unsteady step backward, her eyes hot.

"Then you had best fight with all your abilities in the suns ahead," she snapped.

He watched, bemused, as she turned and fled from him.

37

KIYE KIPI LISTENED disbelievingly as Looking Glass swayed the council. *In spite of everything that had happened to him, they would listen?*

"Your people are weary. Mine are grieving," he pointed out. "The herds need to graze, and we all need to eat. What better place than this? I say we should rest for a few suns, then we can move on for the Bitterroot pass."

"This is a lush spot," White Bird agreed. "And the pass is only five suns' ride from here."

They were still on the far side of the Clearwaters, and the place was rich with forage and winding streams. The slopes were rife with deer and elk. The squaws worked feverishly to dry and pack the meat and fish that their mates were already bringing in. The others gnawed hungrily on bones, replenishing their strength.

Kiye Kipi knew all that, and she knew it was good, but she still felt her skin tighten over her flesh with an itchy, worried feeling.

Joseph alone seemed to share her concern. "I am not particularly worried about those wagon soldiers coming after us. My brother was among those to fight them, and he says our numbers are greater than theirs."

They all looked at Alokot. He nodded.

"Those camped on the other side of this mountain could come," Joseph went on, "but again we are stronger. I only wonder where How-erd might be. We have not heard from him in so long, it troubles me. What is he doing these suns? What is he thinking?''

"You say you left a misleading trail from White Bird," Looking Glass pointed out. "Both west and east of the Salmon. He is probably still trying to track you. He is not a god. He does not have Tahmahnewes's sight."

Pensively, Joseph nodded. "So be it, but I think we should move on to the pass in no more than two suns' time. That is ample opportunity for the women and the ponies to recover."

It was enough of a victory to make Looking Glass puff his chest out. Kiye Kipi saw him look smugly to Twelic, and she let her breath escape hard. She realized that he only wanted to stay because Twelic wanted to go. That, and because he feared the uncertainty of what waited for them on the prairie to the Bitterroots.

She wanted to shout at the headmen, wanted to make them see it. But somewhere beneath her panic, her bones were beginning to ache.

She closed her eyes. If she was wearying from the strain and upheaval of this flight, then she could not imagine how the old ones must feel. No one among them had complained, but their faces were becoming drawn, their eyes haunted. They were being pushed to the end of their endurance to run from the only homes they had ever known.

The adrenaline rushed out of her on a flood of empathy and despair. She turned away, too weary to think anymore. If Howerd appeared, they would fight him. There was nothing more they could do than that.

She made a bed for herself near a chuckling foothill stream, wrapping her old buffalo robe around her shoulders, then she squinted about in the thick darkness.

The moonlight could barely break through the trees, but she knew that there were warriors about. Earth Sound, for one, had come up here just ahead of her. Many of the men were ready to meet the white-skins if they should come in over these crests.

Her hand moved unconsciously for her rifle and pulled it close, under her robe. She settled her back against a tree, exhausted, but not yet willing to sleep.

Where was Twelic? Where was Cloud Singer?

It was another reason she had left the camp.

When she heard footsteps, she stiffened but waited quietly, knowing it was to be a warrior and not a white man coming from behind her. Twelic stepped about to face her, and her heart thumped, but she found she was not truly surprised.

She eyed him levelly.

"Do I interrupt a tryst?" he asked, looking about.

Her heart moved against her ribs again. *Had he finished with his?*

"Only with my gun," she answered flatly.

He came down on his haunches beside her. "Where is it?"

"Safe beside me."

"Let me see."

She wanted to tell him to go away, but it required more energy than she possessed at the moment. As had happened when he had helped her save her ponies, she felt a treacherous vulnerability begin to swim in her gut. She pushed the rifle at him soundlessly.

"It is a good one," he observed.

She shrugged.

"Where did you take it?"

"The canyon."

"When did you have time? Between scattering their ponies and stampeding your own?"

Her heart lurched again. "How do you know what I did to their ponies?" she demanded. She had not thought anyone had been aware of that, had not realized any warrior had seen.

"Wetatonmi told me," he answered.

Yes, of course. She had been there.

They were quiet for a long time; he watched her, and she studied the water. Then she heard herself talking, telling him again, confiding, just as she had a hundred seasons ago, just as she had long ago learned not to do.

Stupid, stupid . . . but the scant moonlight was seductive.

"That was more of a coup than the stampede," she admitted. "When those settlers took the stallion from the Snake, I

could not call him back. I tried, but I could not jump into him
without dreaming. But I think I discovered something at the
canyon. Two things were different there. I did not try to tell
them to turn around. I made them scared.''

She paused, thinking. ''The other thing was that I did not
feel frightened or beaten. I was . . . furious. I have been thinking that maybe anger can carry me into them.''

''You will try it again.''

''I pray Tahmahnewes that I will not have to.''

But it would happen. They both knew it would happen, and
she shuddered.

''It is hard not to be afraid now,'' she admitted. ''It is hard
to keep that emotion out of my heart.''

He shrugged, as she should have known he would. ''Fear
is something that exists in every moment of every life,'' he
answered, so cocky, so sure of himself. ''You use your knife
carefully to avoid slicing your own finger because you fear
the hurt. It is only an enemy when too much homage is paid
to it and it breeds hesitation.''

Suddenly she was angry again, with him, with How-erd,
with herself. ''Caution is a wise thing,'' she snapped. ''It
keeps one from rushing in and making mistakes.''

He cocked a brow at her speculatively. ''You speak like one
who fears she has made one.''

Oh, she had, the most recent being to allow him to stay
here, to talk with him. She pushed to her feet, flinging her robe
aside. That was not a mistake she would talk to him about.

''I have miscalculated!'' she cried bitterly. ''I know my ponies are superior to those *xayxayx* mounts. I know they can
outrun them forever, but I forgot the elders, the women! They
will have to travel as quickly as the horses, or How-erd will
catch us, no matter how shrewd Joseph is. Look about at them!
Look at their faces down there! They are weary and frightened
already, and we have so very far to go! How am I to stand by
them and encourage them when I am needed for this fight as
well?''

''Perhaps you should not try to do both. Perhaps you should
just be a woman and nurture them.''

She reeled back as though he had slapped her. He got to his feet to come after her.

"There are many men in that camp willing to protect you if you would leave the fighting to them." He was watching her face with narrow eyes, studying her.

"What do you say?" she spat.

Go back there. Be safe.

Fear twisted his bowels to think that she had helped save that canyon fight. Fear and something else . . . the same dangerous respect he had felt when she had swept by him on the buffalo prairie seasons ago. He could forget women when they were not in his arms. He could not forget this one precisely because she was so much more than warm, willing flesh.

And that taunted him still.

Yes, he loved her, and that frightened him like no enemy could. Once he had told himself that he feared she would take the wind from him. Now, suddenly, he knew he feared more that she would share it. He thought again that the place they had dreamed of might have been the afterworld. If she fought like a man, then she could die like a warrior.

He wanted her back in the camp, not up here in the hills with a gun in her hand. If he could only infuriate her into going back, so be it.

"I say that you should be safely wed by now," he said gratingly. "I say that you should be warming a man's bedding, not this cold earth by a creek."

Hurt and horror crashed through her. "We have had this talk," she said, strangled. "A hundred snows ago at a treaty talk, when I offered to wed you."

He snorted, but his own gut tightened. "You were a babe then."

"But perhaps wise enough to know that no man would want what I am!"

"Then change what you are!"

Her voice came out in a wild laugh. Change it? Give up the glorious freedom of running with her ponies? Give up the adrenaline, the fire of being *worth* something? She had ached for this fulfillment for too long to relinquish it. She had suffered too greatly on her path to becoming different. She no longer knew how to be the same as every other squaw.

"There is no man worth that!" she gasped.

His face turned hard with fury.

She had never seen him like this before, and her belly roiled. She knew before he spoke again that his next words would change everything, would slash her so deeply to the bone that she would never wholly recover. She tried to step away, but his voice stopped her.

"Or is there no man strong enough to keep you at home in a lodge?" he demanded. "Is there no man virile enough to heat that cold, rigid courage within you?"

She let out a little, keening cry. "Go away."

"Because you cannot bear the truth of what I say?"

The truth? Oh, it was not the truth, but he and Cloud Singer could never know that. They could not know the way she ached for him to touch her again, this man, not any other. They could not know the way her memories of him haunted her. She had always needed him, had reacted to him so strongly it was the one thing she truly feared. She saw the heat lingering in his eyes, and knew that even the burning force of this anger would not match what it would be like to join with him.

He was the one who knew her heart, her past, her need. He was the one who had defied all that to come close to her anyway, to teach her what it was to yearn. Joining with him would be a firestorm, would shatter her and make her whole again.

She wanted it. She would dare it.

But he did not.

A growling sound of fury came from her throat. He would not walk away from this glade telling *her* that *she* was lacking. She had borne it with Cloud Singer; she would not do so now. Cloud Singer was just another obscure face of the many that had always surrounded her, judging and mocking. But this was Twelic.

She stepped close to him again, eye to eye. His breath was

warm on her face, and yes, it made something begin to burn within her.

"*Is* there such a man?" she whispered defiantly. "Are you virile enough, *warrior*?"

Something changed in his eyes, and it made his knees weak, made her fury abate, shimmying into panic again. *What was she doing?*

She was stealing one more memory for herself before it was all over, because not even she knew what was going to happen to them now.

She brought her mouth down on his, hard.

She thought of all the times she had wandered through the herd late at night, stumbling uncomfortably upon young lovers, groping, needing each other. She thought of sharing copses under the moonlight with Wetatonmi and Alokot on a distant prairie. Those others had nibbled, roamed; she needed more than that. Twelic had once explored her skin with his mouth, but she did not need to search now. This time she knew what she wanted. It was not an obscure, swimming need. It pounded through her, reckless, wanton, desperate.

He stood very still for a moment, then he pulled at her until she fell against his chest. Her heart erupted, clamoring. A weakness slid through her at the solid heat of him, pooling between her legs, at the pit of her belly. *This, yes, this.* He took a handful of her hair and pulled her head back so that he could see into her eyes.

"Am I?" he answered, his voice purring now, deadly. "Curse you! Curse you for the one challenge that can make me forget all sense. You think you are a wildcat, but there is much you do not know. This warrior will show you."

He found her mouth again, and this time his tongue plunged, teasing hers, pulling away. She shuddered and groaned.

His hands found her hips and pulled her down. She went like water tumbling over a rock, and then he was full on top of her again, as he had been on the way to Wallowa. His lips still covered hers, moving, tasting her like a man who would die for a drink. This time she drove her fingers into his hair to hold him. She wanted every moment to be hard and sweet and clear, a memory too strong to fade. He *did* want her, he did. In some small way, though she could not touch his heart, there was woman enough in her to make him hunger.

That was enough.

Instinct drove her. She closed her teeth over the taut flesh at his neck, the way she had seen the stallions do, then she slid her tongue there to soothe the hurt, to taste him, salt and smoke and darkness. An unintelligible sound came from his throat, and he pulled up on her doeskin to find her own skin. His mouth fell to her breast and he took her nipple in his teeth, gently enough to leave her frenzied, hard enough to make her cry out.

She needed, oh, how she needed. She wrapped her legs around him, holding her to him, running her hands over him feverishly. The strong cheekbones that had once made him beautiful, that now made him arrogant. The rounded tightness of his buttocks, clenched now with his own need. His flat nipples, his broad chest, smooth and warm . . . hers for this moment, to savor and to crave.

But she could not understand why he was shouting.

Then she knew that he was not. It was not Twelic's voice she heard. It was a white-skin.

A howl of fury rose in her own throat as she realized that they would take this from her, too. She knew even before she wrenched away from him that How-erd had found them.

Understanding came to Twelic more slowly, mingled with the violent, horrible realization that he had been right, she could make him forget anything, everything, even the wary fighting strength that made him a man.

The soldiers had caught him as off guard as it was possible for a man to be.

They both plunged for her gun at the same time, each taking one end of it, tugging desperately.

"You do not know how to use it!" he growled, furious.

"I can shoot an arrow! I can manage! It is mine!"

"This is different! Do not be a fool! I am here. You should go where you are needed!"

Something about his rage made her let go of the weapon.

She tumbled backward, sprawling.

The first *xayxayx* pony came over the hill. She saw him clearly even in the darkness, saw his one sleeve loose and flapping.

How-erd.

She choked back a scream that would have called his attention, going flat on her belly, crawling. *Her ponies.* She had to save her ponies.

She left Twelic, scrambling through the brush, back to the camp to find them and to alert those who slept. Her body still throbbed and her heart bled with the loss of something irretrievable, but her thoughts were desperate and cold.

THE HILLS EXPLODED with gunfire even as she reached the valley. The air cracked and rattled, and flashes of fire showed through the trees like a demented *cewcew* ghost played there. Kiye Kipi looked back at it, and finally, she screamed.

Some of the people had already begun scrambling out of their lodges. At the sound of her cry, the old ones and the infirm emerged as well, blinking groggily, gaping at the foothills. The first keens and moans of confusion came from them. She began grabbing them, hauling them toward the herd, shoving those who would not flee.

"Get your ponies! *Run!*"

She began to follow them and met Joseph's chest hard. He reached a hand out to steady her as she staggered backward.

"How many?" he asked, and his voice was cold, beyond horror.

She opened her mouth to answer, then she shook her head. She did not know.

There was a curdling scream from behind her, and she whipped about. Oh, sweet Tahmahnewes, someone had died up there—horribly, badly, and the sound had come from a Nimipu throat. She had known the tongue, the sound of it.

Who? Which man had it been?

She took one lurching, instinctive step back that way, but Joseph caught her arm.

"We must go!" he snapped. "We cannot fight here. We are too disorganized."

She did not *want* to fight, not now! She had to know who
that had been!

Twelic . . .

Joseph shook her hard enough to make her teeth rattle. "Go
to the herd! Get them out! Without them, we have nothing!"

The herd. Slowly, dully, her head came back to her ponies.
Now, finally, the People would use them to run. The blacks
could outpace those *xayxayx* horses, but oh, Spirit Chief, what
would become of the rest of the herd?

The warriors began to spill down into the valley, yowling
their war cries, shooting behind them. The men who had remained in the camp ran to join them, yipping and screaming.
An impossibly big metal ball groaned through the air over her
head, and Kiye Kipi gaped after it until it landed in a knot of
Kahmuenem lodges, exploding in a ball of flame and sparks.

Sweet Spirit Chief, what were they fighting with?

Squaws ran at her from that direction, dragging their babes
and toddlers, sobbing, groping at each other. She had to get
them out as well.

She looked back at the foothills.

Tahmahnewes, let him be alive. Let him fight well, let him
kill them all. She stumbled back the other way, then she began
running.

She had no choice. He had her gun. In the end, she was just
another woman after all.

The women galloped until dawn lifted the darkness. Then,
gradually, Kiye Kipi was able to see their vacant faces, their
eyes darting in wary shock.

She goaded her mare and got to the front of them, calling
out to them to stop. Her throat was raw and parched. She had
spent all the night yelling at them, trying to keep them moving.

Slowly, one by one, they reined in. They sat dully upon
their ponies, looking at her, waiting. They could not move, she
realized, unless she told them where to go.

But where? In the melee, she had lost Joseph, and she had
no idea where to take them.

She pressed her hands to her temples and looked back the

way they had come. Morning touched the grass now with thin, early light. The spotted ponies were following at a distance, struggling. The blacks had flown so far, so fast, that no one had been able to keep up with them.

She sent a grateful, fervent prayer to the Spirit Chief for that, then Wetatonmi came to her.

"What now?" Her voice was cracked as well, but with exhaustion and despair. She clutched Little Mole close against her breasts, and Kiye Kipi knew she thought of Alokot, but she would not let the others see her terror. If anyone broke down now, uncontrollable panic would sweep through the others like prairie fire.

Kiye Kipi swallowed dryly. "Water? Yes, water. We need to find some for these ponies, for ourselves, and then we can wait."

But who would come? Their men . . . or the *xayxayx*?

They moved on, slowly now. Wetatonmi rode beside her, helping her scan the land. When the sun rose full upon them, they found a low spot on the prairie, the grass marshy and wet with a hole deep enough to sate the herd. The women dismounted, many of them swaying with weariness, with emotion. They squatted down among the ponies, lifting water to their mouths gratefully, splashing it over their necks, their faces.

Kiye Kipi trudged up to the higher ground. The swale— barely a swale—was not enough to conceal them. There were only three or four thin, scraggly trees to hide all their ponies. She dragged her hands through her hair, groaning, so tired. She wanted to close her eyes, sink to the ground, and let someone else care about this.

Find us, please love, find us.

She shook her head dazedly. Stupid, stupid . . . Twelic could not hear her; she did not even know if he lived. But she had been pleading with him, drawing strength from him all through the night, as though *he* were her *wyakin*.

Now, looking out at the barren grass, she knew she was alone.

She went back to the squaws. They were beginning to move

about now, some keening with losses they could not yet be sure of. She gathered up one toddling child, and took another by the hand.

"Hush now, hush," she murmured to no one, to all of them. "It is not that bad."

But it was.

She looked about, her heart chugging. Easily twenty hands of ponies were empty of packs. They carried no lodge covers, no parfleches of dried food, no robes, no clothing. She remembered the explosion of Kahmuenem lodges from that strange, deadly metal ball. Pure, unadulterated rage swept through her for Looking Glass. How many more lives would that headman take from them? She swallowed back a little cry and sank down into the mud to sit, to wait.

The men came again with dusk.

When she first heard their hoofbeats, instinctive terror turned her bowels to water. She looked quickly to where Wetatonmi took her turn watching up on the grassland. The squaw cried out, then she began running, dragging Little Mole by the arm. It was their own warriors. Kiye Kipi gave her own weak whoop and scrambled to her feet to follow her.

Ahead of her, she saw Alokot catch Wetatonmi and pull her and their babe astride. Her eyes darted, and her breath started coming short. *Where was he? Where was Twelic?* So many faces, so many galloping, seething war ponies . . . and then she saw him.

Her legs went wobbly with relief until she thought she might fall. He was alive, not bleeding, not hurt anywhere that she could see.

Suddenly, her skin flamed and her stomach rolled over. He had survived, and now that it was over, she remembered how she had left him. He had scorned her and charged her with being just what Cloud Singer had said . . . and she had thrown herself at him, hungry and shameless.

She keened a sound of mortification deep in her throat.

He rode close enough to her that she could have called his name and he would have heard her. She sank quickly down into the grass instead so that he would not notice her. Oh, what a fool she was!

She got a slow grip on herself as she watched the men reach the water. Their squaws ran to meet them, weeping and howling. Finally, she got up and went back there.

She did not want to disturb Alokot; he was sitting close by Wetatonmi with Little Mole in his lap. Her gaze scanned the others for Joseph, then Twelic's voice came from behind her.

"This belongs to you."

She jolted. Oh, there was no escaping him these suns, now when she needed to most of all! She turned woodenly about to face him.

He held her gun out to her. "I used all your ammunition," he went on.

She could not look at him. She focused on the weapon as she took it from him. "I suppose I will find more, somewhere . . . some time," she managed.

"Yes, I think there will be another fight. How-erd is close."

Now her eyes flashed up to him. "Where?"

"We only stop long enough to gather you women. We must push on."

She did not want to say it, but knew it had to be said. "I think . . . he will know we are heading for that Bitterroot pass."

Twelic's face hardened. "This pass is called the Lolo, and yes, I have thought of that, too. Our trail is plain enough for him to follow easily."

He began moving off toward the others again. *Let him go.*

She could not. She called his name.

He looked back at her, a storm of emotion on his face. What *was* this tie that bound them, that tormented them, that made them act so crazy when neither of them really wanted to be close to the other? Her heart began moving again painfully.

"I—" she began, but then she found she could not speak of what had happened, not even to beg him to forget it. She could not bear to remember touching him, to think of what had almost happened, what she had almost done . . . what she had almost had.

"We lost warriors?" she asked instead.

"Four of them. Six more wounded."

She gave a little cry of horror.

"The dead were all mine, Hasotoin," he went on. "Two of your Kahmuenem took bullets. Burned Tree, Toolhoolhoolzote, and Tenku work over them now."

Still Tenku lived? How old he would be by now! It was all that much longer his distrust of her would have had to fester.

"I would offer to help, but neither Toolhoolhoolzote nor Tenku would like that," she managed.

Twelic shrugged, and for a moment, she almost thought he would smile. "We will have a quick council anyway, before we go. I think you would rather be part of that."

This time when he turned away, she only followed him at a distance.

The headmen, all except Toolhoolhoolzote, sat near the water. No flames crackled in front of them this time; a fire would draw the attention of the *xayxayx,* wherever they were. For the first time she noticed the eerie silence as well, broken only by the deep, rasping voice of a solitary toad. The women did not even dare keen for their dead.

For some reason, that tore at her heart most of all.

"Our pony wife thinks How-erd knows where we are going," Twelic said suddenly.

Her pulse stopped and she stared at him. *What was he doing?* One moment he was deriding her for her part in this fight, and now he would throw her to the council like a foal to wolves?

She looked about, snapping her jaw shut. Joseph nodded.

"Yes," the headman agreed. "That is almost certainly so."

Huishuis Kute's voice came quietly. "If we do not reach that Lolo, we are doomed."

"Is there another way?" White Bird mused. "Could we go south again and cross the mountains that way, near my country?"

Alokot finally approached, shaking his head. "No. The women and herds would not survive that trail."

Silence fell, thick and painful.

It could not end this way! Kiye Kipi thought wildly. They *had* to go on!

She looked to Twelic, against all her instincts, needing his eyes. The truth was there. He knew it, too. The Safe Place was north, still distant. Whatever it was, wherever it was, it lay over the Lolo.

"We all agree that How-erd will try to block our flight," Twelic said roughly. "I think it is strange that we have not heard his hounding hoofbeats already. So where is he? I say he is headed there, to get there first. We must find out."

"What are you saying?" snapped Looking Glass. For the first time she realized that the others did not look at him. Perhaps they had not openly chastised or blamed him for this disaster; too many had agreed that it was a good idea to rest. But few were inclined to tolerate him at the moment either.

"We must find him," Joseph agreed, as though that other headman had not spoken.

"Ride out!" Alokot growled. He waved a hand at Twelic and the warriors to follow him.

Kiye Kipi heard her own voice stop them. "No! That is crazy!" she cried.

She knew any other warrior would have slapped her down for such disrespect, but Alokot's face only went stony. "Say what you must," he snapped.

She swallowed, looking around at all of them. "This land is so open, only grasses. How-erd would spot a party of our warriors as easily as they would spot him. And the country between here and that Lolo is vast." She looked to White Bird. "You said the pass is five suns' ride from the Clearwaters. That is what—four suns from here? We would have to send out several parties of warriors, in many different directions, to find these *xayxayx*. Do you think How-erd is so simple that he will go right to that place? I do not think so. I think you will all be gone looking, leaving these women and children unprotected."

They all began talking at once. She waited, sending a silent plea of apology to Alokot, but he would not glance her way.

"Why not ride straight for the pass, and if they are there,

fight them?" Two Moons demanded. "Why look for them at all?"

"You have no wife," another man snarled. "Would you lead ours straight at those blue-coats?"

Joseph held a hand up. "We will not elude this How-erd by force and our ponies alone. We have done it so far, but I do not think it will happen again. Twelic is right. We must locate him somehow. We must defeat him with our wits as well as our prowess, and we cannot do that if we do not know where he is."

"I will look for him," Kiye Kipi heard herself blurt again. "I can dream for him."

A bellow of outrage came from Toolhoolhoolzote. She had not seen him approach.

"You would trust a rude squaw's magic?" he demanded of the council. "Bah! That is crazy! *I* will dream. I will find him."

Anger gripped her . . . and desperation. Kiye Kipi drew herself up.

"You are an animal caller and a healer," she answered thinly. "You can call game and spirit medicine. Can you send your mind out to look for something? If you can, then I would be glad to see you go instead."

The council went very quiet at the challenge. Their silence made her feel sick. *What was she doing?* But it had to be done. Tahmahnewes, she had never heard that Toolhoolhoolzote could search. All that mattered now were the People, not his haughty, vain pride, not his hatred of her.

The *tiwats* did not answer her. *He will kill me for this.* The sudden certainty of that brought terror, making her feel weak, but she only looked back at Joseph.

"Please. Let me try. I can ride over the land, find out where I can feel him, then send my magic out to search. It should not be too difficult to go to that place and make sure that is where he lurks."

"No!" Twelic roared out.

Her gaze snapped to him, startled. What did he care? She would not take his power, his following, if she succeeded. She knew that he wanted to find How-erd, that he knew it was necessary. Why, then, did fury darken his own face?

"You would go out there alone, like some defenseless doe, knowing that How-erd and his men would willingly kill you?" he snarled. "You are a fool!"

"I will need ammunition," she allowed carefully.

He looked to Joseph. "I will take a few men and go with her," he said stonily. "She cannot go alone."

Joseph raised a brow. "Yes, I would have suggested a party to accompany her. I do not think that she should go unprotected either. If you would like to ride along, so be it."

Looking Glass agreed too easily. She realized that he wanted to be free of both of them.

She balled her hands into fists and turned away. She could not fight this, had to take her limited victory. She had caused too much stir in this council already. But she passed close by Twelic as she went to her pony.

"No Hasotoin," she hissed. "Bring whoever you wish, but no Hasotoin. I cannot dream when those men are all around me, doubting me."

He met her flashing eyes and wondered what kind of insanity he had just put himself into. He did not want to travel through this dark, intimate night by her side. He did not want to fall into the lure of her again as he had in the Clearwaters. Sooner or later, it would kill him, risking everything he fought for. Instead, he found himself nodding grimly.

She went last to Alokot. "I am sorry," she said, demanding that he acknowledge her now.

He looked at her for a long time, then, finally, he gave her a tight smile.

"I am getting used to it," he answered, shrugging. "May Tahmahnewes ride with you."

39

As they moved through the night, clouds gathered low to hide the moon. The air was damp and close, and strands of her hair clung uncomfortably to her neck. Misgivings began to make Kiye Kipi's belly squirm.

The worst of her fears were for the white-skins. Small, dark hillocks became squatting blue-coats, armed, ready and waiting for them. Shadows seemed to move surreptitiously, and the howl of a wolf made her gasp.

Twelic raised a brow at her. His expression was neither tolerant nor kind.

"You could go back."

Her jaw clenched. "And you could find How-erd on your own," she snapped, "but I do not think our elders will live that long."

She could no longer remember why she had not fought for another escort. Her back hurt with the tension of being close to him; her head was thick and befuddled with it. She had been so concerned with getting out of camp, with *looking,* that she had not considered how long and painful this journey with him would be.

"Why could you not have let Toolhoolhoolzote do this?" he demanded, relentless.

"I told the council why. He would have failed."

"Now you have made yourself another needless enemy. Are the *xayxayx* not enough for you?" he grated.

"Toolhoolhoolzote would have hated me either way, even

if he had attempted this and failed.''

''You will do as I say when we are out here,'' he went on as though she had not spoken.

His voice was building in volume, with the rigid anger he had been suppressing since they had left the others. ''You think you are a warrior, but you are only a squaw! You hinder me. How am I to fight when all my cares are for watching over you?''

She looked across at him, her own temper bubbling. ''I do not ask you to watch over me! I can fight as well as I have to. I have done it before.''

''*Curse you!*'' he spat suddenly, swinging his pony around to block her way. ''Do you never listen to reason? You have never killed a man before!''

Her heart began to flutter. ''I think . . . I could do it if I had to.''

''You will not find out,'' he said through grated teeth. ''I do not intend to let it happen.''

They watched each other, their eyes hot, then his gaze slid away. He dismounted abruptly.

''Dawn is coming. We will sleep here until the sun leaves again.''

She began shaking her head frantically. ''No, that will not work.''

''You cannot tell me how to stalk prey!''

''You cannot tell me how to dream!''

She swung to the ground as well, facing him, then her anger slid out of her. There was only desperation. She did not feel as though they had a lot of time. They could not stand here and argue.

''You must listen to me,'' she said fervently. ''When *my* prey is too far away, my *wyakin* ponies cannot take me to it. And I have nothing of How-erd's to touch, to carry my mind to him. That is . . . that is how I do this.''

He was quiet for a moment. ''What are you saying? What about the anger you spoke of? What about crying fear into other hearts?''

''That only works with horses.''

She put her face to the sky, trying to remain calm, to *feel*. He felt every muscle in his body clench suddenly. Tahmah-newes, she was beautiful.

She stood, her spine straight, her head tilted back. Her hair swam past her waist, sleek and unbraided. Her doeskin was tattered, torn at the hem, thin with wear, and it streamed over her body like water. It clung loosely to her breasts, high and round. A memory flashed at him before he could stop it . . . her skin like warm, smooth river sand, tawny and flushed beneath his hands. He remembered taking the tip of her breast into his mouth, and desire pounded cruelly through him again. He thought of her strange, indigo gaze and the way she met him eye to eye.

"I . . . I cannot feel anything here," she admitted quietly.

Her voice shattered his thoughts, but he could not for the life of him think what she had said.

"What?" he demanded hoarsely.

"I cannot dream for How-erd here. He is too far away," she repeated. "Twelic, we must go on."

It was too late. The eastern horizon was yellow-gray. He would have given anything in that moment to accommodate her, anything to keep from having to lie down beside her on this prairie. . . .

He shook the thought from his mind.

"That is impossible," he said.

She realized that his voice did not bite this time. She looked at him again, something odd moving in her belly. "Why?"

"If we travel in the light, How-erd can see us. You said that yourself in the council."

"He is not here. I am sure of that."

"But you would take us to him."

"Well . . . yes."

"In the sun?"

"Oh." She looked at the grass. Tahmahnewes, she did not want to lie down here, so close to him!

Was that what drove her, or did she truly feel as though How-erd was besting them even as they stood about talking?

Oh, Spirit Chief, she just did not know! She could not think clearly now.

She moved mutely to her black again, pulling her robe from her pack. Her movements felt stiff and brittle as she laid it on the ground. She sat upon it, drawing her knees up to her chest, wrapping her arms around them.

Farther out on the prairie, she watched his warriors approach. They had kept their distance as she and Twelic had argued through the night. Only one of them—Thunder Dance—was Hasotoin. He had given her that much.

"Twelic." He was at his pony, and he went very still at the sound of her voice, but he did not look back at her.

"Why are you so angry with me these suns? I have done nothing to hurt you."

She thought at first that he would not answer her, but he still did not move, either. She decided he was thinking, or perhaps he had not heard her because he was listening for something else. She began to repeat herself when he finally spoke, then her pulse exploded.

"Because I want you without wanting you," he said tightly. "Because I would like to spend these long, hot suns sinking into your flesh, and if you have your way you will not see another summer."

She did not know what she had expected, but it was not that.

It was too sweet, and she did not know much of sweetness. It made her want to cry out and run to him, to find her way against him again, warm skin and hotter mouths touching, needing. *I want you.* Oh, how glorious that was!

But he had not said that he loved her. He said that it made him angry.

She lay down very, very carefully on her blanket instead.

Twelic put his own robe down on the other side of his pony.

She could not sleep.

The sun came up high and burning. Insects sneaked hungrily out of the grasses and found succor on her flesh. She scratched and rolled over, and they crawled away again, but that did not help her shut out the sounds of Twelic's sleep, his deep, even breathing and his occasional snore.

Curse him, how could he sleep after what he had said?

She could not stop struggling with it, could not put it out of her mind. She tried to turn her thoughts to the white-skins, and they veered back. She tried to make her head as clean and empty as a snow-deep prairie, and failed miserably.

Groaning, she sat up.

She looked about at the rushing grass, waving and dipping in the hot wind. How-erd was out there somewhere, and she knew, finally, that she was not going to find him, not this way. She would not be able to do it with Twelic by her side, tangling her heart and her mind.

Again, it came to her that they did not have much time. A sense of urgency kept scurrying through her blood. Joseph and the headmen were traveling with the bands somewhere behind them, getting closer and closer to the Lolo, and Twelic would not even allow her to look for a place to dream.

She knew what she had to do, and her blood went cold with fear.

No matter what he seemed to think, she was not eager to meet these white-skins; she had no wish to die. But there was no help for the risk, not this time. She was going to have to leave him and find a place where she could search.

She had her magic to help protect her, and her fingers closed around her gun. Twelic and Alokot had both given her more ammunition. *You have never killed a man before!* She swallowed dryly. She *could* do it if she had to; she could.

She pushed quietly to her feet. None of the warriors stirred.

She had not hobbled her *wyakin* mare; she had not ever been able to bring herself to force such ignominious trappings upon her. Now she stared at her hard and focused her mind.

Go.

The mare looked up, her nostrils flaring as though scenting the wind.

Go out on the prairie. The prairie. Good grass. Better grass.

The mare snorted and tossed her head.

Kiye Kipi froze, looking about, but Twelic slept on. The

pony began wandering, heading farther out from them. Then, finally, she stopped and lowered her head again. That was good. That was perfect.

Kiye Kipi began moving toward her, around the sleeping bodies of the men, holding her breath with each step. She put her moccasins down carefully, watching where they went so the grass would not rustle and no twig would snap. Twelic stirred anyway, clearing his throat. She froze in midstride.

When she was absolutely sure that he was not on the verge of waking, she finally moved again, making it out to her pony. She eased her way up silently onto her back, and they began walking out onto the prairie.

The Bitterroots loomed blue and dark against the horizon to her right. Her eyes narrowed on them, then she shook her head. No, she did not feel that How-erd was there yet. He was heading there; she was still certain of that. But he was moving even now as she searched for him; he was not at the pass.

She looked back to make sure she was far enough away that no one would hear her, then she put her heels to her mare and they began to trot north.

Twelic could not believe he had slept.

His tongue was dry and cleaved to the roof of his mouth, and the sun was merciless. He stirred uncomfortably and sat up, scratching under his hair. He had thought only to close his eyes, knowing the *xayxayx* were somewhere nearby, knowing Kiye Kipi's sweet flesh and flashing eyes were so close. But the fighting and the flight had worn down everyone, even him, and he had fallen heavily and completely into the blackness of rest.

He snorted angrily at himself, then looked to where she lay. *She was gone.*

His heart staggered as he had not known it could do. Something cold and liquid swept through him, down into his very bowels.

His first thought was that they had taken her. He lunged to his feet, wild, a crazed howl building in his throat. But there were no tracks in the grass other than those from their own

ponies. Slowly, slowly, fury began to build in his head instead,
red hot and hurting.

He would find her, and when he did, he would skin her
alive.

Thunder Dance sat up at the sound of his movement. "What
is it?" he asked groggily, then his own skin flushed at the
realization that he had dozed as well.

"Stay here," Twelic snapped. "If I am not back in one
sun's time, return to the others without me. Tell them there is
trouble. I have lost her." He let out a long stream of curses.

Thunder Dance looked at the pony wife's rumpled, empty
robe. If panic had not been thumping in his own chest, he
might well have smiled.

He watched his friend leap astride his war pony. The stubborn, arrogant warrior had finally found his match, he thought.
There was, after all, a woman on Tahmahnewes's earth who
could claim him. He did not remember much of the one they
had called Dark Moon as a child, but he decided in that moment that he liked her.

After a while, Kiye Kipi dropped her reins and let her *wyakin* mare carry her where she would. The pony seemed
strangely alert and watchful, as though she knew what they
were doing. It was as though she had magic of her own and
was guiding Kiye Kipi.

When they finally came upon a stream, she dismounted long
enough to hunker down beside it. She stripped her doeskin off
and drenched it, then she splashed the deliciously cool water
over her skin. She guzzled a drink from her palms and looked
to her mare. The pony did not seem to want to sate herself.
She ignored the water. Her big, dark eyes remained fast on the
northern horizon, her ears pricked forward, and she stomped
one hoof as though impatient to be off again.

Kiye Kipi felt it now, too, an itchy feeling just under her
skin that had nothing to do with her insect bites. *How-erd was
close.*

Off in the distance, the land swelled up a bit. There seemed
to be some water there as well, because squat bushes crowded

the base. She would go there, she decided. That was where she should dream.

She began to struggle into her sodden doeskin again, just pulling it down over her breasts, when something slammed into her from behind.

She screamed, but the sound choked off suddenly. The force of him knocked her flat on her belly, stealing her air, and the water swam into her nostrils as she splashed into it. She fought wildly, choking and gasping, sinking her teeth into the hand that came around to hold her own arms down. A feral, growling sound of fury answered her.

Twelic.

His weight eased enough to let her roll over, and what she saw in his eyes made her cry out again.

"I would like nothing"—he broke off to shake her—"nothing so much as to kill you myself! *Do you know what you have done to me?*" She had made him love her, he thought viciously, she had changed everything, and now she would try to rob him of all that, to leave him broken and alone with her loss.

He ground his mouth down on hers before she could answer, wrapping his fist in her wet, tangled hair. It was brutal and wild and something leaped in her in response. But before she could respond, he tore his mouth away.

"You did not hear me come up behind you, did you? I could have been anyone!"

It was true.

His mouth came back, his tongue plunging to find her own again as though to reassure himself that she was warm, whole, alive.

"You squat here like some stupid squaw, without even the gun that you have no cursed idea how to use!" he went on.

"I—" But she could not argue. Her gun was with her mare.

"*What did you think to do out here on your own?* If you would fight like a man, then do it right!"

He dove into her again, his mouth hot and searching. The agony of wanting him crashed through her again, and she mewled in a voice that did not even sound like her own. His hands were on her damp flesh now, moving over her ribs, over her breasts, finally sliding beneath her back to mold her hips against his. She groped at him frantically, then, as suddenly as he had ravaged her, he went still again, breathing hard.

"So be it," he muttered. "So be it."

"So . . . be . . . what?"

His eyes were still hot, but different now. She had the absurd, impossible urge to weep, but she did not know if it was for something glorious . . . or something too horrible to bear.

Curse him, curse herself, why did she always respond to him?

"We will fight this fight together, Screamer," he said wearily. "You will do it anyway, and I cannot let you do it alone."

He was not one to acquiesce. It violated something inside him. But he knew now that to keep battling her would be to lose her.

And that brought the worst pain of all.

Kiye Kipi turned her head to the side, her throat working. *Fight together. Just another man.* The bitter regret of it almost choked her.

That was what he wanted, no matter what his hands and his mouth conveyed. But at least it was something she could give him.

She struggled, planting her palms against his chest to push him off her. Then, nearby, her mare gave a quiet, urgent whinny.

She looked to her sharply, understanding crashing in on her. "Sweet Tahmahnewes," she breathed.

He let her up. "What is it?"

"I thought—" But there was no time to explain. She had thought she was meant to *dream* at that distant hill, but that was not it at all. Panic made her cold again, and she scrambled to her feet.

How-erd was there. *He was right there, on the other side.* That was what her pony had been trying to tell her!

"We must go." She motioned to Twelic frantically. They mounted again and rode to the place.

At the base of the hill they dismounted again. Even she

knew enough to get down on her belly to creep to the top. They went up, side by side, and then her breath snagged.

The blue-coats were there, riding west. *West?*

''What—''

He clapped a hand over her mouth. She pried it away again and watched more quietly.

They were close enough to see that the *xayxayx* leader was indeed How-erd. They could see his fuzzy face hair, and his empty sleeve rippling in the wind. But she could not understand what he was doing, where he was going.

Twelic pulled on her arm and motioned down the slope again. She scrambled back, following him. He was looking at her the way Wetatonmi had when she had scattered the *xayxayx* ponies at White Bird.

Something moved inside him at the extent of her magic. *How had she known?* Oh, yes, she was so much more than any woman he had ever met before. Stubborn, reckless, intelligent and powerful beyond what he could understand.

And so beautiful it made him ache. Her blue-black eyes watched him quizzically.

He cleared his throat, whispering, ''He is looping around to the west so that it looks like he is going back to Lapwai.''

Her pulse hitched. ''But he is not?''

''No, I do not think so. I think he is feinting retreat. It is the only thing that makes sense. He is not one to give up. If he keeps his present course, Earth Sound's sentinels will spot him. I think that when he is behind those men, he will veer south and cut off the bands' trail. I think he will be waiting to meet them.''

''Then we must get back to Joseph and warn him!''

He gave her a tight, bitter smile. ''There is a small matter of the warriors you forced me to leave behind so that I could track you quickly.''

She flushed, but managed to keep her chin up. ''So be it. We will have to detour to pick them up and ride that much faster to make up for it.'' Suddenly, she grinned, and the look was nearly as condescending and arrogant as his had been.

''It is really too bad you never traded for one of my black ponies.''

40

THEY REACHED THE bands just as Earth Sound returned to give his own report that How-erd was moving west, back toward Lapwai.

A furor of excitement and relief went through the women, and Looking Glass strode forward in good humor. "Then we can camp, and move on with the dawn," he announced.

"No." Kiye Kipi swung down off her pony. She could feel the headman's eyes itching her skin as she gave her reins over to Dirty Dove.

One of the boys rushed forward to take Twelic's pony as well. He met her gaze with a shrug. There was peace between them again, deceptively smooth, dangerously fragile, but she knew he would be glad to argue with Looking Glass in her stead.

"We found How-erd as well," he said, squatting at Joseph's hearth. "He is not retreating."

They had tracked him after rejoining the warriors, and his first guess had been right. "As we speak, he is just ahead of us," he went on. "He has moved south to cut us off."

"Then we have no choice but to meet him," snapped Two Moons, ready and hungry for it.

Huishuis Kute shook his head. "No, I think we should play his own game. Cross his trail, let him see us, and draw his troops after us while the women flee to the Lolo."

"It will not work again," Joseph contributed flatly.

Kiye Kipi felt a cold worm of premonition wriggle in her

gut at his expression. He had been so pensive and unhappy since they had attacked the soldiers on their way to the Clearwaters. But now that look was deeper, weary and almost hopeless.

"How-erd is too shrewd to be fooled three times—if indeed we confused him back at the Salmon," he went on. "I think now only a major ploy will keep him off the Lolo."

"What kind of ploy?" Alokot demanded.

"Something like my surrender."

Howls of horror went up from the Kahmuenem women. The men bellowed in outrage and disbelief. Even sedate old White Bird was angry.

"You would go in to him so the rest of us can run on? Think what insanity that is! All our cunning, all our efforts are needed if we are ever to reclaim our country. If you go in, it is over. If you go in, I will sit this old body down here and wait for How-erd to find and kill me! Why prolong it by making him chase me for a while?"

Kiye Kipi felt herself jostled rudely by the crowd. She stumbled, then her mouth fell open. The woman who had pushed her aside was Arenoth.

She moved heavy footed to her son and stood until his troubled eyes came to her. There was a strange, eerie dignity to the set of her shoulders, though they drooped with weariness. She clutched her heavy robe about herself, though the sun was still warm as it fell.

Kiye Kipi's heart quailed. *What was she doing?*

"Your words are wise, my son, but you cannot go. You owe it to your father to keep on. *I* owe it to him to give up."

Alokot moved to her, his face twisted, reaching a hand out as though to silence her. She looked about at him, at all of the children of her hearth.

"Yes, you see what I am saying. Perhaps you think I am a doddering old fool, but I listened well to my husband through many snow seasons. I learned enough to see what we must do now. Someone should indeed go to this How-erd under a flag of truce. Someone should ask him under what terms you can come back to Lapwai. I would be that person. While he is triumphant and preoccupied with me, all of you can move on to the buffalo country.''

''No.'' Joseph's voice was harsh, low.

''Think, my son. Think as though you were in my moccasins. See my life as I see it, and all the remainder of my snows as they must be. I am too old to be climbing over mountains. I do not want to live out my last suns there. What I would wish for myself is to die in the valley where my husband's own bones rest, but these thieving *xayxayx* have taken that from me. Now I do not truly care where I die, except that it should not be on the buffalo prairie.

''I would go to the afterworld with peace in my heart,'' she finished, ''knowing that I have done something to save my people. I would do that for my husband, so that when I rejoin him, I can be proud.''

The women began wailing in mourning. Joseph's face turned to stone, his eyes dark with torment.

''Whoever goes to him will not return,'' he said tightly.

''No, of course not.''

His next words seemed to strangle him. ''There is no guarantee that we will win this fight. Perhaps we will never get our land back. Perhaps we will live forever in the land of the Crow, and you will live at Lapwai.''

Her eyes softened. ''Then let us say good-bye while I still have the strength to hold all of you.''

Alokot made a choking sound. ·Wetatonmi gave a quick, high-pitched cry of grief.

''Know what I am proud of all of you,'' Arenoth went on.

Kiye Kipi turned away. Twelic made a half gesture as though to comfort her, but she shoved past him blindly. *So many snows of care, of healing . . .* Arenoth had given her that, had allowed her to live on her own and breathe the wind and start over. Those memories were being stripped violently away from her, and she was not ready to let them go.

Another good-bye, and she was not yet ready to speak it.

Her eyes burned and her throat closed. She knew it as well as Arenoth did. How-erd gave them no choice, after all.

*   *   *

They all moved on while it was still dark, Arenoth going east with a handful of other elders who were too tired and too beaten to continue. The bands rode north to veer around Howard while he was busy with their arrival.

There were sporadic wretched wails of grief for the mothers and grandfathers who were lost to them. Each cry was like a knife thrusting into Kiye Kipi's gut. She had hugged Arenoth once, hard and clumsily, before she had left, but she could not bear to look back at her now.

She traveled with her eyes straight ahead, part of a rear guard that fell behind the slower ponies and the children. Near dawn, they passed the place where Howard camped. She looked that way and saw a murky smudge of orange on the southern horizon. She guessed that if the *xayxayx* had fires, then some of the soldiers were awake. Her muscles clenched with tension, but there was no stir or uproar from the blue-coats as they passed around them.

The first morning light was beginning to touch the sky when Alokot rode close to her. "Get ready to drive the ponies," he said quietly. "We will run now."

She looked at him, gaping. "They will hear us!"

"Perhaps. But they are preoccupied with our mother now, and we are faster. We will get to the Lolo pass first, even if we have to fight them off from our rear."

She nodded stiffly. It was, she realized, all the head start they needed.

Good-bye, mother, friend . . . good-bye.

She set her jaw, her throat working. When one of the warriors gave a quiet yipping sound, she goaded her mare and dove grimly into the herd, stampeding them.

The sun was high and strong again when they slowed enough for Earth Sound to catch up with them. He went to ride with Joseph, and she left the herd long enough to get close, to hear. Twelic and Alokot and Two Moons moved in as well.

"Five of them come after us," Earth Sound reported.

Only five? That did not seem right. It was too easy.

"Why so few?" she demanded.

"They are *their* scouts," Twelic answered.

"What do we do now?"

"We must not stop," Joseph advised. "If we do, How-erd will be upon us." He was quiet for a moment. "He knows where we are, knows he has been duped again, but I would guess he is busy interrogating our mother."

Kiye Kipi could not help herself. A little keen broke from her throat before she could swallow it.

"He will come after us as soon as he is through with her," Joseph finished flatly. "That is why he wants to keep sure of where we go."

They were still three suns' ride from the Lolo. If they kept going without rest, they would reach it by sundown tomorrow. Sweet Tahmahnewes, could the weak ones travel that long, that fast? Could the spotted ponies survive it?

"It is not possible," she groaned.

Joseph shrugged as though his shoulders were weighted with boulders. "It has to be."

They reached the pass as the next sun faded, throwing blue shadows over the foothills. Kiye Kipi's thighs trembled with strain; her spine sent up a constant ache, and her eyes were grainy with exhaustion. As soon as they were concealed from the prairie, many of the people swung, staggering, to the ground.

A squaw fell solidly, her legs giving out beneath her. She sat holding her babe, sobbing quietly.

Kiye Kipi girded herself and looked about at the others. Unexpectedly, an immense, fierce pride swelled in her throat. Oh, Spirit Chief, their courage! They clung to their mounts, swaying, moaning, but even the elders' jaws were hard, their eyes were grim and determined, and she knew, suddenly, that if they had to, they would somehow find the strength to keep moving.

It shook her deeply, and she turned away to go into the herd. They had not fared quite so well.

A full half of them were down, their sides heaving. She moaned in despair as she moved among them, squatting to stroke them. She had lost another five hands of them in the ride here, old ones and weanlings who had simply collapsed from the pace and died. Now she saw another five hands who would not be able to go any farther.

She went to find Joseph before she could cry.

He was standing atop one of the first rises with the warriors, looking back at their trail. Huishuis Kute and White Bird had joined him as well.

"When do we camp?" she asked shortly. The women and the ponies had no one else to speak for them. Now, more than ever, she would defy propriety to do it.

"We can stay here until the moon comes," Joseph said finally, looking at her. "Tell them that."

It was not enough, but she nodded.

"Then we will have to divert them again," said White Bird. "Your Earth Sound says those five sol-jers are still behind us."

"They kept up?" She was astounded.

Alokot managed a thin smile. "We did not say that, only that they are still moving . . . more and more slowly. They are a far ride back now. We do not know what How-erd does. We have left him distant as well."

She felt her own heart thump a little. Bless Tahmahnewes for even their spotted ponies, who did not need seeds and had no heavy metal hooves to weigh them down.

"We need you to pick ten of the ponies who will die anyway," Twelic said suddenly. "We need to cut them."

"*Cut* them?" She looked at him incredulously, shaking her head.

"Pick five hundred of the strongest ones as well. We are going to crash open a trail with them. We will mark the trees with the additional blood and the hairs of those we have killed."

She began to understand. "So we will leave two sets of tracks."

"Yes. The obvious, marked one that we hope they will follow. It will look as though we have jammed our ponies through there, over all obstacles. They will believe that, thinking we are desperate, trying to lose ourselves in the mountains. But the People will stay on the Lolo itself. If the soldiers follow *that* trail, if they are not misled, then we will just have to leave some warriors behind to meet them.''

Some semblance of her adrenaline came back, snaking through her. ''Yes, it could work.''

''How-erd will not be fooled by this,'' Joseph said dully.

''How-erd will not reach us first,'' Alokot argued. ''His scouts will. They are not so shrewd or intelligent.''

It was worth a try, Kiye Kipi thought. Anything was worth a try now. They were so very close to buffalo country . . . to the other side of these mountains where they could find the Safe Place without How-erd dogging them.

She nodded, then she thought of her ponies, the ones who would not see that haven. Her heart recoiled.

She could not kill them.

Twelic watched her face. ''Would you take a bullet if it ensured that the rest of these people would make it to safety?''

She groaned and closed her eyes. ''Yes,'' she whispered. ''Yes, I . . . I think I would.''

He felt his own heart twist. *So much the warrior.* She was stronger than many men he knew. He believed her.

''Then let your ponies give the same sacrifice,'' he urged.

In many ways, she thought, it would be harder. She turned away.

''Come with me,'' she said hollowly. ''I will show you the ones you can . . . can take.''

41

THE LOLO WAS lush, tangled, primordial. There were not nearly as many cavernous drops as there had been on the southern pass, but the trail was steep and snarled with rock-slides, fallen timber, and washouts. A branch of the Koos-kooskia trickled busily down the slopes, and the surviving ponies guzzled almost frenziedly at the water, gnawing the thick wire grass on its banks. At least, Kiye Kipi thought, How-erd's ponies would find only thin, eaten-down forage if he followed this way.

After their brief camp in the foothills, the People did not stop again. Then they came upon the hot springs.

Those riding at the front reined in suddenly to gape at the deep, bubbling pool. Thick tendrils of steam snaked up from it, and there was a heavy, rotten smell to the air. A squaw wrinkled her nose and another keened in consternation at something that was clearly magic. But an elder only gave a wide, toothless grin.

Kiye Kipi moved her pony close to that one. "What is it?" she asked.

"Medicine waters," the old one answered reverently. "Bless Tahmahnewes, He watches over us."

"Do we drink it?" If it tasted anywhere near as bad as it smelled, she did not think she would reap its benefits. But the old squaw shook her head.

"No. We steep ourselves in it. I have heard of places like this, long ago, from my father. The bubbles are healing."

And healing, Kiye Kipi thought, cannot be a bad thing now.

The woman dropped off her pony and hurried toward the pool in a trundling, head-forward gait. Other old ones began following her, talking and laughing like a bunch of frenzied crows. Even the squaws were inching close now to peel off their moccasins and dip their toes in. There were oohs and ahs, and much smiling and nodding at the delicious warmth. Kiye Kipi looked for the headmen, and found Huishuis Kute close.

"Can we stop? Oh, how they want this!"

"We *must* stop," Huishuis Kute answered. "I have been here before, traveling east. These waters are indeed strengthening. We need them as desperately now as we need to put space between ourselves and those white-skins."

"The white-skins no longer follow us," Looking Glass said authoritatively, riding up to join them.

It did not seem so, Kiye Kipi thought, but she looked back at the trail doubtfully. There had been no sounds of fighting from the warriors behind them, and they had been riding through half the night and this whole sun. Either the *xayxayx* scouts and soldiers had rushed blindly onto their false trail, or it was as everyone had prayed from the beginning—How-erd had seen that they were leaving the land, and their terrible flight was over.

Either way, much of the desperation was gone from the People. She knew they would camp this night, and her bones ached deeply for sleep as well.

She was getting used to the smell of the water, she realized. Now she only wanted to immerse herself in it with the others.

She watched a moment as they splashed and groaned in pleasure, then she reluctantly turned the other way. Most of the squaws were attempting to settle as word sped among them that they would rest for a while. So many of them had lost lodges in the Clearwater fight, but at least their kin were taking them in.

Then she saw Dirty Dove's mother huddling forlornly in the clearing with a toddling babe and an older child. She dismounted and pulled her own lodge cover from her mare's pack.

"Here. Will you use this?"

The woman looked at her sharply, as though distrusting the kindness.

"It is so important to us all that I dream now," she went on, "and I do that much better beneath the stars. I would like to sleep outside this night. I will ask for my lodge back when I need it again."

She knew she would not, but it seemed to assuage the squaw a little. She managed a tremulous smile and reached for the cover.

Kiye Kipi left the others and went into the herd. For once, her heart flinched as they guzzled and greeted her. She gave another small, wretched prayer for the ones who had died. Some of those who had been used to blaze the false trail had fallen with irreparably torn tendons and cracked leg bones. Twelic had said all the carcasses made the path look legitimate, but, oh, Spirit Chief, they were her *wyakins*!

She began tending to the fresh wounds of the others, crooning to them of their own strength and bravery. Once, as a child, she had wondered if they knew what she said. Now she was sure of it. Many snorted and tossed their heads as though the praise was their due; others rested their heavy jowls on her shoulder with heartfelt groans. By the time she finished, it was late, and she was smiling again thinly.

She looped her arm around her mare's neck. The medicine waters were abandoned now. All the people were sleeping, exhausted, the children curled in upon each other like wolf pups in a litter. Oh, yes, they had all needed this.

"Come," she said to her mare. "I think it will be good for you as well. We will find a place where you can stand."

She started for the water, the pony following. Snorting, shifting sounds came from behind her as others trailed along as well, heeding their instinct to herd. She passed quietly through the lodges.

She went on, leading them into a shallow spot. Then she waded into the deeper part, groaning.

Oh, yes, now she understood why the elders had coveted this spot as soon as they had seen it. The spring was strangely buoyant. Its heat coaxed her heels up from the mud and rocks, and she eased down, belly first, floating into it.

The stench was thick here, and she found that she did not mind at all.

Finally, she stood again, peeling off her doeskin, hurling it back to the bank. She inched deeper, until she had to stand on tiptoe to keep her chin above the froth. Then she lay back in the moonlight, letting the bubbles carry her.

Twelic passed close by the bank, carrying his own robe in a search for a place to rest. He saw her and went very still.

Keep going. The caution came to him, as always, but he could not heed it.

He moved only as far as a rock ledge overhanging the water. He dropped his robe beside him and hunkered down, watching her silently for a long time, appreciation easing the tension in his muscles. Her breasts cleared the water, round and perfect. Her hair fanned out about her in the moonlight, a huge, black halo.

Finally, he spoke. "You do ease my heart, even as you trouble it."

Kiye Kipi shrieked, coming upright again, and he cursed quietly.

"Can you behave like nothing other than a wildcat?" he demanded. "You will wake the others."

"*I* will?" She fairly sputtered with indignation.

"I was not the one who howled."

"Why are you here?"

"Because it looks to me as though we are camping this night," he snapped. Why had he not gone on?

"Are we safe from soldiers?" She looked back as though she could spot them coming up the trail.

He had spent the sun behind the bands, watching for pursuit. Now he let out a deep breath. "They are not close. Two Moons and his Lamtama have relieved my men. Earth Sound has gone out ahead. I am only a man, Screamer. I will gladly kill again and again for these people, but sometimes I need food and sleep and succor."

He stood again, and she stiffened even in the gentle water. *Screamer.*

"Do not . . . call me that." She hated when he did. The name was too rich with dangerous memories. It would always make her remember that she had never stopped loving him even as she had learned to crave his touch.

A small grin twisted his mouth as he looked back. He found he could not resist nettling her any more than he could resist loving her.

"So be it . . . Pony Wife."

She did not like that either. It only reminded her that there were so many who looked to her for salvation, and others whose eyes burned hatred at her because of it.

She shook her head and began moving out of the water, then she remembered that she was naked.

"Go, please," she managed quietly, sinking down again.

One of his brows came up high, and his grin widened. "Would you like your doeskin? I could get it for you."

She would not play with him this time. She knew better. She eased back, crossing her arms over her breasts beneath the water.

"How often you call me a fool," she purred caustically, "when it is *your* memory that is dangerously addled. We have done this before, and you were not any happier about it than I was."

He remembered the creek in buffalo country, so long ago, so many seasons past now. Tahmahnewes, sometimes it seemed as though she had been with him forever, in one way or another. No, he had not been happy after that encounter. It had marked the time when she had first begun tormenting him. But he knew, suddenly, that if he never enjoyed her again, he would be far more miserable.

Succor, he had said, and she alone could give it to him now. He needed a woman, had been long without one through this strife, and he found that he wanted no other.

He did not know how this trek would end. He would fight by her side because he had to. If he lost her, it would destroy him. But perhaps that was in Tahmahnewes's hands, not his own. Suddenly, he was not sure how he could protect himself against it. How much more vile loss could be when that which was wrenched away had never truly been possessed!

Possessed? He almost laughed. No man would possess this one. She would claim him, burn him, mark him.

So be it.

Abruptly, he wrenched on the cord of his breechclout, letting it drop. He pulled out of his leggings, and reaction went through her like an echo of thunder. He dropped down into the water with her, and she backed off quickly, the water and mists swirling about her.

"What is it, Pony Wife? Are you afraid of feeling that way again, of burning the way you did in the Clearwaters?"

"*Afraid?*" She was, oh, yes, she was. But never, ever would she let him know it.

"So am I. Wanting you leaves my soul exposed."

Her heart slammed against her ribs. "Then why risk it?" she asked, strangled.

"Because it is like a good battle. However dangerous, I crave it."

She closed her eyes because she understood that, because the more suns they spent together, the more tangled all this became.

"Go away, Twelic, please. Go to Cloud Singer if that is the kind of succor you need."

He laughed almost bitterly. "That one no longer has anything I want."

That shook her badly.

She pushed out of the water. Curse him, curse her doeskin, she did not care any longer. She had to get away from him, now, while she was still whole. She could not joust with him like this over and over again, and have anything left of herself, anything to give to the people who so needed her magic.

He watched her emerge into the moonlight, water streaming off her bare skin, steam wafting from her like an aura. Her hair was slick and clinging to her back and buttocks. Wanting lanced through him again and made him crazy.

She was the only woman who had ever walked away from

him as often as she had melted over him.

His hands flashed out and he caught her hair, stopping her. She cried out again in surprise and splashed backward into the water. He held her tight against him, his hand still in her hair, tilting her head back so that her eyes had no choice but to meet his.

They were hot, hungry, and her breath snagged in her throat.

"Please . . . do not do this again," she choked out, "to either of us."

"We will resolve this, Pony Wife," he warned quietly. "There is too much between us. It is more than *wyakins,* it is more than wanting, and I am beginning to think we cannot escape it. There was a beginning, a middle, and soon, somehow, there must be an end."

She struggled with him as his mouth came down on hers again, but then it was as it always was.

She wanted him.

She gave a little cry of helplessness and turned into him. His body was smooth and warm beneath the water, like the rocks beneath her feet. His fingers dug into her bottom, and he pulled her hips against his as he had once before. But this time he was hard with wanting her, and there was nothing between them but water, hot, slick, and bubbling. A groan was wrenched from her, and she put her hand to him impulsively, greedily, closing her fingers around him. He gave a growl that nearly shattered her.

She still did not understand what he expected from her. Soon, perhaps any sun now, this flight would be over. They would reach the Crows' grasslands, and he would go back to reclaim Nimipu country for the People. He would leave her again, and somehow, once again, she would have to go on without remembering; she would have to stop needing, but she could not care about that now.

She moved her hand over him, avid, exploring, wanting to learn everything there was to know of him. Her touch galvanized him. He lifted her suddenly from the water and drove her back against the rock overhang. Her breath burst from her and there was no way to regain it. His lips, his tongue, stole her air. She growled a sound of her own and wrapped her legs around him. She felt him hard against her most secret flesh and wanted more, wanted still.

"Ah, woman, what you do to me." She was as courageous in loving as she was in this war, he thought, more so, because she knew how cruel loving could be.

"No . . . talk," she managed. "Just . . . touch me." Yes, Tahmahnewes, she would take this end for herself, and curse all the suns that would follow.

Someone cleared his throat self-consciously in the shadows of the bank, but neither of them heard.

Earth Sound hefted a rock and threw it near them, sending up a violent spray. They did not stop.

The warrior swore and looked back at the camp, his head in a tangle. Finally, he knew why she had never wanted him. Bitter regret and startled, inevitable acceptance filled his throat. He found that he did not want to interrupt them; Tahmahnewes knew they all needed to take what they could for themselves these suns. But the lodges spread out in the glade were all torn and snarled together now, no one more prestigious than another. He knew which one belonged to Toolhoolhoolzote, but he had no idea where Joseph or White Bird or Huishuis Kute rested, and Alokot was equally hard to find.

Finally, he looked back and shouted a sound. Twelic let loose with a hard stream of curses. Kiye Kipi cried out in shock.

"What is it?" Twelic growled.

Earth Sound spoke the one word that could drench them in cold again. "Sol-jers."

Water splashed. Twelic came up from beneath the overhang, looking shaken, his mouth tight. He grabbed his breechclout, and threw her doeskin back into the water, in the direction of where Kiye Kipi waited, breathing hard, her head pounding.

"Coming after us?" she heard Twelic snap.

"No," came Earth Sound's response. "Camped."

"Where?"

The warrior's response stunned her, taking the last of her breath.

"On the trail ahead, blocking our way."

42

CLOUD SINGER MOVED back into the tangled trees on the far side of the spring. Her head reeled in shock as well, but it had nothing to do with those cursed, pestering soldiers.

That one no longer has anything I want.

Gradually, the shock drained out of her to be replaced by unprecedented rage.

He had wanted her through seasons and seasons. She had tolerated the others because she knew he would come back to her in the end. And he had, he always had, until this haughty, fighting squaw had begun stealing his time and attention. She had guessed, in her gut, that it could happen. She had tried to warn her away, but she had not listened. Suddenly, she made a vicious decision.

The pony wife would have to die.

Even if it did not bring Twelic back to her side, perhaps it would scar him deeply. He would pay for what he had just said.

The thought made her finally smile.

Kiye Kipi hurried back into the camp moments after Twelic and Earth Sound. The headmen were spilling out of their lodges. All of them, even Joseph, looked as stunned as she felt.

Soldiers *in front* of them?

It could not be. It made no sense. There was no way Howerd could have gotten around them. Did his power reach so far that he had called soldiers from buffalo country to intercept them? And why? Why would he do that? He had what he wanted now. *They had left their land!*

The headmen talked among each other in quiet tones. Twelic came to her, his face looking hard and haggard now in the moonlight.

"Earth Sound says they are camped half a sun's ride up from the valley," he reported. "They have dug trenches and blocked the trail with trees and logs. They are in the narrowest part of the defile."

She struggled with that even as he spoke what it meant.

"There is no way around them, Screamer."

The People rode out again with the dawn. There was no need to hurry. They all seemed to know that they were not fleeing from death now; they were heading into it.

Kiye Kipi's heart rebelled as she straddled her mare. *It could not end this way, it could not!* She shook her head in denial as they came out on a high part of the trail, then she looked down and saw them.

Sweet Tahmahnewes, there were hundreds of them, soldiers and settlers and even Indians she did not know!

Joseph and the headmen and warriors began putting their heads together again. She rode to join them, still looking over her shoulder at the men below.

"We will not attack them," Joseph said stubbornly. "If you others choose to do so, it will happen without my Kahmuenem warriors."

A red flush spread over Alokot's face but he did not argue.

White Bird only shrugged. "I see no purpose in fighting them," he agreed. "Not yet. I have hunted buffalo many times here. I bear no animosity toward the settlers. They have stolen Crow and Sioux and Cheyenne land, not mine."

"I still cannot understand what enmity they bear us," Huis-huis Kute muttered.

"Perhaps they do not?" Looking Glass suggested. The others looked at him as though he had grown horns.

"I say we go down there and talk to them, find out what

this is about,'' he went on more forcefully.

"It can do no harm.'' White Bird shrugged.

"A delegation of all our headmen then?'' asked Joseph.

"Not Toolhoolhoolzote,'' Huishuis Kute warned. "He has never gotten over his rage at How-erd for incarcerating him. I am afraid he will be belligerent and cause trouble. All white men are enemies to him now.''

There were nods all around. Even Joseph seemed mollified. "Let us go, then,'' he said.

Kiye Kipi pulled her mare back off the trail to let them pass. Looking Glass was wrong again. She could not believe those soldiers did not mean them any harm.

Oh, how she wanted to go with them! She looked for Twelic instead, and realized that he was gone.

Surprised, she glanced around. Both sides of the narrow trail were flanked by jutting, wooded promontories. She found him scrambling up the north wall and rode to him.

"What do you do?'' she demanded.

He looked back at her with a withering expression. "Stay with the women. Surely they are agitated by now and need you.''

Her eyes narrowed, and her heart squeezed. He was acting angry with her again.

He made her crazy.

"The women are stronger than you give them credit for,'' she snapped. "And they have been agitated before.''

He turned away from her and kept going. She let out an oath of her own and swung to the ground.

The wall was more difficult to climb than he made it look. He wore leggings, so the rocks did not scrape him, but she had scarcely followed him before she felt the raw sting of blood on her knees. She grimaced at the pain, but found a handhold on a bush jutting crazily out from a crevice. She began to pull herself up with that when his strong hand closed around her arm just above her wrist.

"Hold on,'' he said gratingly.

He yanked her up hard, and her shin banged squarely against an outcropping. She landed on a ledge on her stomach, then she scrambled into a sitting position to rub the sore spot.

"You did not fight me this way when you helped me save my ponies," she muttered bitterly. "And later you said we would fight together. Now you chastise me for every move I make, push me back—"

"Save your hide," he finished for her. "You condescended to let me help you with that trouble, and there was not yet a war going on." *And I did not love you this way then.*

He bit those words back.

"You are here now," he went on, "if only because I do not wish to spend more time arguing with you."

He spoke without looking at her, his gaze trained down the trail. Finally, her eyes followed his.

"Oh!"

The view was panoramic from this high above the pass. They could see the headmen clearly as they rode down to meet a soldier chief and a translator who came forward to block their way. Other white men waited close behind them with their guns drawn.

She looked to Twelic, and for the first time she noticed that he had his rifle up as well, gripped in a tight hand. Once again she had left hers with her pony. She cursed at her stupidity, her skin heating.

He began crawling forward, following the progress of the men below, and she went after him. The promontory was snarled with undergrowth, and their path was difficult. Finally, they came out into a small clearing just above the council.

Twelic went flat on his belly, slowly and silently. He put his gun to his shoulder and aimed it down.

Kiye Kipi heard a quiet notching sound from somewhere distant, and was startled to realize that Alokot was on the cliffs on the other side. She looked about, wide-eyed, and found Two Moons as well.

She felt so useless!

She balled her hands into fists. If there was trouble, she would do nothing but get in the way here. And her ponies . . . if the soldiers rushed at the others, she would not be there to save the ponies, to drive them away.

Quietly, she eased her way back into the brush. Twelic did not look at her, did not even seem to realize that she went.

She started back down their path, and soon realized that she was lost. She bit back a sound of frustration and pushed on. She thought she had gone too far, but she could not find the place where they had climbed up. Her ears strained for sounds of a fight behind her, and her muscles began to burn with tension.

She had to get back quickly, before someone fired.

Finally, the path cleared again, but it was not the place she had been looking for. She came upright, looking around.

Once again she heard voices, and they were behind her. She whipped around, but they were of her own tongue, soft and fretful and worried. The squaws. She had passed them. She started to go back that way, then she froze.

Ahead of her lay a narrow, sandy trail called the Lolo. She moved up on it, and saw that it vanished into a landslide of rocks and debris. She dropped onto her bottom and slid down it, landing on the Lolo again with a thud that jarred her teeth.

She twisted around and looked over her shoulder at the way she had come. That rockslide. If it could be moved . . .

"Yes, oh, yes," she breathed. *They were not trapped after all.*

She hurried back to where the others waited. The headmen were returning, looking grim. Twelic and the other warriors were still in the cliffs. She hurried to Joseph.

"What do they say?" she asked.

"White Bird told the sol-jer chief that if he allowed our women to pass unmolested, we would not harm anyone in his Mon-tan-a valley. He said that would be good."

Mistrust pooled in her belly. "Do you believe him?"

"Yes, because he also said that he would agree to this only if we give him our weapons, our ammunition, and all of our ponies."

Her head spun. *The ponies. Always the ponies.* "That is to . . . to bow to them, to surrender. We would have nothing left to go on with!"

White Bird and Huishuis Kute joined them. "We cannot

rampage through their blockade with our babes and our elders,'' said White Bird.

"But we cannot go back," Huishuis Kute argued. "Howerd will surely be waiting for us on the other side."

"No! No!" Kiye Kipi shook her head, her hair flying. "We are not trapped."

"What are you saying?" Twelic's voice came from behind her, and she spun around.

"There is another way. I found it when I returned here. We can go up and around these soldiers."

His eyes got hard, but they searched her face. "It is too rough. There is no way for the ponies to get up. You were there with me. You saw that."

"No, there is a trail." Her thoughts raced. "It is not much of one, I will grant you that. It will not be easy. But I think they can do it, the ponies *and* the women."

Joseph rubbed his temples. "Show us," he said finally, wearily.

She led them back to the rockslide, the others falling in behind them.

"It could be possible," mused Twelic, studying it.

There was a snort of disbelief from Looking Glass. "It is nothing but boulders! She is crazy! She lived with us once. I know how crazy she can be."

Kiye Kipi spun on him angrily. "The warriors can clear it!" she argued. "They can move the boulders away. There is sand underneath. The ponies can climb that. The hard part will come once they are up on top."

"I will not ask my old ones to attempt anything so risky," Toolhoolhoolzote sneered.

Curse them both! Her throat tightened. "Then stay," she managed. "I am going to Mon-tan-a Territory, and I will take with me anyone who wishes to come."

She turned away. She felt a hand graze off her shoulder, knew it was Twelic, and kept going. Her head hurt. Looking Glass would scoff at any suggestion Twelic agreed with, and Toolhoolhoolzote would oppose her if she offered his people a feast. In their stubborn enmity, they would lead everyone to die! In the end, she was still a squaw, only a squaw, and she could do so little to argue with them!

She reached the others and squatted down in a spot where Joseph's wives and Wetatonmi were building a small fire to eat. Though they looked at her questioningly, she could not tell them. She would not give them hope only to see Joseph snatch it away from them again.

Where did Joseph stand on this?

She looked back as he approached the fire, tucking her hair behind her ears, waiting tensely. Alokot and Twelic came with him, still clutching their rifles, but then they passed on to talk with the other warriors.

"The Kahmuenem will try it," Joseph said quietly. "We cannot stay here. As long as there is a peaceful way to keep going, I will attempt it."

She did not want to ask him what he would do if there was more fighting.

She breathed again, carefully. "And the Pikunanmu and the Hasotoin? What will Toolhoolhoolzote and Looking Glass do?"

But Joseph did not need to answer. She saw for herself. Those warriors were following behind Alokot and Twelic, going back to the rockslide. Behind them moved women, boys, elders, their jaws all set stubbornly.

Her heart thumped hard, and she pushed to her feet again to help them.

They would all move the rocks together.

They would not surrender.

43

KIYE KIPI GOT ready to move the ponies up the cleared sand path while it was still dark. Dirty Dove and some of the boys waited at the top to catch them while she studied the incline one last time, searching for hidden problems.

She would start with the strongest blacks, she decided. That would give her some idea of how the weaker ones would fare. She turned away to begin gathering them, and found Twelic behind her.

His eyes found hers and held them. "Can I help?" he asked.

After a long moment, she nodded.

She could not scream fear at them to send them crashing up the slope, because that would make them reckless and the going was too precarious. Her only alternative was to lead them a few at a time, and the more hands she had to do that, the more quickly it would be accomplished.

"Will the others be ready soon?" she asked suddenly.

"The squaws are packing up."

"And the men?"

"Smoking, pacing, cursing the white-skins."

"Not nearly as much as I," she muttered.

A smile flickered across his mouth, then was gone. But, oh, how that smile always warmed her belly!

"Here," she said, "let me tell you what I am thinking."

After a moment, he nodded and went back to the camp. When he returned, it was with Hasotoin warriors and a handful of squaws who had finished packing. The men helped the

women up the steep slope, then they waited at the top with
Dirty Dove and the boys.

"You will each have to lead two, three, as many as you can
handle in addition to your own mounts," she called up to them
quietly. "Then head for the valley whatever way you can."

They all nodded and she turned back to Twelic. "Is there a
man up there who knows the paths?" she asked.

"*Are* there paths?" he countered, then he relented. "Thunder Dance will lead. He can blaze a trail where need be."

"That will do." She turned into the herd again and chose
five of the blacks.

She led the first gelding close so that his front hooves were
planted in the sand. Twelic watched critically. She called up
one more time for the others to stand back, and for Dirty Dove
to get ready. Then she smacked him on the rump and clucked
to him.

He plunged up.

His front hooves sank deep and his back legs scrambled.
His powerful shoulders bunched as he fought for purchase,
lunging forward. Then he heaved himself over the edge of the
precipice and Dirty Dove caught him to keep him from trotting
dangerously into the brush with his momentum.

Her grin was slow and spreading. "It will work."

Twelic nodded cautiously. "Yes, I think so."

They began sending the others up. Thunder Dance took the
first of them, heading down through the tangled growth. Soon
the ponies were vanishing as quickly as they reached the top.

Her heart began pounding hard with certainty. Twelic began
to smile.

More and more people came from the camp. She and Twelic
held the ponies back long enough for them to get up as well,
then they began again. The ones with the packs struggled hardest, and some of the weanlings and spotted ponies slid back
for every stride they gained. She scrambled up with those, her
hand tight in their manes, urging them, goading them to keep
trying.

By dawn, they were all up, and only the headmen remained
behind them. Kiye Kipi turned back to them. Neither Tool-

hoolhoolzote nor Looking Glass would meet her eyes. She bit back a retort and let Twelic pull her to the top as well.

She looked about at the snarled rocks, the twined vines, the crazily jutting trees. This would indeed be the hard part.

"They are still moving," Twelic pointed out quietly. "They have not bunched up yet. Thunder Dance must be getting through."

He *would* get through. He had to.

Soon the sun was hot and insects buzzed about them hungrily as the morning dew burned off. They moved steadily through the gullies and the trees, brush and vines snagging at them. They passed the spot where Twelic had watched over the council, and went on.

Suddenly, impossibly, she heard singing. She stopped dead and gaped at Twelic.

It was the squaws.

Laughter came up from the deepest part of her belly, making her eyes tear and her muscles hurt. A grin cracked Twelic's face as well.

"They are taunting them," she managed. "They are teasing the white-skins!"

"Yes, may Tahmahnewes save their hearts."

From up ahead, the voices came stronger, rose higher, and she shivered. She began trudging on again, and finally, they reached a place where they could look down.

Her breath snagged in amazement.

Soldiers, settlers, Indians, all gaped up at them. Occasionally one would heft his gun as a Nimipu face appeared here or there, but as quickly the *xayxayx* could aim, the People were gone again, disappearing back into the forbidding terrain. A few soldiers seemed to realize that their strategic advantage had been turned against them. They dashed clear of the open ground below where they were in plain view of the exiles' weapons. But the warriors did not shoot; they held true, however grimly, to their headmen's promise.

There had been so much loss, so much pain, so much fear, she thought shakily. In contrast, this simple, isolated moment of victory was among the sweetest she had ever known.

*   *   *

One of the *xayxayx* was laughing as well.

He was a volunteer, had come forward for this debacle at his government's urging, but now he moved to his horse and strapped his gun back into place. The officer of the day, Captain Rawn, hurried to intercept him.

"We are not through here, sir! If you leave, you'll be deserting!"

The man shrugged. "I ain't no soldier. Can't hardly desert something I don't belong to. Who you gonna fight, Captain? Seems to me those Injuns is keeping their word."

He had been as dubious as any other man when the chiefs had said they wouldn't harass anyone. But hell, all they were doing up there was chanting.

More and more volunteers began remounting. Rawn's face turned mottled. "I cannot permit you fellows to leave."

"Well, I sure as God A'mighty ain't gonna hang around and provoke 'em," another man said. "Looks to me like they'll pass right through. Shoot at 'em, and they'll sure as hell trash our homesteads. No thankee, Captain. I want no part of that."

"Somebody say a *goat* couldn't pass by up there?" Still another volunteer chortled.

Rawn flushed. Those had been his exact words. "Well, it would seem they are determined," he muttered.

A soldier came slipping and sliding down the Lolo, returning from his inspection of the Indian camp. "Lord, they've even taken all their camp supplies!" he called out. "How'd they do that?"

"Guess they're goats." Someone laughed heartily.

"Either that, or this here is Fort Fizzle."

There were a good deal more guffaws before the volunteers began riding out. Rawn looked about grimly. Only a dozen or so remained, and they looked undecided. He had his Cheyenne scouts, a handful of them, but there wasn't an Indian yet he felt he could fully rely upon. Besides that, he had fewer than seventy enlisted men from his fort in Missoula, still under construction and undermanned.

On the other hand, there looked to be one hell of a lot of Indians.

"What do we do now, Captain?" one of his soldiers asked.

Rawn sighed. "We mount up and follow them, I suppose, although we can hardly engage them. But we might at least find out where they go."

It would be one small, affirmative thing he could report back to Howard when that general learned of this inconceivable achievement of his desperate, relentless Nez Percé.

The snarled brush cleared out just before they reached the valley. For a moment, as Kiye Kipi stood looking down at the sweeping grass of buffalo country, she knew another moment of impossible weariness. Once again, they would be exposed down there. Once again, there would be blue-coats behind them, avid to pursue them.

Once again, they would have to run.

Twelic swung up on his stallion. She looked to him and knew his thoughts mirrored hers, but his eyes were bright, his muscles rigid and ready.

She mounted as well, then she screamed.

A warrior stepped out of the trees ahead of them, at the side of the trail. He was one of those who had been below with the white-skins, and her heart thundered. All his hair was braided, two thick cords of it down either side of his face, unlike the Nimipu men who twined only thin strands, leaving the rest to fall free. His plaits shone with some sort of grease, and feathers and fur abounded there.

He was short and thick, and he wore *xayxayx* clothes.

"Hush," Twelic hissed. "He is Cheyenne."

After a moment, carefully, the warrior laid his rifle at his feet and stepped back. He held his hands up to show he had no other weapons, then he began motioning.

"What . . . what does he say?" she whispered.

Twelic looked uncharacteristically shaken.

"He says . . . we should turn south. More soldiers may come from the north. He says the Spirit Chief should guide our trail, and courage should guide our hearts.

''He says his own people have fallen. May some tribe best these white men before they take all of Mother Earth.''

Dirty Dove and the boys were rounding up the herd again when they reached the valley. Kiye Kipi went to them while Twelic galloped to the headmen.

''South!'' she shouted at their stunned faces.

Dirty Dove pulled her pony to a stop instead. ''But—''

Kiye Kipi motioned behind her. Already the blue-coats who had been on the Lolo were spilling out into the grasses from that pass.

Dirty Dove blanched, and they began running.

As they drew abreast of the others, warriors began passing them, heading back the other way. She twisted around, looking after them, her heart hurtling. She saw no new soldiers on the horizon, but the ones from the Lolo were coming on fast.

A gunshot sounded, so horribly familiar now, and she cried out. *Not again.*

But the soldiers only fell back.

The warriors were firing parting shots over their heads.

A moment later, the men passed them again, galloping through the herd. Kiye Kipi left Dirty Dove and pushed her mare harder to catch up with them.

Now what?

Then she saw, and once again, her heart staggered. *More white-skins.*

She thought at first that the strange warrior had tricked them. Rage closed her throat, pounded at her temples. Then, slowly, she began to understand.

These *xayxayx* were not soldiers.

A small throng of settlers hovered by the foothills, and when they saw the exiles, they ran forward. There were women and men, children and elders. Some of the squaws screamed, sawing on their reins to back their ponies away. Some of the warriors brought up their bows and rifles, ready. Still, the white-skinned people came on. Kiye Kipi reached them and reined in as well, looking about disbelievingly.

A *xayxayx* woman ran to her, pushing a sack at her, waving

her on with her hands. Stunned, Kiye Kipi steadied her mare
and pulled the top of the bag open instead.

Food? There was meat, and cakes of some kind. . . . She
stared at the woman uncomprehendingly.

"Go!" the woman urged. "Hurry! The soldiers follow
you!"

A girl came to them, pallid, with eyes the color of the sky.
She gave her another sack bulging with clothing.

"I will pray for you," she said shyly. "The newspapers say
you have only tried to escape. It is wrong to kill you."

They stepped back to let her pass, but Kiye Kipi only looked
dumbly around at the others. The white-skinned men were
giving the warriors guns and ammunition. Her throat closed.

They were helping them.

Sweet, treacherous hope moved in her belly again. She
dared to believe again. Perhaps they would find sanctuary in
this country after all.

Finally, she looked for the headmen.

Joseph was crying.

44

Near dusk, they found a place to camp.

The tiny, protected valley was neither as pacific as the Clearwater place, nor as lush as the Lolo. There were only trickling waters, and not many trees. But as Kiye Kipi drew in with the others and looked around, she saw that it possessed one very precious advantage over those other camps. It was guarded on three sides by the Bitterroot foothills. Soldiers would not be able to see their fires unless they approached from the crests above them, or from the east. Twelic had said there was no pass through the mountains here. The Bitterroots were treacherous and unpassable at this place.

She let herself relax for the first time all sun, breathing deeply and carefully. Her emotions felt tangled and exhausted, on the very surface of her skin.

She dismounted and took her packs from her pony, peering again at the strange *xayxayx* gifts inside.

"I do not see what good that stuff will do us," Wetatonmi said, looking over.

Kiye Kipi spilled it all onto the ground. "It is good just to know that they do not all try to kill us," she murmured. Perhaps, if these few *xayxayx* saw their side, then others would listen as well.

Please, Tahmahnewes, let How-erd begin to listen.

She began laying the clothing about the ground. A giggle caught in her throat at a long, voluminous skirt. She could never ride in such a thing, could never run or climb or fight.

But in the growing firelight, she saw that the piece was gloriously colored in a way she had never seen before. It looked as though the sky were caught in it, and the green of the grass in spring. There were even bursts of yellow, like the sun.

She rubbed the fabric wonderingly between her fingers. What was this stuff? How did the *xayxayx* make it? She took her knife and began cutting off pieces of it.

Nearby, one of Joseph's wives gagged over the meat that had been given. Kiye Kipi looked up sharply.

"Is it pony?"

The squaw shook her head. "No . . . no. I have had this before once, at one of those council talks. It comes from their cat-tul." She put it aside to give to the dogs.

"This is good," Wetatonmi murmured. She handed around portions of the cakelike stuff.

Kiye Kipi took some, and her eyes widened. It was sweet and melting on her tongue. But somehow, it made her belly roll again.

"These white-skins know much," she mused. "They are not all stupid and rash if they can make these things."

The others went quiet, scowling thoughtfully at that.

She took up the pieces of fabric she had cut, and borrowed an awl and some sinew from Wetatonmi. She pulled her doeskin over her head, wrapped her robe about herself, and began to patch the thin spots and tears in her dress.

The warriors were not so patient or neat with their acquisitions. She looked around to see swatches of the colored stuff hanging crazily from their ponies' bridles; some of the animals snorted and stomped and swung their heads as the pieces blew into their eyes. A Lamtama man had donned one of the skirts. He strutted about one of the fires, tripping and tugging on it. For the second time that sun, Kiye Kipi threw back her head and laughed.

The sound was light and lilting, and it swam hot through Twelic's blood. He stopped behind her, squatting down.

"If only I knew a way to make you safe, you could laugh that way forever."

She started and looked around at him. Something funny

moved in her belly at his tone, at the way his eyes looked in the firelight.

He was being kind again, and . . . and something.

Hungry.

Wanting.

It unnerved her, changed things somehow, skewed the delicate balance of their friendship. She nodded carefully.

"Perhaps . . . soon," she managed. "Perhaps we will all be safe soon."

His strange mood seemed to break. "I will believe that when we get there," he said flatly.

She knew he spoke of the Safe Place, and knew, too, that he would not mention it aloud because of the others. She stiffened again.

"It is north," she whispered. "We are going the wrong way." That truth had been dogging her fragile emotions all sun, but Twelic only shrugged.

"For a time," he answered. "Looking Glass will lead a party backward with the new sun."

"Why?" She was startled.

"His father always had good relations with the Crows. He will ask them if our women can stay among them for a while."

Kiye Kipi flinched. For the first time, she admitted to herself that she did not want to be hidden away, waiting like a helpless squaw while the warriors returned to Nimipu country to try to get their land back. She did not think she could bear it, did not think, after this, that she would ever tolerate such coddling again.

She pushed to her feet restlessly. "We still have a long trail ahead of us," she murmured.

Twelic stood as well. "It will take longer than we thought. The *xayxayx* have built a town here called Miz-ool-a. It is straight north of here. The headmen have decided not to risk passing close by it, no matter what the mood of those settlers we met. We will make a big loop to the south, then veer north again once we are well east of the place."

But they would get there. Sooner or later they would reach the Crow grounds.

She shook her head. For now, there was time, treacherous time, precious time ... for what?

For him to speak to her again the way he had a moment ago? To touch him again the way she had in the medicine waters?

Did she want that?

She gathered up her gaily spotted doeskin and left him, moving off into the shadows to change. For a long time she felt his gaze between her shoulder blades.

She was too tired, she decided. She was too ... worn. She was feeling far too soft and vulnerable.

Another new warrior rode into the camp with the next sun. He was Nimipu, one of their own, and his arrival seemed to breathe new life and fresh adrenaline into the men. They surged along beside him as he rode to White Bird's hearth.

Kiye Kipi pushed to her feet to watch the procession. He was older than Joseph, but not as grizzled as the white-haired Lamtama headman. Twelic seemed to know him.

She left Wetatonmi's fire and went to hover outside the council circle. White Bird's wives began to bring food, but the man waved them away.

"My own women will be here shortly, and they bring much. We have not been running as you have, and we know how to bring down buffalo."

"I would worry for you if you did not," Twelic taunted, his mood strong and good now. "You live in this country. You should know where to find the beasts that remain."

The man raised a brow at him. "The last time I saw you, you were only a calf, eavesdropping on your uncle and me, and not very well. I hope your skills have improved since then."

Twelic laughed, and Kiye Kipi shivered at the sound of it. Then she understood. This man was Lean Elk, the renegade headman who roamed these distant lands not his own.

Her heart thumped. It was said that he had many warriors, some of the strongest the People had ever known. She turned away to find the women again, to tell them, but none of them seemed to share her excitement.

"That is good," Wetatonmi allowed quietly, "since we are not close to stopping."

Another squaw moaned at that. Kiye Kipi's gaze snapped to her. There was grim pain in her eyes as she apportioned among her children the tiny bit of fish she had left.

"His women bring food as well," she said encouragingly. "He says they will be here soon."

The squaw looked up at her and nodded reservedly. Her expression said what she did not speak aloud. That would help for a time, but they needed to camp, to hunt, to dry and pack and store.

Kiye Kipi looked about at the others. Their euphoria of the Lolo had worn off, leaving them dull and dispirited and too weary. They crowded about their shared fires, ripping off small pieces of meat with their teeth, passing the rest on to their little ones and elders. The old ones snatched at their portions, cramming them into their mouths, their seamed faces chewing as fast as their remaining teeth would allow. The young ones wrestled each other frantically and wailed for the remainder. Their mothers did not have the heart to scold them.

Kiye Kipi's good spirits moaned out of her.

She sat among them, pulling one of the children onto her lap. "I will tell you something I have dreamed," she said impulsively. "Perhaps it will help."

Tahmahnewes, forgive me, she prayed, closing her eyes. They need this so badly. I do it for them.

She swallowed carefully and looked about at them again. "A long time ago, Tahmahnewes told me of the place we should go to if this happened to us."

"Crow country?" someone asked woodenly. "If there is food there, then why have our men not been able to find buffalo these past seasons?"

"I . . . do not know what this place is exactly," she admitted. "But I know where it is. It is north, and when we go that way, we will find it."

Others began crowding around, listening, sharp eyed.

"It has deep snows," she went on, and someone keened.

"No, no, in my dream, that was good. There was game anyway. I saw elk walking on the drifts. I saw fish beneath the frozen ice of the streams."

"Could we get to this fish?" someone demanded.

"Oh, yes." The People smiled. "For some reason, I do not think the white-skins can follow us there," she finished. "If we hold on, if we can make it, there will be peace and goodness there. Our bellies will be full, and everything will be fine again. I am sure of that."

Some of them groped for each other, desperate to believe her. She forced a smile for them, then her gaze slid into Twelic's.

He was standing just behind them, listening, watching. Her heart lurched. His gaze was different again, fathomless and yet somehow rife with emotion.

He had learned to accept that she was strong. Now her kindness made him ache.

She had shared her *wyakin.* All of it. He could not remember when any of them had given their people that much, and it shook him deeply.

She gave the little one on her lap back to his mother and got to her feet again. Her jaw hardened and her eyes flashed with the heat of defiance, as though she expected him to chastise her.

"Without hope, you would have no one left to leave with the Crow," she challenged when she reached him.

He only shrugged. "Without you, they would have no hope."

He touched her again, and she was not expecting it. He combed his fingers through her hair as the wind lifted it, knotting it thoughtfully in his fist, holding her. Her heart erupted, clamoring.

"They will . . . go on now," she managed inanely. *What was he doing? What did he mean by this?*

Twelic nodded, and finally, his hand dropped away.

"It will not be long now until they have some surcease," he promised.

Her eyes widened. "We will go straight north then, after all?"

"No. South again. But there is a good place there as well. Lean Elk knows of it. He is very familiar with this country, and he will take us to it. He says there is good hunting, and much forage for the ponies. We can rest again, at least until Looking Glass returns. You can tell the women that as well."

"What is this place?" she breathed.

"He calls it the Big Hole."

The Big Hole. Something itched in her memory, then her heart slammed.

"We were there before."

His mouth moved in a strange smile. "We crossed the Big Hole River to find the buffalo many seasons ago. South of there, there is a stream that runs like ice in the sun."

A beginning, a middle . . . *and an end.*

That was what he had said in the hot spring. A horrible premonition of doom and misgiving filled her throat and made her suddenly cold.

"I remember now," she said, strangled. "We are going toward the place where you once said good-bye."

45

LEAN ELK'S PEOPLE arrived with the new sun.

The exiles fell hungrily on the buffalo they brought, spare pieces just enough to rekindle memories of greasy slabs of hump steak and marrow-rich bones. Then they all rode out again, their bellies fuller, a hundred people stronger. They reached the Big Hole as dark came, and Kiye Kipi's heart could not remain cold.

Perhaps they were close to that place where she had once been scorned and shamed, but this idyllic valley was not the same. She looked about slowly as she dismounted. It was a basin of rolling hills, etched with streams, banked with timber. The grass was strong, still green-gold, and rippling in the wind. She heard a boy cry out from one of the waters, and knew he had found fish there. Already the women were hurrying into the trees to cut more lodge poles, and the men sharpened their arrows and lances, their hungry gazes roaming to the hills as they worked and rode out.

Kiye Kipi went to help Wetatonmi and Joseph's wives settle. The women had put their lodges together, and they swallowed frequently as they watched pieces of antelope sizzle over their big central hearth. Alokot had already been into the hills and back, and he had left the meat with them.

Wetatonmi laughed nervously. "I almost wish Looking Glass would not return. I could stay here. It is much like home."

"We will not be with the Crow forever," Kiye Kipi urged.

If we get there at all. "Our men will wrest our land from How-erd, and then we can go back to Wallowa."

She pushed her portion of the meat unobtrusively at Little Mole. If there was truly more than enough here, then she could eat later. Wetatonmi looked at her without noticing.

"Could this be the place you dreamed of?" she asked hopefully.

Kiye Kipi looked around. There was no snow, but this was still only Tay-ya-ahl, the Moon of Hot Weather. She scowled, unsure how to answer.

Suddenly, she jumped as a bloody slab of rib bones dropped into the grass in front of her. She looked up at Twelic.

"Even magic Dreamers need to eat," he said quietly.

She waved a hand at the fire. "There is plenty now," she pointed out lightly.

He looked at the piece she had given to the babe. *How had he known?* Her belly squirmed as she understood. He had been watching her.

"I have no one to provide for, and the hills are alive with game. Humor me."

"I would think you would have plenty of women to gift," she snapped in spite of herself.

Her skin heated. Why could she not just take it graciously? But she knew why.

His care made something young and sweet leap inside her. It made her want so much more than his companionship and wisdom through this struggle.

Slowly, treacherously, he was beginning to make her dream again, now when she could afford it least of all.

He moved away, his shoulders rigid. Impulsively, she pushed to her feet and went after him. He had pitched his lodge and laid an outdoor hearth farther back from the others, closer to the hills. As the sun fell behind the mountains, the place became steeped in darkness.

She stopped a short distance away, scowling, her heart feeling trepidation. This was wrong, it was all wrong. Why was he not at the headmen's fire with Alokot and the others?

She went the rest of the way and stood over him. "What is it?" she asked.

"Do you see into people's minds now as well?" he snapped. His voice made something quail inside her. He was not just irritated with her for snubbing his gift of food. Something else was itching him deeply.

She kneeled beside him. "I know you," she said carefully. "Something troubles you."

His eyes came to her sharply, but he said nothing more. She sighed and started to rise again. He caught her arm, his grip hot and hard and tight, and pulled her back.

"Has your *wyakin* talked to you lately?" he demanded.

She could not think with him touching her. Everything inside her seemed to flow and surge toward his hand, leaving her head feeling empty and muddled.

"I . . . no. But I have not reached for it."

"Will you try this night?"

Her heart skipped a beat. "Why?"

"Because mine is talking to me, and I do not like what it says."

She blanched. She had not dreamed, but that sense of doom and misgiving flashed back at her, just as it had when she had learned they would come to this place.

"When Lean Elk first told me about this valley," he went on, "I thought it would be good."

"It is good!" she protested desperately. "Look about you—"

"No," he interrupted. He shook his head, and his grip finally fell away. "Now that I have seen it, my spirit guide has started whispering to me. Death is on our trail. It will follow us here."

"Soldiers?" She choked on the word, looking about as though she could spot them.

"I would think so."

They had not seen hide nor hair of one since the Lolo.

"Earth Sound is on our back trail—" she tried.

"I do not think they will come from there."

Thunder rumbled, distant and warning, and she cried out in spite of herself.

Sweet Tahmahnewes, the thunder was his *wyakin*.

Suddenly, she was very cold.

"You should tell the headmen," she whispered.

He gave a snort of disbelief. "And take this from the People?"

She looked around at them again. Their faces were beginning to crease with smiles in the firelight of their hearths.

"Better that than they die!" she burst out.

But she did not believe it, not really, not deep. And when she looked at him again, she knew that he did not either. The Nimipu needed these suns here to live, to keep on.

He pushed more meat at her and shrugged. "We cannot move on anyway until Looking Glass returns. Until then, we will not know where we are going, and there are too many of us, too many white-skins out there, for us to wander about in circles."

She nodded. "He will be back soon. He will."

They looked at each other, both knowing that young Looking Glass had never done anything quickly or determinedly in his life.

She slept for a while at his hearth, knowing it was crazy, but her eyes burned to close and her bones ached for rest. The warm heaviness of the meat swam through her, melting her energy, and finally, she lay down in the grass.

Twelic's eyes moved sharply over the shadows as he fed more wood into the fire, but her soft, even breathing dragged at him, making him look her way again . . . and again.

If they lived through this place, he would take her to Crow country. He vowed that to himself, even if it meant tying her to a tree to keep her safely there.

If he lived through whatever came after, he would go back for her.

There was no fear anymore. Somehow, with death and doom so close, he had begun to realize its worthlessness and had finally let it go.

The decision eased something heavy and cumbersome in his chest. Relief rushed into the void it left. He did not know what lay ahead for them, but he knew that he had been hers since she had smiled up at him from her cradleboard, blue-black eyes shining. She had possessed him since she had galloped past him on this buffalo prairie, her head thrown back, her hair streaming and free, laughter bursting from her throat. She had touched him forever when he had given without taking beside a stream that ran cold in the sun. And now, in this flight, she had become his closest friend and comrade. He told her his fears, and she made him smile. Suddenly, he knew that he could not live on without that. Without her heat, her intelligence, her courage beside him, the wind was cold when it called.

He laughed quietly, and knew Tahmahnewes did so as well.

The sound choked off in his throat as a body moved out of the darkness, into the light of his fire. It was only a Kahmuenem boy, but he checked again to make sure that his rifle was loaded and close beside him.

The youth shifted his weight from one foot to another. "I must speak with the pony wife."

Twelic glanced her way again. Exhaustion had smudged dark circles beneath her eyes. Her chest rose and fell slowly, and he was loath to wake her.

The boy looked back over his shoulder where the horizon was turning luminescent gray. "The sun comes," he went on. "What would she have me do with the herd? They have eaten down the grass here close to the camp."

Twelic opened his mouth to tell him to drive them farther out, then he snapped his jaw shut again. If he made the decision for her and it turned out to be the wrong one, she would scratch his eyes from his face.

He did not want to fight with her anymore. He was learning, reluctantly, that there was more pleasure to be found in giving her her head, like a beautiful, headstrong filly, in spite of all his instincts to protect.

He reached out and shook her shoulder. She came up with a start and a gasp, looking about.

The boy repeated his dilemma.

Twelic saw the turmoil in her eyes. Finally, she nodded.
"Take them out," she said. When he had gone, she looked
back at Twelic.

"If you are right, the soldiers will come here, to the camp,"
she explained wearily. "I think the ponies will be safest if
they are not here as well."

He nodded, and she stood to stretch the hurt and kinks out
of her muscles. She looked back at the crushed grass where
she had lain, where she had rested more deeply than she had
in suns.

She felt so safe with him.

"I should go back now," she managed.

"Why? Everyone sleeps."

"But not you."

"I have been thinking."

There was so much he needed to tell her, so much he wanted
her to understand. He opened his mouth to go on when the
first cracking sound of a gunshot rang out.

"What—?" Kiye Kipi whipped about, looking, but she
knew. Her blood froze.

It had come from the herd.

"Noooo!" she howled. The boy! She had sent the boy
there! She took one running step in that direction, but already
Twelic was on his feet, grabbing her, holding her back.

She fought him wildly, but he was stronger. His fingers bit
into her arms and he shook, again and again until she focused
on him.

"Do not . . . fight me now!" she grated.

A raucous white-skin shout broke the air, then the thunder
of hoofbeats rumbled, shaking the earth beneath their feet.

"The boy is gone," Twelic hissed. "You cannot save him."

"I do not try to! The ponies! *They always try to take the
ponies!*"

She wrenched away from him, stumbling back toward Wetatonmi's hearth. She had taken a few packs from her mare,
and she pawed through them frantically. Her hand closed over
her rifle, but she shook so badly, she could not remember

how to check to see if it was loaded. She took it anyway, and began running.

The *xayxayx* blue-coats came straight at her from the prairie. She veered left, and a storm of them came that way as well. They sprayed bullets ahead of them. The bullets whined past her, spitting into the earth, into the lodges . . . *the lodges.*

Horror and disbelief made her stagger, and for one treacherous moment, she could not move, could not think, could do nothing but stare as squaws came rushing out, howling in shock and terror.

Finally, she spun the other way.

She got only as far as the Lamtama lodges before a woman ran keening from her lodge there as well. The squaw watched in horror as white-skins came on from that direction, too. Then her face changed with a rush of agony as she went down, blood staining her dress, the babe beside her wailing as her hand was wrenched from his.

Kiye Kipi screamed.

Someone crashed into her, sending her reeling. The others were fleeing for the river, but she could not go with them. *Her ponies.* They were stampeding in terror, farther and farther out of her reach, onto the grasslands. She closed her eyes and cried for them silently.

Not that way! Bad, bad, hurt, danger!

She looked again. She was stronger now. She was sure how to move them, and they began crashing into each other, veering aside. Relief made her weak. But where was her own mare? She tried desperately to reach her without being able to see her.

Turn to the hills! Please, Tahmahnewes, let her hear me!

She whipped around again, looking back at the camp. The warriors were beginning to recover from the shock of the pre-dawn attack. Many had fallen into a line between the oncoming blue-coats and their women. Others ran behind the squaws, covering thier retreat. She rushed to the line, found the Kahmuenem men, and squeezed her way in among them.

A hand caught painfully in her hair from behind, dragging

her away again. She howled in terror and twisted around to find Twelic.

"The ponies . . . are gone." It was all she could manage by way of explanation.

He knew now that he would not be able to force her to leave the fighting, but he could keep her away from the worst of the fire.

"Go to the lodges!" he roared over the screams and bullets. "There will be ammunition in there! Bring it to us!"

He pushed her away and dodged past her to take her place on the warriors' line. She hesitated only a moment, then she crawled in after him again.

She would get the ammunition later, as soon as she depleted her own. She brought up her gun. There was no doubt that she could kill these mongrel bastards after all. She pulled on the trigger as she had seen the warriors do.

Nothing happened.

She began keening, pulling again and again and again. It was empty. She hurled it aside, groping forward again. Twelic would have another gun. He always had more than one. She would take that and—

Suddenly, she looked up and howled in an agony of disbelief. *The white-skins were killing the babes and the women.*

They aimed coolly, calculatedly, at every one of them that fled by. A bullet picked a little one up off his feet, hurling him sideways, dropping him again with a grotesque spray of red. His mother stumbled after him, and fire riddled through her as well, making her body twitch and dance before she collapsed atop her child.

Kiye Kipi rolled onto her belly and vomited.

After a moment, she sat up again, dazed. *Where was Twelic? Where were his guns?* She looked about. He was gone.

The warriors were breaking up, spreading out, pushing forward, finally, finally driving some of the *xayxayx* back. That was good, but she needed him now. She came to her feet with a howl, and a bullet caught her in the shoulder, ripping through her, spinning her around, driving her down.

*   *   *

Cloud Singer huddled in her lodge as gunfire riddled it, weeping, ducking with each new barrage. Finally, she crawled to the flap, peering out, and saw the others rushing toward the water.

There would be safety there. She lurched to her feet to run with them, then she saw the pony wife fall.

For a moment she could not believe the pure luck of what she was seeing. Cloud Singer's mother raced past, trying to drag her with her. She fought her off. She had to see. She had to make sure she was dead.

Toolhoolhoolzote watched Cloud Singer from a trench among the Pikunanmu lodges, and he knew a sudden rush of satisfaction as well. He got to his feet, returned the blue-coats' fire for a desultory moment, then ran heavily toward the Lamtama squaw.

He had been watching her for many suns as she crept furtively about the camps, following the Hasotoin war leader, glaring at the pony wife. Now he saw a chance to be neatly and conveniently free of the pony wife's magic with no other man being the wiser.

People died in battle, after all. The ground was already bleeding with squaws' lives.

"That one is not dead," he said, reaching Cloud Singer. "It takes more than a single bullet to kill one with her magic."

Cloud Singer focused on him, startled and wary. "You cannot know that!" she gasped.

He dragged her behind the lodge, into the relative cover it provided. "She has my blood. I would feel it if she died."

Her eyes narrowed. "Why do you tell me this?"

"Because you want her gone."

Her heart lurched. It made her feel cold to hear it spoken aloud . . . but only for a moment.

"More bullets will find her," she protested halfheartedly.

"No. The *xayxayx* are shooting at those who move."

The first doubt crept into her. "I can do nothing about that."

"But you can," the *tiwats* said gently, persuasively. "And you can save yourself."

She bit greedily, avidly, as he had known she would. "How?"

"Take a babe and run to the *xayxayx*. Know what it is to eat again. Know what it is to sleep again without bullets waking you. If you carry a babe toward them, they will see that you mean to surrender, and they will not shoot you."

Yes, yes, she thought. Did they not want the People to go to Lapwai? It was all they had asked, was how this whole nightmare had started. Cloud Singer could live at Lapwai. Oh, Spirit Chief, she could live anywhere where her hair and skin would be clean again, where there would be food and rest and water.

She had lost Twelic anyway. There was nothing here for her any longer. But white men, she had heard, treated their squaws fairly well, with many trinkets and plenty of food in return for keeping them warm on cold prairie nights.

"But how will that kill the animal caller?" she demanded, scowling again.

Toolhoolhoolzote cocked a brow just high enough to make her feel stupid. "She will go after you. You see how she is with the babes and the women. She will not let you steal one. When she fights you, they will kill her for trying to stop you."

Cloud Singer peered around the lodge, looking dazedly at the fighting again. Then she moved around, slowly at first, then running faster and faster into the shooting.

Toolhoolhoolzote smiled.

Wetatonmi pushed Little Mole down between her knees, tugging her hem down to cover him and trap him there. She screamed once as another bullet spit by her, then she groped for the gun of a fallen warrior.

Many of the white-skins were trying to retreat, but some still savaged the camps, trying to set the lodges afire. The warriors were outnumbered, could not kill them all.

But she had hands to shoot, an eye to aim.

All around her, women were beginning to fight as well, pushed beyond complacency now, beyond fear and exhaustion. She raised the rifle clumsily, firing it off in the direction of a bastard *xayxayx* who was close.

It bucked impossibly in her hands, flinging her backward. She fell from Little Mole and howled in horror as he scrambled to his feet and began running.

She staggered to her feet to go after him, mindless of the bullets, then another squaw intercepted him to save him. Thank Tahmahnewes, bless the Spirit Chief! Relief made her sway. She began stumbling toward them, then disbelief and terror crashed in on her all over again.

The woman was taking her babe to the soldiers!

"Nooooo!"

She broke into a run. The squaw lifted Little Mole over her head, as though to show him to the *xayxayx*. Wetatonmi crashed into her from behind, screaming, clawing for her child.

The *xayxayx* poured fire into them.

She felt her chest explode in red-hot agony, but she managed to close her hand around his chubby little leg.

She pulled him toward her, finding strength where there was none. Closer to her breasts . . . closer, safe from the bullets. She twisted about to shield him. He was so quiet and still. He was a good boy, so good. . . .

She sank slowly to her knees, her body shuddering, her blood streaming, and pulled her babe beneath her as she died.

Twelic ripped savagely at the lodge with his knife until it came down. An old one lay inside, his eyes sightless, a black, strangely bloodless hole between his eyes.

He turned away, his head deadly and cold, his heart stonily unreacting. Later a piece of him would die with the man. Now he would kill as well.

He hurled the cover and poles into a breastwork and began to hunker down when he saw Cloud Singer grab a babe and run for the soldiers. He knew a stunning, single moment of feral rage and came to his feet again to go after her.

Alokot's woman reached her first.

Twelic understood then who the babe was, even as he reacted. He reached Cloud Singer, grabbing her off her feet, hurling her to the ground. Her own scream of thwarted fury ripped the air, but he turned away from her to the other woman, to the child. . . .

Dead. Sweet Tahmahnewes, they were gone. He was too late.

Now grief did fill him, clawing around his throat. Fresh fire rained in on him, and he wrenched Cloud Singer to her feet again.

"I should give you to them! What stupid thing did you think?" Then he saw the evil selfishness in her eyes, and he hated her.

He wanted nothing so much as to thrust his knife into her heart. If he stayed here a moment longer, he would die himself.

They were in open, unprotected ground. He dragged her, crazed and howling, to the nearest copse. From the corner of his vision, he saw more warriors pouring up from the water again, where they had been covering their squaws' retreat. They could help him fortify this end of the camp. He screamed a war cry, catching their attention, waving them after him as he dove into the trees.

He hauled Cloud Singer behind him.

He was a warrior again. He would deal with her later.

At first there was nothing but ice, a numb, prickly feeling radiating out from her shoulder. Then came the pain. It exploded suddenly through Kiye Kipi as her body crashed back from shock.

She mewled in pain, rolling, trying to get to her feet again. *She could not die.* She *would* not die. Twelic. She had to find him. He had . . . something. He had a gun, her heart, her courage. Suddenly, it seemed the most important thing in the world to join him.

She staggered about, looking for him, and saw Toolhoolhoolzote approach her instead. Behind him, lodges were ablaze, and he seemed to step right out of the flames and the smoke. She stumbled back, instinctively, warily.

"You look for your warrior?" he asked too kindly.

Her eyes managed to narrow on him. *Why would he help her?*

"He went to those woods."

She could not distrust him now. Her heart filled with savage certainty again. She had to get to Twelic, quickly.

She did not see the soldiers approaching the place even as she did. She staggered into the trees and found him, directing an assault from a shallow depression behind a log. He was alive. She moaned his name and fell beside him, atop Cloud Singer.

Cloud Singer?

A sense of fuzzy unreality swept over her. The woman clawed at her, raking her fingers down her cheeks and her throat. But nothing hurt so badly now as the pain in her shoulder.

Then another bullet found her, slamming into her thigh.

She screamed in agony. There was no blessed moment of numbness this time, just searing fire down her leg, flashing up into her hip. She grasped at the wound instinctively, and felt her own blood slide hot through her fingers.

Someone was screaming.

She looked up, her vision blurring strangely. Soldiers. Always more soldiers. They were coming in to the trees now, firing. . . .

Cloud Singer gained her feet. It was her crazed voice Kiye Kipi had heard.

"I surrender!"

The soldiers spat bullets into her chest anyway.

Twelic and the other warriors rose and spun about, firing at them. The trees exploded with gunfire until her ears sang shrilly with it, until the acrid, searing smoke burned her throat.

Twelic staggered back, his arms wheeling, his eyes rolling. Blood burst from his back, crimson and spraying. She watched the life drain from his body, and she let loose with an inhuman wail. She crawled to him, covering his body with her own as the last of the warriors fell and the soldiers ran on.

She screamed and screamed until her voice was raw, her strength was gone and her own blood drained into the earth.

46

KIYE KIPI HID from the pain.

She found a place inside herself that was deep and so very dark, and she went there. The outside world stayed muted and far. The screams, and then the deathly silence of the camp, did not touch her. Hurt did not writhe and bite through her body, and Twelic could not be dead, not here, not where she was safe.

Then hands pulled at her rudely, rolling her over, forcing her back.

"She lives." She knew the voice, although it seemed different somehow, hard and uncaring.

Alokot?

She opened her eyes. This was not the warrior who had led her with a gentle hand as she had grown into her power. This was a man with a cold, dead gaze who cared for nothing anymore.

"Get up," he snapped.

"Wetatonmi?" She knew.

"Gone."

"The babe?"

"With her."

He wrenched her to her feet. Pain screamed through her, and as soon as she gained her feet, her bad leg gave out beneath her. She fell again, crying out.

Alokot shouted impatiently for a warrior to carry her. A distant flicker of heat returned to her eyes.

"Not yet. Twelic . . ."

"He is dead. Leave him. We have other cares now."

"*Nooooo!*"

She remembered, yet denial crashed through her. She crawled to him, pummeling him, hating him for leaving her. She loved him so desperately that she knew it was useless to leave this copse without him. For what? Why? She hit him again and again, and finally the tears came. She had forgotten how to cry and she gagged with them, choking, putting her head to his chest. *It was over.* They had not won. There had not been a Safe Place after all, and she could not stand it, could not bear it, could not say good-bye this time and go on.

"Curse you!" she gasped. "Curse you . . . with every . . . spirit monster. . . . Come back! *You cannot go!*"

He groaned.

She reeled away from him, her heart exploding. She stared at him, gaping.

He was alive.

"Help me!" she screamed at the others.

Alokot had gone on, but Earth Sound came to her. "Doeskin, something . . . your dress!" he snapped.

She found her knife and began shredding it wildly. The warrior took the tattered cloth and pressed it down into Twelic's wound, then he bound more around him to hold that in place. She brought her fist down on his chest again, because when she had done it before, he had groaned.

Somehow, if he made that sound, she was sure he would not die.

"He needs a *tiwats*," said Earth Sound.

"I will take him to one."

"You are shot yourself."

"I can ride." *The ponies.* Where were the ponies? She looked about frantically.

Earth Sound nodded, coming to his feet again. "If you can take yourself off, that would be good." For a moment, he looked dazed with the aftermath of the battle as well. "There are so many others . . . need to get them . . ." he trailed off.

"Go," she answered. She staggered upright, clutching him

to keep from falling again. "Just find me the herd."

He shouted to one of the other warriors to bring a mount to the copse. "Most of the ponies went to the hills," he told her, and for a moment she swayed again with relief and blessed thanks for her *wyakin*.

"We lost maybe half," he went on. "The soldiers cut those off and drove them away."

Half?

She keened a sound of new fury and loss, but then she saw the other warrior returning. He had her *wyakin* pony.

That was enough. Hot tears slid down her cheeks. She did not feel them this time.

Earth Sound helped her astride. The woods and the sky blackened for a moment, then swam back into focus. The warriors tore up some of their own buckskin and lashed Twelic behind her.

He lay, limp and heavy against her back. She forced herself to remain upright against his weight.

"Where . . . are the bands?" she asked.

"They went east," said Earth Sound.

"And the soldiers?"

"Many died. The rest are trapped up in the hills again."

It would have to do.

"Take me . . ." she said to her pony, ". . . take me to the others."

The mare moved out gingerly with her delicate burden. When they were out of sight of the others, Kiye Kipi laid her head on the pony's neck and let her carry them.

The Dreamers were camped on the open prairie, beside a thin stream of water. Kiye Kipi roused as she neared them. Howls and keens of sorrow ululated over the grass with a kind of stunned grief few of the People had ever known before.

She opened her eyes, looked around, and cried out at the nightmare. Many chanted over their dead, but more wailed at the sky for bodies that had not been recovered, their hands reaching high, pleading with Tahmahnewes. There was moan-

ing and weeping from the wounded, and the stench of blood
and death was strong.

She swallowed convulsively, looking about for a healer.

She saw old Tenku first, and knew she did not have the
luxury of finding Burned Tree. Despite this old one's antag-
onism for her, he would have to do.

She went to where he knelt over a squaw and slid clumsily to the ground, gripping her pony. "Help me," she
breathed.

He looked up, recognizing her. "You will have to wait your
turn. You, at least, are standing."

She motioned at her pony, feeling a good spurt of anger. "I
do not ask for myself. Do it for your Hasotoin. He is one of
your own."

Tenku finally came to his feet and saw his beloved warrior.
She saw then that the *tiwats* was wounded too, and very near
to collapsing. A thin trickle of blood ran down his neck from
somewhere above his ear.

"Tahmahnewes," he moaned. "Not him."

"We have . . . stopped his bleeding." Or perhaps the Spirit
Chief had done that, and he was gone. She could not bear to
know.

She shuddered and closed her eyes. There was no room for
hatred anymore, for suspicion and regret and old hurts. They
were all exiles together, all wretched and hounded now to the
last of their will.

"Just help him," she managed. "Show me what to do, and
I will see to the others. I have healed ponies."

He grunted, but he did not argue.

He pushed some doeskin and *xayxayx* fabric at her, and
some balms and a sack of moist herbs. She curled her good
arm back to hold it all against her breasts.

"Put the weed in the wounds," he said, and she nodded.
"Spread the balm over them, and wrap everything tightly together with the cloth. Start with yourself, or you will be able
to help no one."

"How many . . . are gone?" she asked.

He studied her silently for a moment. "I think seventeen or eighteen hands are dead."

Ninety of them? Sweet Tahmahnewes! She reeled, and he snagged her shoulder to keep her from falling.

"Mostly women, babes," he went on. "Maybe twenty of them were warriors."

Her gut surged with sickness. "Wounded?" she asked.

"Too many to count." His voice hardened again. "Get off with you now. I have work to do."

She went to Twelic instead and helped Tenku pull him from her mare. They sprawled onto the grass with his weight, and pain exploded through her again as her breath pounded out of her. She was up again before it fully came back, gasping, pulling away the skins the warriors had packed him with.

The bullet had gone clear through him. She pressed her ear to his chest. His heart sounded so distant, moving so slowly. . . .

"It is good that it went through," Tenku said, beginning to work. "That is why he lives."

She watched, her hands clenching into fists of frustration. She did not want to leave him! She swallowed carefully, and got control again.

There were so very many others who needed help as well.

She did herself next. The wound in her thigh was at the meaty part, inside. She mewled with pain at the sting of the herbs as their juice spread into her. She bandaged it, but she could not reach her shoulder. She could not do anything for it with one hand, and her bad arm was stiff, swollen, and useless.

She staggered to her feet again, hobbling into the camp. The dead, oh, Tahmahnewes, the dead!

For an unguarded moment, the loss nearly undid her. *Wetatonmi.* Her laughter, her courage, her warmth . . . A cry tore from her throat for another beloved person who had stood by her. How would she go on without her to talk to?

Alone . . . she always ended up alone.

Then she saw Wahlitits.

She nearly stumbled over him as she left the Hasotoin who were huddled miserably together, rocking and keening. Half of his neck was torn away. A woman grieved over him.

He was dead. She waited for some emotion, some satisfaction. He had started this war with his foolhardy anger. He had brought them to this. She remembered the time he had broken her arm, and later when he had taken something precious from her she had not been willing to give.

She felt nothing.

"You will taunt me no more," she managed.

The squaw looked up at her, shocked, then furious.

Kiye Kipi ignored her expression. "Let me fix that hole in your arm."

The night crawled by and dawn came again, as overcast as her soul. She returned to Tenku and laid his supplies at his hearth. He sat at his fire now, head bent, chanting wretchedly for his god to save them all.

"I can find no others," she told him. "All have been tended to for now."

He looked up at her and growled a sound in his throat. She managed to raise a brow to show that she had not understood.

"Thank you," he repeated gruffly.

His words shook her all the way down to her bones.

She nodded, swallowed, then went to Twelic. She kneeled to bend over him, though her leg screamed in protest. She put her ear to his chest, her hand over his mouth. Still, he lived, breathed. That was all that mattered now.

She curled up beside him. Pain throbbed in her head now, and her mouth was dry and parched. Later, she would change his bandages. Later, she would go back to the others and work some more over them as well. Now she needed sleep so desperately and deeply she trembled with it.

Twelic made another sound.

She dragged herself upright again, fighting the urge to shake him. "What? *What?*" she demanded, knowing he could not hear her.

But he did. His lids fluttered, then opened.

Hysterical laughter strangled her, and she felt the eyes of

the others move to her warily. "I should have known . . . you are too willful to die!"

Then he spoke, his voice a barely recognizable rasp, and something died inside her.

"Cloud . . . Singer?" he asked.

She straightened away from him. Her heart thudded sickly. "Dead."

"That is . . . good."

She turned back to him in shock. "*Good?*"

"Justice. She killed . . . Alokot's . . ." He trailed off, not able to finish, but she understood too well.

She thought she could feel no more rage. She thought she knew all there was to know of anguish. She was wrong. Now she wished she had killed Cloud Singer herself.

He watched her face change, watched it flush as her indigo eyes blazed with hatred. Somehow, he managed to speak again.

"You are . . . the only sight . . . more beautiful than the sun . . . setting behind me."

Her heart slammed hard, and she flushed deeper, confusion making her dizzy. "I . . . you . . . that wound has left you addled." It was safer, so much safer, to antagonize him.

She closed her eyes. Safe and good . . . so very good. Tah-mahnewes, she had almost lost him. The truth of that nearly shattered her again. She knew suddenly that she could live with the fear of having him close, could bear the horror of having him ride away from her later, anything, as long as he was alive and whole, rattling her with things he had no right to say.

His eyes moved over her hungrily. When the bullet had caught him, he had thought never to see her again. Now her face was blood streaked, her eyes sunken with all she had seen. Her long hair was wild, tangled. She was half-naked in a savaged doeskin, its gay *xayxayx* patches hanging in tatters.

He loved her more than life itself.

If he had come back from the afterworld, then he knew he had done it to find her.

He managed to raise an arm, his hand finding her hair. He

pulled her closer with a strength that was impossible, that stunned her. It was fleeting, gone as quickly as it surged through him, leaving him breathing hard and bleeding again. But he brought her face close to his, and she did not move away this time.

"If I live through this," he rasped, "I claim you."

Her breath froze. She was wrong.

She could not bear him rattling her after all.

47

THERE WAS NO time left for grief, for healing.

Kiye Kipi woke to a soft, misting rain that seeped all the way into her blood and made it cold. She sat up, shivering. The people still moaned, but more dully now, and the shamans chanted in earnest, performing the Pasapukitse, blowing the ghosts away.

Sentinels were coming in fast from the western prairie. Her eyes narrowed on them and her heart kicked. She wanted desperately to know what they said, but first she went to Twelic.

Moving was misery. Both her arm and her leg had stiffened, and as she straightened them, dull throbbing erupted into shots of hot, tingling pain. She made it to his side, breathing hard.

She put her good hand to his chest to feel his heart.

"Wash your shoulder out before it festers," he said quietly, "and find out what those scouts have seen. Do not worry about me now."

She gasped, snatching her hand back. She wanted him alive; she was not so sure she wanted him awake.

She eyed him warily, thinking again about what she thought he had said before they slept. *Claim her?* Sweet Tahmahnewes, there were times when he had wanted her, and he had condescended to fight with her, but surely he could not have meant that.

Hope leaped in her again, stronger than hurt, wilder than grief. It was no different now than it had been when she had seen only sixteen snows. She was a fool. She knew better now, yet still it squirmed in her belly, aching, needing.

He only watched her with that one arrogant brow raised high.

She pressed her fingers to her temples, and decided it was best if she did as he said, if only for this one time. At least he could not follow her.

She struggled to her feet and limped to the water, splashing it on her wound as best she could, picking pieces of doeskin out of it with her nails. She had to find Burned Tree, she realized, or it would indeed get rotten. She looked around and found him now, and went to his hearth.

The bullet was close to the surface of her skin. She bit her lip to keep from crying out, her face parching white, as he found it. He pushed some weed into the freshly seeping wound, then he looked at her leg.

"That one has gone all the way through," he muttered. "Someone has fixed it well enough."

"I . . . did." She struggled to get her air back.

He gave her a long, appraising look that was almost a smile.

She got to her feet again and looked for the warriors. Those who were not injured had begun to gather at Lean Elk's fire. It had been his men who had gone out to scout. They alone knew this barren country well enough to hide in it.

She went that way, pressing forward through the others to hear, holding her hand against the pain in her shoulder.

"How-erd has reached the Big Hole," one reported. "We left him there not long ago. He is burying his dead, but that will not take long. They do it without talking to their god much."

Lean Elk nodded and looked to the other headmen. "Then we must go on immediately."

Joseph began to protest. "Too many are still bleeding—"

Lean Elk silenced him with a glance. "And they will bleed whether we stay here or whether we ride. If we stay, more will die. How-erd will not carry his wounded with him. This prairie offers no obstructions. He will be coming up on us fast."

Finally, Joseph nodded.

Kiye Kipi felt her heart chug tiredly. She looked about at the women, fully expecting them to start wailing again, wondering how she could comfort them this time. But the ones who were closest, those who had heard, only got to their feet and began loading their ponies again.

It took her a moment to understand.

How-erd had punished them to a point beyond weariness, beyond grief, beyond hopelessness. Now they were desperate. They had seen what he would do to them if he caught them. He was the worst, most heinous kind of enemy. His *xayxayx* did not even spare children. For the salvation of their babes, they would somehow, impossibly, go on.

It was, in its own way, its own sort of courage.

She cried out in despair for them, then she brought her chin up and went back to Twelic.

"What do they say?" he asked.

"We run again," she reported hollowly.

By sundown, she was as furious with him as she had ever been.

"You are a hundred times a fool!" she spat. "Look at you! Do you prove you are strong? They all know that, but they will not remember it after you are dead!"

The rain had picked up to a sodden, drenching downpour. Still the People kept on, their ponies slogging through mud in the lower grounds, the grasses slapping wetly around their legs. Twelic rode his own stallion, though he could barely sit astride.

"I do not die," he grated. "Stop harping. You are worse than a mated squaw."

Her heart stuttered at the inference, but her attention was quickly snagged again by his obvious pain.

He was as pale as any *xayxayx*.

His mouth was pinched and drawn down at the corners. The skin beneath his eyes looked thin and blue. The rain had flattened his hair, giving him a skeletal appearance, and blood was beginning to spread through the bandage around his belly.

"I should ask Burned Tree for something to make you sleep," she muttered.

"You would never hold me down long enough to get it in me," he answered mildly. "Think, Screamer. If the others see me try, perhaps they, too, will find a way to be strong. That is no more than you would do in my position. And I will not have another man carry me."

She snorted. That last was the truest part of all.

"We will have to stop soon anyway, I think," he added.

She could not deny that. The wounded, the aged, and the children had kept up their impossibly grueling pace all through the sun. The air echoed with their groans and their cries. Only their desperate horror of captivity, of How-erd's sol-jers, kept them moving despite their injuries.

She looked around at them, and her gut clenched tightly again.

Few had lodges left.

There was no more food.

Only a handful of the squaws even had blankets.

Finally, they found water, and the women dismounted to scavenge the banks for any roots and weeds that were edible. Kiye Kipi's belly clenched, but she only waited astride with the others. They would still be going on.

She moved up onto high ground, looking back at their trail. Suddenly, her breath caught. Another party was approaching them.

"Looking Glass has found us!" she cried.

Twelic jerked his pony around to watch his cousin come in. His face was livid. She rode quickly, instinctively, to move between the two of them.

"You are late." Twelic's voice was barely controlled.

Looking Glass flushed miserably. "I was there . . . looked for you first at the Big Hole. I saw—"

"You saw!" Twelic snarled. "You did not smell the blood. You did not hear the screams. You did not feel bullets shredding your flesh or watch babes die in bursts of blood! *What kind of a headman are you to leave your people to death?*"

"I could not have known!"

"You knew there were white-skins about!"

"It does not matter now," Kiye Kipi gasped.

They both looked at her sharply.

"She is right," Looking Glass ventured finally. "It is past now."

The shock of having him agree with her should have warned her, even if it was only to save his own pride. She should have known he had nothing good to report, but his next words made her heart fall all over again.

"The Crow will not have us."

The headmen gathered in a crude circle near the water, their ponies hungrily tugging up the grass around them. Once again, their warriors pressed in. Kiye Kipi stayed close to Twelic, feeling both sick, yet somehow unsurprised.

Neither of them had ever truly believed that Crow country was the Safe Place.

"Too many of those people have given up," Looking Glass explained. "They are dependent upon the *xayxayx* now for sustenance. The River Crows live near a fort. They take their food from the sol-jers. They do not dare anger them by offering shelter to us."

"What of the Mountain Crow?" White Bird demanded. "They are no friends of these white bastards."

Looking Glass shook his head. "No, but they are hungry and vulnerable as well. They say there are no buffalo left in their country. The best they can promise us is to remain neutral, and pray that our Spirit Chief protects us. They will not harm us if we pass their way, but neither will they stand between us and the *xayxayx*."

There was silence, deep and stunned.

Finally, Huishuis Kute broke it. "Then where do we go now?"

Joseph gave a sigh that hurt Kiye Kipi's bones.

"While we were fighting for our country, there was reason to fight," he said woodenly. "Now that we are here, I have no will to pick up my bow. This is not my country. Since I have left that, it matters little to me where we go.'' He got to his feet and left them.

She could not let his despair touch the others. She found Twelic's eyes. He knew as well as she did that it would be deadly, that his defeat would snake through all the others like a disease.

They could not give up now.

''More mountains,'' she suggested thinly. They all looked at her, and Twelic nodded.

''How-erd falls farther behind us when we cross mountains,'' she pointed out. ''It is . . . his ponies. They do not keep up in that terrain.''

Toolhoolhoolzote barked a sound of contempt, and she flinched because she had not seen him approach.

''She nearly trapped us in the Bitterroots, telling us that!''

''No!'' she cried, stung. It was not true! ''I did not say to go through there!''

He ignored her. ''Is this woman a leader to show us how to go?'' he demanded.

''She got us down from those mountains,'' White Bird reminded him wearily.

Kiye Kipi looked at Toolhoolhoolzote, struggling to bring her chin up. Then understanding slammed through her, and the blood drained from her face.

''What is it?'' demanded Twelic. He reached for her so quickly he flinched in pain. But he found the strength to hold her, to keep her from falling.

She moved her mouth, but no words came out. Too much was happening too fast. Realization crashed in on her from both sides, and she could not get her breath.

She heard something in Twelic's voice, something too deep for her to credit, and her eyes widened hugely on him. *He loved her.* She might not be sure what he had said before they had slept, but she knew in that moment that he could not bear to see harm come to her. Something wild swam through her, something sweet and elating . . . but then there was Toolhoolhoolzote.

She looked at the *tiwats* again.

He had tried to kill her in the Big Hole.

He had sent her to that copse knowing there were soldiers there. Suddenly, she was sure of it.

She would have gone anyway, had she known Twelic hid in that place, but the headman's evil intent had nearly destroyed both of them. Hatred blazed up in her.

"Perhaps," she answered tightly, "it is not in our best interest to listen to our established leaders."

There were shocked sounds and frowns of consternation. She did not care if they drove her out of this council and never let her speak in one again. She held Toolhoolhoolzote's eyes.

Now you have an enemy, old man. You have something to fear.

Fury made her shake.

"She is right about the mountains," Lean Elk said finally, wise enough and detached enough from it all to step around the squabbling. "We should try to put another range between us. There is a pass through the next Great Mountains. The *xayxayx* call them Rockies. The trail is the Targhee."

"That will take us into Sioux country," protested Looking Glass, not happy about it. But Twelic silenced him with a glare.

"I went through that way once," he said. "We can make it."

Kiye Kipi turned away, needing suddenly, desperately, to be away from both of them.

They camped for the night at the next water hole they found, a shallow place that would have been dry in other weather. Now it was spongy with pools, and the ponies put their noses to it, guzzling noisily. Kiye Kipi squatted among them, cupping water in her palms, hoping some of it would fill her empty, knotted belly.

The skies had finally cleared, and now the moon showed through. The air was thick, clinging. She lifted her hair off her nape and used her fingers to comb through it. She longed to wash, and knew there was barely enough water for the people to drink.

She stood again and hobbled back to the others.

Twelic was pushing wood into her fire.

She went still, watching him, her heart skipping a beat. All around the grass, the warriors were huddled close with their wives and kin . . . and he had come to her. Then her elation was extinguished by concern. His lodge was gone, and something cringed inside of her at the thought of him sleeping in the open, so hurt and so exhausted.

"I am wounded. I am not a prairie flower," he said without looking up at her, and she jolted at the way he knew her mind.

"No." She recovered. "They smell sweet. You stink like a mongrel dog, like blood and mud."

"Would you help me bathe?"

Reaction shivered through her. She sat beside him, carefully. "No. But I will repack your wound."

"This is more important." He pulled a prairie dog from the ashes of the fire.

Her eyes widened and her mouth immediately began salivating. "Where did you get it?"

He inclined his head at a nearby hole in the ground. "Tah-mahnewes sent him. Perhaps I am meant to live on for a while after all."

"You are," she snapped, the alternative chilling her as she remembered the way he had looked at the Big Hole.

Twelic only shrugged. "Will you share with me, or would you be a hardheaded cow?"

Her jaw set. "You need it more."

"And how are you to ride without the strength to hold yourself astride?"

She looked at the scant meat, her body reacting to it, trembling. She was so hungry!

She reached out and snatched a leg off the piece. It burned her fingers. She blew air on it, bouncing it from hand to hand, then she crammed it into her mouth, pulling the meat from the bone with her teeth.

Her gut clenched, then settled again with an ache of almost fullness.

He grinned and began eating as well. "How-erd has stopped

to camp,'' he said at length. ''Lean Elk's men have just brought word. We should be safe enough this night.''

Some of the adrenaline went out of her, and she closed her eyes. ''Thank Tahmahnewes.''

''If we cross over the Targhee and the headmen turn north, I think we will find the Safe Place before the moon is gone,'' he went on, then his next words made her eyes fly open. ''I dreamed of it again.''

''When?'' she croaked.

''While I was in darkness, close to dying.''

She could not bear to ask, but she had to know. ''Did it change?''

He was quiet for so long that that was an answer in itself. Fear bloomed in her.

She got to her feet again, her heart thudding, and scanned the dark prairie as though she could somehow see the place. Her heart screamed for the surcease it offered, and writhed at the thought of finding it alone.

She turned back to him.

Perhaps he did not mean to claim her. If he had indeed spoken those words, then they must have come from the obscure part of his soul, brought closer by the death spirits. She found in that moment that she did not care anymore. There was no sweetness left in life, no traditional hearths where men brought food and women cooked it. That was in Nimipu country, perhaps never to be reclaimed again. All that mattered here and now was that he lived, that in his own strong, arrogant way he loved her, and that they reached that Safe Place together.

''Tell me,'' she whispered. ''Please. Tell me all of it.''

She knew what she was asking, that she had no right. She knew, too, that if his heart was truly bound to hers, he would tell her his *wyakin* dream anyway. She would not ask him to stay forever at her hearth, but she would reach out for this piece of his spirit. It was all she needed, all the courage she had.

She waited, and realized her heart was thundering. He only made a neat pile of his prairie dog bones.

Say something.

He touched the ground beside him that she should sit again.

"I dreamed mostly of battle," he said finally. "The women were running, and the enemy was behind us."

Her breath rushed out of her. She sat because she could no longer stand.

"I heard the fighting behind me," she whispered. "I did not see that part of it. I ran."

"The black mare—"

"She called me into her. That is how I went."

"Yes. You were there." His eyes found hers, so hot, telling her so much now. "You took the People to safety in a final, terrible battle. That is what Tahmahnewes has reminded me of. I am in no condition to fight at my strongest now. Now I understand. I think I am meant only to hold off the *xayxayx* long enough for you and that black mare to go on."

"No!" She keened the word, recoiling from him. He caught her.

"Listen to me," he said harshly. "You must be ready for that. If your own dream can deny it, then tell me now. If it cannot then you must be ready to go on. I told you this once. I never saw this Safe Place. It is you who must take the women there. You must not come back for me if I fall. That is not how Tahmahnewes meant it."

She stared at him in cold horror, nausea threatening to push up her food again.

"Tell me," he repeated. "You saw this land in your dream. Did you see me? *Was I in your* wyakin *as well?*"

She fought his grip off violently. It did not matter. He knew it. He already knew.

"No," he said for her quietly. "No, Screamer. Perhaps you saw elk and snow and fish, but I was not there."

48

THEY WOVE THEIR way into the craggy Rocky Mountain foothills fifteen suns later. More of the wounded took hollow, dying breaths and closed their eyes. The exiles paused long enough to hide their bones from the timber wolves, to pray and to keen over their losses, then they went on until they reached a steep, protected glade.

Twelic swung to the ground with a grunt and a grimace. Kiye Kipe watched him with narrow-eyed frustration, then she turned away.

She went to the edge of the glade. Lush, vivid grass swept down over a fall of rocks there, and another valley nestled below her, ten lodge lengths beneath where she stood. She looked across to the other side in the falling darkness. Water poured over the rocks, foaming white and spraying as it crashed into a pool below.

Twelic moved up stiffly behind her. "Each time I believe Tahmahnewes has forsaken us, He gives something like this to ease my soul."

She started and looked at him. "I would not have taken you to be so touched by sheer beauty," she murmured. Then she saw the way he was looking at her, and her heart slammed again.

"There is something I do not understand about this trail," he went on finally. "I have heard that the *xayxayx* have claimed it somehow, as they have done to our land. But it is obviously not a fort, and there are no iron horses. I have not ever seen any of their big wooden lodges here. They leave the land unspoiled as Tahmahnewes intended it, and that is not their way.''

"No." She frowned. "It is not."

"If they say it is theirs, then there must be some of them here nonetheless.''

Her pulse skittered. "Sol-jers?"

"Perhaps, or settlers. I will keep my eyes open for them, and warn the others.''

He went back to the settling camp, but she only watched the cascade of water until darkness stole it from her eyes.

So close.

She jolted. It was not the white-skins she felt here, she realized. They were, as Twelic said, strangely absent. No, it was the Safe Place. She had never been so near to it before, and suddenly the sense of it filled her. Her skin went cold.

Through so many seasons she had waited for it. Now it lurked behind these mountains for her like some gnarled animal with unknown temperament. They would leave the Targhee, and the headmen would decide to turn north, and then they would finally find it.

What would she do when the got there?

Her *wyakin* would have her go on, would have her leave him, watch him fall. And that was the one thing Tahmahnewes could ask of her that was truly beyond her.

She could not do it.

She cried out quietly and closed her eyes. She knew that she would defy it, the very spirit guide that had given her her power and saved her from being cast out. Terror made her knees weak. She had never heard of anyone doing such a thing, but she thought that once it happened, she would probably die.

So be it. Twelic would live, and so would the People. The alternative, to go on without him, was the one sort of death she could not bear.

Decision left her feeling stronger than she had in suns. She opened her eyes again and looked for him. He was talking with Alokot, but he was watching her, and somehow she knew that he knew at least some of what she had been thinking.

Her chin came up and her eyes got hot. She would fight fate at the Safe Place, but she would take something for herself when she went. Oh, yes, this time she would best these white-skins. They could not take everything from her after all.

He was still watching her, his eyes narrowing now.

She knelt carefully on one knee, the hurt in her bad leg lingering. Her hands shook. She managed to untie her moccasin, then she stood again, found his eyes, and hurled it over her head into a tree behind her.

He would understand that as well. He would remember that once he had tried to steal her clothing beside a cold creek on the prairie, and in doing so he had begun something that neither one of them had ever escaped.

A beginning, a middle, and an end. She shivered.

She backed up without looking away from him. Her blood began to rush crazily, with something almost like fear, but not quite, almost like fury, but hotter. She moved gingerly, carefully, down into the rocks behind her, finding footholes with her bare toes. Then she stopped to untie her other moccasin, and she threw that back into the camp as well.

Twelic felt his heart stagger.

". . . when we get there." Alokot broke off. "You are not listening," he snapped.

Twelic's gaze slid to him, then moved back to the edge of the glade. "No."

She was gone now.

Arousal reared up in him so suddenly, even his skin felt hot. He could feel his blood pumping dangerously at his wound, and could not care. *Now.* With the instincts of a fox, she had known it, had known just when it was right, when it was needed most. Oh, yes, he craved peace now; he needed release and the kind of surcease that only she could give.

He began to move after her, leaving Alokot gaping, and found her tattered doeskin hanging from a branch on the other side of the drop.

The rocks scattered into a thin, slanting creek bed. He found his footing there and followed it through a bend, around and down. The water trickled into the pool that caught greedily at the fall splashing from above.

She was there.

She stood naked just in front of the cascade, the pool foaming and rushing about her hips. Her arms were at her sides, her breasts high, nipples tightening from the cold. Her chin came up and her back straightened as she saw him.

"If I would lose you, then I would have you first," she said plainly. "I do not know if I can go on without you, but no matter what happens, I would have this memory."

He did not hear the warning in her words.

"Once you said you touched me for my own sake." She paused, licking her lips. "Let me . . . let me touch you now for my sake as well. Please . . . do not turn away."

As if he could.

He had tried to once, only to be haunted by memories of her. He had run from her faster than the wind, and found her waiting for him. Finally, near death, he had found the courage to reach out for her, only to realize that to speak of it again would be cruel. He understood now that neither Tahmahnewes nor fate would allow him to claim her. Never again would he torture either of them by talking of what could not be.

But she was right; when he fell, he would have this memory. He would have the sweet, bitter succor of what might have been.

He pulled out of his leggings and breechclout and moved down into the water. The cold bit into his flesh, but it could not reach his blood. Hunger was tumultuous inside him, making his heart pound louder than the fall. But when he reached her and pushed his hands into her hair, his touch was reverent, not hard, gentle where it might have been unrestrained.

He curled his fingers into the tangled mane on either side of her head and lowered his mouth to hers.

The mewling sound she made staggered him.

"This . . . way," she whispered when he would have dived into her. She pulled back from him, taking his hand, and led him behind the crashing water. There was a hole in the rock there, a cavern. She slid inside onto a cool slab of stone.

He went onto his knees in front of her, then leaned toward her and covered her mouth with his own again. She cried out and wrapped her arms about his neck. Finding her way against him again was everything it had been before, but this time no *xayxayx* would find them. No one could find them. No anger or fear throbbed between them.

His tongue was hot and seeking, and it was all she had ever wanted, the only caress her mouth had ever known.

He caught her around the waist and brought her beneath him. Then his body covered hers, trapping her between his heat and the smooth, cold stone. Finally, his mouth moved over her, as it had once before, a lifetime ago.

He closed a hand over her breast, cupping it, holding it for his tongue, and she began trembling. Need, hungry and impatient, screamed through her. She arched herself into him, but he held her down.

"No, Screamer." He almost laughed. "This is not rutting. It is perhaps all we will ever have."

He had had so many others, enjoying the heat of them for the moment, then riding away. This was not, could not, be like that. Yet she was as wild and demanding as he had ever been in those times, writhing beneath him, her hands stroking and seeking. In so many ways, she was his counterpart, the braver, more passionate and compassionate, part of himself.

They would not do this his way. He realized that they rarely did.

She drove her fingers into his hair, dragging his lips back to hers. Then she let him go because she wanted his mouth on her body as well. Her hands stroked him, urging him on. His muscles flexed and tightened, and still she demanded, still she gave. He was the wind, rushing over her skin, pausing long enough to lick and tease and taunt. She wanted to fly with him, now, high enough to touch the clouds. She wanted all of him, now, before she could never have him again.

A growling sound came from her throat. It undid him.

He thought fleetingly of Wahlitits, of taking care not to hurt her, but she would not even allow him caution. She wrapped her legs tight around him, drawing him in before something could happen to rob her this time. It took a kind of strength he did not possess to deny her. He slid into her, and she was hot and ready and waiting for him.

Kiye Kipi shuddered all the way down to her soul.

This, yes, this was what she had always needed, and no, it was not like the ponies rutting at all.

He filled her until there was nothing left inside her but him. Then he began moving, steadily and hard, making everything coil within her. Her strong, eager cries filled the cave. She held him, rocked with him, loved him, craved him, laughed aloud with him in great, gasping breaths until satisfaction crashed through her like the water tumbling by outside the hole.

He left her body tingling and throbbing, depleted and brimming all at once. His breath was hot on her neck, his arms hard around her, and she felt a last tremor move through him as well.

Her voice, when she found it, was scratchy. "Now . . . what?"

She wondered only how she would live through these last suns if this did not ever happen again. But his answer was all it could be, and she had to close her eyes so that she would not weep from the loss.

"We take the rest of this night for ourselves," he murmured. "Then we find out what waits for us, Screamer. Then we go on."

49

OLIVER OTIS HOWARD stopped his cavalcade inside the mouth of the Targhee and swore with all the color of a sailor. His men moved cautiously backward.

He was a very religious man, but he was not praising his God at the moment. He was staring at the third broken wagon axle of the morning.

"How the hell did they get this far?" he demanded. "They have their wounded, all their camp gear, their herds—"

"I don't know how they did it," interrupted his second-in-command. He'd been whining since Howard's troops had picked his men up at the Big Hole. Now he dabbed worriedly at the seeping arrow wound at his shoulder, looking around at his subordinates as though to defend himself against them.

"We had them pinned down for the better part of the day," he insisted. "Even their bucks were running down the river. Then they came back at us like a bunch of hornets."

"Of course they did, Colonel. You killed their women," Howard snapped. He moved away from the wagon, rubbing his temple with his good hand.

"Only way to fight the bastards," someone muttered.

"That may very well be, but the fact of the matter is that they got out of that hole when they should not have, they are still moving on, and we are no closer to capturing them than before," Howard replied in a voice that grated. "Now, suppose one of you gentlemen who is familiar with this terrain tells me how in blazes we're going to get these wagons over the Rocky Mountains.''

"We're not, sir," a brave man said.

Howard was quiet for a long time. "Very well, then. Disengage them."

"Jesus, General, that's our *food!* That is ... I mean, gosh—"

"It's quite all right, sir. Jesus is aware of our predicament as well as I. Move the wagons."

He looked up the trail again, into the mountains, shielding his eyes against the glare of the sun. There was, indeed, no possible way the horses could drag the conveyances through those canyons. The beasts would have to make do without their oats, and now his men would have to cut back on their already short rations as well.

How in blazes was Joseph getting through? he wondered again. What was *he* eating? His people had pulled too far ahead for his bucks to be taking the time to hunt.

If he could not catch up with them, his reputation was ruined; he was growing uncomfortably aware of that. Already the newspapers back East were buzzing between sympathy for the heathens and scorn for his own ineptitude. That was not even to mention the support the Indians were beginning to garner from many of the locals—as though those people had never once clamored for Nez Percé land and opened this whole, illogical can of worms.

Yet his government said to push on, and so he would.

One of his scouts was coming back down the trail now. He straightened authoritatively again and moved to meet him. Perhaps *he* had a good word to report.

Howard knew as soon as he saw the scout's face that he did not.

"We got real trouble now, General. They've turned into the Yellowstone. Good Lord, they've gone into the tourist park!"

As they neared the mouth of the Targhee, the exiles were forced to dismount again. Kiye Kipi swung to the ground, her head hurting with the impossibility of it all.

The land here dove into chasms; brush parted only to reveal more rockslides. There was no time for the warriors to move them, and there were no prairie grasslands to receive them anyway, only more gullies and ravines for perhaps another sun's ride.

She turned back to look at the people waiting behind her. "I think we will have to lead the ponies over and through these places by hand," she told Joseph. Sweet Tahmahnewes, it would take forever! Panic closed her throat, but Joseph only nodded and passed on the word.

Oh, how she wished, just once, that he would mull over her words again, discuss them with that sharp-eyed look the way he used to! He was, perhaps, the weariest, most beleaguered of them all. When he spoke in council now, it was to fret and gnaw over the one thing that stymied all of them. *Why was it so imperative to the* xayxayx *that they be placed on that little plot of land at Lapwai?* Why was it worth so much death and horror?

But there were no answers to that, only the impossible truth that How-erd still followed them no matter which way they turned, no matter how far they ran from the country he coveted.

She jumped down from the rocks, coaxing her mare along behind her as she kept one critical eye on the others. No man, woman, or child struggled with more than two ponies now.

So many gone. And the remainder were chisel ribbed.

"Can we camp?" she asked when they were all down. "There is forage here."

Joseph shrugged. "We will talk."

The headmen moved together again while the ponies grazed briefly. Kiye Kipi moved behind them more slowly, her thigh aching, her feet sore. Twelic caught her arm and helped her ease down to sit.

Impossibly, in spite of her exhaustion, something shuddered into life inside her again.

She looked up at him and managed a thin smile. His touch was different now. Now it was hot and alive with memories; now it distracted her, made her yearn, in a whole new way.

She would still die hungry, but now she would know what she needed to fill her.

Lean Elk spoke first. "There is a river near here. The white-skins call it the Yellowstone. I think we should go that way. If How-erd follows, there is a fork there as well, in a canyon. It is an excellent place for defense if we can get in there ahead of them."

"And then?" Joseph asked dully. "Where can we possibly go?"

North.

Kiye Kipi waited. Of course it would be that way; she and Twelic had known it since the Big Hole. Yet she was unprepared for the sense of shock that flew through her when Tool-hoolhoolzote began to complain.

"There is nothing beyond that Yellowstone, nothing! Where would you have us go when we pass through that can-yon? Would you have us travel all the way to Old Woman's Country? What is for us there? I say it is time for us to turn about and fight."

"Would you tell the women to pick up their dead mates' bows?" asked White Bird.

"I say we should—"

"Wait!"

They all looked about at her. They had not stopped her from listening in on councils since she had defied her grandfather, but neither had she tried to participate.

"I . . . what is Old Woman's Country?" she asked carefully. "I have not heard of this."

Toolhoolhoolzote did not answer. His eyes were small, hard chips of stone.

"Where is it exactly?" she persisted.

"Due north of here," Joseph said finally. "There is a Sioux chief there. Sitting Bull. He went there after his own people fell."

"And is he safe there?"

"No sol-jers followed him."

Her heart staggered, then erupted. She looked at Twelic.

That was it.

"It is a place for cowards," Toolhoolhoolzote snarled.

"No," she gasped. "No, it is not."

White Bird raised a brow. "But you said you had not heard of it."

She got to her feet again, though her legs trembled. "I dreamed of it. We must go there. We can reach it in triumph, not shame, and How-erd will stop chasing us."

There was a long silence. "You are sure?" Joseph asked finally.

She managed a deep breath. "It was my *wyakin.*"

The council erupted in murmurs. She turned away.

They had found it . . . and she would send them to it, the People, the ponies.

And Twelic.

She took only a few steps before she was running, flying into her ponies, the death spirits chasing her. *Tahmahnewes, sweet Spirit Chief, what had she done?*

She worked in a fever, readying the herd for their last dash for freedom. Her skin felt cold, then hot, in summer's sultry last air. A high-pitched, strangled laugh caught in her throat. The warm season was ending, and if they turned north, soon the snows would come.

Elk and snows and fish. I was not there.

Twelic touched her shoulder as she bent over a black mare's leg. She yelped, coming upright again. There was a storm in his eyes as well.

"It is . . . decided?" she managed. *Please, tell me no.* But that was ludicrous.

"They voted," he said. "It was unanimous, except for Toolhoolhoolzote. We will go to Old Woman's Country, turning north with the next sun."

She nodded, forcing herself to breathe. "How far is it? Did they say?"

"Joseph thinks about ten suns' ride."

It was not enough time. She wanted more.

She wanted to scream against the injustice of it all. She had waited for him forever; now, when finally he loved her, she would lose him. Rage rushed in her, and she hurled her parfleche of medicines aside. The weeds scattered over the grass, and she stared at them for a long time, breathing hard.

"So be it," she whispered savagely. "They will have it. They will take it all from me. I know that now. But this last time is mine, *mine*!"

She looked back at him and claimed his mouth suddenly, hard.

He understood. He did not try to gentle her.

He dragged her closer, his hands in her hair. His mouth moved to her cheek, her ear; his tongue tasted the tangy, salty tears beginning to bead at her eyes.

She pulled at his clothes, strewing them, then she wrestled out of her dress as well. His skin was still warm from the sun; if she held tight to him, it heated the cold death within her.

She traced the lines and contours of him with her palms, then followed with her mouth. He tasted of smoke and sun and fires.

She did not know she was crying.

They tumbled together into the short, shaggy grass, already clipped by the ponies' hungry teeth. She did not feel it scratch at her skin. There was him, only him, from now until forever, and forever would come too soon.

He moved atop her, his own desperation making him greedy, hungry. Still, she was ahead of him, greedier, hungrier. Before he expected it, she arched her hips upward. She captured his body and caught the wind again, if only for another short, precious time.

50

HOWARD'S HORSES STAGGERED off the Targhee. A full handful of them went down among the rocks, their ribbed sides heaving. The men watched them silently, exchanging skeptical glances, then someone shouted.

Howard looked sharply beyond the last gulches to the distant grasslands. Fresh cavalry appeared there, the blue of their coats strong and clean.

"Move out again!" he ordered.

His troops remounted, slapping quirts and rifle butts against the weary, welted hides of their remaining horses. When they reached the incoming soldiers, Howard moved to the commanding officer.

"Colonel Sturgis."

"General! I have good news to report."

"Tell me you know where the heathens are," he responded dryly, "and I will surely sit upon this horse and weep." He did not anticipate any such thing, and he felt his heart strengthen unexpectedly at Sturgis's response.

"I do indeed. They're moving north. Toward Clark's Fork, I believe."

"You've engaged them?" Howard demanded.

"Not yet, sir. We received word that you were headed through this way. I'm reporting for your orders."

Howard looked at his spent men and horses, and he laughed bitterly. "Go after them, Colonel."

Sturgis nodded eagerly. "Will you accompany, sir?"

"Impossible. Where is the closest civilization?"

Sturgis thought. "That would have to be Cooke City, sir."

"Good enough. Detail a small party to that place. I need fresh mounts, supplies. Have them sent down to me here. Oh, and Colonel . . ." He paused, then he nodded once, as though to himself. "Wire Colonel Miles with the Department of the Colorado. Instruct him to join this chase as well."

"Colonel *Miles,* sir?"

Howard went on as though he hadn't heard him. "You say Joseph is headed for the fork?" *If he was Joseph, where would he go from there?* Suddenly, the answer was as clear to him as the nose on Sturgis's face.

"Canada," he mused aloud.

"I beg your pardon, sir?"

"Tell Colonel Miles to intersect that country between the fork and the Canadian border. You take your party and pursue the Indians to that place. In effect, you'll be pushing them right into Miles's path. As soon as I receive fresh supplies, I'll join you."

And that, he thought, would be that. It was over.

Miles was a hungry, ambitious man, a career soldier. With his fresh horses, fresh men, and knowledge of the Indians' route, there was no doubt in Howard's mind that he would find a way to end this debacle.

Surprisingly, his satisfaction and adrenaline ebbed, leaving him with only a headache. He wondered suddenly what harm could possibly come from allowing the exiles simply to leave the territory. They could come back, but he seriously doubted they would. And if they did, they would not bring their women and children. Then, at least, it would be a fair war.

He turned away, feeling uncomfortable deep inside himself. He knew what bothered him the most, what unsettled the man in him as well as the soldier. He had come to respect Joseph too much over these past several months to destroy him easily, to rob him of everything he had strived for. It seemed a moral sacrilege to bring him down now.

He had tried to warn him that he could not outmaneuver the

strength of the American militia. No tribe had done so yet.
But he had. Joseph very nearly had.

A knife-sharp edge of finality and triumph began to grip the
People. Kiye Kipi saw it in the way they rode: leaning slightly
forward, eyes hungrily scanning the land. Soon the country
was changeless again, swell after barren swale of golden grass,
rolling out forever. It chilled something in her soul, but the
squaws' and the elders' voices rose in satisfied murmurs at
each tree they passed, each creek bed they splashed through.

She saw the mouth of the canyon at the precise moment
Lean Elk's sentinels shrilled a warning behind them.

Now?

She twisted around to look over her shoulder. It could not
be; it did not make sense! They had not ridden ten suns yet.
They had not even ridden two. *It was not time.*

She rode to the place where the headmen and their warriors
had reined in. Lean Elk's men had reached them.

"Sol-jers," a warrior reported. His tone was clipped, tense,
and it made fear shimmy in her belly. "Half a sun back, but
with fresh ponies."

"You are sure?" snapped Lean Elk.

"They make strong time."

"Where did they come from?" Joseph wondered, appalled.
"This cannot be How-erd."

Lean Elk looked at the other headmen. "We must move
into the canyon. Quickly."

Kiye Kipi looked at it again, so very distant. It was barely
more than a dark smudge on the horizon; had she not known
it was there, she would not even have noticed it. Rage moved
suddenly in her heart, sweeping up into her head, pounding
red hot at her temples.

She was prepared to lose everything to them. She was not
prepared to lose yet.

She looked at Twelic. *She had eight suns left!* No, she
thought wildly. No! She would not let them steal that last
precious time, too!

"Give me one of your guns," she demanded.

He looked at her blankly, then his face hardened. "Go ahead with the squaws. Drive them on. Make them hurry."

Her heart slammed hard. "No."

Not this time. This time, she would not run, would not coddle the elders, would not hide the ponies. This time she would kill every cursed, vile white-skinned man who thought to take it all from her.

Twelic looked into her blazing indigo eyes, and loss and fury choked him.

"Another man will give me one," she told him. "Let me fight with yours."

He could not do it.

He turned his stallion away, heard her behind him, felt the very heat of her as she rode defiantly back to his side. Yes, some other man would arm her, but it would not be him; he would not hand her her own death.

"Tahmahnewes!" he snarled at her, reining in savagely. "Think what you ask of me!"

"I ask from you life!" she hissed. "I ask from you a little more time."

She did not know why it was so important that she have his weapon. It was a gut feeling, a certainty, churning deep in her bowels. If she fled, this would not end right. She would die, they would all die, here and now.

"You cannot shoot," he grated.

Her chin came up. "Then show me how."

He could not protect her anymore, and he felt sick.

She could not lose him yet, and something burned in her belly.

"Please," she gasped, her throat tight. "Please. There is no time to argue."

They looked back at the southern horizon. The soldiers were visible now, a shadow too distant to show the blue of their uniforms, but their dust was clear, churning up above their heads, their ponies. Twelic wrenched a rifle free of his saddle. He threw ammunition at her so suddenly she had to drop her reins to catch it.

She had won, but the prize made her shake.

''Put the bullets in there.'' He stabbed a finger at the weapon to indicate the place. ''Touch that hook with your finger. Do not pull it. If you pull it hard, your shot will go wild. Coax the bullet out of it, do not force it.''

''I—'' She choked off the response, and merely nodded.

''When it goes off, the gun will slam back into you. There is no weight to you anymore. It will drive you down. If you hold that butt end against your shoulder, at least you will not lose it.''

He rode away from her. She wanted to cry out, wanted to call him back, to give him the gun. He was right; she could not do this. The ponies, the women, needed her.

Then she swallowed and cradled the gun against her breasts instead. There was no choice anymore, none at all. They were so very close to freedom, and they were still alive.

They were too far away yet to run to the Safe Place.

She rode back for the squaws, howling at them. Many looked startled and befuddled, but more eyes widened in a kind of resigned understanding. They all obeyed mindlessly. Somehow, impossibly, they got their ponies to move faster, toward the black shadow of the canyon on the horizon.

Where had Twelic gone?

She looked around, but she could not spot him anymore. Most of the warriors had held back to form a rear guard behind the herd and the women. Ahead of her, the smudge of darkness that was the canyon widened, spread, began eating up the horizon as they drew closer. She could see crags now, rocky promontories sweeping up on either side of it. Behind her, she could see the soldiers now, too, a blue haze under the sun as their uniforms became clear, silver sparking as their weapons caught the light.

They came on hard, but her own ponies struggled.

She keened aloud, feeling their loss already, a pain that went so deeply into her bones she could not breathe. They were skeletal, gaunt, too many on the verge of fatal lameness. How much they had given her over these last moons! Not even the black's could endure forever, but they pushed on gamely now, their nostrils wide and red.

She could not let them go, could not let the white-skins eat and destroy them. She owed them that, and so very much more.

The last of her doubts fell away.

She reined in hard, screaming at the squaws and elders as they passed her. "That way! Run! Go on without me!"

She whipped her *wyakin* mare around again. She heard the first bullets pop even as she turned back for the warriors. The blue-coats came on again as they had at the Big Hole, strong, charging lines of them from the east, the west, the south. *So many.* For a moment, a sense of doom froze her.

Then the warriors broke up into a circle to meet them. From somewhere behind her, a squaw screamed.

The warriors began backing up even as they fought. They would let the *xayxayx* drive them into the canyon, she thought, and from that protected defile, they could kill them all.

Adrenaline and desperation crashed through her again. She howled a war cry and rode in among them.

She brought Twelic's gun up, laying it carefully against her shoulder. *Coax it.* She heard his voice from somewhere inside her, and it made her strong again, made her hands stop trembling. She found the little metal loop he had shown her and put her finger there.

The gun exploded in her grip, the shot going wild.

Her mare reared, terrified at the sound so close over her head. Kiye Kipi tightened her legs around the pony but could not hold on. Her air whoofed out of her as she landed in the grass, the ground punching into her. She crawled upright. She had not lost the gun.

She put it to her shoulder again, this time watching the soldiers, following them with it, waiting, waiting.

For Wetatonmi.

She touched the trigger again. The second explosion only knocked her back onto her bottom. Pain screamed through her arm, but, oh, Tahmahnewes, she saw a white man fall. She screamed again, in revulsion and triumph.

The warriors moved back a little more, and she scrambled with them.

She did not know where her mare was, could not look.

Suddenly, she realized that the *xayxayx* knew of the protection of the canyon, too. They shot at the warriors haphazardly as they tried to push through them, trying to get to that place first. She brought the gun up and shot them down again and again and again.

For Arenoth, for me, for everything you have taken when you had no right, no right at all!

The gun began to click emptily.

She howled, still coaxing the trigger mindlessly. Where was the ammunition? Someone began pulling at her, dragging her, trying to get her to her feet.

"Nooooo!"

"It is empty."

She twisted around to see Twelic. There was a careful, controlled sound to his voice now, almost kind. She groped for his arms.

"I . . . did . . . it."

"Yes." He swung her onto his pony. She struggled around as he came up behind her. A bullet sliced the air over their heads and she screamed and ducked.

"Killed . . . them . . ." She gasped again. "Told you I could."

She began shaking.

He wrenched his stallion around, heading back for the canyon. The other warriors were still retreating, somehow keeping the blue-coats back. As the *xayxayx* broke through, they were brought down, one, then another and another.

The People would make it.

Twelic shoved the reins into her hands and turned around to take a final shot. Then they galloped into the shadows, safe between the rocky walls of the canyon.

Too many of the ponies were still behind them. They milled crazily, confused. Her black *wyakin* mare was with them. She howled for her, aloud this time, and the pony's head came up.

"Go through! Come into the dark!"

The canyon shadows were frightening her. Kiye Kipi felt the mare's fear tremble in her own muscles, felt the burst of

terror and panic that drove her into them anyway. She cried
out in triumph.

The rest of the herd began following, stampeding. Then
more blue-coats came in from the east.

They drove cleanly through the last of the herd, cutting them
away. She fought Twelic violently, trying to dismount. He held
her in implacable hands.

"It is too late," he grated.

"No, no!"

But it was.

She wailed with loss, with fury, then her voice shattered
into silence. She let him leave her in the canyon. She wrapped
her arms around her knees as she collapsed against the rock
wall and mourned.

The white light of the moon began shafting down through
the towering rock walls before she finally pushed to her feet
and went to find the herd.

There were so few of them now, scarcely enough to carry
the People the rest of the way. She had lost another half of
them. *Gone. She had failed them.* She turned away again to
keep from crying.

Tahmahnewes, she felt dirty. She rubbed at her arms com-
pulsively, at the dust and dirt there, at the spattered blood that
itched where it had dried. But worse was the cold, soiled feeling inside her, the sense that the blood would be with her
forever, no matter how much she washed, how much she
scrubbed. Nothing could touch it. Nothing could reach it.

She needed to find Twelic.

She looked about. The People did not camp; they had little
left to camp with. They huddled together around an occasional
fire, hollow eyed, disbelieving. *When would these white men
give up?*

Back at the mouth of the canyon, the warriors worked to
block the way with logs and brush. She shook her lethargy off
and went that way.

She found Alokot, Earth Sound, Two Moons, even Thunder
Dance. Twelic was not there.

Her heart skittered. Where had he gone, what had happened to him, after he had left her?

Her eyes flew frantically around the chasm. She found a steep, rocky trail running up one side and went that way, hauling herself up.

He was at the top, alone, sitting quietly with one of his rifles on his lap. He watched the southern country, and she followed his gaze.

Fires.

The blue-coats waited out there for them, like badgers at a prairie dog hole. She gasped, and Twelic looked around at her sharply.

"Do not stand there. They can see you in the moonlight."

She hurried to him and hunkered down.

"Why?" she breathed. *"Why do they do this?"*

He shook his head slowly. "I am not sure. I think they would prevent us from going back that way."

"We do not want to!"

"They do not know that. They want to make sure we keep going forward."

North. Was it conceivable, was it possible, that How-erd knew about the Safe Place too? *Could that white man dream?* The idea staggered her.

"They could be waiting to attack us again at dawn." She scrambled, desperate, for another explanation.

"No. They know they cannot get in here. They want us to come out the other side."

She looked that way from their view up high. There were no fires there, but that did not mean anything. If the warriors were to lay an ambush, they would not lay fires either.

The cold inside her grew again.

He looked at her, his eyes softening as much as they could. "You did well enough out there."

"Are you still angry with me?" It could not matter, not now, but it did.

Angry. He laughed, a harsh sound. "No. I was never angry, just desperate, helpless to stop you. I do not like that feeling."

Neither one of them said it, but they both knew it. Soon,

somehow, this horror would be over, and one way or another, her fighting would not trouble him again.

"I did not like it either," she whispered wretchedly.

His eyes narrowed at her tone. He knew then what was wrong with her, what was hurting her. Death was an evil, black monster, even when it was invited to one's hearth as an ally. He had learned that long ago, but for all her courage, she was only now meeting it.

She had killed because she thought she had to. But she possessed a soul born to nurture, to create, to heal. She had taken life, something only Tahmahnewes should do. Now she needed desperately to reaffirm it.

He loved her. He would have given his life to have killed those men for her. Perhaps he still would, in the few suns to come before they reached the Safe Place. But now, all he knew how to give her was hope, rebirth, memories to take into a shadowy future. "Long ago, when I was young in Nimipu country, we had a game," he said suddenly.

"A game?" She looked at him strangely. Why did he speak of this now?

"At feasts, at communal camps, we would go to the river. The boys bribed the girls to take off their clothes."

Her eyes widened. "Why did I never know this?"

Because you were different, magic, a rare bird that one watched swooping, but would never try to capture. The Kahmuenem youths would not have included her. He suspected that was it, but he said only, "You were young, and then the white men came to change our world."

She nodded pensively, looking out at the *xayxayx* fires again.

"I bribe you, Screamer."

She laughed tightly. "You do not need to do that."

No, he did not, but he wanted to. There was so much he wanted to give her yet, and so little time.

"1 would give you peace," he went on quietly, as though she had not spoken. "I would give you gentle suns, and blanketing snows, babes at your hearth, and all the ponies in the land."

Her throat closed suddenly, hard. "Stop."

He would not be there to share it. Without him, all of that was nothing.

"I bribe you, Screamer," he said again. "Take off your dress, and I will make sure that all of that will be yours."

She looked at him wildly, hating him for taunting her, because he could not give her that, not if Tahmahnewes meant him to fall. She would try to stop it, but she was still sure, so very sure, that she would be cursed forever for defying Him. There was no way Twelic could give her peace. The white-skins had stolen it.

Then she saw the heat in his eyes.

One more time.

It did not matter that he would not be able to pay her the bribe. All that mattered was that it was dark now; the *xayxayx* could not see them if they stayed low. They had this one last time for themselves.

And she would grab it.

She pulled her dress over her head, and his breath went still. For a moment, he remembered Cloud Singer, so long ago. He thought of that one's arrogance, her conniving greed, the way she had turned, showing herself, luring them all in. How had he ever gone again and again to her, when this one waited for him? Where Cloud Singer had been smugly confident of her beauty, Kiye Kipi waited, straight-backed, trusting, and unabashed.

The moonlight spilled over her skin. She was far too thin now, and her smooth flesh puckered at her shoulder, the mark of that *xayxayx* bullet. But she was the most beautiful woman he had ever known, good and pure, and so very strong.

"Lie back," he rasped.

She cocked her head, unsure.

"As you did once before."

Understanding, memory, made her nostrils flare and her eyes widen. Slowly, gracefully, she did as he asked. She kept her eyes on him, and her breath snagged as he bent over her.

It was like before. The sweetness of that, of a recaptured

time when life had been good, was almost more than she could bear.

He brushed her hair back off her forehead, trailed a finger down her cheek. She closed her eyes. He traced the outline of her wound and covered her breast with his palm, and there were buffalo again, and a home to return to. It did not matter that that other time had ended badly; when it had happened, she had been happy. There had been a strong sun and hope, all the hope and awakening that a young girl's heart had been able to hold.

He had not lied. He gave her peace after all, but it was a memory, not the future. It was Old Joseph and her *wyakin* dance, and mists over the Wallowa, all the things that had been before.

She bit down on her trembling lip and cried.

He touched the salty tear with his tongue, stealing it so that not even that could hurt her. Then his mouth followed his hand again, down over her breasts, over the notches of her ribs, so stark now. It ran along the sharp angle of her hip bone, and this time she opened her legs without being told.

The first touch of his tongue there shocked her. She gasped, then groaned, closing her thighs again, panicked and unsure. Some things had not changed after all.

"Trust me again," he said quietly.

She did; she always would, whether it was sane or not.

She opened to him again, needing him, needing this, more than she dreaded shame. And in the end, as always, there was none with him, after all.

His mouth coaxed the last of the death and the fear out of her, lingering and making every sensation in her body pool there in the center of her. It tightened and ached until she cried out his name and dug her fingers into his hair.

Twelic smiled. There was no need to restrain himself this time. Now, always, he was hers. He had simply not known it before.

He came up over her and entered her suddenly. The moon exploded as the sun once had, but now they shared it.

One more time.

51

THE EXILES LEFT the canyon before dawn, picking their way stealthily and quietly through the last light of the swollen moon. Kiye Kipi and Twelic stayed on the cliff, watching the distant fires of the soldiers.

The fires were dim now, a dull glow. They remained after the People were gone, and there was no stir from the southern horizon.

Finally, Twelic came up on his haunches. "They do not follow."

She almost wished they would. Then they would know, at least, that the *xayxayx* did not merely urge the People on into a trap.

She hugged herself against a shiver and pushed to her knees as well. They crawled back to the trail leading down. Their ponies waited for them. They mounted and went after the others, and she felt as though she were leaving the last goodness, the last peace, that she would ever know.

They caught up with the bands as the sun began to glow gold-blue in the eastern sky. There was still no sign, no sound of pursuit behind them. There was nothing to the north either, only windswept grass still pitched in darkness.

If How-erd waited ahead of them, then he was as stealthy and invisible as a spirit monster.

The People began galloping, running one last time.

*   *   *

The tenth sun came, but they did not find the Safe Place. They rode instead into a kidney-shaped valley ringed by mountains and coulees and sage. Kiye Kipi reined in behind the others, pushing her hair from her forehead, looking around.

There was a distinct nip in the air now. They had been climbing up into foothills throughout the whole sun.

"Why do we stop?" she asked, looking at Twelic.

He scowled, shrugging, and rode to the headmen. Kiye Kipi followed.

The chiefs and their warriors were at a creek, dismounting. Joseph sat wearily, but the others stood.

"My people cannot keep up this pace any longer," Looking Glass said querulously. "They need to rest, to eat. Surely there is game here."

"There is," Lean Elk allowed. "It is a fertile place."

"What is it?" Joseph asked. "Where are we? I do not think this is Old Woman's Country."

"No." Lean Elk shook his head. "We are a sun's ride from there still. These mountains are the Bear Paws. We call this Snake Creek."

"Look at my people," Looking Glass said again obstinately. "They need this."

Kiye Kipi glanced around at the bands. Some had built fires against the mountain chill. The old ones lay beside the hearths without robes or bedding, too tired to care. Squaws moved between them and the ponies, rummaging to the bottom of their parfleches for some scrap of old fish or antelope.

The babes cried, weak and sniveling. Her heart squeezed, but she knew Looking Glass was even less concerned for his people than he was tired himself.

"We are not safe here," she whispered.

The headmen looked at her, then their gazes snapped beyond her. Lean Elk's sentinels were finally coming in.

"No one follows," one reported.

"There. She worries needlessly," said Looking Glass. "I say we stay here for a few suns."

A few suns? Kiye Kipi stared at him, aghast. "No!" she protested. "We must not do that! We are practically there!"

"All the more reason to rest," Toolhoolhoolzote said coldly. "If trouble comes, the women can easily run on. Our warriors can finally turn about and fight."

For a wild moment, Kiye Kipi wondered if he had dreamed of the Safe Place, too. "Yes, that is exactly how it would be," she managed. "You are a fool if you think it will end well! A fool!"

"You overstep yourself, squaw!" the *tiwats* snarled.

"Enough." Something implacable flared briefly in Joseph's voice again. "This is not a time for squabbling. We have no choice."

They all looked down at him.

"Looking Glass is right," he went on. "Perhaps some of our people could ride one more sun, but too many are wounded. Old Woman's Country will offer them no comfort if they die before they see it, and many are dangerously close to doing just that. We have been riding hard for ten suns now, sleeping only in snatches. We have not hunted, have not eaten. I do not think the ponies can manage another sun either."

He paused, watching them. "There is also the matter of Sitting Bull. Old Woman's Country is his home now. He has claimed it. We should send a party ahead to find him, to tell him that we are coming his way and to ask for his hospitality."

Kiye Kipi bit back another protest.

She looked at their faces. They had made up their minds.

She looked wildly at Twelic. He knew. He could argue, but she saw at once that he would not. His face was haggard, pinched with weariness. His wound was healed, but his strength was not yet the same.

"If we fought this sun," he said to her quietly, "I do not think I would make it."

She shook her head in mute denial.

"I need to rest, Screamer. It is the only way I can think of to try to change what the Spirit Chief has decreed. I must get stronger."

She grabbed his arm, digging her fingers in deep. "If we go on to the Safe Place now, we might not have to fight at all," she tried.

He watched her levelly, waiting for her to see how foolish that was. She moaned softly.

He pried her grip away and looked to the headmen. "Yes, we must stay here for a bit," he agreed. "But it would be foolish not to send sentinels back to the south."

Looking Glass's jaw hardened; not even he could deny the sense of that. "So be it."

"And if the party going ahead to Sitting Bull does not make it through, then we know this is a trap," contributed Alokot.

Kiye Kipi flinched. So he had thought of that, too.

She did not think the party would get through. A fight was inevitable. Both she and Twelic had dreamed it. They could not prevent it; they could only alter the way it happened.

Maybe . . . maybe they could do at least that much.

She turned away, feeling sick.

Colonel Miles stopped his men in the eastern foothills of the Bear Paws. The order was met with incredulous gapes and insubordinate mumblings.

He silenced them with a glare. Most of the soldiers moved their eyes to their boots, studying them as though they were the most fascinating objects on earth. Only the Cheyenne scouts continued to stare at him sullenly.

One of the Indians motioned in sign language, *We can smell their fires.*

Miles nodded curtly when the translation was made for him.

"So we can. That is precisely why we must stop here. We cannot allow them to become aware of our presence."

"Kinda hard to fight them otherwise," someone dared to mutter.

"Quiet!" Miles snapped. "Let me think." He began pacing.

He was grimly aware of the many subterfuges General Howard had suffered at these Nez Percé hands. He could not allow the same fate to befall him. The United States Army did not have the luxury of one more defeat. To lose this battle was to lose the exiles entirely. They would scurry over the border like squirrels, and then they would be unreachable.

A less ambitious man would have balked at this assignment.

It was fraught with failure. But Miles seriously doubted if glory could be had easily, without treacherous risk.

He looked at his Cheyenne scouts again. "Deploy to the western side of the range," he ordered them. "Creep up on them, but do not, under any circumstances, show yourselves. Report back to me with any alteration in their routine, no matter how innocent it might seem. We will be moving steadily north, here on the eastern side of the range. Provided nothing changes, we will move through the crests and attack at dawn."

He would keep the mountains between them. There was no better concealment than that.

He had studied Howard's records of pursuit very carefully. When the exiles knew they were being followed, they ran with a speed he would have thought was impossible. When Howard fell back, or when they lost track of him, they stopped. Now that they had camped again, Miles did not think they would move on unless they detected his troops.

"Move out," he ordered his soldiers. "And no hunting. I don't care if you see the last goddamned buffalo this godforsaken land has to offer. These Indian bastards are like animals themselves. Kill one of their brothers, and they sense it. I swear to God they do."

Night settled over the valley as inexorably as death.

Panic itched at Kiye Kipi's skin because she could not see. Tahmahnewes, they could be just beyond her fire, and she would not even know it! She stood up to pace there, stepping over Twelic's sleeping form. She looked down at him briefly.

Sleep well, my love. Grow strong.

But he could not grow strong in just a few suns. She could not believe this time would change anything.

Where were the sol-jers?

She looked up at the mountains. She knew they were there; she felt them somehow, sensed them, smelled them. The wind seemed to carry a taint, like something rotten.

She bent down for her bow, taking it with her into the night shadows.

She did not know what she was looking for; she only knew

that she could not rest. She wandered down to the creek. She did not undress, but moved into it clothed, splashing the trail grime from her skin. The water was bitingly frigid, making her teeth clack together. She scrubbed out her hair and knotted it at her neck, then she got out again, shivering.

Tahmahnewes, it was cold.

She set off toward the hills. The moon was still large enough that she thought she might be able to see game. Dawn could not be far off. The animals would be gathering to drink. She would bring something back for Twelic to eat.

She considered dreaming for prey, then shook the thought from her mind. No. That would mean letting go, losing touch, floating off into that moon where she saw things. She could not risk that now.

She began climbing the hills, and then she saw the Indian.

For a wild moment, she did not understand. She gaped at him, her head swimming. He only stood there in the moonlight, watching her solemnly. *Cheyenne*. She knew his kind now.

Lean Elk's sentinels were watching for rash, bumbling soldiers. These Indians must have crept in through the hills.

She opened her mouth and screamed.

She backed away from him, stumbling, falling with a thud that jarred her teeth. Frantically, she scrambled up again. She kept her eyes on him, but he did not move.

He was warning her, giving her a chance to alert the others, a small chance, a breath of a chance. . . .

She turned and fled.

She screamed again as she reached the camp. The warriors came awake. Twelic caught her as she passed him.

"Sol-jers!" she gasped.

"Where?"

She did not know.

Not south; the sentinels had not picked them up. North, then. They had to be barring them from the Safe Place. They were doing that after all.

She saw the realization come to him as well, saw it change his face. He grabbed his weapons and ran that way.

She looked about, her head whipping back and forth. All around her, the warriors rushed into the coulees, ducking down behind the sage. *It could be done.* Please Tahmahnewes, they could win this one, too. She had to believe that. It was just like White Bird Canyon; the blue-coats would have to come down into this valley to get them, and the warriors would be waiting for them.

But no blue-coats were coming. The crests to both the north and the south were silent.

The warriors began to move more slowly, confused now, looking about. They could not kill men who were not there.

She became aware of distant thunder . . . Twelic's *wyakin.* She cried out again, then choked on the sound. It was too cold for thunder. She spun, looking east, and finally she saw them.

"Noooooo!"

The *xayxayx* came at a trot over the grassy tableland there. The rising sun limned the mountains behind them. One of their horns bleated eerily in the dawn, and they broke into a gallop.

There were no warriors on that side.

She heard a pony whinny shrilly as she turned back into the camp. The herd crashed into each other, milling crazily as some of the boys tried to drive them into a small glade. She took a staggering step toward them, then she stopped.

She could not go to them. If she did, it would happen.

Twelic had gone north. She had to find him, had to warn him, to bring him back. The ponies were her *wyakin,* but she knew, had always known, that she would have to deny them now if she were to save him.

She turned, running the other way. She found him hunched low behind some brush, taking aim on more Cheyenne who had appeared there. She gathered her voice to scream again.

"Stop! No!"

He looked around, focusing on her slowly, disbelievingly. Fury touched his face as she had never seen it before.

She motioned at the camp. "They come that way!" she cried before he could open his mouth to chastise her.

She stumbled back, allowing him to pass, then she followed him. He veered around again at her footsteps.

"You must go now!" he hissed. "You must lead them on, go to that place this time. *You know that!*"

"I . . . I will." And she knew it was a lie.

She watched him run back to the camp. She let him go, squirming down behind some bushes. She would wait until he did not expect to see her amid the fighting again.

Tahmahnewes, please grant me that much time. But she was praying to a Spirit Chief she intended to scorn. He would not hear her this time.

She keened aloud as the warriors lost their entrenchments on an east bluff. *This could not be happening!* They had held the *xayxayx* that way before! But this time they were confused, scattered. Soldier ponies overran the crest. She saw Earth Sound go down and came to her feet again mindlessly, screaming.

Sweet Tahmahnewes, still more soldiers came in behind them!

The squaws were stumbling, running for the herd, dragging the weak ones, the elders, their babes. The blue-coats followed them. She thought they would cut them down, as they had done at the Big Hole.

"No," she wept. "Please, please, no!"

The soldiers passed them. They went into the herd, stampeding them, cutting every precious pony around to the *xayxayx* side.

The squaws began wailing in inconsolable grief. *The whiteskins had the ponies.*

Kiye Kipi began running, but she was not fast enough. Her breath tore from her throat as she strained, lengthening her stride. Oh, Tahmahnewes, she had left the herd, had turned away from them willingly, but now she knew she could not lose them! She had never meant to let them go, had never meant to destroy the People with their loss! In the end, she could not do it.

Her foot hit a boulder and she went down, the breath slamming out of her. She struggled to her hands and knees again, weeping.

Her magic. She still had her magic, her *wyakin*.

But if she used it, she knew that Twelic would die. It would be as they had dreamed. If she did not turn away from her *wyakin,* if she did not defy it now, she would lose him.

She tilted her head back and cried a sound of agony and denial, and knew that it had never been her choice at all.

Tears blinded her, but she could still see the faces of the women and the babes, smeared and distant. *No! She did not want to see!* She scrubbed a hand over her eyes and looked for her warrior instead, the man who shared her dream, and finally, so much more.

Forgive me, my love. I cannot kill them, not for myself, not even for you. I am so sorry.

She stumbled to her feet. Bullets spit around her, digging up the dirt at her feet. She began to walk through them, feeling dead. Then Toolhoolhoolzote slammed into her.

She reeled back, away from him.

"Now, too late, we learn you have no magic!" he bellowed. "I curse you for the charlatan you are!"

She stared at him uncomprehendingly, and he gave a cruel, triumphant grin, looking to make sure the women watched them. "The ponies, *your ponies,* are gone!"

Emotion slid back into her slowly. Red-hot fury started in her belly, then rose to pound at her temples. All he could think of now was his following? All he could consider was shaming her, pulling the People from her side?

She snatched his rifle from him. His big jaw dropped.

"Then use *your* magic, *tiwats,*" she snarled. "Bring them back if you are so strong."

The women began keening, their eyes moving from one to the other. She did not hear them.

Twelic was surely lost to her; Tahmahnewes had decreed it. She could not care for anything else now, except getting the women to safety. If Toolhoolhoolzote could do that, so be it.

She watched him, her eyes blazing, her breath hurting in her throat. He opened his mouth to speak, then snapped it shut again.

He could not do it. They both knew he could not call the herd back.

She stepped closer to him, standing straight, her head back to keep his eyes. "If you are so secure in your own magic," she said sharply, "then come with me. But leave your weapon here. The women need it. We will bring the ponies back, protect ourselves, with our power."

She hurled his gun to the nearest squaw. Her grandfather's face mottled. If he was strong enough, if he did this thing, he would never have to fear losing face to her again. But if he did not dare it, no one would ever heed him.

Finally, in the end, without meaning to, she had trapped him in his own ego. She felt no victory.

"You hope I will fall," he snarled.

"No," she replied baldly. "I do not care."

"You, too, could die."

"But I do not fear it." Oh, no, not anymore. It was all that was left.

She turned back to the soldiers. After a moment, she heard Toolhoolhoolzote behind her. She did not look back. Her eyes scanned the soldiers, searching, trying to find a way. Her heart thundered. Both the warriors' rifle pits and the blue-coats' entrenchments were between her and the herd now. The ponies swarmed and crashed together, confined behind the soldiers' ranks.

You think you have them, white-skins. You think you have beaten us because we cannot run on again.

"We will see," she breathed aloud, viciously. "We will find out."

She could not stampede them forward; that would only send them spewing onto the southern land, farther out of reach. Somehow, impossibly, she would have to bring them back toward her.

She had not ever done that before.

A bullet screamed into a bush beside her, scattering leaves and debris. She hunkered down again quickly, looking ahead for more cover. She made a little sound of determination, and darted to the next clump of sage.

Again, again . . . past the warriors . . . farther, on and on. *Now.* She was as close as she could get. She rose to her feet again, palms up, as though to capture Tahmahnewes's blessing from the sky.

He would give it to her this time. He had sent her for this, and she cried a sound of loss as she accepted it.

She felt it fill her, *power*. Stronger, different, than it had ever been before. It burned and hummed under her skin, hurting; oh, Tahmahnewes, it hurt! It hurtled her over the grasslands, spinning in her head, blinding her without a dream.

And some part of her conscious held back. *No, no, no, no! Twelic, good-bye.*

She screamed aloud in grief, then her silent plea to the ponies roared through her mind, tearing through her. Pain exploded behind it. She strained to touch them, to touch all of them.

The wind sprang up, battering her. She felt it whipping at her hair, her doeskin, and she shrieked again with it, falling into her black mare, running . . . running north.

Behind the soldier lines, the Nimipu ponies crashed past the guns of their captors. She did not hear their shouts of confusion. She felt her lungs burn with the mare's energy, felt her hooves pounding, tearing up Mother Earth. Then, as though the wind rushed right through her, the vision released her.

She sank into the grass again, sobbing. The herd thundered past her, but her black mare stopped, rearing over her.

A bullet hissed by both of them, taking her grandfather with a moist, meaty thud. Toolhoolhoolzote staggered down to his knees, his hands stretched out to the Spirit Chief who had finally forsaken him.

52

TWELIC WATCHED HER go down, stunned. His rifle fell nervelessly from his hand.

It was not supposed to end this way. She was supposed to go on to the Safe Place. *He* was meant to die.

Then he knew. She had defied her power to save him, to find him on the north side. Tahmahnewes had taken her magic back, had taken her ponies, had given her the bullet meant for him.

A roar of anguish tore from his throat. He came up from the warriors' line, running for her. He had accepted his own death. He had thought he could meet it.

He could not accept hers.

He closed half the distance between them before the *xayxayx* bullet caught him, the one that was his, that had always been meant for him. It spun him around, dropping him into the grass, as agony exploded in his chest.

Colors swam before his eyes, like the ones in his *wyakin* dream. They ran, smeared, cohered, and he saw her there in his mind, her black hair streaming free, her long legs pumping, the way she had always run to greet him as a child. He saw her grown tall and proud, her indigo eyes blazing as he had left her on the buffalo prairie . . . and beautiful and arrogant, fighting him, loving him, changing all he had thought he needed in this world.

So much wasted time . . .

The colors turned black.

Perhaps, if Tahmahnewes was kind and forgave them, he would find her in the afterworld.

Perhaps, in the end, they could start over.

Her *wyakin* mare nudged her with her muzzle. The touch was warm, soft, insistent. It whiffled over Kiye Kipi's face, then came more strongly against her shoulder.

She did not want to wake. She knew, somehow she knew, there was nothing left to wake for anymore. *It had happened.* It had happened as they had both known it would. She had used her magic, and Twelic was gone. The instinct of truth left her feeling hollow and ice cold inside.

A hoof grazed her shoulder, pawing. The pain finally made her open her eyes, and she saw her pony.

The mare trembled, white eyed, as gunshots burst around her. Her black coat shone with nervous sweat, and again, always again, Kiye Kipi felt her terror as if it were her own.

"Go . . . on," she rasped. "Go. Run. Save yourself."

This time, the pony did not move.

It screamed instead, rearing up to thrash the air, coming down so close to her head Kiye Kipi had to roll. She did it instinctively, not wanting to, wanting to die.

It was over, but the mare would not let it end. *Why would she not let it end?*

Her hoof came up again, caked with mud and grass, ready to strike her one more time. Kiye Kipi sat up away from it, her head swimming.

"Curse you!" She wept.

If she stayed here, the mare would stay with her, and the white-skins would surely shoot her. She could not let it end that way for her, not when she had gallant life left in her, fire and intelligence still burning in her eyes. Curse her! she thought again. The mare knew what she could not accept; it was not finished until they found the Safe Place, and Tahmahnewes said they should go on together, as they had come through this nightmare side by side.

She choked back her grief and struggled up to find the pony's mane with her hand. The valley spun, darkened, then came clear again as she hauled herself astride. She lay down against the mare's neck, closing her eyes, and felt her gather herself beneath her one last time.

They flew out of the battle, leaping over the prone form of the man she had loved, the man she had not been able to save.

She did not see him, did not look again until the mare stopped, still shuddering. She pushed herself up. All about her, the women screamed. Their cries were tangled, wretched, yet strangely jubilant. They gathered up their ponies and mounted again.

The ponies were back.

Finally, dully, Kiye Kipi looked around at the fighting.

Alokot charged out of a coulee, keeping low, then his arms flew out and his rifle dropped from his hand. He fell backward in a spray of red.

"No," she choked. "Tahmahnewes, no."

Looking Glass stood up from his spot of hiding, shouting in impotent rage. A bullet caught him in the forehead, and the mirror he wore there exploded in ghastly, sparkling light.

She could bear no more.

She thumped her heels against her mare. The others would follow, or they would not. She had done all she could. There was nothing left she could give them anymore.

As she raced out of the valley, gentle white snow began to fall, the strong wind carrying it from the north.

Someone was dragging him by the hair.

The new pain brought Twelic back. He was supposed to be dead, wanted to be dead, and he cursed Tahmahnewes for not even granting him that.

Why? Why would the Spirit Chief not let him go?

He twisted around savagely, with the last of his strength. The hand he found in his hair belonged to Thunder Dance.

"Leave me," he snarled, fighting him.

The warrior fell hard to his belly beside him as a bullet whined by too close.

"Stupid mongrel, I would if you would walk," he snapped.

"If that shot did not kill you at the Big Hole, then this bullet will not take you either."

Finally, Twelic looked at his chest. Blood chugged slowly from a spot above his heart. *Too high. Too cursed high.*

The pain was abominable, and not enough. It did not burn through the cold in his gut.

"Go on. Fight. I can get back on my own."

Thunder Dance snorted as they both began to crawl. "There is nothing left to fight for."

Twelic looked at the carnage around him. Too many red bodies. So few white.

Rage exploded in him, that they had come this far, that they had won everything, every battle, but the one that mattered. For the first time since he had found his *wyakin,* something hot, something like tears, burned at his eyes.

He looked at his comrade, his friend, then he looked away again quickly because he could not bear to see. Something shone too bright at Thunder Dance's eyes also.

They reached the camp. They had to move around Lean Elk's body, but his gun was beside him, loaded and ready. Twelic grabbed it.

"Tell me," he grated. "The pony wife?"

Regret shafted through a place deep in Thunder Dance's belly, a place he had not thought could hold any more emotion. He had seen that one run, leaping over her warrior's body, leaving him, this man who had finally learned to love her. He did not want to tell him, and knew Twelic would not let it rest until he did.

"She is gone," he answered tightly.

Gone. He knew it, had seen it happen. But he had had to hear it before he could try again to die himself.

He came up with a roar, staggering, going down on one knee then rising again. He brought Lean Elk's gun up and ran into the last of the fighting.

For you, Screamer. For the wyakin *we shared.*

She had not let it end as it had been meant to, curse her sweet, stubborn hide. But it would end, and he would take with him the men who had destroyed them.

He bellowed again, charging close to the white-skins' ranks, firing. He took down one, two, then three, their eyes wide in disbelief as they watched him approach. One waved at him in an impossible parody of surrender.

"You do not understand, *xayxayx,*" he sneered. "We are going to die together."

He shot him as well.

Now it was over.

Lean Elk's rifle clicked emptily. He threw it into the grass. He left it there, smeared with his own blood, and walked straight backed toward the Nimipu ranks, waiting to feel the last bullet between his shoulders.

This time his own men kept him from the death he craved.

Those who remained ran howling to meet him, spitting their own fire into the blue-coat ranks, covering him, ignited anew with his own reckless fury. Twelic reached the camp behind them and sat, laughing bitterly until he finally cried.

The white-skins' gunfire slowed as night fell, spitting out with less and less frequency. Finally, their shots were only occasional flashes of orange in the darkness.

There was no answering fire from the warriors. Only three headmen gathered by a cold hearth as the snow began coming down heavily. The few men they had left gathered around them.

Twelic looked at all their drawn, defeated faces. Joseph lived, but his gaze was strange. Huishuis Kute was stunned and vacant eyed. Only White Bird sat straight, pensive, his seamed face tense.

Twelic spoke to him. "Tell me what you want me to do now," he demanded. In the end, it was up to him, as his *wyakin* had deemed long ago. All the others, Alokot and Two Moons, all the other war leaders were gone.

Joseph lifted one shoulder. "The Colonel Mi-yuls sends word that we must surrender, or fighting will resume again with the light. He tells me I can go home." Something shuddered visibly through him. Twelic flinched at his obvious longing.

"I do not believe him," said Huishuis Kute. "But to fight

on is to die. We cannot win now, not this time. I do not care for myself. There is nothing left. But there are those behind us.'' He waved a hand over his shoulder.

Twelic did not want to look, and could not stop himself. Some women, some elders and babes remained, mostly those too injured, too weary and broken and grief-stricken to go on.

And the others? Someone had said they had run. He wondered distantly if they would find the Safe Place without their pony wife to guide them, or if they, too, would die.

Pain shimmered through him. He could not tolerate it yet. Later he would grieve; his heart would bleed and die. Now these others still needed him.

He would see it through for them.

''I will take my people to this Mi-yuls with the dawn,'' Huishuis Kute was saying. ''I will let them live, if they wish, now that everything is gone.''

White Bird shook his head. ''You go to Mi-yuls. I must head north,'' he said. ''The white men will kill me if I go in. This fighting started in my country with that Wahlitits. They know that. They will neither let me live, nor die with honor. All I can do is go on.''

He looked to Twelic.

His response strangled him. The irony of it tortured him. He would see the Safe Place after all . . . alone.

''I will follow you and cover your people in case there is pursuit.''

General Howard and Colonel Miles stood side by side on the snow-crusted grass, watching the decimated remains of the Indian camp. They were surrounded by a shivering handful of aides-de-camp and translators. Miles was rock jawed, as he had been since Howard's arrival just before dawn.

Howard finally waved a weary hand at him. ''Take the surrender, Colonel. It's yours. You've earned it.''

One of his aides looked at him, stunned. *Miles* had? Howard had been on Joseph's trail for over three months. Miles would not even have known where to look for the exiles if Howard had not informed him of their whereabouts, if Sturgis had not driven them right into his lap.

But the colonel looked relieved and pleased all the same, as though this had not occurred to him, and Howard merely shrugged when he made a token protest.

"You *are* senior officer, General," Miles said stiffly.

"A very tired senior officer, sir, and one who wants nothing more to do with this dubious victory."

Miles scowled, perturbed at the response, but he had nothing to gain by pursuing it. Together, they looked back at the camp and watched the surrendering headmen come on.

Two of them. Howard's gaze dismissed the short, stocky one and went to the man who was his nemesis, his strong and proud adversary, one of the most courageous soldiers he had ever known, white or red.

Joseph.

The chief rode a stumbling spotted pony, one of the few beasts the Nez Percé had apparently saved, though Howard could not imagine where the others had gone. He sat with his rifle across his thighs, his head bowed. He wore buckskin leggings, and a gray woolen woman's shawl.

As he drew closer, Howard saw that the shawl was burned with bullet holes. The stub of his own long-absent arm itched.

Joseph straightened himself with the last dignity of a free man. He swung to the ground in front of them. The Indian wept silently, tears tracking down his haggard cheeks as he held out his rifle.

Howard felt his throat close.

The general steadied himself and spoke to a translator. "Tell him . . . tell the chief I cannot take it. Tell him to give it to the colonel."

He looked back at Joseph. For a long moment, their eyes met. Joseph nodded, and handed the weapon over, but he did not speak to Miles.

He, too, looked at the translator.

"Tell General How-erd I know his heart. I am tired of fighting. Our chiefs are killed. Looking Glass is dead. Toolhoolhoolzote is dead. The old men and *tiwateses* are all dead. It is left to the young men to say yes or no in council, and my brother, who led them, is dead. It is cold and we have no blankets. My children are freezing. My people, some of them, have run away. No one knows where they are. Perhaps they freeze to death, too.

"Hear me, my chiefs. I am tired. My heart is sick and sad. From where the sun now stands, I will fight no more forever."

Epilogue

THE SIOUX GAVE them robes, shelter, food. There was a great deal of food.

Kiye Kipi sat against a thick-trunked fir, her back painful against the hard wood. Snow banked deeply on either side of her. It caked her brows, her hair, her lashes. Occasionally, she reached a thin hand up and wiped it from her eyes.

So this is the end, she thought dispassionately. All of the running, all of the fighting, all of the hunger . . . for this, to be here among Tahmahnewes's riches, alone.

So many were lost, were gone.

One of Sitting Bull's squaws came to squat next to her and harass a fire into fresh flames. "We sent men," she said. "They had nearly reached you when the Cheyenne scouts met them and told them it was too late."

Kiye Kipi shrugged. It did not matter anymore.

"Perhaps more of your people will come in yet," the woman offered.

Kiye Kipi shook her head. It had been two suns now, and the last of this light was falling. No one else would come.

But then she heard the commotion.

The camp was a sprawling one of the damned and the banished. No fertile hunting, no lush forage, could spare either Sioux or Nez Percé hearts their aching memories of home. But some of her own people were shouting now, moving to the southern edge of the clearing, and there was something in their voices she had not heard in a very long time.

Happiness. Ecstatic surprise.

She pushed to her feet, swaying as they tingled, as her life-blood returned to them. Her heart squirmed, then jumped, then her jaw dropped.

White Bird?

She could not credit it, could not believe it, but more, still more of the People came in. They rode limping black ponies, and huddled into themselves against the cold. But they were alive, *alive.* The ponies had brought them on.

Then she saw him, and she knew why her *wyakin* mare had not let her die.

Twelic rode into the valley behind the others, his eyes flinty and unseeing until they fell upon her. Then he stopped, stunned, and moved with uncharacteristic clumsiness to the ground.

Finally, he understood why Tahmahnewes had refused to take him.

They came together, but they did not touch. They stared.

"I never . . . saw you . . . fall!"

The magnitude of that realization struck her for the first time, shattering the last of the cold within her. She reached out for him convulsively, touching his face, his chest . . .

. . . and she found blood. It was dried and crusted, but he had taken another bullet after all. But she could heal that; she knew how now. Oh, yes, this was something she could do to save him!

She put her head against the good side of his chest and wept.

Finally, impossibly, she felt his arms come slowly around her again, still hard, still strong. "I saw you go down." His voice was strangled, disbelieving. But she was warm, alive; *she was here.*

"I used my magic."

"You defied it."

"I tried to." She looked up, touched his face again. "It would have killed them. I could not. . . ."

He shook his head, silencing her. It did not matter now. She had done what the Spirit Chief had decreed, and He had, in the end, smiled His blessing upon them.

"I give you gentle suns," he managed.

She laughed, a choked sound. "Give them to me in the spring. We have time now, and it is too cold to take off my dress."

Still, he went on. "I give you babes around your hearth."

Longing chugged through her, stronger than she had ever known. Her eyes widened. "Oh, please," she breathed. "Oh, yes."

"I claim you, Screamer. Finally."

She had never truly dared to believe it, but she knew in that moment that they had made it.

They had won.

She would have it all.

Together they looked around at the People. She saw then what she had not been able to see before, through her despair. Yes, they had lost their land; too many had lost their loved ones. But they were whole, and they would heal, and Howerd would never find them again.

They would go on.

She found Twelic's hand and held on hard.

The blanketing snows kept falling. There would be more ponies.

And the People smiled.

Author's Note

WITH APOLOGIES TO the true course of history, and to those Nimipu men and women who lived and breathed and fought so hard, I confess that I have altered a few minor details of the Nez Percé's historic 1877 flight for freedom.

While Wahlitits was indeed responsible for the bloody raid from Tolo Lake that began the war, he was a member of White Bird's band; he was not Hasotoin. And while history does not reveal him to be a very endearing character, there is no evidence that he ever molested a child.

The same holds true for Toolhoolhoolzote. He was indeed a *tiwats* shaman, a devout disciple of the Dreamer faith, and he was a headman. He was an arrogant and strong personality, but to my knowledge, he never threw a daughter out of his band, nor did he have a granddaughter with power stronger than his own. In the Bear Paw battle, it was his own determination that led him to his death.

The Nimipu did not breed black ponies; they were, however, renowned for their fine herds and their innovative breeding concepts, unequaled by any other tribe in American history. They raised Appaloosas, coveted for their strength and endurance, and for the colorful spots and blankets mentioned in this book. They did indeed introduce Arabian blood to these herds, increasing their stamina, but not at the expense of the fine coloring that is an Appaloosa trademark.

Lastly, while most textbooks would have us believe that General Howard triumphed over the Nimipu and that they were ultimately brought to heel, the inaccuracy of this is something I did *not* alter. While Joseph was never permitted to return to Wallowa despite Miles's promise and Howard's legitimate efforts to arrange it, in fact two hundred and thirty-three Nez Percé men, women, and children did indeed elude American military pursuit, escaping into Canada to begin again in a safe place. The exiles never, at any time, had more than three hundred warriors, yet they engaged in all some two thousand soldiers, holding them off until the end, until their women could flee over the border.

BEVERLY BIRD
MAY 8, 1993